Between the Darkness and the Light

CHRONICLES OF THE NIGHT BOOK ONE

G L HOUSER

THE BLACKEN...

THE TWISTE...

SMOKING PLAINS

FORGE WART...

TORN FLOWAGE

THE STEPS OF GLASS

THE VALE LA...

RIFFS CROSSING

BLACK...

LEAF WATE...

THE LIGHT LAN...

LANDS

ORCS RUN

THE DARKENED GATES

SHADOW LAKES

ANDS

TH

ROC`NAR

TAIN

THE LOST ROAD

THE GREAT ROAD

OANORS FIELD

LUCS RANGE

LOST KINGS HIGHWAY

THE HARBOR CITIES

S

RAVENHOF

TWEL FORAS TRAIL

THE GARDEN WOODS

HIGH GATE

SCALE B

HAVEN

Between the Darkness and the Light, Chronicles of the Night Book One

Published by G L Houser

ISBN: 9798223878803

Dedication

"I dedicate this book to my father and mother, who have always believed in me. To my father, for his boundless love, enduring patience, and his belief in accepting people as they are. He instilled in me the tenacity to never give up and the drive to work hard. To my mother, whose care and unwavering positivity taught me that falling is simply a step in learning to navigate a world full of obstacles."

Contents

Preface

Mission Log: Captain Mark Adams is in command. The USS Titan has arrived at Alpha Centauri, a trinary system located 4.3 light-years away from Earth. The most distant sun resembles a faint orb in the night sky. We landed on the smallest planet near the equator at twilight, where the continent touches the sea. This planet orbits the nearest two suns.

During our exploration, we discovered the remnants of civilization amidst the ruins. Among these fragments, we found a chronicle written on a new type of metal native to this system. Further analysis of its spectral and metallurgical properties will follow. This chronicle is a record of a calamity that occurred in this system. Our AGI has partially translated the text, revealing the following cursory interpretation:

Note: Due to challenges in translating the writing, the computer replaces less defined text with human words believed to approximate the meaning, ensuring better understanding on our part.

We have high hopes that this chronicle will serve as a guide to uncovering archaeological sites elsewhere on this planet as we continue to translate it. USS Titan out.

Artificial General Intelligence Interpretation Date: 03/25/2089

The world was in chaos as mortal beings waged war with ancient Powers, disrupting the delicate fabric of creation and pushing it into disharmony. Amidst this turmoil, birth, life, and destruction unfolded. The Mages, wielding the Powers of Darkness and Light, strained the fabric of creation and shattered the balance.

Driven by greed, the Mages sought to create their own utopia by eliminating the opposing faction tipping the balance. However, the fabric of creation couldn't recover faster than the war brought changes, resulting in fractures at the focal point of our reality, tearing it in two.

The mortals on our planet soon discovered the devastating cost of their reckless pursuit of Power. Gods emerged, turning our planet into the primary battleground in their struggle between Darkness and Light.

Our planet became divided into two fronts, with the forces of Darkness and Light clashing on either side, leaving the Grey Area as a purgatory-like demilitarized zone in the middle. The aftermath of this shattered balance left our planet in ruins, with civilization crumbling under its weight. Those who used the arcane Power at the time of the rupture perished.

Among the survivors, those with the talent to wield this Power now sought to restore balance. The Order of the Light aimed to restore the previous equilibrium, while the Order of Darkness sought to overcome the Light entirely and establish a new balance. These two factions conspired against each other, manipulating their followers as pawns in a grand game for domination fueled by greed.

The gods influenced the intelligent races of the world, who unleashed horrors with increasing ferocity. Mortals harnessed this Power to create new breeds of beings and adapted existing races, perpetuating an endless struggle. There was no turning back. Ages came and went, civilizations rebuilt on both sides of the conflict, and in the middle between Darkness and Light, people lived, died, and prayed for the balance to be restored.

This passage is a fragment from the lost author's Third Chronicle of the Shattered Age.

Chapter 1 Shadows and Whispers

"It was only a dream. We were never in control. Thinking of ourselves as wise, we became fools. Darkness can dwell in the heart, that deep well of rejoicing or despair. Sometimes we call what is in our heart our world. Darkness entered our world, and we were too blind to see it. Some could see it but had mistaken it for the Light and they fell from the Light. If you mistake Darkness for Light, how great is that Darkness?"

Death wasn't so different from slumber, except for the smell. Tara inhaled sharply—pungent and empty. It clung to her, a hollow sensation, like an unforgettable memory, a shadow, or a whisper. It was a heavy emptiness that had lingered in the room for years. At twenty-five, Tara's memory of his lifeless body remained hauntingly clear. Her father slumped over a writing desk, white hair disheveled, his head resting on an open book. Nearby, a quill lay beside his ink-stained fingers, next to a candle burned to a stub. That much was normal, but the green foam at his lips? That was not. She struggled to shake the memory, forever etched in her mind. Every attempt to banish the image only intensified its grip. Anger rose like a furious tide within her, squeezing her chest and igniting a heat that threatened to boil over. Her hand went to her heart, tears welled in her eyes, and she closed them, reaching desperately for happier memories.

As the memories washed over her, she found herself transported back to her fifteenth year—darting through narrow streets on a chilly morning, her thin clothes offering little defense against the biting wind. She moved swiftly, like a feral creature, her bare feet slapping the wet, gritty cobblestones, and she caught the scent of rain in the air. Her filthy fingers snatched goods from unsuspecting shopkeepers and vendors. In this unforgiving city, every stolen morsel was a desperate bid for life. Spotted, she ducked into a nearby bookstore, seeking refuge from the city watch. Back then, Duncan, the old owner of the store, caught her by the arm. Stained fingers gripped her like iron. Her eyes found his wearily; and he saw the spark raging inside. Every memory brought her back to that moment. Just five years ago, she was twenty, and he was already gone. In the end, the written word consumed him; the irony lay in his demise—death by an assassin's poison concealed within the very pages of the books he cherished. Tara shook herself from her thoughts.

Her life revolved around his bookstore. It was a sanctuary of ancient tomes and volumes that held the secrets of a shattered past. She spent countless hours poring over them, seeking answers that remained elusive despite her thirst for knowledge. The question: Creation torn in two—how do you put it back? She had shared her love of books with a man who had become her father. His death left her with unanswered questions, the kind that would determine her fate.

It was one of those nights when Tara saw a man stalking about the bookstore. He did not make a very good burglar. Fearing he was the killer, she lunged at him with knives from her hiding spot under the counter. He disarmed her, but it cost him a little blood. There would have been more had he not told her he was there to help her find Duncan's assassin.

Antoff Grant was his name, a retired Priest Knight, arrived after the death of her father, having served with Master Duncan for years in the campaigns. Antoff received a letter from Duncan predicting his imminent demise at the hands of the Dark Order. According to Duncan, Tara was an aberration of a kind seldom seen; he was hiding her from the Dark Lords who would use her, though Antoff wouldn't say for what. Duncan was digging into forbidden histories of the Lands of El'idar, trying to piece together a lost truth about the Breaking of the Balance, and if he had found it, it could be restored.

It all came down to one undeniable fact: Duncan had loved them both. It was comforting to know she was not alone in her pain; together, they were going to finish the work and find her father's killer. Over the five years since Duncan's passing, Tara had grown to love Antoff, but it had not been easy. He tried to embrace a fatherly role in her life, but unlike fighting, this did not come naturally to him. He was grumpy and a man of few words, to put it politely. She had no question; he loved her, and after relentless efforts, she had cracked the hard steel of his Priest Knight's armor. But Antoff was not telling her everything. He kept secrets. Tara knew he held back information—something concerning her, and whatever it was, it was terrifying him.

Together, they managed Master Duncan's bookstore, *Lost Lyrical*, a coffee shop with tables and chairs where customers indulged in rented books, coffee, and honey cakes from the baker. The shop flourished, offering a haven of words and treats in a town where books were scarce and expensive. Secretly, trips buying books served as a cover for their investigations.

Recently, an invitation from an unknown associate of Duncan arrived, heralding a new adventure that began with a message from a courier boy sent by the owner of the inn of the Old Rusty Bucket.

Antoff stood at the door of the bookshop. All the customers had long since gone home and it was time to meet Ivan, the man that sent the invitation. Tara tried to follow him out, but Antoff blocked her way. "You should stay here. It will be only a short while."

Tara's eyes narrowed. "Antoff, you can't protect me from everything you know? I am coming."

"No, But I can limit your exposure to unnecessary danger. You don't need to be there."

Tara pushed past him. "I'm going, Antoff. If things go sideways, you'll want me there. Remember, I'm not a child anymore."

Antoff fell in behind her, irritated, and muttered to her under his breath. "You can be such a stubborn girl."

The skies darkened as night storms descended, enveloping the town of RavenHof in a cold, wet blanket, casting its buildings in shadow and bathing them in silvery moonlight. Ancient gothic towers reached skyward like skeletal hands, memories of a grander time, when myths say they soared through the heavens in great ships. All lost in the breaking. What persisted were the abandoned structures and wasted towers strewn throughout the town of RavenHof.

Coth'Venter, a crumbling and abandoned metropolis, surrounded RavenHof on three sides, as if it was trying to devour it. Locals claimed they rebuilt RavenHof upon the ruins of the larger city destroyed when the balance shattered. Remnants of ancient gothic architecture stood decaying among the sprawling new construction that had only just begun expanding beyond the city walls.

Cloaked in darkness, Antoff and Tara left the bookshop and headed toward the Rusty Bucket Inn. An invitation from a mysterious sender awaited them. The streets bustled with townsfolk, their conservative garments barely shielding them from the rain. They navigated through the crowd, ignoring the curses from a startled wagon driver. Sheltering under a porch, they took advantage of the warm light spilling from the nearby windows to navigate a path.

Tara inched nearer to Antoff, her voice scarcely above a whisper. "This is risky, Antoff! We know nothing of this man. How do we know he can even teach us anything that might bring us closer to Duncan's killer, much less help us discover the reason they killed him?"

Antoff leaned in, his voice a soft murmur that carried a note of intrigue. "Tara, this man knows of a place that Duncan was obsessed with. Whatever mystery it holds, it could be the very reason he's no longer with us. Unraveling the secrets of that place might lead us to the elusive killer."

"Sure," Tara said, "but how will you know this guy is not working for the killer, or is not the killer *himself*?"

He gave her a guarded smile. "I am a Priest Knight, Tara. I can discern these things."

She raised an eyebrow, rolled her eyes, and shook a finger at him. "You always say that kind of stuff when you don't want to explain something, Antoff. I just wanted you to know that I know that," Tara muttered to him under her breath about frustrating Priest Knights and secrets.

Antoff responded with a muted chuckle, his eyes twinkling momentarily with amusement. She knew that meant he had no intention of discussing it further.

The wind gusted, blowing a hawker's hat off. He gave chase, his sales pitch still echoing from beneath the overhang, and shopkeepers worked late to sell their goods. The occasional echoes of a blacksmith's hammer rang out in the cold, wet night, singing the end of a long, hard day of toil. Signs hung swinging in the breeze outside the old flagstone two and three-story buildings, marking the storefronts with colorful emblems or portraits identifying what they sold.

Red paint edging the porch roof distinguished the inn from the other buildings. That and a wooden sign swaying under the porch with a picture of an old rusty bucket. Music drifted outside, along with the smells of good food, wine, and beer carried into the streets with laughter.

The old, whitewashed oak door squeaked open, letting a rush of cold air into the bustling common room of the Rusty Bucket. Skepticism ran high in the cities within the Gray Area, with wary patrons shooting quick glances over their shoulders. Eyes above clay mugs of beer scrutinized while they whispered to each other. Pipe smoke lingered, mingling with the aroma of spilled pints and sizzling meats from the kitchen at the inn's rear. A fire roared in a river rock fireplace at the back of the common room, its warmth driving away the chill of the early, wet spring. Antoff followed Tara in, and the music washed over them. Witty and lyrical voices went high, and the tambourine shook as the tune peaked and the crowd roared with laughter.

The serving women, dressed in matching light blue dresses that reached to the knee, and wearing long white aprons, smiled as they skillfully delivered meals and drinks to awaiting customers. They deftly avoided over-friendly patrons who were looking for more than just drinks. Musicians played harps, lutes, and tapped tambourines while customers in the din kept the rhythm with their feet and sang along with a tall blonde woman who stood posed upon a chair, reenacting an inspired scene. Deeper into the common room, they spotted the innkeeper who had sent their invitation by a boy, and she waved them closer.

A large, round woman of middle age, wearing a clean white apron over a gray spring dress, the owner greeted them. Her black hair framed a pretty but stern face that brooked no nonsense. She ushered them through the hall to the private dining rooms connected next to a set of stairs leading up to the patrons' bedrooms.

"Thank you, Mrs. Devens," Tara said, her face still cloaked from under a dripping hood.

"You're welcome, Tara. Be careful; that man in there is dangerous." Her lips compressed, a mix of fear and anger, but she still tried to smile.

"We will be careful, but thank you." Mrs. Devens had known Tara since she was a child running the streets. Tara grabbed her hand and gave it a squeeze to ease her fear before heading into the door of the private room.

Their private dining room, only large enough for a table to sit six, was lit by polished brass wall lamps, trimmed to emit a minimum of light. Shadows played on the walls, reflecting the outline of two men. The first, a large man with a black cloak fringed in red, sat at the head of the table. His well-muscled arms, white and ashen, rested on the table. The atmosphere was cold and dangerous, and a younger man sat next to him on the far side.

Tara's gaze slid over the young man sitting across from her, noting his strong features. His short, blonde locks framed a face lit by eyes the fascinating color of sea green. His brooding expression as he frowned into his ale did nothing to diminish his charm. Her eyes traced the hint of muscles beneath his shirt. He was undeniably handsome. Involuntarily, her cheeks flushed with warmth as his eyes met hers. He had noticed her staring.

Quickly, she averted her gaze. Her heart pounded in her ears, attempting to appear nonchalant. Her mind darted back to the time she unexpectedly encountered him in town. At that moment, his brooding good looks struck her. He was being fawned over by mothers with their daughters, the same ones that talked about him like he was a stray dog when he was not around.

With a mental shake, she reminded herself of his notorious reputation for carousing, a subject of many cautionary tales whispered by concerned parents to their daughters. The stories of his daring escapades were widely known, as were the rumors that spread among the married women. She couldn't deny knowing who he was.

Tara furrowed her brow, lost in thought. *I can't help but wonder if it was a stroke of luck that he never displayed an interest in me. Every man I've ever been interested in seems to have vanished—as though they think I'm some kind of freak*, she mused quietly.

In a raspy voice, the figure in the dark cloak spoke softly to avoid being overheard outside the private room. "Thank you for coming. I invited you to take part in something that should prove interesting to each of you individually and guarantee the knowledge you seek. Master Duncan contacted me, and with him dead, I contacted you. He was researching an old bastion of the Light, and I found it with the help of his notes and a lot of searching. I want to enlist your help to open it. I will pay your expenses if you are interested."

Antoff's eyes, a piercing ice-blue, and chestnut brown was hair secured in a leather tie at his neck that shook when he answered with a nod. "We are interested,"

His nod appeared a touch too hurried, in Tara's opinion. Her head still hooded, water dripped onto the floor. She spoke up. "What are you?" Tara's voice wavered despite her best effort to sound assertive. "What should we call you?" That's when his eyes—spots of swirling silver and gold—met hers, sending a chill down her spine. She wanted to be brave and so she didn't back down.

The dark figure rasped, "Mortality puts so much emphasis on names. For the sake of your curiosity and to allay your fears, you can call me Ivan. As for *what* I am, you would not understand." Ivan tugged back his cloak and his raven-black hair fell at his shoulders, accompanied by a strong jawline and a prominent brow as pasty as bread flour. His eyes touched hers again, and Tara shivered as if an icy wind was blowing across her wet flesh.

"I am Tara," she bravely introduced herself and threw back the hood of her cloak.

Edward's gaze lingered on her from behind the rim of his ale, partially concealed by the glass. Her black hair flowed in wild waves down her shoulders, raindrops glistening on the obsidian strands. Her white bangs nearly concealed the arcane markings, a delicate tangle of swirling, deep grey lines etched from the corners of her eyebrows to the peaks of her cheeks, vanishing down the graceful curves of her neck. They looked like washed out tattoos. He clenched his jaw, willing himself to not stare. *Her eyes, such a pretty shade of grey. I could stare into those eyes and trace those marks until we both lose track of time,* he mused.

Ivan's smile was brief, almost undetectable, as he answered her. "Well met, Tara. Here's your map and the gold for your provisions. Meet me at the marked location. I have other business to attend to first or I would accompany you." As Ivan stood, he dropped a leather-bound folder and a bag of coins on the table, causing a clank. "The location shown on the map is abandoned, as far as I know, and I will wait for you there. Follow the path, and you should have no difficulty." With that, Ivan exited without another word. Tara's eyes followed his predatory form. The feeling of danger left with him, leaving them staring at the items on the table.

Antoff took the bag of coins, bouncing it appraisingly before taking the map from the table. "We should get going. It's getting late, and we need time to find quality gear and horses. They don't come cheap or easy."

Edward, across the table, stood up. "Ivan has hired me to escort you. The name is Edward of Haven, also known as Edward the Dark. I would recommend the Stinger breed of warhorse. They can survive a run and are nasty in a fight." With that, they were off.

The horse and gear purchases took a while, and they decided to start fresh in the morning, leaving the animals stabled at the inn. Tara stood by the stables, watching as Antoff handled the boarding of the Stingers and stored their gear. Soon, Edward emerged from the stables and approached her.

Tara waited for his words, her nerves fluttering like restless *Hornbees* in her stomach. All the while, he leaned against the stable casually, his hands in his pockets. She wanted to scream, "*Speak*!" He was just standing there being handsome, and she hated it. *Besides, if he glimpsed the arcane markings etched into my skin, a rush of fear would likely eclipse any intrigue he felt. I've seen it before — the way they look at me, as if I were a puzzle to be solved or, worse, a harbinger of danger. Their glances shift from curiosity to cautious retreat, leaving me stranded in my skin, a mystery they'd rather avoid instead of discover.*

"Something bothering you, Tara?" He drawled, his eyes ensnaring hers again. Tara flushed and just about managed to shake her head. *Reading a book? Solving mysteries? That was her forte, talking to handsome men? It made her want to throw up.* He let out a low chuckle and straightened. "Good night, Tara. Sleep well. I will be waiting for you in the morning." Edward's lips curled into a mischievous grin, his sea-green eyes sparkling with amusement.

The brightness of his smile spread to every corner of his face, casting a spell of charm that Tara found hard to resist. *Can a man be too good-looking? Stop that!* Tara admonished herself. "Good night, Edward of Haven. It was nice to meet you." She called out, willing her voice to not tremble. *I am as bad as the rest of these girls and their mothers. Mooning over a man. Get a hold on yourself, woman. Stop acting like a girl waiting on the wall at the dance.*

Edward nodded, his sea-green eyes lingering on her, before he turned and strolled back to the inn. As he opened the door, the music enveloped him and reached for her. Tara felt an urge to follow him, maybe even ask for a dance.

Antoff startled her, watching her watch Edward go. "Don't sneak up on me like that!" she said, her hand coming to rest on her heart. *This man has a knack for showing up at all the wrong moments.*

"Come, Tara," Antoff continued, "Let's go home."

Home for them was the loft above the bookstore in the attic. They each had a gable room with a window. Tara's room overlooked the street. It was simple and cozy, with a bed, wardrobe, chest, and a washstand. Nothing fancy. She lay on her bed with her eyes wide open. Her mind buzzed with questions about the mysterious Ivan, the charming Edward, and the ancient bastion of the Light they were about to explore. It was as if her life was on the brink of transformation, and for a moment, the world held its breath, waiting for the secret untold.

Chapter 2 Twisted Places

"Uncertainty is at the heart of every beginning. When we place our feet on the stone and carried away to places unknown. While the allure and thrill lie in the newness and changes, remember: as everything around you shifts and evolves, so do you. You are not immune to changes."

The Elder Brother, the first sun, peeked above the horizon, bathing the landscape in brightness and outlining the rooftops in a warm glow. The morning air was frosty, and warhorses exhaled long, vaporous streams, while grooms tightened saddle girths. Edward was outside waiting when they arrived. He loaded the fourth horse with gear, tying it to his saddlebow, before leaving the stable. Antoff gratefully pressed coins into the head groom's hands. They put their feet to stirrups and hoisted themselves onto the broad backs of dancing Stingers that always challenged new riders. Each quickly brought their mounts under control. Stingers trained as war mounts, bonded with only one rider. Dangerous creatures in light armored scale. They were fearless, loyal, and had bladed tails. If their owner died, you had to put them down; you couldn't sell them to another.

Mounted on Stinger warhorses, they rode down Main Street, where cobblestones glistened from recent rain, and the air resonated with the clatter of steel-clawed hooves. Shop owners bustled about, arranging their wares and exchanging hushed greetings about trade, markets, and taxes with fellow merchants and hawkers, before the second sun, the Little Sister, had even crested the sky.

Guards in grey livery and leather armor swung open the large, iron-banded oak gates, which groaned in protest. The chill of the damp spring air smelled of pine, fir trees, and freshly plowed farmers' fields. A long, grassy meadow waved like an ocean in the wind as they flowed toward the trees that bordered the road. The golden sunshine kissed the many-colored leaves, outlining them in the warmth of a new spring day.

Before them, the Great Road stretched out, a ribbon of promise leading to the Lost Kings Highway crossing. It reached northward to the bustling Harbor Cities and southward to the various communities, towns, and cities nestled within the mysterious Grey Area.

Antoff took the lead, his long, dark cloak draped over his mount's flanks. A round shield hung over his left arm, and the hilt of his sword peeked out. His Stinger, sensing his mood, pranced and broke into a trot. Tara followed, picking up the pace. Edward of Haven wore smoked plate armor, a knight's shield slung over his back, and his hooded cloak displayed the emblem of a hand gripping two lightning bolts. A broadsword, secured by a sturdy leather belt, hung at his waist.

Tara found comfort in knowing he was brooding back there; she didn't know why, save that the lands they would be traveling through were dangerous and all manner of twisted things lived there. *Another sword would certainly be welcome*, she told herself, looking back over her shoulder at him. He gave her a smile and a nod that caused her stomach to flutter, and she quickly looked forward.

New construction and smaller homesteads gave way to dense forests of fir trees, oaks, and Redleaf, which thinned as they neared the lands twisted by the Shattering, close to the border of the Blackened Lands. She remembered the wide swift river, the Torn Flowage, that contrasted bleakly with the wastelands terrain as it flowed by. The river, originating from the mountains called the Steps of Glass in the south, ran its snaking path toward the sea. It was beautiful in a stark kind of way. But it would be days before they would see it.

They traveled straight through to avoid lingering in anyone place, taking only brief rests to allow the horses to recuperate. After a long, hard day, Antoff called a halt with a raised gauntleted hand. "We are going to give the Stingers a rest," he shouted above the howl of the wind, his cloak flapping.

Edward and Tara dismounted side by side. He looked across his saddle at her, and she tore her eyes away as he spoke, pretending to check her Stinger's saddle girth. She didn't want to appear too forward or direct. That was a problem she often had, according to Antoff. He had told her that she was always too direct or literal with people, and it shocked them.

"We should not stay in the Twisted Lands longer than we must, Tara. It invites attacks from minions of the Dark Order and those malformed things that roam this forsaken land. So don't go wandering off without someone with you," Edward advised her with a grin. *Maybe if I give her a reason, she will ask me.* Edward thought hopefully.

He stumbled a little. The wind tangling his broadsword in his cloak. She wanted to laugh.

Tara smiled back with just a little sparkle in her eye. "This is not my first trip into the Twisted Lands, Edward of Haven." She replied haughtily, "I have been here before, and not that long ago. I am in no more danger than the rest of you," she assured him. "Edward of Haven, if *any* of us go anywhere, it should not be unescorted." She hinted.

"Just Edward is fine, Tara." He gave her a nod in return for her answer and went about tending to his Stinger.

Tara was a strange girl, at least as far as Edward was concerned. *Well, all women are mysterious,* he thought, but Tara was different. He just could not decide what it was. First off, she was a mage of some kind. *Not exactly normal.* He had met one at his father's court once, but that one did not have the marks that swirled from eyebrows to cheeks and down her neck like Tara did. He looked at her from the corner of his eye while pulling off his saddle. She wore black leather thieves' armor, matching knee-high riding boots, and had two short swords belted to her hips. And she looked like she could use them, too. *Definitely not a normal girl.*

Antoff set up a campfire in a clearing with large rocks on one side for seating. Nearby, he prepared a lead between two trees, intending to secure the Stingers with precise military order once Tara and Edward had finished tending to them. He had done it so many times he just did not think about it anymore; he could do it in his sleep. *These younglings are going to require some direction*, he thought, watching them.

Antoff raised his voice, "Get your gear stowed so we can move out quickly if we have to. Edward, you need to spread the load between those two Stingers better in the morning. It's trained for fighting, and if we get into combat, half of it is going to be spread out all over the trail. Believe me when I tell you, boy. I have never known the Dark Order for letting you come back and pick your gear up. That gear is life and death out here, so split it up."

Edward tensed at Antoff's commanding voice, not used to being ordered around by anyone. He gave Antoff a look of weary arrogance, his voice tight as he replied, "*Relax*, Antoff, I know what to do."

Antoff narrowed his eyes the way he did when measuring a pupil. "You can show me you know what to do by actually doing *it* from now on. If I have to tell you, that means the job was not properly done. You get me, lad?"

Edward's green eyes flashed with annoyance as they remained locked with Antoff's ice-blue ones. "Yeah, I get you. Just give me a chance and lay off, Antoff, I will do better. Ok?" He shook his head. *This old Priest Knight is as hard as stone, with a tongue that stings like a salted whip!*

Antoff gave a grunt in answer. He brought a water pot to the fire and began heating it. *The boy's spoiled and had it way too easy on his father's gold.* Besides, he wanted to know what the young man was made of, before metal had tasted meat, preferably. It was an old trick, but it usually worked. Put the heat on them and see if they melt. "Tomorrow is a new day and a new chance, Edward. What you do with it is up to you. But just so you know, I will be watching."

Edward's face was red. He did not bother to answer, but his eyes flicked to Tara and then away irritably as he finished hobbling the horses.

Tara sat across from Antoff, balling one fist and planting it firmly on her hip. "Did you put that armor on too tight or something? What are you doing, Antoff?"

Antoff didn't bother to look up from his cooking, "and what am I doing Tara?"

"You're testing him." She huffed.

Antoff raised his eyebrows, "And? Is there a problem?"

Tara folded her arms together under her breasts, pursing her lips. "Edward is new to your ways. You cannot expect him to be perfect."

Antoff finally raised his head and gave Tara a look that spoke of his experience. "I know that, Tara. I am just checking him out a little. You don't want to find out he can't deal with a little stress when the blades come out, do you? That boy can fight. I can see that in the way he carries himself. What I am saying is, he doesn't need your protection."

Her look was firm, and voice was a furious whisper that bit off each word. "No. I don't want to wait until there is trouble to find out. I want him to choose us over himself. But he must have a reason to be loyal, and you are not giving him one, Antoff. And I am not protecting him."

Antoff grunted a sigh. "That part comes later, Tara. Trust me, I know what I am doing. It worked on you, if you recall?"

"Did it?" Tara asked, "Yes, as I remember, I tried to stab you for it?" She raised an eyebrow and grinned. "You should think about that before you push him too far."

After five days of travel, they journeyed through farmland, lush forests, and rocky crags, and arrived at the dusty, oppressive expanse of the Twisted Lands. Here, they encountered distortions of nature, lurking out of sight, warped, and twisted, hungry for survival. Creatures skittered across ridges, and some animals settled into positions resembling plants or rocks. Shapes and colors shifted, and the creature stilled and to the eye at least they were gone.

The Elder Brother ascended to its zenith, hotly pursued by his Little Sister across the brilliant spring sky. Below them, the Torn Flowage raged beneath the towering, abandoned rampart, supporting a fragment of a stone archway. The bridge gates loomed, half-open, serving as the entrance to the Twisted Land, an alluring mystery, a fusion of promise and menace. Crossing this bridge was fraught with danger.

The territory was infamous as a hunting ground for Roc'Nar's marauding barbarians, who reveled in ambushing and seizing opportunities against unwary wayfarers. The distinct clatter of steel-tipped hooves on stone signaled potential danger, spurring the party to scrutinize their surroundings with increased concern.

Yet, as they reached the bridge's crest, their hopes for a peaceful crossing quickly evaporated. Their adversaries had cunningly concealed themselves, laying a strategic trap with deadly precision. Tara spotted movement on both banks. Crag Lions, aptly named for their cliff-top stalking grounds, were crafty predators. Settling high upon craggy precipices, surveying their territory, patiently waiting until their prey was vulnerable. Exploiting the landscape's natural features like ravines and narrow passages, they ensnared unsuspecting victims, demonstrating their cunning and adaptability. Tara, accustomed to their deceptive tactics, shockingly; she had never seen them use a bridge for an ambush before. Tara cursed to herself for not closing the gate.

These formidable creatures moved with lethal elegance, their serpentine, scaled hides catching the sunlight, resembling a textured bed of sand painted with dark, bold stripes. Their heads were an uncanny fusion of feline and reptilian features, topped with showy frills that flared ominously, enhancing their snake-like allure. Their large, curved fangs were as deadly as they were intimidating. Despite their imposing stature, they weighed only between eighty and a hundred and twenty pounds, the largest reaching only up to one's waist. Tara's stomach dropped, particularly when she spotted the pack's alpha, a commanding beast leading at least a dozen of these fearsome creatures. A confrontation with this daunting alpha and its squadron appeared inevitable. The odds were against them, but retreat was not an option. Her mind raced, formulating an action plan as she steeled herself for the imminent battle.

"Antoff!" Tara yelled.

"I see them. Dismount the Stingers," Antoff ordered.

"What?" Edward exclaimed. "We can charge toward the other bank and run. That's insane, Antoff."

Antoff dismounted his Stinger and positioned himself in front of it, unsheathing his sword. "It took us five minutes to trot out here, Edward. They'll be on us in one. Do you truly think we'll outrun them?"

Tara descended from her mount and pulled a leather case that held a bone-white short bow with a built-in quiver teeming with broadhead arrows, slinging it over her shoulder. She drew an arrow and nocked it. "Antoff is right, Edward. We can't outrun them; there are at least a dozen, and they're much faster. This will give them seven targets. It'll divide their focus."

"For the love of the gods, Tara," Edward unsheathed his menacing broadsword and then his shield from his back, positioning himself beside Antoff and providing room for a swing.

"Watch your tongue, boy. Do you really want to anger the gods of Light right now? I think we'll need at least one of them on our side, don't you?"

"Can't you just conjure something up, Tara?" Edward's voice was strained; there were six Crag Lions approaching from the direction they headed and at least as many from where they had come.

Tara stepped up behind them, preparing to draw her bow. "Edward, there are things far worse than Crag Lions out here. Some drawn to the Power like a dinner bell. If you think it looks bleak now, just wait until a Dragon Hound arrives, and they seldom travel alone."

The Crag Lion's elongated bodies were closing the gap, their terrifying yet graceful strides consuming the distance. Sinewy, powerful muscles flexed beneath a layer of palm-sized scales, an interlocked fluid mesh of armor. This natural defense system rippled from their shoulders to their flanks, tracing the ridge of their backs and cascading down to their snake-like underbellies. The scales then thickened into sturdy chest plates at the front, their texture contrasting starkly against the sleekness of their bodies.

Their claws, thick as fingers, scraped against the stone blocks of the bridge like a blade dragged across a whetstone, resounding in the eerie quiet. However, the

Crag Lions moved nearly noiselessly, except for the occasional sharp intake of breath, inhaled into lungs designed for endurance. These creatures were evolved hunters, built for relentless pursuit and efficient ambushes, and it was in moments like these that their deadly silence was most foreboding.

Tara closed her eyes. She needed the connection. She needed the image to form before the onslaught. Tara let it rush over her, the higher reality, the storm others couldn't see. Raw Power gushed out, a vast reservoir of Light and blackness lashing, twisting, and churning against each other, vying for supremacy, each striving to extinguish the other. It was a kind of fractured balance, a fabric torn in two. Tara summoned an envelope of reality in her mind. An image of white-hot fire from a forge solidified. She was now visible, and these opposing poles of living Power would strive to devour her, to absorb her, adding her essence to their own. She reached for both and allowed the tendrils of Power to lash out and touch her. Tara drew; she pulled.

Opening her eyes, and the lower reality was there in every detail, every fiber of its complex construct interwoven with threads of energy into matter. The higher reality was a storm threatening to unravel the world, each pulling at the other's portion of the construct, trying to consume it and add new threads of its own. The first of the Crag Lions, running along a raised edge of the curtain wall meant to prevent people from falling into the river, had come into range.

Tara drew the arrow to her cheek, hearing the creak of her bone-white short bow. Her whisper was only for herself, not intended for anyone else to hear. The words were not necessary; they just helped her visualize the arrow in every detail as she altered the flows of the fibers of its construction and introduced a new one into reality.

Edward's heart pounded as he watched Tara from the corner of his eye. They flickered between her and the fast-approaching creatures, covering the ground with each stride. Whether from excitement or fear, his voice trembled. "Come on, Tara, do something. They're almost on us."

"Oh'Mas Flam'Meer," the whisper left Tara's lips, and the arrowhead burst white-hot, as if pulled from a smoldering forge fire. She loosed the arrow, and in a streak, it arced high and struck as Tara pulled another smoothly from her quiver and whispered again, "Oh'Mas Flam'Meer." The broadhead squeaked white-hot in a wash of reality that rippled out like a stone thrown into a pond.

The first broadhead struck, its white-hot tip having lost neither its glow nor heat when it sunk deep into the neck of the nearest oncoming Crag Lion. It penetrated the scale as if it were butter. The cat let out a screaming yelp and rolled, tumbling off the side, followed by a splash of water.

Edward stepped back as the heat washed over him. He was going to have to reassess this girl. The Stingers had spun to face the other direction and tossed their heads, preparing for the rush. Edward bolted for the rear to defend against that portion of the ambush. He weaved his way past the horses, his shield raised, and caught sight of the first cat as it launched into the air, leaving the ground, its momentum carrying it toward the closest Stinger. He just had time to intercept it as it struck.

Edward raised his knight's shield high to deflect the weight of the creature's blow. His broadsword followed with a stroke that had a lot of "what if's" and "hope so's" in the calculation. The Crag Lion struck with all its weight, multiplied by the speed. It clung to the shield, and they were going down, nearly bowling him over.

But the worst part. The clawed paws rapped the shield, and the head was coming over the top. His sword struck across the ridged back of the scaled cat and took a bite, but it was not deep. What's more, the cat did not let go of the shield, and now Edward had a problem. He was going down under the weight of a pissed-off cat with teeth like curved daggers sticking out of both sides of its open mouth.

He collapsed under the weight of the aggressive feline, the thin, long creature perched on top of his shield, exerting crushing pressure. The world seemed to close in around him, the weight pressing against him, his every move restricted by the force of the cat's attack.

A metallic blur just missed his head and armor as he slid shield-mounted by the Crag Lion toward his Stinger. It was the warhorse's clawed shoe that was the blur, and it struck the head of the cat, launching it in a powerful thwack against the bridge wall that nearly dislodged Edward's shoulder from his arm due to the shield strap.

Edward peered up at the Stinger with gratitude, and it rolled its four eyes with the look of *"Get up, dumbass, there are four more, and that one is not dead."* Now, Stingers can't speak, but if it could, that would have been pretty close to what it said, he thought.

A trio of Crag Lions advanced with deliberate precision toward Antoff and Tara. Antoff, with swift grace, hoisted his round shield into a defensive stance, and with a flourish of his longsword, he shaved a piece from the nearest feline foe. In the next fluid motion, he spun low, driving the horizontal edge of his shield into the skull of the bewildered beast. His maneuver culminated in a seamless repositioning back into a defensive stance, his shield resuming its vigil over his torso. The cat's four yellow-gold eyes fixed upon him, meticulously flanking him on either side.

Tara tempted to assist Antoff by launching an arrow, yet for a man of the cloth, his movements mimicked the lethal elegance of a viper and the fluidity of a seasoned dancer. The close quarters combat was a risky scenario - she was just as likely to hit him as the cat. With a swift, practiced move, she slid her arrow back into its quiver and stowed the short bow. Retrieving two short swords from her hips, she moved to stand by Antoff's side, creating a barrier against the cats' flanking.

The third cat, struck hard by the edge of Antoff's shield, lay there on the cold stone of the bridge. Its limbs twitched in a futile struggle to rise, but it remained prone, its senses stunned by the blow. The one facing off with Antoff looked to be the alpha, as it was the largest. Having lost three of its number already, it was none too happy with them.

Edward's voice came from the rear. "Hey! Little help back here!"

"We are busy, Edward of Haven!" Tara yelled back; her voice strained behind the clanging of swords.

Edward was on his feet again, staring down the teeth of three pissed-off cats; the wounded one had run off. Apparently, steel-clawed shoes left something to be desired, and that one at least did not want a second course.

The four Stingers were a combination of facing every which way, looking for something to slash with a bladed tail or to kick, and Edward was doing his best to fend off a Crag Lion that had removed some significant weight from his rear exterior plate mail and one of his ass cheeks while he was trying to get up. That left a mark stinging wet with blood, and *"We are busy, Edward of Haven!"* was not helping. He mouthed Tara's words mockingly.

The cats appeared shaken, likely from the Stingers' threat, Edward mused. He, on the other hand, was bleeding, looking more like a morsel. The closest cat, the ass-cheek swiper, went for another chunk of his hide. Edward returned the favor by removing part of its foot with his blade. Well, that did it for that one; it was off and running, limping away.

Edward heard a loud scream from a cat and then a growl, and the cats turned with regret and retreated toward the banks they had come from. It looked as though for now, he was off the diet.

Antoff broke through the Stingers, an angry gash sliced across his thigh, followed by Tara.

Tara was going to a saddlebag. "Let's have a look, Antoff, you're first."

Edward spread his arms wide. "Right here in the middle of the bridge?"

Tara looked at him with a raised eyebrow, her cool steel-grey eyes running over him with a smile. "It's safer than the bank at the moment, Edward of Haven. When I am done with Antoff, you are next." *Seeing him helpless like this is only adding to his charm.*

"I can stitch the boy up," Antoff grunted through his teeth as she worked on him.

Edward gave Antoff a nod of appreciation. Tara looked like she would enjoy it a little too much, and right now, he felt, well, vulnerable. He turned his bleeding cheek to the bridge, which only brought a brighter smile from Tara's face. *Yes, this girl was definitely not normal.*

Chapter 3 Lost Time

"There is something wrong here. We should never have come. This blasted land is twisted because of our folly and our fall. Nature, torn asunder, and remade into half-truths: a broken and misguided reality."

In the desolate valley, their horses thundered through a dry riverbed. Dust billowed up around steel-shod hooves that rang like a smithy against the dark, yellowish stone. Rock shards and disturbed dirt sprayed, leaving a hazy cloud streaming in their wake. A red misty moon hung partly shrouded by thick clouds. The glow bathed the valley in hues of red and orange that disappeared into the shadows of rocky outcroppings running the length of the valley. Darkness concealed their figures as they rode. Glimmers of steel armor peeked from beneath heavy woolen cloaks, dark black or woodland green, rippled across their horses' flanks.

Antoff studied the map, his finger following the vivid red line that mirrored the terrain before them. Amid the howling wind and thundering hoofbeats, his voice pierced through. "Go right!"

Just off the old riverbed, a trail veered sharply up the mountainside. Jagged remains of long-petrified trees sprinkled the ridge randomly, giving a ghostly outline of the long-extinct forest that existed before the Shattering of the Balance.

Years of weathering cast shadows from rocky ledges and boulders, causing the trail to disappear as it snaked its way up the mountain's face. High above, the smallest pinprick of firelight danced on the cave mouth, a sight that would have eluded the eye entirely had it not been for prior knowledge of its existence.

The trail angled upward, away from the old riverbed, traveling higher and ever higher. The loose, rocky trail would have proved too difficult for any normal horses. However, Stinger warhorses, necks arched, with powerful muscles pulling and hooves prancing, fought their way upward. Steel-clawed shoes tore their way up the mountainside trail with effort, kicking loose rocks off the trail's edge, causing them to cascade down the side, echoing as they fell. Hooves plodded and clattered, huge muscles strained. Minutes turned to hours as the Stingers tossed their heads and rolled their four eyes. The rigors became too much for them, even their valiant hearts.

They dismounted to lead the warhorses the rest of the way on foot, pulling them along with effort. The winds whipped cloaks, streaming behind them like torn sails. Blown sand needled them, coarse and stinging their skin, while pebbles blew in from the track above.

Finally, they reached the cave, tired and worn from the long climb. The mouth edged in a soft glow, the width and height of a horse and rider. Antoff Grant signaled with his upraised fist and handed the reins of his horse to Tara for safekeeping.

Antoff pulled his painted round shield tightly to his body and drew the ornate longsword from its sheath as he entered the cave. Keeping to the shadows, Antoff all but disappeared into the darkness of the inner cave wall that curved quickly to the right. After a moment, Antoff soundlessly came back out, waving them in while simultaneously taking their horse's reins. Tara, perched on a high, narrow ledge overlooking the valley below, trying to ward off the icy wind, her left hand clutching the cloak drawn tightly around her. Tara's companions guided their mounts into the cave, disappearing within.

In the valley below, the pale light of a false dawn broke over the horizon, a prelude to the imminent day. Two dark red Dragon Hounds stood watch, their eyes gleamed red, reflecting a non-human intelligence. They moved with deadly beauty, sensing their prey through the air, their acidic drool hissing and smoking upon contact with the dusty soil of the dried riverbed. The dark gods of this world dispatched Dragon Hounds to hunt prey and prizes desired by the Lords of the Night. These large creatures possessed transparent, leathery, blood-red wings and bodies covered in reddish scales with black edges. Their heads resembled lizards, adorned with small, dagger-like teeth that shone white in the soft light. Their broad chests tapered down to their flanks, and a long, scaly, spiked, and bladed tail completed their dragon-like appearance, making them twice the size of a horse. As they moved with lethal determination, their overlapping, scaly armor blazed red in the early morning light.

Tara furrowed her brow, narrowing her eyes in irritation. *Just that little use of Power on the bridge drew them? This cannot be. They must have already been searching or hunting nearby,* she mused. Releasing ancient words in a hushed, exasperated sigh, the syllables escaping her lips in a murmur only she could hear. A dusty wind, imbued with Power, roared down the mountain trail. It erased any trace of their presence, sweeping across the dried riverbed. The Dragon Hounds turned into the wind, their translucent, blood-red, leathery wings snapping open with a pop, lifting them into the sky as the gust of wind passed by. Sniffing keenly, hissing and screeching in frustration, they pivoted, wheeling in the direction where the arcane wind blew away from the concealed path. Their departure dispersed into the dusty morning sky. Tara nodded in satisfaction and, after a few minutes, rose wearily to her feet, brushing herself off. She entered the cave without a backward glance as the last remnants of the night faded away.

A fire blazed in the center of the room, casting fitful light on the rough cave walls, surrounded by rocks forming a circle almost three feet across. The room spanned fifty feet round with a ceiling that reached twenty feet or more above, with stalactites and stalagmites that reached towards each other, looking like apple cores, for massive natural supports. Entering, Tara moved from the cave mouth and surveyed the subterranean room. Except for Antoff Grant, who was hobbling the horses in an anteroom, the men sat on large rocks that surrounded the fire, taking in the warmth as small cut sticks and dried dung snapped and popped, giving a less than desirable odor mixed with the smells of moss and the dankness of the cave.

Tara's gaze found Edwards, his eyes like beacons in the dimly lit cave. Her heart quickened. In that shared moment, an unspoken connection that made her feel seen. A silent message passing between them, as if whispered, *you are not alone.*

She chose to sit across from a shadowy figure covered in a black heavy woolen cloak edged in a deep red border, with only his bare, heavily muscled arms and legs sticking out, exposing flesh that appeared a pale, almost white color. They had agreed to meet a week earlier in the town of RavenHof, at an inn called The Rusty Bucket. Even now, his cool deadly composure and the color of his pale flesh marked him as Half-Dead, causing a shiver as a cold bead of sweat trailed down her back between her shoulder blades.

He called himself Ivan and nothing else. His grey and marbled gold eyes were cold and unsettling whenever they brushed you or looked into yours, leaving you with the feeling that you had just been weighed and measured in a way that calculated your value to mortality and whether you would be missed if you did not show up again. Ivan had raven-black hair that fell at his shoulders, accenting a strong jawline and a large, overly prominent brow. He spoke in a raspy whisper that still seemed to carry above the crackle of the fire. "As I told you in RavenHof, this cave is unknown to any that are still living that I am aware of. It has been more than eight hundred years since its use, and except for the Dire Wolf that I had to come to accommodation with for us to share the space, I have seen no other signs that would show otherwise."

Edward the Dark abruptly looked up, his interest in the conversation suddenly piqued. "Dire Wolf! No one made any mention of any Dire Wolf before. Some of them can weigh as much as a horse and are hard to kill even with our number." Edward looked questionably at Ivan. "And where is said Dire Wolf now?" *Crag Lions and now a Dire Wolf, what's next, Dragons?*

Ivan's gaze shifted to Edward with a subtle lift of his eyebrow, a half-smile playing at the corners of his lips. "He's here in the cave, concealed behind a column," he said, his voice carrying an air of gritty nonchalance. As he spoke, he gestured casually over his shoulder in the general direction.

Antoff Grant strolled towards the fire after tending to the horses. "That certainly explains the smell of dry dirty dog combined with that wonderful aroma of burning dung." Antoff sat down on the big rock next to Edward. He pulled a leather-lined burlap bag out and set it on the ground in front of him. Antoff rummaged through the bag. He produced dried meats, cheese, and a small kettle for tea, all in quantities that could satisfy the rumbling in their stomachs.

Tara watched as Antoff passed the meal out to each of them and made the tea. The tea was not fresh and even if it was, the overpowering aroma of the mysterious Dire Wolf and smoking dung ruined the flavor, causing her to wrinkle her nose at the taint left in her mouth.

As she sipped her tea, her mind wandered to a time not that long ago, when she grappled with the elusive image that only she could see—an image representing a higher reality, invisible to ordinary eyes, a realm where the forces of good and evil took on tangible forms. This higher reality once existed as a unified fabric, a harmonious balance where opposing powers coexisted balancing each other.

As a young thief on the streets of RavenHof, Tara's life changed when Master Duncan, an observant bookshop owner, saw the latent potential within her. He recognized the "spark" of power that lay dormant within, the potential to tap into the vast resources of the higher reality. Master Duncan took her under his wing, nurturing and guiding her until his untimely death, which she had vowed to avenge.

Master Duncan's voice reverberated within her thoughts, his words assuming a patient, lecturing cadence. "You have the spark. Magic girl, there were all the usual kinds before greed caused the breaking and some even called it a technology. I am not saying that the other does not work anymore, only that they have become lesser forms. What I am saying is things are different. Now the greater magic in this world derives from the Fabric of Creation, a higher reality where the forces of good and evil, light and darkness, take tangible forms. Yet, the world changed dramatically after the balance shattered. It split the unified fabric into two distinct paths of Power: The Path of Light and The Path of Darkness:"

The Path of Light drew strength from positive emotions—love, joy, hope, and empathy. Wielders of the Light could create protective shields, heal wounds, and illuminate darkness. However, their energy drained with each use, risking exhaustion and vulnerability. They had to maintain emotional positivity for their abilities to work.

Conversely, the Path of Darkness harnessed negative emotions—anger, fear, despair, and hatred. These wielders manipulated shadows, induced fear, and could create illusions. Their powers required emotional negativity and could consume them if used recklessly.

Grey Walkers, much like Tara, possessed the rare gift of blending both paths, serving as a bridge between the realms of Light and Darkness. Their unique status allowed them to perform incredible feats, but the balance was delicate. Leaning too far towards one path risked losing access to the other.

Tara heard herself as a child weeping. *I don't want it, father. I want to be like everyone else. Everyone hates me, and I don't have any friends they are afraid of me. I'm a freak!*

Duncan's voice whispered to her mind again, "You can't change what you are, girl. But you can choose to do the best you can for everyone around you. I can ask no more than that. Besides Tara, I will always be your friend." Duncan's voice echoed and then was gone.

Tara's anger grew hot. *Accept it. You are a freak! It's no wonder men run away from you.*

Tara knew she was like one of these rare beings. An aberration. Grey Walkers can blend the energies of Light and Darkness to create a temporary balance, enabling them to perform incredible feats like creating powerful energy blasts, telekinetic abilities, and reality-warping on a minor scale. However, this comes at a significant cost. The balance is precarious, and if a Grey Walker leans too heavily towards one path, they risk being consumed by that energy, losing their ability to tap into the other path. Grey Walkers must always maintain emotional and mental balance. And that was the part she had difficulty with.

The Power is accessible through intense mental focus, visualization, and emotional connection. Mages visualize the higher reality, reaching out to it mentally, and channel the energies down into the mortal plane. The more vivid and precise the visualization, the more potent the effect.

The Power can also be utilized to manipulate the world's creatures, creating new breeds, and altering existing ones. However, this comes with the risk of creating uncontrollable monsters if the balance is not appropriately managed.

There are physical limits to how much Power a person can channel. Overuse can lead to fatigue, physical harm, or even death. As such, mages must train their bodies and minds to increase their magic-bearing capacity in order to reach their potential.

Every mage's goal should be to mend the Fabric of Creation, restoring the balance between Light and Darkness; however, the path to achieving this remains uncertain, with the forces of Light and Darkness in constant struggle, each striving for domination. The ultimate power lies with the one who can fully command both paths, a feat yet to be accomplished. *There is still so much greed and the desire for Power, the very thing that destroyed us, still runs rampant in the world.* Her mind echoed.

Now, at twenty-five, and five years after the loss of her mentor, Tara still clung to the Power as she clung to his memory. It served as a reminder of the father figure she had known and lost, fueling her determination to seek justice for his death. Yet, another presence had emerged in her life, Antoff, bringing new challenges and revelations about the fractured reality she grappled with.

As she sipped her tea, Tara felt the weight of her responsibility in this turbulent higher reality. The torn fabric of creation beckoned with intense energy, pushing her to navigate the boundaries between Light and Darkness, struggling to find her place in the eternal battle. *Can the war be stopped? Can the fabric be mended?* These are the questions that she needed answered.

"Tara, Tara," a voice in the distance called.

Tara's eyes fluttered and refocused. "What is it?" Tara replied, maybe just a little too angry.

Ivan watched her knowingly; *This girl is smoldering with Power.* To his eyes, she glowed like a furnace. "I asked if you saw anything outside; it took you some time to come in?"

Tara answered slowly, only half in lesser reality, "Below in the valley, Dragon Hounds were hunting us, but they are searching in the wrong place now, and besides, the day is breaking and the Power of the Night Lords is waning." Tara replied, distracted, then looked away, hiding her inner turmoil.

Antoff's gaze lingered on her, the frosty edge in his icy blue eyes giving way to a softened expression. Memories carried him back to that distant night when he had trailed her to the bookshop, the weight of time making it feel like ages past. He had watched her since arriving in RavenHof after the death of his old friend Master Duncan, a retired cleric of the same Order. Antoff had left the Order of the Light as a full Priest Knight after engaging in campaigns against the darkness along the boundary in what they called the Grey Area. Now the Grey Area was where he lived and searched for the assassin that killed his friend.

Antoff knew about the girl who captured Master Duncan's heart, the one his friend had written to him about and begged him to watch over her should he be assassinated by the Lords of the Night. Duncan had said that the Dark Lords wanted her and were looking for her to use as a vessel. Old Master Duncan was trying to figure out the depth and width of her talent. It was obvious to Antoff that he had found the daughter he had always wanted but never had before fate had brought him, Tara. Antoff, the old knight, had had to corner Tara in the bookshop. After taking away two small, simple blades she had stuck him with, he held her weeping form to himself.

Tara investigated Antoff's eyes and said, "You loved him too?"

"Yes, and I am here to help you find his killer." That was all Antoff could make himself say. Any more than that would have caused his stone exterior to crack and reveal the man beneath the Priest Knight. Antoff slowly looked away as she met his gaze, raising an eyebrow questionably, but the old knight did not speak. *Whatever vengeance she thinks she needs, I will see that she gets it.*

The darkness faded to light as the wind blew steadily, kicking up dust that blustered into the cave entrance, adding insult to the already haggard air within. Daybreak always brought new hope as the darkness lost its strength and light gained power over the night, ruling the circumstances that governed fate, even if only for fifteen hours of the day.

Edward lowered himself onto the gritty stone floor, wincing as the rough texture bit into his palms. The cave's cool embrace clung to his back as he leaned against the wall, watching the light that cascaded through the cave mouth, showing the particles of dust and sand that blew in from the mountainside trail. Edward daydreamed. *How have I fallen so far? The son of Lord Lars Haven and the future of my family's fiefdom, and now all lost.*

That day so long ago started like any other. He had broken his fast on eggs, fresh hot buttermilk bread from the stone oven, and honey, all prepared by his father's Haven manor staff. Edward had hurried to dress, picking only his best clothing out to impress the women of the court. Lord Haven sat in judgment, hearing the locals' problems. Problems always needed to be solved, and his father had been teaching Edward from an early age to rule well. The few times he had sat on the high-backed chair in the throne room, raised above the court so that all eyes and ears were on him, he had judged well and had the respect of their people, his father had told him.

He sat beside his father, and his mind drifted away from the tedious arguments of merchants or farmers concerning goods and unpaid contracts or whatever else. He stared at a young woman who smiled back at him with an obvious interest that did not evade his father's notice.

Lady Martins showed interest in anyone that gave the least bit of a smile, but she was young and attractive, and that all by itself sufficed for Edward. After court, they ran off together, spending time at the local inn drinking and dancing until late in the night. One thing led to another, and Edward had fallen asleep. When he was startled awake by the watchmen and guard surrounding him, the constable stood over him, gasping with his mouth hanging open. Edward could still see the blood covering his clothes, and his ornate silver inlaid dagger plunged into her heart. Stab wounds had covered her upper body, and her face frozen with terror.

The old, wrinkled-faced constable said, "You've done it this time, boy, and there will be no saving you by your father's position." Edward tried to shout that he did not do it, nor could he remember anything. But all evidence pointed to him alone. They clapped him in iron, bruised, bloody, and held him at the Haven prison yard; he waited until his father had come.

Lord Haven came with an entourage of loyal arms men that looked ready to kill. His father gazed down on him from between the bars of his cell and said, "The law is the law, son, and not even we are above it. To save your mother, I will spare Haven the trial. You are guilty and sentenced to death or a coward's banishment; it is your choice, son."

Edward's eyes widened, his lips parting as his thoughts stalled, grappling with the astonishing jolt. His father had refused to grant him a defense. "Then banish me, Father, if I'm not even allowed an honorable defense," Edward said. Tossed out and banished to the Grey Area with only his armor, weapons, clothes on his back, and a stipend of monthly gold. Without honor and abandoned. Set up and betrayed. Edward's fists clenched, his gaze locked on the walls of the cave. The futility of the situation sank in. But if he could restore his honor, the honor of his house, and his family, he would do it. *I am so ashamed. I was so spoiled. An embarrassment to my family. Until I recover my honor, I am no good to any of them or anyone else. Who would want me if they knew?*

Movement in the cave caused Edward to startle back to reality. His companions had unloaded the Stingers while he daydreamed. Hopping to his feet, Edward brushed himself off. Wordlessly, he headed toward his mount in the antechamber to get his gear.

Ivan spoke quietly to Tara, "The cave is obviously artificial because the size and shape are too uniform and naturally made. And look at the spacing of these columns, Tara."

Tara's fingers brushed the cool cave wall as her gaze swept across the room, her brow creasing in thought to puzzle out the room's purpose. "It doesn't make any sense," Tara said aloud to herself. "Why bother creating a room out of solid rock, which does not even go anywhere?"

Ivan gave a slow, almost indecipherable smile and said, "No, it does not make any sense, does it? You must remember Tara; we are not dealing with the thinking of today or our rudimentary practices of hiding things. What we are dealing with here is a Mage of some type. That is for sure. And Tara, of course, you know what it takes to figure out what a Mage has done, don't you?"

Tara gave Ivan a questioning look before answering, "Another Mage." She glanced at Antoff, hoping for some confirmation, and he responded with a grunt and a nod. Exhausted from the journey, Tara closed her eyes and focused. Taking deep breaths, she steadied both her nerves and her mind. Tara knew she was pushing it too far, stretching her abilities to their limits. Her powers, like a double-edged sword, cut through the fabric of reality, but they also exacted a toll. Fatigue gnawed at her, the weight of her choices sinking in. *Just this one last thing, and then I will rest.* She promised herself.

Creation, torn in two halves and battling for balance, was on the brink of destruction. Tara's mind ignited like a tapestry unfurling; she visualized the intricate dance of creation and sculpted its threads with the brushstrokes of her thoughts. She was the balancing force, but the strain was immense. It was a lot to hold in an image, what the higher reality looked like.

Summoning her imagination, Tara visualized the torrent between Darkness and Light: shadow fighting to consume molten sunlight, struggling amidst powerful waves in a higher reality. The immense Power threatened to overwhelm her, to absorb her into its depths. She was already bone tired, but she pushed on.

Initially, forming this image and grasping reality took time, but with practice, it became quicker. Tara worked meticulously, unraveling time and creation, searching for inconsistencies in the structure of the cave room as she pushed the image further backward in time. She compared its current state to its past, aligning the two images until they perfectly overlay the room's current state.

Using such arcane Power drained her, and she knew she wasn't at her peak potential. Time-stretching strained the barriers of her imagination.

Master Duncan said that with time, she would grow in strength and expand her imagination and ability to affect reality using the flows of Power. But it seemed to be so slow and arduous a process. Tara was in a hurry to mature into her potential. Scanning the room, columns appeared where natural supports now resembled men with arms raised and hands supporting the ceiling, their stone armor bearing gilded, overlapping plates painted in gold. The room, finished in stone tile, and colorful frescos covered the walls, depicting scenes of trade and warfare. The frescos showed a wide river swiftly flowing beneath the mountain in a lush, forested valley, with huge stone docks that jutted out into the water like fingers. River ships lay moored, and traders loaded and unloaded cargo with cranes. Now all long gone after the Shattering of the Balance. Ivan stared intensely at Tara who, to his eyes, blazed like the sun's molten and burning with Power that he could never touch. Tara pointed and said, "The door lies there in the rear of the room." Antoff and Ivan looked at a solid wall of stone where a door should be.

She walked weakly towards the location. As she approached the hidden doorway, Antoff and Ivan followed. She retrieved a piece of chalk from her pocket and marked the outline of the door, reaching only as high as she could. "The doorway is at least fifteen feet tall," she declared, her voice wavering as dizziness overcame her. Finally, strength gave way as her knees buckled under her weight. Antoff tried to reach for Tara as she collapsed, only to find her already missing from the spot where she had stood only an instant earlier.

Ivan moved with supernatural speed, a blur of motion scooping the limp Tara up before she could fall. His eyes changed to a deep shade of blood red and gold that seemed to swirl together and glowed with a dim, angry light. "Get a blanket!" Ivan shouted as he cradled her gently. Holding Tara affected him. *She is raw Power, but barely trained. She is vulnerable. I need this girl to access this place.*

But it was too late. Antoff moved with the reactions of the Priest Knight, drawing his ornate longsword with the smooth elegance of a veteran swordsman. "Unhand Her!" Antoff's voice was furious, his words biting off behind clenched teeth. Antoff's thoughts churned like a tempest within. His responsibility for Tara weighed heavy on his shoulders, a constant reminder of his failure. He couldn't shake the feeling of letting her down, a wound that cut deeper than any blade. *She falls and I am not the one to catch her. I have failed her. Tara was pushing herself too hard, and I didn't put a stop to it. Damn it! She needs me to be strong. Needs me to say no. She won't do it for herself.*

Antoff's ice-blue eyes locked onto Ivan's, a brewing storm of tension swirling beneath the surface. Like two opposing forces hurtling toward a collision. But for now, the storm remained on the horizon, its distant thunder a warning.

Ivan looked sullenly at Antoff and the two men stared at each other with danger thick in the air, but then Ivan shook his head and laid Tara down gently. "I am only helping her! Be calm, I will get her blankets, Priest Knight." Ivan said angrily. Then ran for the antechamber to retrieve blankets as Tara slipped into an unnatural slumber and the world faded away to fitful dreams. The last scraps of awareness ebbed from her sight.

Chapter 4 The Deep

"Beneath the foundations of El'idar, there's a profound disconnection from the familiar, unfolding across the threshold of a new realm. Above ground, you navigate within familiar rules and norms. If you lose your way in the treacherous domain below, do not worry, you will eventually be forgotten."

Tara awoke to the sounds of steel ringing on stone, echoing throughout the chamber. Men in shirtsleeves worked feverishly with pickaxes and hammers to clear the entrance. Dust hung in the air, settling on her companions like soot on chimney sweeps. She stood and looked at the rubble piled knee-high on both sides of the door, its blackness hollow like a void. Lantern light flickered, pooling inside the doorway.

Turning her attention, Tara noticed someone had placed her gear beside the wall where she had slept. With blankets still wrapped tightly around her. She approached the working men, looking as if she'd emerged from a dust storm, powder shedding from her blankets with each step. Astonished, Tara observed the clean line that marked the boundary of the wall, as if time froze and the damage of the Shattering of the Balance had not extended beyond the doorway. The floor tiles remained covered with undisturbed dust, sloping gently downward and vanishing into darkness. The walls and columns showed no signs of wear, just as she had seen them while using her time-viewing Power. Fascinating frescos decorated the walls, depicting scenes of trade and warfare, offering a glimpse into the grandness of bygone nations.

After quickly dusting themselves off and washing to preserve their limited water supply, they prepared for the underground expedition. Antoff Grant donned battle-scarred chainmail over boiled leather. He secured a longsword at his waist and carried a shield emblazoned with a black hawk on his left arm. His heavy crossbow, loaded with a quiver of bolts, was slung over his cloak. Water-skins and a large black leather travel bag holding provisions draped over his shoulder, with ample room for items discovered.

Ivan moved with deadly grace, resembling a wolf covered in boiled black leather armor adorned with small steel plates that overlapped like black dragon scales, fringed in red. A large double-bladed axe hung from his back, complementing his matching black cloak. The tension between Ivan and Antoff remained. Ivan was distant.

Edward brooded in silence, clad in smoked black plate mail armor. A two-handed broadsword rested on his left hip, bearing the signet of his house on the hilt and pommel. His cat-scratched knight's shield, emblazoned with the emblem of a fist holding two lightning bolts, was slung over his back, matching his sword's house standard. *I won't get between my Half-Dead employer and a salty old Priest Knight—a recipe for disaster.* He told himself.

Tara reviewed her equipment lying against the stone wall where she had slept. Removing her dusty blanket, she picked up a lavishly carved, bone-white short bow and slid it into a specially designed leather case. It also held a quiver bristling with broad-headed arrows. After strapping the bow and quiver over her shoulder, she added two small water skins. Tara inspected her twin short swords and secured them to her hips. Antoff Grant had gifted them to her when he started her sword training. Now, after five years, she had become skilled in their use, though they were not her primary weapon. She also found a large black leather bag with a strap, which she heaved over her other shoulder.

Antoff warned everyone in a low voice, "There is an evil here that sleeps, and we must take care not to wake it." His ominous sincerity caused a pause in the small group, him being a Priest Knight, one that held favor with the Light.

Ivan took the lead, followed by Antoff, Tara, and Edward at the rear. As they crossed the threshold of the door, a chill washed over them, as if submerged in ice water—a dark reminder of the Mage's presence and the potential surprises that lay ahead.

Gloom settled around them like a thick veil, as the lantern light pooled, oppressed by an unseen force. Its glow struggled to escape, thwarted by an unknown Power resisting the light. The air was still musty and chilled, evoking the feeling of a forgotten tomb—an ancient glory long passed.

They moved deliberately down the corridor, their footfalls muffled in dust as untouched as fresh snow. Pillars shaped like warriors in battle dress emerged from the blackness, standing sentinel. Lighting the torches that hung in wall sconces spaced at intervals of fifteen feet, their flames flickered, casting a weak light throughout the passageway.

Near the end of the corridor, light fell upon a solitary figure in a dust-covered cloak sitting atop a three-step dais. At the top of the stair set into the stone wall stood a large metal door, with chains looped through hefty iron rings secured to the wall.

Ivan bent low before the dust-covered figure, and Tara moved beside him, holding her lantern low for a better view. He reached toward the motionless man, but Tara's small hand grabbed his wrist. "Wait! He's warded," she warned.

His hand closed into a fist, only an inch away from what could have been death. "Thank you," Ivan said sorrowfully. "Poor old fool. He waited all this time for my return. Co Ádean, why?". It was fleeting, but there was sorrow in his eyes.

"How long has he been sitting here?" Edward asked.

Ivan looked away, his voice only a raspy whisper. "Six or eight centuries, maybe an eon, I can guess." Ivan shrugged his shoulders in uncertainty.

"Guess?" Edward retorted. "How can you only guess, given that you led us here in the first place?"

Fury flashed in Ivan's eyes. "I slept for a long time. I don't know how long."

Antoff stepped between them, locking his ice-blue eyes on Edward. "Let it pass, man. Can you not see he suffers for a lost friend?"

A cold moment stretched, but Ivan finally gave Antoff a sympathetic look. "It's okay. I did *bring* you here, and you deserve some kind of explanation for something that must seem so strange for someone of your years." With a sigh, Ivan began to tell the sad tale of Co Ádean, a High Mage, and his connection to the grand experiment called the Melding.

"This structure was a remnant of the previous age and a bastion for defense against the Dark Order before the Shattering of the Balance. The Mages used their craft to mix creatures from creation into new life. In their distress, they used the Powers of Darkness mixed with that of the Light to create this new life."

"Like what?" Tara breathed.

"Like me and things much worse," Ivan said, his expression dark. "They called forth and then captured a Dominion, a dark-winged beast, breeding other races of beings twisted by the evil lineage of the donor. Somehow, these Mages separated the creatures from the souls that would have been born in them and injected the soul of someone who had lived before. They used these creatures to infiltrate the Dark Order and gain access to their plans. Unfortunately, no one could be in contact with that kind of evil for long without being affected. Our former heroes betrayed us and became our enemies, telling all our secrets to our foes."

Tara gave Antoff a fearful look. The evil described left her at a loss for words. "So, what happened to this place?"

"The Shattering happened. Dark forces, knowing the locations of their enemies, tried to destroy them. Likewise, the forces of Light resisted with all they had. The tide of Power was too much, or at least that's how I understand it," Ivan explained.

"So how did you come to be?" Tara asked, curious about Ivan's origin.

"Co Ádean created my body from a mixture of Demonian and Vam'Phire. As to whom I am, I never found out beyond knowing that I lived before and was still in the Well when this body was created."

"The Well? What's that?" She asked, intrigued.

"It is a device that uses both arcane Powers to capture the life essence or the souls of people and creatures that have passed or destroyed without it. An evil twisted technology of terrible Power, from a time of desperate insanity. The device was still functioning when I found myself outside of this place with no way back in."

Antoff reached over and placed his right hand on Ivan's shoulder. "So, this undertaking is as much to find out what happened for you as an investigation for us?"

"True," Ivan agreed, appreciating Antoff's understanding. *This Priest Knight truly cares for everyone. A rarity in an evil age.*

Edward glanced at Tara, raising an eyebrow dubiously. "So, Tara, can you remove this ward?"

"Perhaps I can, but it looks difficult, and the chains on the door are warded as well. I will try, but first, I need to rest. I have not recovered from earlier, and I'm weak."

They ate dried meat, nuts, and drank cold water, taking turns to keep watch. Tara napped under blankets. When she awoke, torchlight danced as they quietly sputtered and popped from the putrid oil that had gone bad a long age ago.

She found Antoff Grant, her old Priest Knight, watching her quietly with his typical hard face and ice-blue eyes, always grading a pupil's performance and judging if they had studied their lessons to his satisfaction. Yet, they were also like a loving father's eyes, soft and watchful, but only "soft" for him compared to river rocks.

Tara smiled slyly at him, earning a grimace and a grunt. She always found it funny and laughed musically to herself, which darkened his expression even more. While teasing Antoff, Tara noticed a pungent and somehow familiar smell. Her mind raced to recall where she had encountered it before, and it finally locked on what gave off such a consuming odor.

She caught Antoff's gaze, which bore a deeper understanding.

He mouthed the words, "DIRE WOLF," just as a wicked smile formed on the hard planes of his face. Tara swallowed hard and tried to look everywhere at once. Snoring came quietly from the corner. Next to Ivan lay what appeared to be a big mound covered by a very large, hairy rug, only it moved with regular breathing, accompanied by a soft, snoring sound, almost like a rumbling growl. With the awareness of a wolf, the Dire lifted his head from its curled body, stretched, yawned, and acted aloof to everyone else, looking completely at ease.

Tara's face went pasty white, while her body went rigid and still as the great wolf's eyes settled on her. Tara stood slowly, trying to look regal, but the dire knew she was scared. The scent of her fear permeated the air, leaving a thick, almost palpable taste in his mouth. With a snort, the Dire Wolf licked his chops and laid his head back down, overlooking her sensitive state.

Tara's steel-grey eyes were angry, and her lips pouty. She focused her ire on Antoff and placed her hands on her hips. "You did that on purpose!" she whispered to him. *Does everything have to be a test?*

Antoff gave a wicked smile. "Yes, I believe I did."

"You are pushing it, Priest Knight." *This man can be infuriating. It is a good thing I love him or he would be the one learning the lessons here.* Tara took a slow breath to calm herself.

Antoff's eyes twinkled.

Ivan lay quietly, enveloped in a brown wool blanket, with his eyes shut, listening to the voices of his companions echoing softly in the deep darkness of the hall. He eavesdropped on the mortals interacting with the great wolf. The living always has connections, so tangled and messy, yet harmonized, flowing with deep-running emotions—an eternal spring cut short by a mortal existence. The commotion of beings and the sound of voices murmuring to each other caused Ivan to stir and sit up.

Tara and Antoff looked at the form of Ivan's old friend, Co Ádean. They murmured almost inaudibly to each other, not entirely clear to a mortal ear, but the hearing of a Half Dead is not so limited. Ivan listened motionless as Tara spoke to Antoff. "No, it's not too dangerous if I study it first! You can't protect me from everything forever, you know?"

Antoff responded with a grunt.

Tara concentrated on the sitting cadaver of the long-dead High Mage until he suddenly became lightly illuminated with a soft greenish-blue glow that pulsed angrily with Power as her hands passed over it. As she worked, the glow begrudgingly faded away and then winked out with one last bright flash. She stood up and moved towards the door chains. The chains looping the rings looked unblemished, with the exclusion of the centuries of dust deposited over the long years. She spoke again under her breath. "Jud 'elm Bar 'lush." And the chains glowed with a deep red energetic light. "THE GODS!" Tara shouted. "The ward is not just trapped. It's an alarm." But it was too late. The alarm sounded, like a low battle horn's blast, accompanied by kettle drums awash with arcane power, echoing like a beacon.

"Baha, Baha, Bang, Boom, Bang Boom!" The room became awash in energy that prickled the skin.

Deep in the heart of the Blackened Lands, winged, demon-like figures in red and black, scaly armor, and matching skins watched the blinking of an arcane symbol on a map table. It seemed to construct three-dimensional terrain, landscapes, or cities out of black sand. The demons, all underlings of the Dark Order, were bent over the map table with interest. The room was dark, lit only by a single lamp emitting a fitful glow that smoked and sputtered with a hiss, adding a sweet, nauseating, corrupt smell. They all bore long, curved, jagged swords bejeweled with dark-colored bloodstones, rumored to be sentient, with the blackest of blood thirsts only matched by that of their masters.

The largest, a black-colored demon, pointed and spoke in a hard, guttural speech. "Send scouts, Narean. I want reports within the day."

"Yes, Lord Modred," one of the red demons said.

Out of a dark corner, a dry voice came low and threatening. "Lord Modred?"

A chill seemed to permeate the air, raising Modred's hackles.

"Great Lord Amorath, forgive me. I did not detect your entrance," Modred said with hesitance and a cringe, shuddering from the cold undead chill. Modred knelt on his right knee and bowed his head subserviently. "How may I serve the Great Lord Amorath?"

The shadows seemed to shift like a mist around the ancient, undead Mage called Amorath. He shuffled with a limp toward the kneeling, black-clad demon, whose powerful wings spread behind him like a huge, leathery cloak. The smell of the undead Litch Mage gathered in the room like an open grave, a side effect of using the dark powers, gifts from his gods that unnaturally extended his life. No one besides the Great Lord Amorath himself and the dark gods recalled his age or real name. Modred had no intention of asking either. Amorath favored by the gods and was a member of the Dark Order, rumored to be given the ability to drink life directly from anyone who displeased him. Lord Modred had seen that only once, and he still trembled at the Great Lord's presence with the thought of the images printed indelibly into his mind.

"Lord Modred, can you tell me what you're doing about the glyph that's blinking and who's responsible for setting it off?" Amorath asked. His voice dry and creaked like a millstone grinding grain.

"Great Lord, I'm sending scouts to report on it," Modred stammered.

Amorath's bald head held a taunt gray color of the necrotizing tissue drawn over his face. Its expression of intolerance was a good match for his pale, dead eyes. "Modred, do you have any idea at all what has transpired?"

"No, Great Lord," Modred admitted, still staring at the floor, unwilling to move or lift his head.

"You are a *fool*!" he hissed. "Send more than scouts. That is the glyph for a Torrent Mage, and I want that Torrent's Power. I would recommend that you send a complete fist to retrieve the Torrent."

"Yes, Great Lord, as you command!" Modred acknowledged as he rose to do his master's bidding.

Ivan looked at Tara when the alarm fell silent. "Is Co Ádean safe? Maybe the old fool will have some clues to help us out still hidden about his body?"

"He should be safe," is all Tara said. She looked unnerved by the alarm and effects of the ward.

Ivan carefully lifted Co Ádean's cloak and looked. The High Mage had an amulet hanging around his neck. The amulet had a large translucent piece of quartz in the shape of a teardrop that appeared to have a light moving dimly within it. In the lining of the Mage's cloak was a small book that hummed a warning when Ivan tried to touch it.

"Tara," Ivan asked. "Will you come and look at these things? I do not dare handle them. I think them protected somehow."

Tara looked at Ivan and raised her eyebrow dubiously. "OK. He looked safe to me. What did you find?" She moved tiredly from the chains she was studying to where Ivan was. "Yes, they are warded and very interesting. I missed it. This mage was very good at disguising his effects," she whispered a few words, taking the items and then handing them to Ivan. "What are we going to do?" Tara asked Antoff.

Antoff shook his head, "It's obvious at this point that we must wait to go in as we have set off an alarm and I can feel that a great evil is waking. If I can sense him, there is little question that he can sense me."

"No!" Ivan shouted. "It doesn't matter. This trap gave off a burst of Power that was likely detected by the Dark Order. They knew of the location before the Shattering and they would monitor it. There are technologies from lost ages you are not aware of. Things you do not know and we can do nothing to escape their view now. It is a tracking device. They have us. The best we can hope to do is get in and out as quickly as possible. We will not get a second chance to retrieve whatever is here first."

Edward looked at Antoff with conviction. "I, for one, didn't come all this way for nothing. Let them come, we will deal with them, and if we can't, what difference will it make, anyway?"

"A tracking device? What's that and why is there nothing that can be done?" Tara asked Ivan.

Ivan sighed. "Because it's done by mages using arcane Power and other devices, I don't understand how it all works. I am not a mage. There are only two places that I know can purge it. Forge'Wrath Keep, a ruin, and the town of RavenHof, both have warding against these things from before the Breaking and once the wards sever the contact, they are gone."

"How far is this... Forge'Wrath Keep?" She asked.

Ivan looked away gloomily. "It's just a day or a bit more down the old riverbed, but it's dangerous and anything could be living there by now."

Antoff grunted. "We will finish here, then run for the old ruin and try to double back when we are out from under this 'Viewing' or whatever it is. Waiting around after a spell goes off is never a good idea. Tara, get those chains off now!"

She raised an eyebrow at him but said nothing. She walked a few strides to the door and closed her eyes. The image formed in a rush, and Tara struggled to hold against the onslaught of Power that rolled in against her. She looked intently at the chains, her eyes alight with excitement. She spoke in a barely audible whisper. "Ex'Treema Oh'Mas Flam'Meer." The chains grew bright red and then white with heat, causing all but Tara to step back away. Then, with a louder voice, "In'Sindra, Um'Freeha." The chains glowed blue over red, squeaked, and cracked as frost suddenly covered them, and then they fell away, shattering on the floor like glass. Tara, still filled with Power, stepped back away from the cold smoking chains aglow with the residue of remaining energy.

"Well, that's one way to do it, I guess," Antoff said, amazed. *This girl can do the most incredible things.*

Ivan pulled the massive double-bladed axe from his back and planted his feet, placing himself between Tara and the closed door. The broken remnants of the chains still smoked and hissed quietly as residue from the unnatural light all but faded out. Tara could hear the rasp of steel as blades slid loose from their scabbards. Antoff moved to the door and waited for Edward to place himself to Ivan's right.

Antoff spoke with grim certainty. "When I open the door, you be ready for the rush." Antoff slowly and firmly took hold of the door's heavy steel rings and gave his companions a nod. Then he pushed to one side, causing it to swing open outward with a low squeak that echoed into the vast depths of an enormous, darkened chamber.

Out of the void loomed a massive seven-and-a-half-foot-tall pale man. He dressed in a black leather long coat that flared out and hung at his ankles, with a curved two-handed longsword hanging from his hip, exposing the hilt and pommel. White hair fell below his shoulders and his face lined with age, but he moved with a lithe grace that declared him unruffled by their appearance. white ashy hand moved with security and almost perceptive comfort as it came to rest on the hilt of his splendid blade. His gold and blood-red eyes studied them intently, judging each one of them.

Antoff slid smoothly into a warrior's stance and brought his shield up, his blade ready with the elegance of a Priest Knight. Antoff pointed his blade and spoke, his voice on the edge of violence. "Vam'Phire! Foul thing, get back!"

The pale, bloodless lips curled into a smile as it spoke with its dry, emotionless retort. "I am Lord De'von, and it is you who desires to enter my realm, not the other way around. Perhaps a little civility in your tongues may be in order. Yes?"

Its voice was so compelling that Tara took a step forward and raised her hand in readiness. He looked at her, seeing the heat of her body like a vapor radiating. The blood pounded in her small shape with a rhythm like thunder that spoke of sweet life. Wreathed in a bright light that blazed like fire, she caused him to stare with infinite hunger.

Ivan glided in front of Tara, breaking their eye contact. "We will both enter, slug, and we shall come out again. As to your condition, that is entirely up to you." Their eyes locked, the other man easily overshadowing Ivan by a head's height or more.

"Half-breed maggot, mind your tongue or I will cut it out and hang it around my neck for a charm." Lord De'von snapped.

Edward took a step toward the doorway as if to enter, but Antoff held out his sword to bar his way. "Mind yourself, boy. You don't have so many years under your belt as to deal with the likes of him alone," Antoff said.

"Lord or coward? Why don't you come in here, slug?" Ivan yelled.

The Vam'Phire's deliberate stride brought it to the very precipice of the doorway, its voice dripping with contempt. "Perhaps it would be easier for you to come in here; it's rather cramped in there and that can lead to all sorts of—*unfortunate* accidents. Just give me that book and amulet you found, and you can have safe passage in and out of the portal. You can have your fill of all the gold and jewels you can carry. You have my oath on it." He gave a bloodless grin.

"An oath, is it?" Ivan mocked. "The oath of a slug is worthless."

Tara stared at the imposing thing. "He can't enter. He's undead and they cannot cross time when it's compressed like this. I thought this was a hallway, but it was not. It is a compression portal."

"A very perceptive child you have here, Priest Knight." The Vam'Phire said.

Antoff answered him dangerously, "You shall neither have her, my friends, the book, nor the amulet for us to have an entrance. You will make way or be destroyed by the Light." And with that, in a bright flash, Antoff's ornate longsword grew white hot and emanated a bright, pure Light. The Vam'Phire backed away as Antoff pushed forward into the darkness.

Chapter 5 The Pale Man

"In the heart of darkness, it births emotion from its very void—crafted not from what can be seen, but from the haunting mysteries that lie concealed within. It's the ever-present yearning to uncover the hidden, and the chilling realization upon finding it."

Antoff pushed forward into the gloom, feeling a chill as he passed through the portal. Edward and Ivan followed closely behind him. The Vam'Phire backed away from the advancing trio, his bitter smile widening as he slid his blade from its sheath with a deliberate rasp. The undead chill permeated the vast emptiness, fear emanating from Lord De'von and chilling the air around him like a wet breeze blowing over flesh.

The massive horse size Dire Wolf stalked through the portal's entrance. Its stride was a deadly menace. Yellow-gold eyes absorbed the Light from Antoff's sword, reflecting the beast's predatory nature. Lowering its head, the wolf gave a deep growl as its hair rose on its back and neck, causing hearts to skip a beat from the intimidating display. The Dire Wolf stalked forward, flanking the undead.

Tara entered, shivering from the portal's cold. The undead presence tainted the very atmosphere. She raised her hand, preparing to act, but as the last effects of the portal left her, so did her connection to the arcane Power that had filled her.

"A dead zone!" Tara's voice cracked as she yelled, her hands trembling. Her heart pounded in her chest as the realization hit her: *If this effect lasts for long, we are dead.*

Pure Light emanated from Antoff's longsword, burning and sizzling the Vam'Phire's exposed flesh. His tissue smoldered as he backed away. The darkness of the chamber pressed down on them; the Vam'Phire moved to the edge of the blackness alongside the closest column. Shadows stretched out like liquid pools that moved across the floor, sliding over him. He disappeared, embraced, enveloped by shadow. Like smoke, wisps of shadow lingered, dissipating slowly.

In the distance, whispers danced through the hall's shadows, a haunting melody only the wolf seemed to perceive. There were watchers. Something or someone else was out there and it was closing in. The perception of the wolf is not so limited and while he could not break from combat, he knew they were not alone. Other things lived here, and they were moving closer. His pack continued unaware. Antoff moved forward, followed closely by his companions, while the Dire Wolf circled the columns, flanking them. They closed in on the location where the Vam'Phire had slipped into the shadows.

Antoff's longsword dimmed to a candle's glow. "He's aided by a dark Power—a demon or a lesser god!" he hissed.

Edward's brow furrowed; his words were a mix of resignation and anxiety. "This is not an adventure. It's a death trap." He clenched his fists around his sword hilt until his knuckles were white, his thoughts echoing with self-doubt—*Why did I suggest coming in here in the first place? Oh yes, I remember, to impress the girl.*

Ivan's voice was grave. "They have waited many long centuries to snare someone or something in their trap."

The Vam'Phire emerged from the blackness, shadow trailing like tendrils from a dark sea. His blade sliced towards Antoff, a red radiance pulsing hungrily from the bloodstone in its hilt.

Ivan caught the movement from the corner of his eye. Time slowed, stretching out as he raced toward Antoff with immortal haste, the flat of Ivan's double-bladed axe barely deflecting the blow in time. The Vam'Phire's blade flashed, sparks flying as he withdrew a step, preparing for the next rush. Antoff fell into a guarded stance, steadying himself after the attempted attack.

Tara moved with the fluid grace of an Elp'har. She slid her bone-white short bow from its sheath, knocked a broad-headed arrow, drew it to her cheek, and then released it in one smooth gesture. The arrow streaked through the darkness and struck the pale man in the back with a fleshy-sounding thump.

Lord De'von screamed with pain and outrage. "That will cost you a child, Knight!" He became a blur of motion, covering the distance between himself and Tara in a half-breath, faster than Ivan could move. But it was too late. The Vam'Phire appeared in front of Tara, a menacing smile on his face, wisps of shadow trailing behind him like dissipating spider threads. The pale man's bloodless lips parted in a smile, his red and gold eyes investigating hers with a hypnotic gaze. His eyes were aglow with hunger, causing her to shiver. The hairs on her arms rose in time with the fear freezing her heart. *He had her.* Tara knew it.

His fingernails extended to sharp points, aged and as hard as steel. Tara instinctively reached for the Power; it was not there! She screamed, raising her arm to cover her face, but it was already too late. Lord De'von backhanded her with a monstrous blow and spun to face the others in a single motion, sending Tara flying through the cold air, careening into the darkness with a thud.

Holding his elaborate sword in one hand, while shaking a finger at Antoff, he made a 'tisking' sound before giving his blade a swish. Lord De'von leveled a look and said in a mocking tone. "Tisk, tisk, tisk. Poor, poor misled child, a shame. I wonder, Priest Knight, will she love me as she has you after a thousand years? Will she remember you at all?"

Anguish filled Antoff's face as he bellowed, "You shall not have her!" He lunged forward with all his Power, the glow of his blade intensified by his love for Tara. The others ran with him at his side, their weapons held ready. But where was the great wolf? It was nowhere to be seen.

The Dire Wolf loped on silent paws and found Tara. Small dark figures approached. Wolves are not so limited as other kinds of life; their senses tuned beyond anything others could hope for. The great wolf could hear and smell the small, dark creatures well before he had seen them.

Reaching Tara, he could smell her hurt, and he cried quietly for her. He was young, but memory did not work with the wolf as it did with others. His memories were from far older times. He could recall shadowy dreams of ages long past, when they hunted in packs with mortals. Lowering his head, he sniffed her hurt, disturbing her hair so that it fell around the point of her ear. He groaned mournfully, *A Keeper! The pointed ears made her a Keeper! How had he fallen afoul of a Keeper?* Ages seemed to pass before him as memories spun out their tale. He could see the Keepers coming to the Dire packs, helping to give birth to pups during particularly hard labor and caring for the sick, taking old wolves into their villages until they died. He had a debt as old as the ages long past, and this was a debt that he had to pay. A deep warning growl left his mouth.

The small, dark creatures came to a sudden stop, chattering among themselves, possibly deliberating their strength and the prospect of overwhelming the wolf to get to his Keeper. One small brave dark figure stepped forward, shrieking something he didn't understand, and pointed a shiny stick at him, then into the darkness. Another turned his head toward where his pack was engaged in battle, hearing the ringing blows of their shiny, sharp sticks clanging together as they coordinated their attacks against the foul-smelling creature. However, he couldn't leave the Keeper's side. Whining, he turned.

Deep within the halls of the old bastion of Light, an alarm had clamored, reminiscent of banging drums and blaring horns, drew them in. Its reverberations pulsed through the halls, charged with Power. *Darklings;* beings, mostly timid. Useful for tasks like excavating the lower halls or tending to the fungal farms. The Vam'Phire had enslaved them. Their freedom was thanks to Va'Yone, who, after years of fumbling, had mastered just one spell: 'Mage Strike'. This singular ability had allowed him and a few companions to break their bonds. Yet freedom was illusory, as they still found themselves trapped with no way out.

Va'Yone, a Darkling, stood no taller than a twelve-year-old child, despite his maturity. His hair, a tangled cascade of dark colors, reached his shoulders, while distinct ridges framed his face, extending from his nose to elongated eyebrows.

As the battle rang, Va'Yone led his band of rebels, hoping that the long-anticipated uprising his kind had schemed was now in motion. However, their designation as "kind" was contentious. Crafted by mage Power, Darklings deemed flawed by their creators for not possessing strength or arcane prowess. This inadequacy reduced them to mere laborers, perpetually under the thumb of the Order of the Light.

With the Breaking of the Balance, however, left only Co Ádean, a High Mage, the Darkling's, the terrifying Dominion, and Lord De'von. Now the High Mage's actions trapped them, and in no time, the Dominion and Lord De'von subjugated the Darklings. The horrors they endured under Lord De'von, from being fodder to clearing collapsed halls, haunted them; the scars on Va'Yone's body were testaments. Their existence had taught them one brutal truth: *the strong exploit, the weak*. Yet, His true strength lay in his intellect.

Va'Yone rallied his group, with freedom's true taste on the horizon. "Spread out!" he shouted amidst the uproar. Though they were smaller and their gear modest — black leather crafted from Dur-Bat hides and rusty daggers which, because of their size, looked like short swords — they were prepared to face the odds. Death was preferable to mere existence.

From the darkness, a Dominion emerged, adding a new and terrifying front to the attack. With an earth-shaking roar, it moved between the Great Dire Wolf and the Darklings. The menacing figure flared its huge black wings, spreading them wide, and slammed its long, heavy tail on the stone floor with a crash. It shifted its weight, transferring its bulk to the stone tile floor through spear-sized curved claws that protruded from its feet. The stone splintered, causing floor tiles to erupt in a spray of shards.

The Dominion, a fifteen-foot-tall demon weighing over twelve hundred pounds, emerged from the darkness, its very presence serving as a reminder of the peril they faced. Its flat black scaly armor seemed to drink the inky shadows, and its eyes glowed red with demonic intellect, a gaze that pierced through their defenses. With an earth-shaking roar, it spread its huge wings and slammed its tail on the floor. The demon then turned and lumbered towards Tara, bellowing. "RAAAHAAAAAA!"

The Dire looked back at Tara, its heart pounding with a wild instinct to flee but bound by a deep, ancient loyalty. It turned and growled, baring its teeth, every muscle quivering with violent resolve as it stood protectively in front of the motionless girl. The Dire leaped forward, paws pounding the tile in powerful strides.

The Dominion swung a huge, clawed hand at him. He ducked low under it, and bit the creature hard, sinking his fangs deep and tearing the flesh of its right calf, barely missing its hamstring.

The Darklings did not attack him! They fanned out, shiny sharp sticks in hand, and supported his attack on the enormous, bad-tasting thing. It was like the combination of charcoal and rotted meat in his mouth.

A small male Darkling stepped forward, his hands surrounded by a blue flame. An electrical charge was slowly building, resulting in an energetic glow that crawled across his fingers. Va'Yone rolled the blue fiery ball back and forth in his small hands and then threw it at the Dominion. The flaming blue charge grew in fury as it struck the huge demon with a fiery flash of electrical Power, causing the wolf's hair to stand on end everywhere at once. It shrieked. The Dominion's charred wound emitted plumes of smoke and smoldered, filling the air with the acrid scent of sizzling flesh, a nauseating mix that heightened the already tense atmosphere. The black demon screamed in defiance, struggling to break free from the effects of the weakening Mage Strike, revealing its desperation. Residual Power, like fading embers, crawled across its form, weakening the once-mighty Dominion, a testament to Va'Yone's unwavering determination to be free.

Chapter 6 Sounds of Strife

"The clash of steel, the cries for mercy, the taste of fear: all these form the bitter symphony of strife."

Tara's eyes fluttered open to clashing steel, a cacophony echoing in every corner of the underground hall. She shook her head, trying to clear it. It throbbed on the right side badly, and only one eye could focus properly. Her veins burned with rage as her gaze fell upon the Vam'Phire, its malevolent form coiling like a predator ready to pounce on her companions.

Her gaze shifted, revealing a completely separate battle unfolding near her. Fear and awe coursed through her as she beheld an emblazoned Dominion battling the Dire Wolf! She reached. Shutting her eyes against the incoming vision, a tempest raging between Light and Darkness, a torrent of Power that threatened to overwhelm her. She struggled to hold against it. Tara raised her hands; a ball of molten Power formed, crackling. With a single inaudible word, lightning flew in a long bolt, forking outward, striking the demon in the back. The lightning staggered the Dominion and dropped it to one knee, a crash of cracking throwing shards, like an eruption. Tara turned a smoldering gaze on Lord De'von, a static charge of the liquid Light building in her hands. As she whispered, spilling images from her mind in a forgotten Old Tongue.

Edward the Dark fought alongside Ivan the Half-Dead and Antoff Grant, the Priest Knight. The undead Lord towered over them, emitting fear and despair as it fought with supernatural speed and immortal strength. The Vam'Phire's dark shroud of shadow billowed out behind it everywhere in wispy tentacles and webs of smoke connecting it to the blackness.

Edward lunged forward, broadsword held with both hands, his knight's shield hanging on his back like a burden. A longing surged within him to free his shield and wield it for protection. *I dare not withdraw. How long can we last against such speed and power?*

Antoff shifted gracefully, his movements carrying the elegance of a seasoned swordsman. Clean, smooth-flowing strokes. Moving from one form to the next, unbroken and effortless. The pure glow of his ornate long sword seared the Vam'Phire lord with harmful Light, causing the Vam'Phire's skin to smolder and blister when he pressed an attack.

Lord De'von's curved blade moved with fury and struck like a viper with each advance; Ivan could barely intercept the blows that the mortals could not.

They fought as a unit; each striking, each moving to defend as they danced sword forms. Sparks flashed, causing the pillars to replicate the shadows that played out the battle like reflections on a dark pond. A sudden flurry of powerful blows—The Vam'Phire feigned an advance before striking at Antoff with swift precision.

Ivan reached but missed the blow; the blade slipped through the Priest Knights' defenses, grazing his left side and slicing through his armor like butter, causing Antoff to groan. The blood-red gem glowed deep crimson with pulsating light as the blade drank Antoff's life, leaving a blood seeping wound as it withdrew. Antoff staggered back and went to one knee. His sword fell with a clatter. His hand was at his side to stop the flowing blood.

Lord De'von stepped back with a triumphant gaze; renewed strength given to him by Antoff's precious life energy. Ivan moved in concert with Edward, closing the gap between Antoff and Lord De'von. "Pity, I expected more from you, Priest Knight, but I shall remove you one by one and still take your Mage! Besides, you will all join me, forever dead with the next moonrise," the towering Vam'Phire gloated.

Tara watched in horror as Antoff's side was sliced open, blood spilling from the wound. An overwhelming surge of liquid electrical charge coursed through her as she unleashed her attack on the shadow-shrouded Vam'Phire. With all her fury and love combined, a brilliant bolt of terrible Power arced forth, striking Lord De'von. The impact sent him hurtling against a column, his body crumpling like a discarded doll. Tara's rage fueled her, enabling her to maintain control over the immense arcane Power she wielded.

As the light from Tara's bolt that had filled the cavernous hall faded, Ivan and Edward struck together. Moving in perfect unison, Edward surged forward, driving his weapon deep into Lord De'von's heart. Simultaneously, Ivan severed the Vam'Phire's head from its malevolent form. They were both thrown back by the residual energy, sending them sprawling limp as fish out of water on the dusty tile floor.

Tara watched the Vam'Phire lord's head tumble to the floor, away from the falling body. *The Vam'Phire Lord De'von was no more. He deserved it.* A satisfied smile graced her lips. She turned to confront the Dominion. Tara drew upon the Power with all her might. Between her palms, a ball of liquid energy arced and swelled, its brilliance intensifying with each passing heartbeat. Va'Yone walked toward the massive demon; blue globe of angry living fire glowed as he rolled it back and forth between his hands. The Dire circled and moved to Tara's side, snarling intimidatingly at the huge demon.

The massive demonic creature stood, raised one hand, and spoke in guttural demon speech. The Darkling shouted, "It said it's not after us. It just wants out!"

Tara yelled back, "Well then, tell it to move on, and this can be over! I am not releasing it upon the world."

It roared with rage and anger, turned, and walked back into the vast void of darkness whence it came.

Tara ran for Antoff, tears streaming down her face. "Are you okay?"

Antoff winced. "I'm going to be fine, Tara. It's okay." His mind whispered. *I can't tell her he has stolen a measure of my life in years. She would not understand.*

She pulled his hand away from the wound to look at it. The wound was red, swollen, and blood still seeped from the slice. "You're hurt, bad. You're not okay!" she sobbed.

Edward and Ivan argued. Edward pointed at Ivan threateningly. "What in the name of all the gods are you talking about? Did that Vam'Phire hit you on your head or something?"

Ivan looked at Edward. "No, Edward, the amulet is the *key*. That is why Co Ádean had trapped himself, and now we have the thing they want the most. It's not a key, it is a curse."

Antoff grunted. "Great! Good news for them. We won't stay, and we won't leave that 'cursed key' here!"

Tara looked at Antoff with fear in her eyes, but Edward answered. "We will not remain here laying in a hole too fearful to go outside. Hang it around the Mage's neck, or take it with us, it makes no difference to me!"

Ivan spoke after. "It's too late for that. The portal is open, and regardless of what we do now, they are coming, and we cannot leave the key here."

Lord Modred, "The Great Black Demon of Legend," sat brooding in his black, high-backed chair. His chin propped on his hands, and his elbows planted on the lavishly carved, demon-headed armrests. Its wings spread wide, finishing the chair-back that broadened out above his head. A fire blazed and crackled in the hearth constructed from black volcanic stone, and the room was lit by a single lamp casting shadows that leaped and played on the gray stone walls.

Heat radiated from the fireplace, leaving the air of the room hot and dry. A slight haze hung eerily from back drafts created by wind constantly gusting in sudden, changing directions, blowing smoke back into the room. Bonded leather books bearing arcane markings sat on the gray marble mantle above the fireplace. One book, blackened with age, lay open on a large slate map table. A glyph blinked with an irritating rhythm, marking the location of a Torrent Arcane Mage. The table, in a three-dimensional landscape, constructed a map out of fine black sand using the Power.

Lord Modred spoke threateningly. "Narean, Great Lord Amorath wants my report. What word do you have from our scouts?"

A large door stood open to a balcony that overlooked the heart of the Blackened Lands. From their high perch in the tallest tower of the sprawling fortress, they could see for leagues. The tents and banners of Zoruk tribal symbols flapped in the breeze as the horde spread out across the black and red soil of the plains below. Height caused the Zoruks to look like thousands of insects teeming around a hill, working endlessly, preparing for a season that must come. *A season of war.*

Narean's red leathery wings spread wide as he landed on the gray marble of the balcony. He bowed low and spread his arms wide when he entered his leader's study. "The Dragon Hounds are watching the entrance, my Lord, and the Zoruks advance at a run. They should arrive by nightfall."

"That will not do, Narean!" Modred bellowed. "The Great Lord Amorath wants that Torrent in our hands by nightfall. I will not be the one that ends up a dried husk on the floor if you fail. Do you understand me, Narean? You will be, if you fail!"

The red demon answered, still staring at the floor, his wings folded behind him like a long, red leathery cloak. "Yes, Lord Modred, it shall be as you say."

The morning suns had just broken the horizon as Dragon Hounds circled high above, riding the currents of wind that blew in a steady stream over the mountains of the Twisted Lands. They watched the cave mouth and the approach of a fist of a hundred Zoruks, arrayed in a long line, two abreast, and their scouts that ranged out ahead in a band. The wind swirled around the boulders and rocky ledges of the valley below where the old, dried riverbed meandered, adding lift to the Dragon Hounds as they watched, circling.

Zoruks ran on swiftly pounding feet, hastened by the brutal leadership of their sergeants and captain. Their battle standard flapped in an unrelenting wind that now grew hot with the breaking of the dawn. Captain Um'elik rode at the head of his unit, upon a large Camolisk Lizard, its hard-scales, hide changing with the desert surroundings, camouflaging as it ran in a dizzying display.

Its powerful claws tore at the rocky soil as it snaked along. Captain Um'elik, Commander of the Revenger Scouts, the image of a Zoruk captain. The skin of his face tinted greenish, scarred in a line starting from his right forehead to the left cheek, ending at his neck and jaw. The scar raised in a pink, puckered swell that reminded everyone under him of his berserker bloodlust. Clad in all kinds of scavenged armor ranging from hide leather, chain, and bits of scale mail. His large muscular exterior covered in greenish hide, and his hair was the color of the blackest night.

He rode like a Zoruk that had spent too much time in a lizard's saddle, steering with his right gauntleted hand and resting his left hand on a battle-axe that nested in a loop belted at his left hip. Revenger Scouts ranged forward and searched for a trail scrawled hastily on his map by his Lord Commander, Narean. A Torrent Mage was the prize his master wanted, and he would guarantee that he got it. This prize would see him promoted and guaranteed more power and every pleasure that went with it. He would have that Torrent Mage if he had to sacrifice every Zoruk under his command to do it!

Va'Yone cleaned and bound Antoff's wound and applied a salve of his own making. His face contorted with pain as he spread the mixture on the open wound, and then bandaged it, winding the cloth around his middle. Helping Antoff back into his armor.

The only parting gifts that Darklings could give them in thanks for their freedom was a small wooden box of gold and gems found over long years of exile from the world and, of course, they got Va'Yone.

Antoff stowed the gift. "There's no time to search or explore with the threat of the Dark Order. I am sure they already must be searching for us because of this—Viewing, and while there may not be much need for treasure in places like these, miles deep in the crust of El'idar. It will be of use once we are outside."

Ivan had carefully searched the Vam'Phire lord's clothing and took all he could find: a heavy gold signet ring with a bloodstone set in it; a necklace of gold linked with a medallion in the shape of a bird's claw clutching an enormous diamond; and a bejeweled dagger with a hilt that made it look like your hands were gripping a bat's body under its extended wings and a long blade that glowed red if held too close to Antoff. All of it of little value to him, but he could sell it for good coin. Ivan also belted Lord De'von's scabbarded sword about his waist with distaste. He hated the thing, but dared not leave it behind.

Va'Yone's slender form had almost finished placing the last of his possessions into his backpack and was trying to position it on his back when he felt a hand lift it in place.

It was Tara. "Are you sure about wanting to go Va'Yone?" she asked him, snugging a strap with a nod and folded her arms beneath her breasts. Her accent seemed crisp when she spoke, and she raised a questioning eyebrow.

"More than sure," Va'Yone stammered, his fingers nervously fidgeting with the strap on his small pack, "I have been down here my whole life Tara, and I thought I would only ever be able to dream of the world above. Now I can see it. My people are not free here and now that you opened the small portal, some have escaped. One day I will return and free them. I just can't right now. I am too weak and I need to find someone that can train my type of magic. Tara, you met that Dominion, he will kill me if I stay. I helped you and he won't forget about that."

"We are glad to take you with. I just wanted you to understand the dangers, Va'Yone." Tara's voice laced with caution.

A smile played on his lips. Va'Yone's little face was brave. A flicker of determination gleamed in his eyes. "I will take the risk if it is all the same, Tara?"

They said their goodbyes to the Darkling rebels, warning them to be alert, and left the cavernous hall and entered the compression portal. A chill washed over them as they crossed through into the smaller hall portal, which moved them between the depths of the complex and the surface cave. Ivan stopped only for a moment to view his friend Co Ádean in silence one last time before he stood. "I will be back and properly honor you, Co Ádean, but for now, please understand that there is no time."

Recovering their gear, they crossed through the cave room with columns like apple cores and then into the anteroom with the Stinger warhorses. They packed, readied for travel, fed and watered the horses. They shared a quick meal of dried meats and fruit, each of the companions giving part of their meal to the Dire Wolf, who hardly chewed at all before swallowing. Everything was new to Va'Yone, the animals, and even the food.

When all was ready, they stepped out of the cave. Greeted by the caress of sunlight on their skin, the scent of the desert breeze, and the soft crunch of sand underfoot. Va'Yone followed along behind the group with a small pack on his back and covered his eyes with a thin cloth as they led their reptile horses out of the cave mouth into the light of the early morning sun. The Dire Wolf ghosted ahead of his pack, and Antoff Grant led his warhorse out of the cave mouth, followed by Ivan, Tara, Va'Yone, and then Edward to the rear, the small trail no less hazardous on the way back down.

The wind whipped cloaks and sand pelleted their faces, leaving a sting. High above, what looked like two red birds circled in the dusty haze of the early morning hour. Below, in the dried river valley, Antoff spied ten Zoruks moving fast along the rock ledges of the trail's entrance. He pointed wordlessly and then mounted his Stinger, removing a long boar spear from a sheath beneath its saddle girth. Ivan pulled his huge double-bladed axe from his back and limbered his right arm before mounting his Stinger. Edward unslung his knight's shield, not wanting to be without it against such odds. Pulling his two-handed broadsword from its sheath, he heaved himself into the high-backed knight's saddle. Tara tiredly lifted Va'Yone's small child-like body onto her Stinger and mounted in front of him.

He smiled warmly and wrapped his arms around her, burying his face in her back with a sigh. Va'Yone was in the world, living a long-ago dream, and the grand adventure of his life had finally begun. *I will become a real mage and when I am, I will be back to free them*. It was a silent promise to himself. One that he intended to keep.

Captain Um'elik rode at the head of his unit, his Camolisk Lizard color-shifting with the desert terrain. The clanking sounds of Zoruks running echoed off the canyon. They were fifteen leagues or more away from the trail that led to the cave mouth high above the ancient river valley floor.

Um'elik yelled, "Sergeants, you drive them with a whip until their hide bleeds, for all I care. If one of these dogs drops, leave him where he lies. Let the lands creatures have him and be done with it. He is not worth the rations or even calling himself a Zoruk!"

"Yes, Captain!" they replied in unison. The Zoruks ran faster under the lash of their sergeant's tongues and the sting of their whips.

Chapter 7 The Path of Ruin

"There is a path that leads to ruin, and rarely do you perceive it before it engulfs you. Exercise caution in the direction your desires steer you, for the shimmering path can swiftly desert you."

Antoff Grant sat atop his Stinger warhorse, his face taut, suppressing pain from the earlier wound, throbbing with every beat of his heart. His fingers tightened around the grip of his spear. He felt the sun's warmth on his skin. A breeze sent a chill through him, stirring the familiar anticipation of conflict within. Abrasive sand pelted him, and unease gnawed at his gut, overpowering the discomfort of perspiration trickling down his gritty skin. Messages from the gods of Light bore an ominous weight, often foretelling the imminent clash of battle like dark omens.

The Dark Order's scheme was unfolding, and despite the world's serene veneer, Antoff perceived threats lurking just out of sight. He and his allies were now in their sights, at the heart of a rising storm. A tremor ran through Antoff as he sensed the impending battle. His mount felt the tension, its hooves dancing, sent rocks tumbling down the mountainside. All motion paused when the path cleared, unveiling the Zoruk scouts near the riverbed's entrance. Yet, their hesitation wasn't solely because of the adversaries they faced.

With a terrifying grace, the Great Dire Wolf lunged its ground-eating pace and dove off the mountain's steep embankment. Landing with a cloud of dust, the creature circle toward the trail entrance. This movement alone wasn't distressing to the Zoruks. No self-respecting wolf would stay between them, but it was clear the Dire Wolf was an ally of the Torrent Mage and was flanking them.

The Zoruks' hearts hammered as Antoff, Priest Knight of the Light, gently touched his massive Stinger warhorse with his knees, launching forward with an angry scream. *How many battles had he survived? How many more would he live through?* As these thoughts raced through his mind, he saw the Zoruks, clad in ragged armor, charging forward with cleavers, spears, and bows in hand.

Roaring, the Revengers' battle cry, they met their enemies' advance. "Scout Revengers, let your shadow cover the Light," their leader commanded, his voice heavy with rage. They bellowed their vengeance, fear, and hate, a fury that seemed to boil their very blood.

Antoff spurred his steed toward the foremost Zoruk, who fired an arrow in his direction. With a clang that echoed across the valley, his hawk-shaped shield met the incoming arrow, deflecting it away. The vibration of impact traveled up his arm, sparking an electrifying surge of adrenaline that coursed through his veins. Seeing that it missed, the Zoruk turned and ran, allowing the next line of Zoruks to advance.

The Stinger's clawed hooves clattered on the stone, a deafening sound. Antoff's boar spear lowered in concert with his Stinger's head, coming into perfect alignment in a well-practiced maneuver. The spear struck with a crunch, penetrating bone and armor, as Antoff lodged it deep into the first Zoruk's chest. With a ferocious whinny, the heavy horse crashed into the enemy, its momentum unstoppable, cleaving through ranks like a hammer slamming into a steel wedge, its bladed tail swept back and forth through the ranks of Zoruks as it burst out of the chaos.

Ivan swung his massive double-bladed battle axe from side to side. Bone smashed, flesh split, blood splattered across the blade and ran down his arm, coating his mail as he fought with untiring ferocity.

Tara rode bravely through the chaos, short sword in hand, batting away attacks. Meanwhile, Va'Yone held on for dear life, arms wrapped around her, head buried in her back. Warhorses kicked and screamed, bladed tails slicing and teeth biting as they rode through the opened breach.

As the Zoruks staggered back, the Dire Wolf darted among them, biting and snapping at them, cleverly creating a path for the oncoming charge of horses. Edward's battle cry reverberated through the air, his blade finding its mark and severing the head of his foe. They bashed those Zoruks unable to evade off the path, their screams echoing as they plummeted. The Dire Wolf, having done its duty, retreated, occasionally snapping at any Zoruks in its path, while the riders pressed forward on the treacherous trail.

Zoruks lay scattered about the trail, bleeding, stunned, dead, or dying. Some knocked off the trail slid down the mountainside's rocky slope, dust still trailing them in the wind. High above the valley floor, the two Dragon Hounds observed the battles unfolding. The first one, and then the other, wheeled in the wind. They folded their wings tight to their body and dove toward the valley floor with abandon. The wind whistled as they cut through it. Finally, two hundred feet before the valley floor, the Dragon Hounds' wings opened with a pop as they pulled up, leveling off.

The lead Dragon Hound broke away to survey the battle-scarred Zoruks, while its companion soared into the sky, bound for the Blackened Lands. Dragon Hounds did not speak like other races of beings. They used thought to communicate, conveying messages in streams of images. The first Dragon Hound surveyed the battle site and said, "Are'Nok, go inform the Zoruk captain Um'elik that his scouts have failed to hold the protectors of the Torrent Mage."

"How much longer must we endure serving these lesser beings, Gor'amk?" the second Dragon Hound inquired, wheeling away.

"We endure only as long as necessary, Are'Nok. Once the Old Ones awaken, we'll be free. Now go, before the gods overhear our treason." To dragon's eyes, the terrain lit up in images depicting heat and the temperature of the surrounding environment. The bodies cooled in the early morning breeze, but were still white with heat where the Zoruks lay dead. The surviving Zoruks glowed hot like coals, stark against the cool, dusty valley trail and rugged mountainside. Are'Nok watched the other Dragon Hound soar toward the fist of Zoruks approaching the old dried-upriver valley.

The Stingers galloped down the old riverbed. Dust and dry soil streamed behind them, windblown and swirling into devils. Antoff watched as the Dragon Hounds fell toward the valley, then flattened their course a hundred spans above the ancient riverbed.

They adopted a systematic pace: they would gallop for a stretch, then trot, dismount to walk their horses, and then mount again to start the process over. This rhythm allowed them to cover ground without pushing their animals to exhaustion.

Throughout the day, they rode and walked, eating and drinking in the saddle. As the journey wore on, Antoff noticed Tara beginning to sway in her saddle. Va'Yone was holding her upright as their horse walked. Tara's face was ashen, her eyes glazed, her body swaying with every step of the horse. Antoff's heart tightened as he saw Tara's pallor and weariness; she had pushed herself to the edge, and it gnawed at him. He looked at her, thinking; *You have heart girl, but need to learn to use your sense.*

Antoff yelled, "We need to take a break to feed and rest the animals. Edward, get the horses fed and watered. We will get our meal ready."

Edward looked at Antoff with a sullen look but said nothing. Not used to being told what to do by anyone except his father, but he did it while grumbling under his breath. Antoff ignored the childish show and wordlessly walked to Tara's horse. He lifted Tara from her saddle and sat her on the ground, followed by Va'Yone, who sat down on a river stone next to her, saying nothing. Ivan dug through their saddlebags, producing some blankets, which he gave Tara and Va'Yone to rest on.

Antoff glanced at Ivan, worry in his eyes. "That was too easy," he said, his voice edged with suspicion.

Ivan's brow furrowed in agreement as he continued to work, watchful, aware that danger could strike at any moment. "Yes, they let us go, or they are just that inept. I'm leaning toward the incompetent. The Dark Order will want the key outside where they can get at it. There is so much we do not understand about the old technologies that lay locked away in the forgotten places of the past. The thing that bothers me, Antoff, is that we are now going to be chased by the Dark Order and the Dominion's creatures that live in the depths of that complex. He has access to allies that we are not ready to defend ourselves against. Allies that even the Dark Order does not know about."

Antoff locked eyes with Ivan, his gaze flickering with purpose and reflecting the internal battle they both faced. "It does not matter, Ivan. They are coming, and we must face them, or the world will suffer for our failure. The weight of this responsibility is heavy, and the dread looms over us. If we fail, we condemn all people to the blackness of the Dark Order's plans. Her importance goes beyond just being a Torrent. A Lord of the Dark wants her as a vessel. Master Duncan confided in me; I don't know which Dark Lord wants her. And I don't know how he knew. I know he is looking to take her and it is likely that those creatures that are chasing us are his."

They left Va'Yone and Tara sleeping quietly next to a small dung fire that Ivan had started with a flint and steel. The last sun now hung low in the sky, a smoldering red ball heralding the approach of night. The scorching sun caused sweat to stream down Edward's face as he sat, stirring a bland mixture of watery potatoes and dried meat on a metal plate. He took a bite. It smelled and tasted as grainy as the desert sand.

Edward's thoughts circled back to Haven; his own father had banished him. His longing for his old life battled with the thrill of adventure, leaving a bitter taste in his mouth. The adventure and risk he now embraced meant he wasn't stuck in the same life his father had been. The murder of Lady Martins still hung over his head, and he didn't know how he was going to fix it. Even if he could, would he still want to return home?

Edward was watching Tara sleep. He couldn't help it. *She is like an angel curled up in that blanket, sleeping on the dust of a dried riverbed. What would a girl like her want with a man like me?* His thoughts accused him, reminding him of his past.

Antoff allowed them only two hours' rest, and then woke them up, handing them each a tin plate of stew and a cup of tea.

"How long did we sleep?" Tara asked, using her hand like a visor as she looked up at the last setting sun.

"Only two hours. We can't rest any longer until we reach Forge'Wrath Keep," Antoff replied.

"Neither I nor Va'Yone will be of good to you until we rest, and I dare not touch the Power. The risk of scorching my mind is too great." Tara said.

Concern crossed Antoff's face. "Don't worry about that. You just stay in the saddle, and we will handle the rest, Tara."

Tara was beyond tired. "Ok.", is all she murmured. Her attention had already turned to Ivan.

Ivan packed the teakettle and put out the rest of their fire when she spoke.

"So ... Ivan, what of these other creatures in the Dominion's control? What are they?" she asked.

Ivan stopped briefly to address her. Even now he looked dangerous, "Tara, not every demon or minion of the dark has a form like a Zoruk, Dominion, or animate demon. Some are spirits that have the power to affect the surrounding environment, and some demons are visible 'normally' only on other layers of existence. These types of demons try to incarnate their existence into that of a host creature. Possession is what some clerics have called it. When they find a host and overpower their minds, usually the sick or insane, they can then take over that person's life, subsisting off the host creature's life energy. They live out the creature's whole life and then discard them at death. It is very hard to detect before the actual damage is done."

Tara took a deep breath. "The Gods! ... How can you get rid of them?"

He smiled again weakly, and pointed at Antoff, "That's what Priest Knights and Clerics are for Tara."

The Dire Wolf left his pack, and ranged out before them, keeping ever watchful for any foes that might lay a trap. He had a place in this pack, and he would keep her safe. He would keep them all safe.

They rode through the night, with the dust kicked up by the pursuing Zoruks trailing behind them like a lingering specter, carried by the wind. Edward watched and said that he estimated the distance to the Zoruks to be fifteen or twenty leagues away. Va'Yone watched now, in the final failing light of the day, as dusk settled over the world and the Darkness took its Power back from the Light.

He was tired, and his legs hurt from being unaccustomed to riding on a horse. He wanted to sleep, but he could not. His eyes were too valuable in the night, and except for Ivan, he could see the best.

Va'Yone wanted to contribute to the group, and in his current weakened state, this was where he could be most helpful. He marveled at Tara's strength and ready access to the Power that lay between the Darkness and the Light. His magic did not work as hers did; he had to absorb the Power that he used until his potential was full. Then he could use it, but only as far as the spells he knew. She had ready access and could draw as much as she could use at one time. Tara seemed to create reality from her imagination while using raw arcane Power. *How could she stand amid all that chaos and the struggle that existed between the Light and the Darkness without being destroyed by it?* Va'Yone could not fathom it. He had needed his whole life just to become proficient at using Mage Strike. *"How could she do so many things without ever being taught?"*

"Tara?" Va'Yone asked.

"Yes?" she said tiredly.

"Why is using the Power so different for you than it is for everyone else? I have tried my entire life to get better at the magic I have learned and even tried to learn new things, but there was just not anyone to teach me. I just tried until something worked." That question spoke to Tara. It was a plea for some kind of teaching, a lesson. Anticipation played on Va'Yone's smiling lips. He was hungry for knowledge and this question was eating at him.

"Well, let's see Va'Yone." Tara was trying to help. "I am a Torrent Mage, and I use the Power differently. You store it up and use it for the specific spells that you know like a purpose-built tool, and I use it as long as I can imagine it and I can withstand the storm of Power needed to bring it into being. It must make sense, and I must be able to visualize it for it to work at all. You do not have to see it before you do it, Va'Yone. Just wait for enough Power to build up. You choose between the Power of Darkness and the Power of Light, though I could use some of each if I wanted to learn it. I stay away from choosing between them, but one day maybe I will have to make that choice. I hope not." She turned her head away. However, not before he saw the anguish on her face. Making that choice was one she was dreading.

Chapter 8 Forged From Stone

"Dining when hungry, resting when sleep is most desperately needed—such pleasures are things an adventurer rarely knows. If you care for your comfort, you'd best stay home."

Out of the night's blackness, a fortress loomed. Its walls were ochre, echoing the valley's earthy hues, its gates forged from bronze, banded in rusty steel. They gleamed faintly under the full moon's light just risen above the mountaintops. The battlements atop the circular wall looked as though carved from solid rock, jutting from a sheer ridge nestled in a cove.

Around that time, the Dire Wolf returned, emerging from the darkness to sit on the sand of the riverbed, waiting for the party. His yellow eyes glowed in the light of the silvery moons, his tongue hanging out one side of his mouth. Tara smiled at him fondly, and he stayed close to her, watchful. He felt her fingers tangled in his coarse hair.

As the party approached the fortress on foot, Antoff held up his hand, stopping them. Before any of them could comprehend why, Ivan snatched an arrow from the air just before it could pierce his shoulder. Raising an eyebrow, his fangs glinted in the moonlight. "Next time, aim for my heart." Ivan yelled.

Bows creaked from atop the walls as six archers seemed to materialize from the very stone of the battlements, aiming their arrows at their hearts.

"Stop!" Antoff commanded. "We are not here to cause trouble."

The graceful figure of a cloaked woman slipped out of the open gate. She approached them slowly, stopping a short distance away, hands spread as she bowed deeply. "I am Cur'Ra, and I welcome you to our fire." Above, on the battlements, figures moved and slowly released the pressure on their bowstrings.

Antoff spoke, "Our thanks, Cur'Ra, but you would feel differently if you knew what's following us."

She pulled back the hood of her earthy brown cloak, revealing her pointed ears. A mature female Elp'har, in the prime of her beauty, with dark hair and skin kissed by the sun. She wore britches, and a blouse made of earth tones. Her green eyes took Tara in. "We are Desert Elp'har and have been since the Breaking. You are welcome to our fire."

Tara pulled back the hood of her cloak, and when it fell away, it revealed the markings of the Torrent Mage. "You honor us," Tara said.

"It is we who are honored. Torrent Arcane User." Cur'Ra bowed.

The Dire Wolf sighed mournfully. *Another Keeper! How many can there be?*

Leading their chargers into the gates of Forge'Wrath Keep. The sounds of horseshoes echoing through the porticos. The Desert Elp'har had a fire lit on the broken cobblestones of the courtyard. They smelled the aroma of cooking meat wafting toward them, making their stomachs rumble.

Elp'harean warriors that sat around fires stood when they entered, and the bowmen on the wall watched intently. There is always a moment that hangs there; you wonder if things truly are as your host insists. This was one of those moments. The Elp'har moved their hands to sword hilts reflexively. Cur'Ra moved in front of the group, held up her right hand, and everyone relaxed. The stress drained out of the Elp'har warriors, as if never there. All at once, they were welcome, and all was well.

The environment became tense for only an instant when the Great Dire entered and stood next to Tara and Va'Yone. His yellow-gold eyes brushed past them, gauging each Elp'har one at a time, but did not move or act anxiously. He had a responsibility to watch over her, and they gave no outward signs nor scent of danger. The warrior Elp'har smiled but said nothing as if they believed it was a normal thing.

The view from the inside was even more impressive. Four large, rounded towers built evenly along the walls, topped with battlements. Wooden rooftops had fallen in long ago, and the outbuildings stood lonely. The castle itself was not large but serviceable, with a big gate that hung open. The fortress towered to the height of the mountain, with a high block tower cut from the same stone. Winds moaned and whistled above the walls and throughout the great heights of the castle.

Elp'harean women took their Stingers, housing them in the abandoned outbuildings, fed, watered, and hobbled for the night. Antoff and his companions took a place by the fires. As the Elp'harean warriors handed out wooden trays of roasted meat, they made small talk with the group. They all watched Tara with interest and treated her with the greater prestige of a healer or priestess.

The Elp'harean people, slight of build, resembled Tara. They were also shorter than other mortals, yet much more graceful in the way they moved. They wore earth-tone colors matching the terrain. Everyone, from the warriors to the women and children, carried a bow and quiver bristling with arrows. The warriors carried short swords in Elp'harean style, and everyone wore a curved dagger, which worked for war or skinning animals. The Desert Elp'har had horses, and from the look of their encampment, they packed light for a nomadic lifestyle.

They all sat around the small fires that roasted desert lizards and ate; the atmosphere was friendly and relaxing. Cur'Ra, their host, moved around the group, making small talk, listening to the story of the adventure from RavenHof to the Forge'Wrath. Concern filled her face, but she waited for the whole of the tale to be told before speaking. Antoff got up, excusing himself politely, and walked toward the outbuildings to check on the animals.

Tara settled beside a crackling fire, her silhouette illuminated by its dancing flames, the flickering light casting intriguing shadows across her face. Cur'Ra came and sat beside her and placed a hand over hers in comfort. She looked into her eyes for a moment before speaking. "Tara, you have many arcane markings for one of your years, leading me to believe that your potential is quite vast for one so young."

Tara stared back into Cur'Ra's eyes, unblinking. "They grow on their own the more I use the Power, and their shade grows deeper and deeper as I age. In the beginning, people thought they were tattoos, so they believed me a strange and unruly child, and I played that for all it's worth, but the truth is.... it scares me."

Cur'Ra smiled at her mysteriously. "Tara, the marks declare you to the world as being a Torrent Arcane User, and they make you difficult to hide. You cannot hide who you are. It is because you belong to the entire world that you need to be protected." She reached up and touched the swollen dark mark on her cheek, where the Vam'Phire lord had struck her. Cur'Ra's hand felt hot on her cheek, and she gasped as the healing rushed through her body. When Cur'Ra took her hand away, the purplish mark was gone.

Tara put her hand to her face in wonder. "How did you do that?"

Cur'Ra smiled warmly. "It is a gift, Tara. The gods of Light watch over us and keep us whole. In the ages before the Breaking, we were once El'idar Elp'har. Keepers to all creatures that knew us. We cared for the forests and woods, not until the Breaking of the Balance that we became Desert Elp'har. We stayed in our valley praying to the gods of Light to make it whole. It appears it is not their will to restore it in our generation."

Tara looked once more into Cur'Ra's eyes. "It is not for you to remain here waiting for the change to come, Cur'Ra. The gods use us in this battle, and we cannot hide out and wait for others to do our work. We are Keepers, but not Keepers of what was. We are Keepers of what is and what can be for our children and the world."

Cur'Ra smiled. "You are wise, Torrent. We are with you." She winked.

That shocked Tara. That was not what she had intended! These Elp'har were so literal and deliberate in their interpretations of her communication. *I will have to be careful with my speech. I cannot be so direct.* She told herself.

Antoff Grant returned after inspecting the horses. His steps marred by a noticeable limp, and despite his attempts to appear nonchalant, lines of pain etched across his face with each movement. Tara pointed a finger at Antoff and spoke to Cur'Ra. "That's the one that needs your attention. He will not admit to needing help. He also has wounds from fighting the Vam'Phire, and it looks serious to me."

Cur'Ra nodded back. "Tara, it is best not to ask too much of men. They are stubborn and act impervious to pain. Perhaps I will have a look at him." She stood with a mysterious smile. Removing her cloak, she walked towards Antoff, looking like a wildcat after a rabbit.

Antoff saw Cur'Ra almost right away. He was in for something. He just did not know what it was. "Cur'Ra." He nodded.

"Priest Knight." She looked into his eyes. "Are you injured?" she asked.

"Not bad," he answered.

"You are limping from pain," Cur'Ra raised her eyebrows at his attempted subterfuge.

"Am I?" The Priest Knight started raising an eyebrow questionably.

"Yes, you are." She shook her head at his stubbornness, invoking the power of a female Elp'har in the full bloom of her womanhood.

He looked back into her green eyes, which were like deep reflection pools. She took his arm. He did not resist. Cur'Ra led him to the steps of the castle and told him to remove his armor. He resisted. She insisted. Before long, it was clear to Antoff she outmatched him, and since she was not giving it up he gave in, following her requests. Antoff stripped to his britches. The wounds of so many past battles created hatch marks, like a map of his painful youth.

She removed the blood-soaked bandages and hissed when she could see the wound. "Fool of a man, why do men never ask for help?"

Antoff sighed like a man bested by a dragon. "It would have healed; I have had worse wounds." She ignored it, placing her hand on the seeping wound. Antoff gasped and his muscles went rigid as the heat and the cold hit him like a wave, visibly shocked from the healing.

The whole time Tara sat watching in a state of amazement. Antoff had become her father. He was clay in her hands, and his icy exterior reduced to sighing and grimacing. When Cur'Ra removed her hand, the wound was closed, if not completely healed. They both looked tired as she stood up.

She looked him dead in the eye with a commanding note to her silky voice. "Now go get some rest." He tried to speak. She cut him off while raising a single finger, saying. "And if we need you for anything, I will wake you."

He rolled his eyes and grunted, but carried his gear to the abandoned outbuilding with the horses and bedded down.

Tara's jaw dropped, and her eyes widened in astonishment. *Do I even know this man? He is not acting like the man I know.* Then a hint of curiosity crept into her face. *Does that work on all men?*

Cur'Ra looked at her knowingly, as if a pupil had just picked up the first lesson on a new subject. Their eyes met, and a silent understanding passed between them, and they shared a smile.

Ivan sat across from Edward, a small fire snapping between them. While Edward devoured another plate of roasted lizard, Ivan barely touched his; he required little mortal food.

"Edward, would you like some more? I have had sufficient for tonight," he offered the plate to Edward, who took it happily.

"I can always eat more," Edward agreed with a mouth full of lizard and a half-smile, juice leaking down his chin.

Ivan nodded. "You know you're not too bad with that blade of yours. If you had some instruction, you could be great," Ivan commented.

Edward raised an eyebrow and retorted, "Ivan, you don't even use a sword," he said, chewing as if vindicated.

"Because I don't use one, Edward. That does not mean I can't. If you can defeat me in a sword fight, I'll know you don't need help, but if you can't. Will you agree to let me train you?" Ivan asked. His voice was a raspy whisper.

"I accept your offer of a demonstration and some training, if that is what it is." Edward's voice was cocky.

Ivan stood up, needing to put the boy to the test. He had already seen him fight. He was valiant and strong, but his movement was a choppy waste of the economy of his energy. True, Ivan preferred the axe, but that was because using a sword made him ill, almost dreamy, and lethargic when he held it. It was going to be a task to use it. But he would if it would save Edward's life in the future. "Very well, Edward. I can see you want to test yourself against me." Ivan smiled like a wolf. "I will be gentle; you look like you bruise easily."

Edward put his third plate down, this one only half eaten. Still chewing, he stood up and acquainted himself with Ivan's size. The Half-Dead overtopped him by more than a foot, and he was spring-loaded muscle. Edward tried to sound brave as he noticed that Tara and the others were watching. Ivan unsheathed his sword, its bloodstone pulsing.

"Hey, take care with that thing; it nearly killed Antoff, remember?" Edward proffered a hand, pointing at the sword.

Ivan answered only with a swish and a nod as he stepped back, the dreamy mood already struggling to take him. Memories of an elusive past kept slipping through his fingers. A former life viewed through a dirty window. Blurry and undefined.

Edward drew his broadsword and looked longingly at his shield.

"Won't need that shield, boy," Ivan rasped. "Learn to rely on the sword in single combat. You use the shield like a lame man uses a walking stick."

Edward nodded, "However you want, Ivan." The show was more for Tara than the others. He wanted to impress her, to show her he could be her protector... if she ever let him. Edward watched Ivan; he almost swooned on his feet, and then his blade spun, the edge of his sword gleamed sharp. He touched the tip to the ground, placed a foot forward, and bent his knee. His silver-gold eyes closed, and all he did was stand like that, frozen, and breathed.

Edward shook his head. *He can't even see me.* Edward lunged and struck with the flat of his blade to land a hit on Ivan's shoulder. He didn't want to hurt him; he just wanted to get it over with. Tara was watching him closely from the other fire, and he wanted to impress her. *Why do I need to impress this girl? Every time she looks at me, I want to shine.*

The blade would have struck Ivan, and it would have been over, but his movement was a blur, and so clean that it startled Edward.

Ivan felt and heard Edward's grunt on swinging the blade, and he opened his eyes, sliding to the side, and slapped the boy's blade away, almost removing it from his grip. He took the stance again and closed his eyes. "Two hands, Edward, and use the edge. Control is what we're working on here," Ivan said.

Edward felt the tremor of the impact going up his arm, almost losing his grip. He placed both hands on his broadsword, hoping to acquit himself better the next round. He flicked his eyes toward Tara and offered her a cavalier smile. She laughed. Ivan slapped his blade in mid-flirt, stinging his fingers.

"Pay attention; you can court the girl later." A small smile curled the corner of Ivan's lips.

Edward did not like being embarrassed like that. "You ask for it, Ivan. Remember that." Edward swung his blade upward in a guarded, striking stance he had learned from his father's master-at-arms and advanced. His blade swung in even controlled forms. He was serious now, and Ivan was going to get it.

Ivan matched him stroke for stroke, parrying, tossing an attack in the middle or at the beginning or end of his rhythm to throw him off and test him a bit. Ivan was only just holding on against the dream, as the weight of another man's memories were crashing down on him.

Edward withdrew and wiped some sweat from his brow. "I will be right with you," he sucked air raggedly into his lungs. Begrudgingly, he had to admit it; Ivan was good and taking it easy on him, to boot. Ivan showed no signs of tiring. Edward took his guarded stance again, and Ivan, seeing him ready, took his and closed his eyes, and breathed.

Edward was about to unleash when Ivan spoke, bringing him to a halt. "You know I don't need to have my eyes open; you grunt like a Hurdbeast before you swing," Ivan said.

Tara rolled with laughter, arms clutching her sides; she was enjoying his lesson a little too much.

Edward looked at Tara challengingly, "Well, you're welcome to join instead of laughing," Edward retorted sarcastically, and it should, at the very least, take her down a bit. That, however, is not what happened. The girl rose, drawing her twin short swords and twirling them.

She smiled at him like a Crag Lion inspecting a meal. "Now, Tara, take it easy. I am injured, and we are only practicing here, okay?" Edward warned.

"Of course, Edward. I would never think to hurt you." Her predatory smile deepened.

Ivan whispered a mirthful warning, "Now you are in trouble, boy."

"Yeah, my mouth does that sometimes." He whispered back out of the side of his lips. "Okay, is this going to be a free-for-all, or are you both on me?" His voice shook a little. He told himself he was still trying to catch his breath. It was strictly untrue, of course, but it made him feel better.

Tara answered for them both. "Definitely a free-for-all, Edward of Haven. I would not want it to be unfair." That last part said with interest in his reaction.

Edward bowed formally and gave her a roguish smile. "Whatever you wish, my lady?"

Tara ran her eyes over Edward's body and struck like a viper, her blades spinning and slashing at him. He barely caught the blows; she sent one spinning at Ivan as well, which he parried. There was a smile on her lovely face, and her grace was like a dancer. Ivan attacked back, not full out, but testing. She slid smoothly, not catching the blow, only deflecting it. Edward attacked Ivan, and he deflected that somewhat more sternly. Before long, it was a circle of clanging and spinning metal, reminiscent of a meat grinder, in Edward's opinion. One slip and that was it!

A crowd surrounded them, watching with unbridled interest. It was a good thing Antoff was sleeping or else they would have all been sore losers. Besides, he is competitive. It would be a dangerous match between him and Ivan. Tara mused.

Tara landed a blow with the flat of her left sword that slapped flesh beneath his shirt and across his ribs. Edward regretted removing his armor before the meal. "Hey, take it easy, Tara, okay?" Edward's hand instinctively went to his ribs, fingers pressing gently on the tender area where Tara's blade had landed. He lifted his shirt. It was not bleeding, but it was going to leave a mark.

Tara's eyes danced with amusement. "I am sorry, Edward of Haven. Do you need me to look at it?" She sheathed her swords in a whirl and approached him. As Edward was adjusting his shirt, the sharp sound of a slap echoed—it was Ivan playfully smacking Tara's rump, causing Edward to stifle a chuckle.

An expression of surprise and outrage reddened her face. "Ivan, what was that for?" She breathed, taken aback.

Ivan's face was trying hard not to laugh; she could see it forming on his flower-white face, "You said free-for-all, did you not? Perhaps if you were paying as much attention to the lesson as Edward, you would have seen it coming."

The nerve of that man, Tara almost said out loud, and then thought better of it and blushed even brighter. "You are right, Ivan. I apologize. He just has that effect on me."

"What did I do?" Edward asked, puzzled.

Tara's steel-gray eyes chilled him. "If you figure it out, Edward of Haven, you let me know." Tara turned for her fire but shot them both a glance over her shoulder. "Next time, Ivan, watch your back. I won't be so distracted, I promise."

"You were lucky to survive that, boy. The girl likes you," Ivan whispered.

Edward rubbed his sore ribs and met Ivan's gaze with a wry smile. "If that's her being affectionate, I'd hate to see her angry. The idea of that scares the seven hells out of me," he chuckled.

"It should." Ivan laughed and went back to their fire.

Edward walked back, his sword sliding smoothly into its sheath. His stomach rumbled with hunger, a half-eaten plate of lizard still beckoning to him. However, disappointment flickered across his face as he realized the plate was empty. An ironic smile tugged at the corner of his lips when he spotted the Dire Wolf, haunches settled on the ground beside the remnants of the meal. Its golden eyes met his, an air of lasting satisfaction in its posture. Edward shot Tara a look.

Edward's thoughts raced as he met Tara's gaze. There was something about her, an allure he couldn't quite untangle. Whatever it was, it twisted him up inside.

Amidst the quiet of the sleeping camp, the warrior Elp'har kept vigilant watch, their presence a constant reassurance. The night was hushed, broken only by the occasional chirping of insects. Then, a sudden urgency rippled through the air as Cur'Ra's voice cut through the stillness like a clarion call, jolting everyone awake. Her words carried a sense of urgency, slicing through the tranquility of the morning. "Priest Knight, the Zoruks approach in force."

Antoff's eyes snapped open with a mixture of alertness and lingering pain, questioned, "How close?"

Observing the distant sounds of the approaching horde, she replied, "A league at most, judging by their clamor."

She gave him a look that had a raised eyebrow in it, but declined to speak. Cur'Ra woke each member of the party and helped them get their armor donned again. The Elp'harean troop numbered sixteen, including warriors, women, and children. Antoff ordered everyone to saddle their horses and be ready to ride and set some men to dig the sandy soil out from under the gate, closing and barring it with a bronze brace. The horses loaded and brought to the courtyard. Antoff ordered everyone but the children to the battlement atop the circular wall. The pre-dawn sky was a tapestry of dark blues and purples, a foreboding omen. The wind, almost still, occasionally disturbed their cloaks. Antoff and his troop stood arrayed across the battlement's bows drawn and broad-headed arrows knocked. Tara and Va'Yone waited atop the wall, ready for battle, as the first silhouettes of the Zoruks pierced the horizon, their outlines distorted by the rising heat waves.

Chapter 9 The Lost Road

"How can we struggle against such madness? It's madness motivated by its own pain—a pain shaped by its circumstance and ever-changing nature. We're fueling its development, like a farmer unwittingly nourishing a feral animal with his crops. The more this war grows, the greater our enemy becomes and the more we spend in lives to sustain it. Peace cannot stop it now. The tide of madness is too great. It's too late!"

A remnant from the lost author of The Third Chronicle of the Shattered Age.

The Zoruks spread out before the mighty walls of Forge'Wrath, some carrying heavy crossbows as ranged weapons while the majority brandished spears, cleavers, swords, or axes. Yet they posed little threat to the walls, especially since they didn't out range the Elp'harean longbows.

Captain Um'elik deployed his forces in a holding action to prevent Antoff and his troop from leaving the fortress.

High above, bathed in dawn's golden glow, a Dragon Hound glided on the wind. It unfurled its red translucent wings with a resonating pop and landed gracefully on the valley floor. Its landing sent sand and dust billowing, enveloping Captain Um'elik and his Camolisk Lizard. The dragon-like creature stretched its neck, its head coming to within inches of Um'elik's face. Locking eyes with the creature, his mind flooded with visions.

Saliva dripped from its maw, sizzling as it contacted the sandy soil of the old riverbed.

"Captain Um'elik," began the dragon-like creature, "Lord Modred informs you he has dispatched five fists of Zoruk and one fist of mortal heavy cavalry. These troops should arrive at first light in two days. Lord Modred commands you to hold the Torrent Mage here until then."

In his mind's eye, Um'elik saw vivid images of Zoruks sprinting and mortals atop heavy Stingers, charging through familiar terrains. The events of an entire day flashed before him, condensing into mere moments.

Cur'Ra stood with Antoff on the battlements, both watching a Dragon Hound wheel in the air and then fall from the sky, its wings folded tight against its body. Its wings opened, flashing red in the light of the first sun. It swooped in and landed, causing the ground to erupt in a cloud of dust. It stood before the Zoruk commander, unmoving for a time, before it took off, bounding down the riverbed a few strides, and then leaped into the sky, its powerful wings beating at the air.

Ivan walked up behind them on silent feet and spoke in a raspy, hushed voice. "That Dragon Hound's speaking to the Zoruk commander using mind talk. It does not look like they will attempt to dig us out of here."

Antoff did not turn around to respond to Ivan, but continued to scan the terrain. "It is likely they won't try to come in, Ivan. They will wait for reinforcements to arrive, and then they will starve us until we are too weak to fight or just overrun us if they have the numbers. They care little for the life of their own soldiers."

Cur'Ra spoke softly, so they could only just hear her words. "There is another way."

"What other way?" Antoff asked.

Ivan made a sign with his hand to hush her. "Cur'Ra, it's too dangerous, and the rumors of an Old One living within these depths? Honestly, it leaves me wanting to face these Zoruks rather than a dragon."

Antoff looked back and forth at them questioningly. "What are you two talking about? What other way?"

Cur'Ra spoke gravely. "There is The Lost Road that cuts through the heart of the keep and runs the deep depths of the mountain to the other side. At one time, this was the only road used to get to the keep. The cove once filled with water, was the only way to reach the keep by river or through the mountain road that runs for miles beneath Forge'Wrath Mountain and lets out into the Springtide Valley just beyond the Twisted Lands, thirty leagues from the Plains of Vale and the town of RavenHof."

Edward and Tara stood nearby, waiting for their chance to speak.

Edward spoke up first. "We could attempt to defend this keep, and there's a good chance we would hold out for a while before they overpower us. But they will eventually overwhelm us. They will take Tara, and the world will pay for our decision. That's certain if we stay. However, if we follow The Lost Road, there's a chance at survival. We might live."

Tara shielded her eyes from the twin-suns, "Antoff, fate has left us with little choice. We must take The Lost Road."

Antoff, taken aback. There was determination in Tara's voice. He felt a surge of pride in her conviction, knowing that she was unafraid of sacrificing her life for a greater purpose. She wanted events to unfold, allowing fate to take its course.

Tara appeared weary as she spoke, as though she was carrying the weight of the entire mountain on her back. "This is not our land, Antoff. There is no value in holding it." She gestured toward her newfound people, "we have others now to watch over. I will not needlessly put their lives in jeopardy."

Cur'Ra turned and smiled at Tara. She followed this girl, hoping for the sake of her people that, with guidance, she could learn to lead. Today Tara showed the sparks of that promise and Cur'Ra was proud.

Va'Yone looked up at Tara. He slid his hand into hers. "I will go with you into the dark, Tara. I will take The Lost Road with you and keep you safe."

Tara smiled down at him and gave his hand a little squeeze as an answer to his bravery.

Ivan did not like it, but he agreed begrudgingly with Tara. At the very least, this way, they would have a chance. He smelled the air of the early morning hour and felt the breeze and sunlight on his face. He knew perhaps this would be the last time that he felt the wonders of the outer world. The last time that he saw the light of the suns, he would enjoy the moment regardless of the dangers that lay ahead.

Antoff turned towards Edward and commanded, "Get the troop organized. We are going to leave as soon as we are able. Inventory the rations and the water. We will keep a presence on the wall and not withdraw until the last moment. We don't need to let them know what's going on one instant before it's necessary."

Edward did as Antoff commanded, with less grumbling than before. He was getting used to taking orders from Antoff, and somehow it felt right. Midday had come when they withdrew their Elp'harean forces from the battlements atop the walls. They entered the gates of the keep. Antoff led the troops and then followed in by Ivan, Tara, Va'Yone, and Cur'Ra, then the troop with the women and children in the middle and Edward bringing up the rear. The Dire Wolf, always watchful, hunted ahead of his pack.

Inside the castle, only light from murder holes pierced the darkness. They entered the Main Hall, the clang of steel horseshoes echoing on The Lost Road's cobblestone.

The road was as wide as a city thoroughfare, designed to allow streams of cart or wagon traffic to pass by in both directions. Empty torch baskets, constructed of black iron bands, mounted along both sides of the road. The torches were long since missing from a hurried departure. There's an unwritten rule that went with Forge'Wrath Keep, and no one violated it until today. *Forge'Wrath Keep's gates were to be left open, and its first come, first serve for whatever force needed it.* They lit their lanterns and lamps as they closed and bound the main gate and barred the doors to the inner keep.

Antoff thought that it would hold undefended until nightfall, but no longer than that. The Dragon Hound would fly in unhindered over the walls to open the main gate. Although the Dragon Hound would allow the Zoruk troops through the porticos, it couldn't access the castle as easily as it could bypass the battlements and curtain walls, flying over the first two defense lines. He could imagine the Dragon Hound's claws click on the paving stones of the road leading to the front of the castle and beyond.

The Zoruks would batter the keep's old, weathered doors with rams. Failing that, they'd use a flame barrel, like those for siege equipment, to blast them open. Antoff looked at the keep doors one last time and thought about how little time it would take to blow that door down and invade Forge'Wrath Keep. He took one last look out over the dry cove from the doorway.

He knew there was no time to dwell on what might happen. The road before them filled with dangers and behind Tara's captivity and their death. They had to press on, guided by the light of their lanterns and a determination to face whatever lay ahead.

Forge'Wrath Keep had many doorways that led right and left of the road, which sloped downward at a slight angle. The chamber used to hold court so many years ago sat vacant, coated with centuries of dust. Cold breezes gusted through the castle, whistling with lonely sighs. A feeling of foreboding lingered in the halls of the keep, as if the ghosts of the past still held court, unaware that their own mortality had long ago faded away. The place, alive with memories of death and battles long forgotten by the world outside, felt like it was still under siege, struggling endlessly after having been the property of both the Light and the Darkness. Over the years, it had been taken and lost many times.

Their hushed voices and clattering horseshoes disrupted The Lost Road's silence. Overhead, the tunnel, constructed from block archways in heavy mountain rock, artfully buttressed, crafted by Dwemerin stonemasons long ago. A curving passageway that flowed in a straight line, sloping ever downward. The troop led their animals, Elp'harean longbows in hand, with broad-headed arrows knocked and ready to let fly. They walked at a steady pace; the darkness of The Lost Road was oppressive, the weight of a mountain pushing down.

Cold pockets of air turned their breath to vapor, causing a shiver to run down their spines as spectral shadows played in their peripheral vision, exaggerated by the fitful light of their lanterns. The shadows formed and moved fluidly, resolving themselves into solid shapes of mortals and monstrous forms from the distant past, locked in battle, frightening the living with feverish voices and unheeded cries for mercy. Water dripped, and stones skipped off the walls, echoing down the tunnel before them, thrown by an unseen hand. As their fear grew, the phantom forms became more visible, moving into plain sight.

"Ignore them!" Antoff shouted above the din of battle.

Horses rolled their eyes with fear, causing them to dance uncontrolled in every direction. In the grand rooms and halls, ghostly battle spilled out of each space. The sounds of wartime struggles echoed as they passed by. The hearts of the living almost froze as history was made manifest in greenish, wispy glows. At the very depths of the stronghold, huge iron banded brass doors were barred from the inside to keep out any unwanted visitors.

Tara shouted above the haunting sounds of battle. "How long has it been like this?"

Ivan yelled back, "Who can know when it was last barred? No one enters the inside of this fortress and then has come back out to talk about it I know of."

Finally, as they approached the immense doors, a shadow moved in the corner where the light flickered from lanterns, revealing a squatting man-like creature; it was naked and all alone. Its head turned down towards the floor, and its arms rested on its knees. Its flesh was greenish-grey, and its white hair hung disheveled about its chest and back, shaking as it laughed to itself soundlessly.

"Old Grim!" Ivan spat out its name like a curse. "It's causing these nightmarish dreams to become a reality by feeding on our fears!"

The Old Grim stood up slowly, lifting its face to see them. Its eyes were white, and it looked like it had been dead for a long time.

"It only has sufficient energy to animate itself for a short period to attack or feed on the flesh of the living. It is our fear energy that gives it the power to take physical form and allows it to attack, leaving its victims in the state of death and a ghostly existence. Do not let it touch you! Its attacks will do frost damage to living flesh and freeze your limbs," Antoff said while he drew his ornate longsword.

Old Grim looked at him defiantly as the sword ignited into a bright, pure blaze of light, and then shrank backward, climbing up the wall trying hard to avoid the pure light of Antoff's blade. It stopped at the ceiling like a four-legged spider, moaned and hissed at Antoff, and then pushed its body through the ceiling, disappearing. A frosty residue remained behind on the face of the stone, turning its surface white with ice crystals. All the phantasmal sounds of battle and the voices of the dead crying out had gone silent with its departure.

Edward and Va'Yone caught the motion of the Dire Wolf entering from a side corridor. Aggravated by things he did not understand and creatures that vanished as he passed through them when he attacked. His hackles were up, and he was jumping and snapping at anything that moved. At the very least, it was clear that he had a bad day.

Antoff spoke, his voice angry. "It's not gone. It just wants us to think it is, so be alert."

Ivan and Edward lifted the bronze bar from the closed gates, and then slowly pushed it open with a loud, echoing squeak. The Lost Road led downward at an increasing slope. Wide stone cut from the mountain rock replaced the cobblestone paving. The left side of the road hugged a large natural stone wall that climbed beyond the fitful flickering glow of their lamplight.

The right side dropped off into sheer blackness. Edward kicked a rock off the side and waited for it to hit the bottom, but it only bounced down the sides of the endless depths of the rock wall until the sounds of echoing contacts faded out.

Ivan pulled Edward back from the edge and growled. "Stop that! You do not know what lives in these depths, and I do not care to announce our arrival in their domain. Stop playing the fool, Edward, or you will get someone killed. And if you do that, be sure that I will drain you and leave your desiccated husk drying on the floor."

Deep within the blackness, a dragon slumbered. Her sleep did not mask vibrations that came from the usage of a god's pure Power by a Priest Knight, and the attenuation of the threads shifting in the fabric of reality that divided good and evil and in the place between the Light and the Darkness. The Great Gold Dragons' eyes opened, glowing yellow in the blackness of a mountain's depths. She's old, a mammoth specimen over three hundred feet in length. Her right front talons flexed sword sized curved nails. She raised her wedged shaped head, two straight horns extending from the top between large curved upright pointed ears. Then, lowering her snout, she sniffed the two golden eggs resting in a clutch between her scaled arms. She thought to her brood, *"So the one that carries the gift of your spark has at long last arrived.* The golden head laid back down and waited. *"We have time, children. Be patient, your wait is almost over.*

Above the mountain of Forge'Wrath, a Dragon Hound glided on the wind currents that gave lift to tired muscles of aching wings. Like a rumble of thunder in Are'Nok's head. "One of the Old Ones has awakened! We are saved!" Are'Nok wheeled into the sky, flying towards the Grey Area. He disobeyed the dark gods, and he didn't care. He would no longer serve these lesser things for dark gods and cruel masters.

Below, the Zoruk captain watched the Dragon Hound go, leaving him without the view from above or fast long-range communication with his lords. "Why were the gods so unpredictable?" He talked to himself. His troops stirred uncomfortably as they watched Captain Um'elik talking to no one in particular. *Is he going mad?* They argued and speculated quietly with each other.

The great fortress of Are'Amadon, in the heart of the Blackened Lands, sat as a stark reminder of the Power of Darkness against the backdrop of the murky soil that spread out beneath it for leagues, like a carpet of dark red and black. Zoruks moved like ants in the plains that stretched out into vast fields that required great effort from the innumerous slaves that worked them to produce meager crops. Banners flapped in the wind with symbols of the Zoruk tribes proudly displayed each one defining the boundaries of wicked, barbaric, and territorial societies.

Great Lord Amorath lay still upon a stone slab resting his old dead bones. His body, forced to live long past the creator's intended design. However, bones were different it seemed, and his right hip had ground down, causing him to limp. Next to him on the raised dais lay a mage's staff, all twisted and disfigured, blacked with age. A single large crystal flickered with Power. These types of arcane devices stored up Power to be unleashed, extending the Mages abilities beyond his potential.

In the darkness of Great Lord Amorath's tomb, a streak of light formed like a ribbon, blossoming into a purplish globe that stretched out above the height of a man, illuminated the stark surroundings of the tomb. Great Lord Amorath sat up, putting his hand on his staff, lifting it, placing it on the polished stone floor, using it to support his weight as he stood. A mortal in a dark, well-cut wool cloak walked out of the Mage Gate. The purple glow flickered like a strobe, reflecting the outline of Great Lord Amorath's visitor.

The man was large and had a bronze skin tone, tanned by the sun. Hair black hung around his neck, held by a golden band. His face was unlined, unnaturally handsome, with a square jawline and high cheekbones of nobility. His eyes, a pale blue in the weak light.

Great Lord Amorath's eyes blazed brightly, wreathed in dark Power, causing his breath to catch. "Great Lord EL'Keet; Why do you disturb my rest, bypassing any semblance of normal etiquette?"

The man beamed a patient smile and chuckled. "Well, let's see Amorath. It could be because you have been keeping secrets from the Dark Order, *Old Friend*."

Great Lord Amorath breathed finally, "There is nothing to keep '*Old Friend*', and it is you who are disturbing the sanctity of my lair. I will prepare a report for the Dark Order when there is *something* to report. For right now, there is not."

Great Lord EL'Keet's smile slid from his face. "Perhaps you could share that *something* with me lest I accidentally slip and let the Dark Order know of your—secret. Purely out of ignorance, of course." Great Lord EL'Keet didn't back down. Amorath stared at him, willing him to yield. He stepped forward with a less than satisfied smile on his face. "Or—we could work together on—the report, Lord Amorath?"

Amorath sighed to himself, aware his deceit was discovered. "Very well Lord EL'Keet! I will tell you what I know. There is a living Torrent Mage trapped by my troops at Forge'Wrath Keep. I have her contained and will take her into custody and transport her here in chains in two days."

The Great Lord EL'Keet's face twisted with rage when he responded. "You would seize this power for yourself and use it against us, making you the overlord?"

Amorath sighed again; the deep intonations of his voice driving home the point. "No, I would not. I would use her as we must. A Torrent Mage, turned to our side, would shift the balance. Finally, allowing us to destroy the Light. Just as originally planned from the beginning! You remember the plan, do you not, Great Lord EL'Keet?"

"I do, Lord Amorath." He replied in a condescending tone. "I hoped we could talk before, as you stated it, we can prepare *our* report for the Dark Order. What do you think? Should we not have a conversation first and discuss our options?"

Great Lord Amorath hesitated for a moment and then spoke. "What are you suggesting, EL'Keet?"

Lord EL'Keet looked into his eyes while allowing his Mage Gate to wink out. Only the glow of Lord Amorath's staff remained to light the room with a dim, flickering nimbus.

Lord Modred paced back and forth on the gray stone balcony of his tower room, situated high above the fortress of Are'Amadon, his movements like a hungry wolf. Time pressed him, and Great Lord Amorath's threats echoed in his mind. The Dragon Hounds remained silent about why one had abandoned its post. The replacement Modred had asked for hadn't yet responded with a report on the Torrent. Lord Amorath's patience was wearing thin.

Uttering curses in a guttural demonic language, Modred flared his black wings and leaped from the balcony of the fortress's highest tower. Riding the wind that rose from the sunbaked soil, warmed and then seared by the intense midday sun, he circled the tower. Unsteady gusts challenged his flight as he glided towards the fortress's inner structures. He landed softly in the courtyard, where the rhythmic hammering of Zoruk armorers and smithies filled the air. The scent of hot oil and sweat lingered, undisturbed by the inconsistent winds that barely touched the air beneath the walls.

Walking through the fortress's central gate, Modred's black scaly hide and armor gleamed under the sun. He moved to the guardhouse, descending the spiraling gray stone stairs to the first dungeon level and the levels below. The tortured screams of captives, taken from battlefields and villages of the Twisted Land, echoed upward. These captives helped them infiltrate enemy territories and gather intel on troop movements through the Grey Area.

Reaching the bottom of the stairs, Lord Modred entered the first cell. A man knelt on the cold, wet stone floor, surrounded by dim light and the hissing of a lone torch. Manacles chained his wrists and ankles, all connected to an iron ring in the center of the room. A brownish-black, wingless demon loomed over him, brandishing a thin, hooked razor. Despite the demon's lanky appearance, suggesting its frailty, it moved with a menace. The kneeling man appeared middle-aged, fit as if he were a warrior or skilled craftsman. Sweat and grime matted his black hair, the signs of long days in the dungeon under the cruel attention of Master Tormenter Be'elota.

Lord Modred stood by the prison chamber's entrance, absorbing the scene. Be'elota's deceptive tales of freedom whispered seductively to the broken spirits of the damned. The unfortunate souls who struck deals with this master tormenter would unknowingly serve darker forces, strengthening Be'elota's Power.

"Will you relent and make the bargain, Ja'eam?" Be'elota hissed.

Wounded and exhausted, Ja'eam struggled to maintain his posture. Blood oozed around the rusty shackles, and his torn clothes bore evidence of brutal treatment. His parched voice cracked as he spoke. "I will take the bargain if you grant me time with my family—time under my control."

Master Tormenter Be'elota sneered, his smile a grotesque twist. "Done and done then! You agree to this now?"

"I will," Ja'eam rasped, his voice shaky.

From a dark corner, a shadowy presence moved, manifesting as black smoke. Be'elota grabbed Ja'eam's head, forcing his mouth open, and the smoky tendril slithered down the man's throat. Ja'eam convulsed under the tormenter's grip, then fell motionless, his eyes momentarily vacant before revealing a newfound malevolence. A brief, sinister laugh escaped his lips before exhaustion pulled him into slumber.

"This man will be invaluable in our quest to control the Torrent Mage," Lord Modred declared. "Clean him up and provide him with gold for his mission. He should return to his former life and family at the earliest. Under circumstances, we craft."

Captain Um'elik scrutinized the empty fortress walls for hours, his frustration growing. He dismounted with a muttered complaint. *What should I do? Lord Modred's orders are clear: keep the Torrent Mage captive. But I cannot risk her escape. I will not lose what belongs to me to another. I want that Torrent!* The Dragon Hound was gone and had not returned. Another hour had passed, and his frustration level grew with the lateness of the hour. It was nearly dusk, and there were still no Dragon Hounds! He would wait no more. "Sergeant, I want three Zoruks with grapples to scale that wall and open the main gate now! Dispatch two scouts also to our approaching forces, and ten troops will remain to secure this location as ordered. I will not deny Lord Modred his prize. That Torrent will be ours!" *Nor will they deny me my reward!* He thought to himself.

Captain Um'elik gave the command, and three Zoruks armed with grapples rushed toward the walls. In a short time, the main gates creaked open, and the Zoruk warriors charged ahead to secure the keep. Forge'Wrath keep had exchanged landlords once again.

Chapter 10 Mountains and Dreams

"The dreams dragons are a universe, interconnected by ethereal streams of visions and emotions that flow seamlessly from one majestic creature to another."

Tara watched Edward and Ivan wrestle to secure the bronze doors from the outside. A sense of unease crept over her, accompanied by the weight of being watched. Deep within, she recognized the identity of the watcher. Engaging her imagination, she recalled every nuance of the Old Grim, meticulously re-sculpting its form in her mind, refining each intricate detail. She closed her eyes and conjured an image of the realm existing between Light and Darkness. Amidst the clash of good and evil, she stood at the center, the equilibrium between these warring forces slipping through her fingers.

The currents of Power swirled around her. Tara reached into the depths, anchoring herself in the present layer of reality, and waited. The image she had crafted of the Grim waited in the recesses of her mind, waited to be used.

Edward and Ivan aligned the bar horizontally across the center of the entrance. Ivan's voice emerged raspy, laced with exertion. "Tara, can you fuse these two together?"

"I can. Just release it when I tell you. Understand?" Tara answered.

Edward and Ivan exchanged glances. "Agreed," Edward said.

Tara's focus narrowed on the bar, sensing its material density and weight through an arcane flow of Power. With a surge, she pressed against the bar, prompting the massive metal doors to shudder. "Let go," Tara commanded. Uttering incantations in the Old Tongue under her breath, she invoked, "Vem'lar Du'ha Ex'Treema Oh'Mas Flam'Meer." The bar emitted a squeal as it blazed molten red. Edward and Ivan retreated as a wave of searing heat washed over them, radiating from the bar. "Due'ae Im'Singular." The scorching heat extended outward, fusing the two substances.

"I believe this will suffice for the moment. Don't you think?" Tara said with a satisfying smirk.

Edward stood stupefied, while Ivan scrutinized the smoldering door. "It appears sufficient. The bond seems strong." Ivan nodded, Edward still gaped at the door. Ivan let out a low chuckle and slapped his back, "come, lad."

They regrouped, assuming their positions, advancing along the road, with Edward at the rear. Tara still held her connection to the torrent of arcane energy, coiled like a serpent poised to strike. The specter of the Grim materialized in the void, awaiting its inevitable invocation. The sensation of being watched intensified as Old Grim slithered from the very rock face of the wall that embraced The Lost Road, leaving behind an icy trace of crystalline frost where it emerged from the mountain stone. On silent footfalls it followed behind, a hand stretching toward Edward.

Antoff's senses detected the malevolent aura trailing them, just as its strike hit. A glacial chill jolted through Edward's arm, freezing his skin solid against his clothing and the armor enveloping it. His cries pierced the air, forming a frosty mist. Antoff pivoted, wielding his longsword high. Radiant brilliance burst upon the smooth walls and cobblestones, their gleam casting eerie, dancing shadows. The Old Grim projected indistinct shadows, a perplexing blur, like anchored in a different layer of time. Only halfway in this reality, its substance wavered between two places.

The Elp'harean archers, fortunate enough to have a clear sight, released their broadhead arrows in one seamless motion, reloaded before the arrows struck their mark. The Grim pried its frosty grip from Edward. Antoff lunged towards Edward, but the damage was already done.

The Grim convulsed, hampered or wounded by the arrows that feathered it like a pincushion.

Brimming with arcane Power and smoldering wrath, Tara turned her gaze upon the Old Grim. It was trying to vanish. Elude this existence; it sneered and laughed soundlessly. Its form became less substantial, allowing the arrows to pass through it. They fell to the ground with clatters. Anchoring the image in time within her mind, Tara perceived the connection bridging the two realities. A vortex of energy swirled around the entity, tendrils of Power at her command. She lay hold of these currents and sealed the vortex with ropes of Power. Channeling the image of the Grim that she had sculpted in her mind. Tara injected it into the swirling maelstrom of the creature's existence. The Old Grim solidified, laughter faltering, its countenance paling as a second volley of Elp'harean arrows plunged into its form, causing it to stagger. The realization dawned—it was no longer in control of its transit between realities. Tara's voice resounded, "Ivan, take its head!"

Ivan swung his massive axe through the air, lunging at the fully manifested adversary. The weapon hissed and then cleaved the head from the entity's frigid shoulders, leaving a mist of blue-gray ice crystals suspended in the air. An expression of astonishment crept upon the Old Grim's visage, its disembodied head rolled, vision spinning, plummeting off the precipice into the abyss flanking the right side of The Lost Road. Tara released her hold on the interdimensional aperture. The vortex shrank, accompanying the vanishing of the headless body, returning to whence it came. The Grim had slipped from an alternate recess of existence, exploiting the vulnerable for life energy. Now, together, they had banished it.

Cur'Ra dashed to Edward, sprawled upon the road's rugged, wagon-wheel-rutted surface. Gently, she turned him onto his back, her palm finding its place upon his chest. His breath surfaced shallow and ragged. Cur'Ra shut her eyes momentarily, producing a hiss before beckoning Tara to her side. "Tara, you must gradually infuse him with warmth, using your Power, while ensuring not to scorch him. Your touch must be with precise control, lest you worsen the injury and kill him."

"Kill him?" Tara hesitated, but Cur'Ra guided her hand to Edward's frozen arm, sensing the temperature rise through her touch. "I'm worried about inflicting more harm. Such delicate manipulation of Power upon another is unfamiliar for me," Tara admitted.

Cur'Ra exhaled wearily. "In times of yore, healers and mages collaborated harmoniously in such endeavors. It's high time you master subtle control. Your command over the Power is untamed, a hazard. Perhaps with a life other than your own at stake, your attentiveness will sharpen."

Tara nodded and focused her energies, weaving fine threads of Power towards Edward's injured arm. "Only the surface remains frozen; the underlying flesh is unaffected." Gradually, she introduced minuscule currents of fire, first to the armor, adjusting it to the ambient temperature, then to the flesh beneath. Slowly and deliberately, beads of sweat glistened upon her forehead, her efforts exhaustive. "This demands greater finesse than using the Power in larger quantities," Tara confessed, but in her inward thoughts she was pleading with Edward to stir. *I refuse to lose you. You stubborn, foolish boy.*

"Indeed, child," Cur'Ra agreed, her tone akin to a mother's guidance. Her eyes remained closed, her assessment of Tara's efforts unfaltering. Merging the healing currents of her own being and her deities with those at play in Edward's body, Edward's muscles tensed and then relaxed. His breathing, erratic earlier, harmonized into a deep, tranquil slumber. "It is done," Cur'Ra declared.

They shed Edward's armor, stripping away the necrotic tissue to expose the nascent, rosy skin beneath. As they met each other's gaze, they found themselves encircled by the entire assembly, mesmerized and awestruck. "That, my dear, is the artistry of healing," Cur'Ra uttered with weariness.

"Thank you, Mother," Tara replied. They shared smiles. Tara radiating eagerness.

Cur'Ra maintained the connection. "Much is attainable through this approach. Marvels can be accomplished by merging our streams." *This child carries an ember; I sense it! How does she straddle both conduits? It's not possible. Only the Elder Gods embody such duality. But can she access it?*

"I want to learn," Tara pleaded.

Cur'Ra replied and promised her, "You will, child, and I will teach you what I can."

Antoff's voice broke their moment. "We can't stay here. We need to move."

Cur'Ra nodded, "Give him an hour, Antoff. Any sooner might do more harm."

Ivan had been quietly observing Tara and Cur'Ra's diligent care for Edward. Their presence by his side, their attentive eyes as he slept, demonstrated a compassion that was new to Ivan. He struggled to remember a time when someone had shown him such kindness. In the deep recesses of his mind, blurry recollections of people he once knew would briefly appear before disappearing again. Transient memories of a former life flickered tantalizingly close, yet remained frustratingly elusive. Ghostly images of a woman, children, and a home that used to be his haunted him.

That life had vanished, leaving only pieces of a hidden reality deep in his mind. He mourned these unknown, unrecognizable specters, shrouded in the mist of forgotten memories. A wave of loss stirred in his heart, igniting a need for understanding.

On the faintly lit road, Ivan contemplated the circumstances that had birthed this emptiness within him. Each fleeting image concealed a story he was eager to uncover. The fragments of affection and love he discerned in these remnants were a painful reminder of what he'd lost, fueling his desire to decode the mystery of his past and reclaim his stolen life.

As he watched over Edward, Ivan resolved to discover the missing fragments. The path ahead was uncertain, but he held onto hope that somewhere along this path, he might find the answers he needed and rebuild the fragments of his forgotten past.

"Are you okay, Ivan?" Tara's voice, filled with worry, broke the silence of the road.

Ivan had not noticed her standing there, which bothered him. He was always on his guard in case of an attack, but he didn't know when his subconscious stopped thinking of his companions as threats. He sighed deeply, "I'm just... reflecting. I remember so little of my past, Tara. Co Ádean from the Order of the Light told me that forgetting was a mercy, allowing me to focus on my newfound purpose. The memories of a tragic past could hinder my ability to perform the duties required by the Order."

Tara's eyes softened. "That's not fair, Ivan. You're a person, not a tool. To know you had a life, loved ones, only to have those memories taken from you... it's wrong." She reached out, her hand touching his, and then drew a hug around him.

Ivan went stiff, then relaxed into her embrace. "Thank you, Tara. Your care means a lot. But for now, we need to keep you safe. We'll worry about the rest later." He patted her head awkwardly, not knowing how to show gratitude, much less affection. *How can this be? This girl only sees me and not the monster.*

An understanding passed between them as Tara looked up at him. "Ivan, you're part of our family now. You're cherished here, not just as a warrior, but as the man you've become. We'll fight for you, just as you've fought for us. And I will help you, Ivan, in any way I can." Tara felt his arms enfold her and hug her back.

Behind the sealed iron doors, they could hear the rhythmic pounding of heavy wood on metal. The Zoruks launched their assault by battering the castle gates with a ram. Their dark, guttural chants accompanied each impact of the ram as they synchronized their efforts to its rhythmic booms with each impact of the wooden ram. "Boom, Boom, Boom!"

And so it went; the ram's impacts reverberating throughout the covered halls and down the Lost Road as the Zoruks worked feverishly to overwhelm the castle gates. It was about an hour when the first gate gave way with a brutal crash, followed by a cheer from a Zoruk horde. Once again, the hammering soon started and echoed throughout the vastness of the halls hauntingly, like the heartbeat of a struggling creature.

Antoff looked at Cur'Ra as if asking to go. Cur'Ra still sat next to Edward with her hand on his chest, feeling him breathe in and out deeply. "Very well, Antoff." She placed her hand on Edward's forehead tiredly and then closed her eyes.

Edward's eyes opened wearily. He looked at Cur'Ra questioningly. "What happened?" His left hand moved to his arm without thinking. When he flexed it, his arm felt weaker than usual but serviceable.

"You were injured and suffered trauma, but we must go now, and there is no time to rest," she responded urgently. She helped Edward sit up and then get to his feet and back into his armor.

"Boom, Boom, Boom!" The sounds echoed the impacts of the Zoruks hammering. The fear of the pursuit hurried them along as they formed up and moved down the road.

Ivan looked around as he rasped sarcastically to no one in particular. "Well, there is no hiding being here now with all this Zoruk racket and Mage Craft being thrown about. It's a wonder the Old One itself is not up here right now having tea with us."

Below the mountains keep, a golden dragon, Al'amire, cradled her brood. She sensed both the imminent and distant threats, the Zoruks, the Old Grim, a god's Power kindled within an old Priest Knight, and more. Yet above all, she sensed an essential spark in a unique Torrent Mage, a spark that could grant her offspring a life beyond mere existence.

This spark was akin to the Power she herself had received from her bondholder, a mage who had filled her with life and immortality. Through this bond, both the dragon and the mage grew stronger, transcending into a single divine entity in the eyes of ordinary mortals.

This union, however, attracted greed, as both dragons and arcane users were scarce and their combined Power coveted. The Torrent Mage, positioned in the gray area between Dark and Light, would bestow her brood with an unprecedented choice, to serve either side.

When a dragon and mage successfully unite, they transform into a formidable force that reflects the core nature of each being. Sadly, such unions could often lead to conflicts embodying the timeless struggle between Darkness and Light, influencing the universe's delicate balance.

Now, a moment of decision looms, as the old equilibrium has been shattered, and only the rarest among beings can restore it. This wisdom is an ancient prophecy shared among dragons, a secret memory dating back to the first dragon-mage bond.

If either of her two offspring were lost before the balance was restored, the sole survivor would set the course for all time—an unnerving prospect for Al'amire, as the details of such a scenario were not contained in her ancestral memories. If the one filled with Darkness lived, then there would be covered in shadow. And if the Light lived, then illumination and no choices.

While the ancient gods slept, Al'amire dared not rouse her bondholder, De'rious, a powerful yet potentially dangerous entity who could inadvertently awaken the old gods and provoke a devastating war. The younger gods, powerless compared to their predecessors, schemed in the shadows, striving to restore balance in their own flawed ways before the old ones awakened.

The young gods' efforts were futile without a dragon's bond. Dismissing it as mere myth, they focused on hoarding relics of Power from a forgotten age, thus disrupting the balance further. Without the Torrent Mage and her broodlings, there would be no hope for harmony.

Tara wrapped Va'Yone's little arms around her middle silently, holding on. It was a kind of comfort that told her she was not alone. He snuggled in.

Cur'Ra rode beside her and asked, "Tell me of your childhood, Tara," her voice a soft echo in an underground filled with darkness, only the lamplight of the troop to illuminate their way.

Startled out of her reverie by the cool, moist air, Tara answered, "There is not much to tell. I am an orphan. I neither remember my mother or father." She looked straight forward, not looking at Cur'Ra, trying to hide the sadness and hurt that always accompanied this topic.

Cur'Ra nodded, understanding. "What is the first thing you remember, Tara?"

"I was alone, abandoned, and forced to steal to survive. I tried to fit in and seek..." she breathed out, and her eyes searched as if she was hunting for a word, "a connection to the world. No one wanted me because of these." Tara touched the scroll that marked her eyebrow to cheek and down her neck. She blinked a tear and wiped it away bravely. "Because I am a freak, and things kept happening around me. Everyone was scared of me."

The Elp'har fell in close around her; all of them did, from the eldest to the smallest child. They reached for her, touching her leg and then their heart, saying, "You are ours. You are alone no more." There was compassion in them for her, and more importantly to Tara—true love. *They love me.* They wanted her connection.

Tara could only smile and touch a hand to her heart while murmuring a thank you. Nothing more—she was on the edge, ready to burst with tears. *They want me. They need me. I need them too.*

Cur'Ra waited a long moment for the full awareness and significance of that interaction to sink into Tara. She let the tears come and the closeness with the Elp'har to take hold. Finally, when they melted back into the ranks of the troop. Tara was silent and except for the rhythmic banging and clomping of hooves, the stillness of the caverns deep lent it solemnity to the thought that echoed inside. Cur'Ra had waited for her to settle. Waited for Tara to find that point of reflection and spoke before the world could awaken her with all its fear and problems.

"Tara, that place you are in, the things you are feeling right now. You feel surrounded by love and a greater oneness with something. A oneness with life and love and connections that flow deep into places that you only glimpse in those special moments of tenderness. That is where healing comes from."

Tara's eyes lit up with questions. She leaned closer, her eyes wide and filled with an insatiable curiosity. "Tell me more, Cur'Ra. How does it all work? I need to understand everything about it. Do you mean the sharing of true love and the giving of self to each other, like between a man and a woman?" She blushed as her thoughts went to Edward.

Cur'Ra nodded, "Yes, but it isn't just between a man and a woman, it's also between family and community. It is a place of tenderness and giving over self for the sake of another. It is that place of solitude in the depths of our being, where love and compassion well up. That is the channel of life. The means by which you communicate, transfer and union. It is a place of trust, and just as you responded to your families love and tender care of you, it is the truest and rawest form of life and it responds to the communication that comes from that deep place that is within each of us."

"I don't understand, not really. If it's the place that the language of healing comes from? How does it work?" Tara was not just interested she was hungry for that knowledge.

"That is a place of trust and compassion that life responds to. And when you reach, first having love, and then the compassion, the channel opens."

"Put your hand on your chest," Cur'Ra instructed. she placed her hand on her own heart.

Tara followed her instructions, mirroring her.

Cur'Ra gave a nod. "Now close your eyes. Don't speak or think Tara, just feel, from that place of tenderness, reach with compassion toward yourself."

Tara closed her eyes. She felt with tenderness and compassion. She waited and held out her love and compassion like a hand to the fallen and felt it. The finest thread. Like the trust of something wild. It was like an injured animal trying to trust for the first time. It was life, and it touched her. She waited. Tara did not withdraw; she pushed compassion toward. It had been waiting for some act, some reason to withdraw. Tara only met that with tenderness and love. More tendrils rapped the channel until it ached with life, pulsed with the flow. "I feel it!" She laughed.

Cur'Ra smiled to herself. She had known it was in the girl she just had to experience a moment of sharing at that depth and it could be drawn out of her. "What you are feeling is your life. It can be shaped and entreated. Those are other lessons, for now just talk to it. That flow speaks Tara. It is that way for every creature in our world. There are subtle differences from everyone because it knows things about them and shares their state. To every creature, only a measure of life is given. That is why it is wrong to take it from one to give to the other. It is a robbery and a betrayal of that trust you feel right now. You must never do this Tara, and taking from yourself is the theft of your own promise. Do you understand?"

Tara was still except for the swaying that came from riding and she only nodded, trying hard to hold the connection. That connection was important and deep inside, she knew it must be maintained and not just within herself, but with all life. "What about the creatures attacking us? And the ones I've destroyed? I just... don't know how to feel."

Cur'Ra smiled, "Yes, it is a conflict, is it not? To carry something precious. We cannot replace it. Choice is part of the equation, Tara. Deep inside, we all know when we make that choice, don't we? What the outcome could be? Yet, when we push forward, whether out of ignorance or knowing inside, we know that the choice was made. Life will not judge you for that. If you withdraw healing when compassion is required. For *that,* life will judge you."

"I understand. Why does war and hate exist if everyone has this life within them? I mean, the connection is so overwhelming?" Tara asked.

"Not everyone can feel it, Tara, and not everyone wants to. Compassion reaches to heal. Some people love so little, even themselves. They do little other than destroy. Compassion and love are required so that you can get outside yourself long enough to see others. Most people cannot see beyond self and how other actions affect their space in the world. It is a small thing that in ages past people called it a point of view. They even called it a world view. Well, that is your first step into a wider world child. You must learn to walk before you can run."

Edward and Ivan rode behind Tara and Cur'Ra, watching the exchange. Though Ivan hadn't meant to eavesdrop, his Half-Dead hearing was sharper than other mortals. He grasped the undeniable power of Cur'Ra's teachings and now understood why his kind, or at least part of his being, was so abhorred. *It is not that I have never thought of the taking of life as a theft. In fact, I knew it was, but it was necessary for my survival. Mages make a mockery of life for the sake of greed, and his existence was the personification of that mockery. And yet, Tara still shows me love. Cur'Ra, with all her knowledge, did not condemn me. Antoff trusted me with his precious mission and the young lad, I dare say, liked sparring with me. It*

was Tara's connection to life and the compassion that spared me her judgement. It is a hard thing to understand.

Chapter 11 Where the Gold Lay

"We played stones upon the grid. I chose white and you black. For every stone placed, there was a response in turn. A struggle to block the other's advance and at the same time to push forward with our own plans to win. It is the portrait of the struggle between Light and Darkness. Opposite poles forever embroiled in battle, they diverge along the edge, fighting to gain some advantage while struggling to find a lost balance. It does not matter who plays the game. The game is always in play, with someone ready to choose a color and another to place a stone."

The troop continued down the Lost Road to the cadence of the Zoruks, crashing through the last gate and breaching the entry to the keep. Followed by rhythmic banging on the bronze door that Tara had melted shut. With time, the Zoruks would spill onto the Lost Road, leaving only one way out.

Edward's brow furrowed as he gazed into the distance, lost in the tangle of his own thoughts since he woke. He knew that Tara and Cur'Ra were watching him from the corners of their eyes, ensuring he didn't fall off the road or get left behind. They soon found him a few paces behind, murmuring in a low voice, careful not to be heard by the others.

Edward stammered, "I wanted to tell you now before the Zoruks come. Thank you both for saving me. I would have died or, worse, been maimed for life without your help." Both women smiled at him in response.

Tara fixed him in her gaze. "I am sure you would have done what was necessary if the situation was reversed. Wouldn't you?"

His sea-green eyes met Tara's, a hint of vulnerability in their depths. "You know I'd risk it, but wielding divine Power to perform a miraculous healing—it's a league beyond our usual challenges," Edward replied, his face filled with a mixture of awe and gratitude. "It's just that I have let so many people down in my life, Tara, and I am afraid-" Edward looked away but steeling his resolve, to get the words out, "I am afraid I will let you down as well."

Tara's eyes sparked with fiery anger. She thrust her hands onto her hips, her stance rigid, her unspoken response like a lance through the air. "Then I guess, Edward the Dark, you have a lot to learn about, friends and family. We are Elp'hars. We give people their place in life by how we feel about them, not by blood relation or birthright. You have much to learn. The first thing you'd better learn is that you are important to *me*." Despite her face turning red, she paused before moving on. "What I meant to say is you are important to all of us and you have responsibilities, and I will hold you to them. Do you understand me?" She felt the pain of his confession and his vulnerability touched her. *If he wasn't such a lout, I may have considered naming him something else closer to my heart, but as he was so hardheaded, he could just forget about that. Well, at least for now.* She told herself.

Edward looked surprised. His voice showed a hint of shock when he answered, "Yes, I understand. It is my honor to serve; you have my blade and my friendship if you need it. I will strive to be worthy of both. You are important to me, Tara—all of you are." He hesitated.

Tara rose on her tiptoes and kissed his cheek, whispering, "Make sure that you do. I'm counting on you. I know you can be that man of honor."

He hastily touched the spot where Tara's lips had met his cheek, then redirected his hand, feigning a casual scratch. A small smile appeared on his lips. The exchange left him invigorated, the warmth of their connection infusing him with a newfound resolve. This, he realized, was the cornerstone on which he could rebuild a legacy of honor. Tara was giving him a priceless gift. *Family.*

As Tara turned, she caught the appraising eye of Antoff and his curt nod. He knew what she had done, and he would honor it by giving Edward a place as well. Ivan's low, husky voice came from behind them. "I guess I could tolerate you for a little while longer, pup."

Edward narrowed his eyes playfully. "I will beat your skill, Ivan. It will just take some practice and time—lots of practice and time." Edward admitted.

Ivan let out a chuckle and placed on his back.

From the road ahead, out of the curtain of Darkness, sauntered a woman clad in shadowy, form-fitting silks, moving with grace and allure. A woman of such dark beauty catches one's breath. Long hair the color of midnight fell down her back below her shoulders and captivating eyes so brown that they glitter like dark pools that would swallow a man's soul if he gave her, but half a chance. Antoff's longsword leaped into his hand, ablaze with divine Light, before her second step fell. The Elp'hars were faster with arrows pulled to their cheeks, waiting silently for the smallest sign from Tara or Cur'Ra to let fly.

Her voice was as silky as her garb and even more charming, giving a haunting feeling, like a dark angel hiding in the deepness of shadow. "I know what hunts you, Priest Knight, and I know who they hunt," she purred, directing a smile at Tara, already burning with arcane Power.

Antoff's voice was on the edge of violence. "De'Nidra, Daughter of Shadows, I sensed you before. I know who you are, but I didn't think you'd be foolish enough to actually show yourself."

"Then you know that I could have destroyed you with a glance from those shadows. Yet here I am, talking to you, rather than burning you to ash." She looked at Tara. From behind De'Nidra, the Great Dire Wolf growled low and guttural, its eyes soaking in the Light.

He crept from the shadows of the Lost Road on silent paws. *Shadow Sister.* His mind whispered.

De'Nidra's eyes widened with surprise, and even more annoyance, she went on. "That includes the pup. But I'm here to help you, not to destroy you."

"And why would the Daughter of Shadows have any interest in helping us? Don't insult us, you are only interested in helping yourself. You're a liar, De'Nidra. You were a liar from the beginning and have always been." Antoff spat back at her, his blade glowing ever brighter.

De'Nidra's smile slipped slightly, but she remained placid. "You call me a liar, Priest Knight, but I was never a liar. I was a student, and I wanted to do research. Yes, maybe your Conclave of the Light did not believe that the areas I was interested in should be pursued because they deemed it dangerous or forbidden knowledge. As if they controlled every intellectual discipline for every intelligent race. And meanwhile, the Dark Order, originally just a group of researchers that held the alternative belief that study should be open and unhindered by faith, had been demonized. That was how this situation had devolved to this point ages ago, not the religious diatribe they feed you in the Halls of the Light."

"Do you want the truth? Let me share some truth with you. I want to keep your Torrent from the Dark Order, at least for now. It suits my plans that she survives a little longer. Yet I will burn you down before I see them hold that kind of power over the rest of the Order, of which I control a small part."

With a swift, determined step, Edward positioned himself in front of Tara, his broadsword held aloft like an unyielding bulwark against an approaching tempest of danger. "You will have to kill me to take her."

De'Nidra let her eyes pass over him. "Ah, it is you, Edward of Haven. Would you not wish to know the truth and be restored to your place? Don't you want to know why your own father acted so strangely? Don't you want to know how a man who was never capable of abandoning anyone tossed you aside without a backward glance? Don't you want to know how it was done? I can give that to you if you would but serve me."

Edward did not even hesitate as he responded. "No, I will not serve you. I serve the Torrent! You cannot offer me more than she has already given. Nor can you pay the debt that I owe her." *This goddess can burn me down, but I will not betray Tara. She has my life and my sword!*

"We shall see about that in time." De'Nidra smiled. *The girl is already shaping them and they don't even know it.*

Tara's eyes gleamed with love as she stepped out around Edward, a ball of liquid fire forming between her hands. She drew deeply on the Power, and the surrounding reality shook, distorted by the image forming in her mind. In the envelope of her mind, she fed the torrent of Power into her desire to protect the ones she loved. The more she fed into the envelope of reality, the more Power she needed to resolve the image of De'Nidra's destruction. It seemed limitless.

Though Tara whispered, her voice seemed to boom from all directions, emerging from the shadows. "Do not threaten those whom I love. Do you think that you are the only one who can burn things down? *Do you?*" She drew more deeply. The liquid ball of Power grew and crackled as lightning crawled across its surface, the arcane swirls from her eyebrows to cheeks blazing like fire-etched ash down her neck. Her face was a mask of concentration and struggle. Her teeth gritted into a smile as she drew on the power unheeding of the consequences.

"Careful, girl, you will scorch your mind and burn yourself out! No one living can teach a tenth of what I could if you would *just* listen to me. If you would serve me, all my knowledge would be open to you," De'Nidra replied.

Va'Yone stepped up beside Tara, a blue ball of lightning rolling from one hand to the other. "And what will you offer to me, Daughter of Shadows? You have nothing with which to pay."

Ivan moved with deadly grace, appearing to flow through the Elp'harean troop. Longbows aimed at a single target, and their animals parted like the sea before his predatory advance. In only a single breath, he had covered the distance of the troop. His eyes, golden swirls of blood, gathered the Light as he took in the scene; the heartbeats all around him thundered in his ears. He focused on De'Nidra and hungrily watched as her blood, wreathed in a red hue, pulsed in her form.

De'Nidra watched Ivan as he slipped like running water through the crowd, his eyes aglow with a fire and hunger for her blood. He emanated death and fear like the old legends reborn. He was not even aware, but she could see it as if some former ghost of a hero long forgotten by mortals spilled out in time. She recognized that walk, the controlled power ready to be unleashed, the form, the grace.

Pictures of battlefields covered in blood floated in her mind. Realizing that her composure had slipped somewhat, she steadied herself before speaking. "Ivan, is that not what you call yourself now?" Ivan paused momentarily. She continued, "You were not always called by that name, but I know your name from the days of old. I know your history, and if you will but serve me, I alone can restore you and what the forces of the Light have taken from you. There is little doubt in my mind that you would repay me when your memories returned."

Ivan's voice was a rasp, a blacksmith's metal file sliding across steel as he spoke even before he could think. "You have only one thing you could provide me, Shadow Sister," he said, hungering while watching his prey's liquid life pulse through her veins.

De'Nidra beamed a warm, unoffended smile, her dark eyes feigning compassion. She spread her hands expressively. "Look at you, your hand poised upon the hilt of that blade. Why not the axe, Ivan? Do you even know? Of course, you do not. That knowledge was taken from you to hide you from us, but from the looks of you, none of the skill hidden in that transplanted soul of yours has lost its potency. Yes, you can hide from our servants, Ivan, and I will keep your secret for now, choosing to let your story play out. However, *Ivan*," she smiled as she spoke the name mockingly, "only as long as it does not interfere with my own plans."

Ivan made a move to respond, but De'Nidra cut him off with an upraised hand. "I will not waste my breath to offer you service any further. It is clear from our little chat that none of you are ready... *Yet*... Besides, you have other interested parties that you have chosen to deal with yourselves. Perhaps you can parlay with them as you have with me. Remember, you decided your own fate."

She pointed into the darkness in the direction of the doorway that they had left behind in the last ten minutes of their travel. All but Ivan turned toward the commotion. His mind reeled, stunned by her words and the feel of his shaking hand resting on the pommel of the sword he hated.

In the darkness and chill of the Lost Road, they heard a final crash as the battered bronze doors gave way to a monstrous blow. The echoing howls of Zoruks spilled into the vastness of the Lost Road, and the light produced by torches filled the darkness behind them. The dire wolf watched with a start as the silk-clad woman faded from his view like dust being blown away by a storm.

Torchlight moved toward them in a fitful pool as shifting shadows stretched beyond the opening of the hall and deep into the keep. Zoruks that looked like angry ants spilling from a hole breached the doorway. They tried to count them.

Antoff Grant yelled, "MOUNT UP!" above the din of the horde.

Tara stood in the face of these odds with her chin raised, eyes alight with a glow that looked like she was inwardly battling an unseen force.

Ivan watched, face contorted with confusion as he was trying to master himself, not yet having the strength to pull his hand from the sword that felt like it could burn a hole in his iron grip. He shook himself sober as he watched this madness. One small Elp'har girl holding off a fist of Zoruks.

The air around Tara stirred, and reality shook with a wash of energy. Then a molten globe appeared, more than a span across, floating high above the Zoruks. A bluish-purple tendril of lightning crawled across its surface. The first Zoruks to enter the roadway passed the door.

Their eyes widened with fear as they recognized what was about to happen. They tried desperately to skid to a stop, but the mass that pressed in behind them forced them into the open road. The ball that hung above them arced a flash. A blinding streak of lightning slammed into the mass of Zoruks spilling from the hall. Where the bolt struck, death came with a crash. The Zoruks turned to ash or thrown like rag dolls in a circular spray whose epicenter measured the width of the road. Tara's troops struggled with horses that were desperately trying to pull free to run, but held fast by veteran riders as they worked to gain their footing.

Again and again, to the sounds of howls echoing in the deep, the globe belched lightning that left arcs of blue energy crawling across the stone. Each time the lightning struck the Zoruks, only cinders remained where they once stood, or hurled into the air by the explosions, only to be slammed against the rock face lining the road or tossed, disappearing from view as they arced over the open l edge.

Tara turned to run for her horse, but Edward was already there, holding it confidently. He grabbed her around the waist and lifted her into the saddle in front of Va'Yone before vaulting onto his own charger. "Go, Tara!" he yelled, and they thundered away, steel-shod hooves ringing on stone, echoing through the vast blackness beneath the mountain. Ivan broke free of his nightmare state and leaped onto the back of his Stinger just as the horses lurched ahead, pounding down the Lost Road. Their path lit only by the lamps, held in upraised hands.

Chapter 12 Price to Pay

"Blood and treasure are the prices of peace. A people willing to pay both, have the grit to keep it."

Mounted on his Camolisk Lizard, Captain Um'elik watched with anticipation as the bronze door resisted the relentless pounding of the Zoruks' battering ram. The torchlights flickered over the rough walls of chiseled stone and the aged bronze door, the green patina bearing marks of heat, warped and bent horizontally across the middle.

The lizard's scaly color shifting skin fluctuated between craven red and the shade of the keep's stone walls, sniffing the unseen and tasting the air with its flicking tongue. Despite having ridden this mount through countless perils, Um'elik found its current unease both tangible and unsettling. "Ridiculous beast," Um'elik muttered, his frustration etched onto his face, "It's bad enough that I have to drive these Zoruks every moment. Now I'm riding a creature that can't make up its mind whether to blend in or stick out. If it loses my prize, it's going into the stew pot." *This journey has already stretched beyond tolerance.*

"Swift progress is essential. If we delay, I risk losing my prize." The Zoruks around him, perplexed by their commander's words, exchanged nervous nods. They debated whether a response was expected from them or whether their captain was still rational. Their captain was losing what little he had left of restraint. If the berserker blood lust took over, some of them would die to make a minor point about obedience. A trigger of any kind was all the excuse he would need. Once that rage released, it would be about the killing, using some of them to workout pent aggression.

A Zoruk wielding a cleaver whispered to another who was carrying a spear, and both edged away from the escalating and uncomfortable situation. "He's gonna blow; I can feel it in my bones!" Barrot, laying his cleaver across his forearm. He shot Um'elik a glance to be sure he could not see. "Three years under him and only a handful of us left," Barrot said, his eye sagging from an old war wound.

Letwin nodded. "Aye, we gotta look out for ourselves. There's no shortage of idiots to die; won't be us, though."

Barrot watched Letwin's lips quiver, a sign he was struggling with what to say. "Well, out with it, Letwin!"

Letwin met his gaze, allowing himself to be drawn toward the wall. Propping his spear on his shoulder, he nodded. "We will watch after ourselves. There are fools enough to die here. It need not be us."

His sergeant's voice broke the tension. "I've seen a lizard act like this before, near an adult bull's den. But here, it makes no sense..." He shook his head.

With a thunderous crash, the mighty bronze door gave way. The lead Zoruks surged forth, charging into the opening with zeal. Lightning belched forth in streams, casting blinding flashes that illuminated the tunnel and road ahead. Tendrils of blue-green energy crawled across the bronze of the fallen door.

"Fools!" Captain Um'elik's roar sliced through the chaos—his voice a sharp blade against the crashes and flashes. "Charge!" he bellowed, his urgency mixing with the thunderous onslaught. Every rush met with blinding flashes of Power and death. As the relentless cycle continued, they watched his elusive quarry vanish down the Lost Road, the flickering light and clattering hooves fading beneath the cacophony of wounded and dying.

Captain Um'elik's voice cut through the chaos. "Move forward, you cowering maggots!" His command echoed as the sergeants cracked their whips, spurring the Zoruks to press ahead.

The cracking whips stung flesh, driving the Zoruks' fear of pain propelled them beyond the gateway. The carnage that the Torrent had wreaked upon them left marks and bodies strewn about the road. She had accomplished something else as well. She had left a mark impressed on the mind of every Zoruk present for the slaughter. He would indeed have to elevate the fear these Zoruks had for him far above what they had just encountered. Otherwise, he would pay hell for trying to force the next engagement.

As the first ten Zoruks emerged unscathed, the others mustered their courage. The sight of their comrades surviving bolstered their resolve. Advancing with determined steps, torchlight illuminated their path. Renewed momentum pushed them forward. Yet there was a reserve there, as if they would turn and run at any sign that the Torrent renewed the attack.

Captain Um'elik's unyielding will would push them to their limits. If he let up, he would lose his prize, and that would just not do. Already, he was down to sixty Zoruks. He had come with a full fist, and ten left behind. If he did not recover this prize, he would pay at the hands of his demon Lord Commander Narean. He shuddered at the thought of having stood and watched the punishments being doled out in the past. In fact, many of his promotions are a result of these punishments. He would not become a leg up for one of these usurpers waiting in the wings for his demise.

The Lost Road is dark, and every sound echoed through a dank air, wet with cold. On the road, one could hardly see beyond the pools of lamplight that were ringing their small troop. The right side of the road had no railing and fell away into the bottomless void. Tara pictured a horse getting spooked and running blindly off the edge. *Stop that! We are all going to make it out of here together.*

She tried hard to focus on the task at hand: getting away from the Zoruks. They could hear them back there, the crack of a whip and an angry bellow accompanying it. However, the Zoruks also seemed more subdued than before, not as willing to pursue at their full speed. At the same time making a good show of it, as if they were trying their hardest. Nevertheless, they were gaining on them

little by little, and Antoff believed it would be less than an hour before they caught up
.

They were all tired. Tara needed rest, as did Edward, riding next to her, putting
on a brave show. Tara, however, knew better. If they engaged the Zoruks now, he
would die bravely. She wasn't sure how much more she could wield her Power.
*None of us will die in a battle we can't win. I will do whatever I must do to keep
them safe. If there are gods of Light, I pray they watch over us.*

Ivan stared off into the distance, his mind grappling with memories. Tara let
him wrestle with his inner thoughts, recognizing the need for him to find his own
peace. The rhythmic clomping of steel-shod horseshoes on the stone road made
it impossible to hide their escape.

Ivan could almost put a finger on a vague memory. He could almost touch it
before it slipped from his mind's eye. His hand kept creeping to the hilt of that
sword without him thinking about it, as if his hand had always belonged there.
Or worse yet, as if he had always carried one, which he never had. *Had he? He
could not remember.* He would snatch his hand away from the hilt, and no sooner
had his mind gone back to trying to figure out the words that were haunting him,
then finding his hand resting on it again. Giving up, he stopped trying to pull his
hand away from the sword. Perhaps it could help him remember what had been
taken from his mind by Co Ádean. *What did De'Nidra say?* He thought. *Look
at you, your hand poised upon the hilt of that blade. Why not the Axe Ivan? Do you
even know? Of course, you do not. That knowledge was taken from you to hide you
from us, but from the looks of you, none of the skill hidden in that transplanted soul
of yours has lost its potency. Yes, you can hide from our servants IVAN, and I will
keep your secret for now, choosing to let your story play out.*

Ivan knew one thing from the encounter with De'Nidra: she was afraid of who
he had been with a blade. That in his book meant a good thing. That meant that
if he could recapture what he had lost, combined with what he was now, it could
very well be a potent combination indeed. *Every fragment of that puzzle I recover
is going to bring me closer to being whole. It's like having a ghost living in the same
body. Each part I get back brings me closer to being who I truly am.*

Ivan rode his Stinger just behind Tara. Occasionally, he would peer back toward
the Zoruks at the rear. Oh, he could see them. He could see the heat emanating

from their mortal bodies, and it awakened his hunger again. He hadn't consumed anything living for some time now, and the blood coursing through the living bodies all around him was singing a seductive song. Not so far gone that he was going to lose control, but he would need to slip away before long, or an issue would come up in the party that he was not ready to explain away. At best, he would kill a horse or two. At worst, an Elp'har, or a friend. He would not let that happen. He was making everyone uncomfortable in an already dangerous situation. *I will slip away before it comes to something worse.*

Across a stone bridge, the Lost Road passed in front of a large stone door opening cut from the rock face. Parapets and battlements threatened high above. The cold currents of air that drifted out of the void raised fear bumps on the flesh.

Cur'Ra called out above the sound of the horses, "It is an old Dwemerin city. They inhabited it when the keep and road were being constructed. They were the builders and allies of the Light. Many mighty weapons of the Light were forged at the heart of this stronghold centuries ago."

Antoff replied, "Maybe we can use it to ambush the Zoruks. I can assure you, we will not outrun them before we find the end of the road, and a better place is not likely to present itself before they are on us."

Everyone agreed. The wooden gate had rotted away, leaving only a few thin boards hanging on rusty hinges.

Narean circled above Forge'Wrath Keep. It looked the same as he remembered it, ages ago. Ten Zoruks stood on its battlements, their captain nowhere to be seen. Narean glided and then landed softly atop the battlements, his great leathery wings folded behind him like a long-hanging cloak.

The Zoruk scouts all bowed deeply on bended knees.

"Where is your captain?" Narean's voice boomed, laced with a note of threatening anger.

A corporal hesitantly replied, "Lord, he instructed us to wait here for you. He pursued the Torrent inside. Captain Um'elik feared the Torrent would get away, and he would lose the master's prize if he did not give chase."

Narean's voice dripped with false concern. "Did he now? Pray tell, did he have a plan beyond *'stay here and wait?'* What was he to do if they escaped? Hmm? I can guarantee one thing: I'm not coming back without her. Of that, you can be sure. Moreover, corporal, this was his attempt to disobey me without looking like he was disobeying me. In any case, and without regard to his success, there will be punishment. And if he loses her after disobeying my orders... *Death!* We, on the other hand, will not be enduring the ghost-ridden madness that dwells within that old ruin. The very reason I told him to wait here, I might add. We are going to use a little-known pass that will take us to the other side. I can only hope the fool slows them down before madness or death takes him. That is the least of the services he can offer at this point. As for you and your scouts, corporal, you will join the rest of the army ten leagues west of our position." He finished with a gesture regarding the direction they were going.

"Yes, my Lord," the corporal answered as he started at a run and bellowed for the others to follow.

Narean liked blind obedience better than the initiative shown by Captain Um'elik. *You will pay dearly if you lose my Torrent, Um'elik!* Narean thought menacingly and stared after the departing Zoruks and whispered. "Five fists of Zoruk, and one fist of human heavy horse, and it may not be sufficient. The old Lord's right, as always." There was more at play here than Narean understood. Something was driving this, something beyond mere mortals. Narean spread his leathery wings and leaped into the sky.

The troop advanced, soaked in the glow that emanated from the Dwemerin estate. Above the door, the word "entry" was etched in the Dwemerin script, as if drawn by a magical quill. "Deep Rock" - or "Mora'Da'Dune" in the native Dwemerin dialect - held a revered place among the stonemasons of Dwemerin. The Hove of the Hammer was one of many translations meant to honor their gods of stone. They had the art of shaping stone coursing through their veins, much like the Elp'hars' innate ability to decipher the signs of nature. They perceived the Deep Rock as a living entity, drawn from El'idar like water from a river. Mora'Da'Dune, an echo of the ancient Dwemerin magic, could draw fire, metal, and stone from El'idar.

Torches illuminated the long-abandoned home of the Mora Clan. The seamless stone walls were a flawless testament to the art, save for the decaying gate. This gate was little more than a service entrance leading into the functional sections of the dwelling, purposely excluding the private living quarters. These areas cordoned off by magic, reserved solely for trade with other races. Here, the Dwemerin magi built their metalworks, foundries, and workbenches to forge their mighty creations.

The troop's leader, Antoff Grant, turned his gaze from the entrance to survey his followers. His people huddled in the flickering light as the oppressive darkness threatened to consume them. The deep drafts stirred their lamps and torches, causing the flames to dance erratically. Distant sounds of approaching Zoruks filled the air, and the nervous stamping of a horse's hoof was the only sound breaking the silent anticipation. *There is always hope, if you know where to look for it,* he thought.

"Come," Antoff instructed, his voice steady despite the uncertainty flickering in his eyes. He needed to be strong for his people, to guide them through unknown danger. He gestured with his sword, leading his horse inside the massive entrance. The inner wall rose at least ten feet overhead, reaching an intricately carved stone ceiling. The ceiling seemed to breathe with life, bearing almost living vines of stone that shimmered as the light brushed across their leafy edges. This was a peace offering for the Elp'harean people, designed to set them at ease. The artists had carved elements of each race's homeland into the panels of ceiling and wall. This created a comforting refuge under the weight of the mountain's Deep Rock. Yet the echoes of footfalls and the clatter of steel-shod hooves resonated through the lonely halls. The place felt cold and desolate, like an abandoned home longing for its inhabitants. An indescribable consciousness, an awareness of presence that had lingered alone for ages.

"The structure is alive with magic, and it is glad that we are here," Tara whispered, breathless, as they entered a cavernous room. The room buttressed by towering columns that extended upwards for twenty feet, supporting a ceiling adorned with expensive metals and glinting semi-precious gems. A peculiar, pungent odor permeated the air - reminiscent of a snakeskin freshly shed. As they ventured further into the hold, the stench grew stronger.

With every step they took, the chill replaced with rising heat. At first, it was comfortable, but as they ventured deeper into the hold, they began to sweat. The air stirred as if the structure was breathing, adding to the sensation of being in a living entity.

"We must be getting close to the furnaces," Antoff said. Just then, they reached an entrance guarded by two colossal Dwemerin statues, each bearing blacksmith's hammers inscribed with runes. The warhorses, however, refused to proceed any further, displaying an uncharacteristic fear.

"Secure them to the columns in the far corner," Antoff ordered amid the chaos. The temperature grew fiercer as they advanced into a vast circular room. At its center was a volcanic vent shaped like a giant furnace with arched openings and massive iron doors, seven in total.

"Where are Ivan and the Dire?" Edward asked, noticing their absence.

One of the Desert Elp'hars replied, "They ghosted away. Only his horse followed. We never saw them go."

Edward, shocked, thought. *They ghosted away, and the Elp'hars missed it? That's impossible. They see and hear everything.*

In the darkness, Ivan concealed his Stinger, distancing himself from the others. Silently, the troop gathered before the ancient Dwemerin ruins. Observing from the shadows, his insatiable thirst for blood overshadowed his friendship with them, fading into oblivion. Hunger consumed him, threatening to relinquish control to the overpowering instinct of self-preservation. Dismounting his warhorse, he caressed it gently while his fangs gradually extended, piercing the curved edges of his pallid lower lip. The horse flicked its tail as his fangs penetrated its flesh. Ivan projected a calming influence, suppressing the horse's instincts. To the Stinger's perception, it was a mere insect bite. Ivan's eyes now emanated a muted glow of pale red as life coursed into his being. He maintained control, having no intention of killing the animal—only taking what he required. Nothing more.

Beside him, the dire wolf stealthily approached, yet then remained motionless, refraining from interference. Wolves comprehended the rituals of sustenance. They harbored no judgment. The wolf seemed to grasp the importance of extracting only what was necessary from nature—a predator's prerogative. Like Ivan, they were about to relish the exhilaration of the hunt, together, reminiscent of days long past. Vam'Phires and other menacing creatures of the underworld permeated his thoughts, the very essence from which they had emerged. Other races of the world perpetually failed to acknowledge the connection—the imperative of maintaining order in the world. The elimination of the weak formed an intrinsic part of the circle of life, ensuring that those who endured would be robust and resilient. Nature could not afford to squander resources on the feeble or elderly. Such was the course of nature, the way it preserved itself. Ivan was an integral component of that circle. He comprehended why Vam'Phires regarded other races akin to how a wolf viewed sheep—*mortality plagued by an all-consuming dread of death.*

Ivan watched as the troop entered the ancient dwelling, the ruins whispering of a long-extinct Dwemerin society. Still linked to the horses, his mind suggested that his own horse follow the others inside. The proposition felt instinctive to the Stinger, and he embraced it without question. Ivan and the wolf stood in the frigid darkness, observing the horse slip inconspicuously into the group—the last creature to enter the fortress.

Leading his troop between the statues of the godly Dwemerin blacksmiths, Antoff felt the air grow hot and alive, like great lungs blasting. From the bowels of the volcanic thermal vents below, the area inhaled and exhaled great blasts of heat. Rivers of molten lava traveled beneath the furnace, supplying the heat that melted metals pulled from the rock, allowing them to be worked. Sweat trickled down his back and dripped from his armor.

The only life left to this once vibrant place of the Dwemerin artisans was a continuous audible breathing of the mountain deep and the hot air that blew in through the furnace vents, making the heat almost unbearable. They approached the center of the Dwemerin furnace hall and there lay what looked to be a giant pile of gold glittering in a reddish light. Except there was something else. The pile seemed to heave. And there was a smell that accompanied that area of the room and permeated the hall. Pungent and acidic. It smelled like a snake that had shed its skin during molting, but was more pungent. It was the smell that caused the Stinger's refusal to advance. At first, Edward began to walk forward toward the gold pile enthusiastically. *Finally, a reward for all their efforts,* Edward thought.

"Wait!" Tara's voice quaked, her eyes wide with a blend of awe and terror. "It's not safe. Can't you feel it? It's alive! Watch out Edward, it's awake." Her mind race for what she was going to do if it became violent. *We are going to get eaten for sure if that happens. We're stuffed in a pickling barrel with a Crag Lion. The only hope we have now is that she is not hungry.*

As Edward moved forward, he suddenly froze as the head of a huge golden dragon rose from its slumber. Behind the dragon, at the rear of the hall, a massive section of the wall was destroyed leaving only the red glow of the main volcanic vent that must lead to the surface of Forge'Wrath Mountain. *God's!* Edward thought, *Why is it always me?*

"Welcome, mortal children," a resonant voice reverberated in their minds, eclipsing all other senses. The golden dragon's eyes gleamed as it spoke, emanating a blend of wisdom and sorrow. "I am Al'amire, known as the golden shadow. Fear not, for I have awaited your arrival." Her voice flowed into their minds.

Antoff's voice shook with fear as a chilling realization dawned on him. "This cannot be! De'rious, the god of dismay and sorrow, your bondholder fell!" The disbelief in Antoff's voice was palpable, his faith in the world's order shaken. The words echoed in his mind, tearing at the fabric of what he thought he knew. *How in the name of all the gods is that possible?*

She turned her gleaming gold eyes on Antoff, appraising him. "De'rious did not fall; he sleeps. We dare not wake him," Al'amire replied. "I am afraid that it was a necessary ruse that required me to stay hidden for a very long time indeed. But that is not why you are here."

"We're pursued by Zoruks and seek refuge. Will you assist us?" Tara inquired, "please." She added, just for good measure, her voice tinged with desperation and fear.

Al'amire's gaze shifted to Tara. "Welcome, Torrent Arcane Mage. We can help each other. That is why fate has spun you out and you are here now. I will help you as a gift and you can give your gift in return."

Tara, taken aback. "What could I offer you do not already possess in abundance?"

The great gold pulsed with Power as she replied. Tara could hear Master Duncan's voice pulled to the surface vividly in her mind. "*You have the spark, girl.*"

Al'amire continued. "I was given the spark by my bondholder long ages ago. But we cannot give life. We can only receive it from a mage, and without it, we are little more than intelligent beasts. You have that spark, Tara."

Tara stammered. "But if you have a bondholder already, what can I do?"

Al'amire unfolded her arms and revealed two eggs covered in golden skin. "Come and see, child."

Tara walked slowly toward the great golden dragon and her brood. "Be warned, there is a price, Torrent. A price that we all must pay. You will be a bondholder of not one but two dragons and while they are young, you all will be most vulnerable. Linked to them, mind and body. You will hear their thoughts, and they will hear yours. Feel each other's pain and share each other's Power. You cannot hide from them. They will always know where you are, and you will find them as well in the same manner. And if they die and do not release your spark before their death, you will die, Torrent. That is the price. Now, will you bestow the gift?"

As the Dragon spoke in Tara's mind, all the vibrant imagery played out, making it difficult to distinguish the visions from reality. "If I do not give my spark, will they be like beasts?"

The Dragon's tone saddened. "Yes, or worst yet, the dark order will find them and defile them in ways I cannot bring myself to speak of."

Tara looked at the gold dragon with compassion. In the background, she could hear the pleading of Antoff and Edward to stop, but she did not heed, nor would she. They cannot understand. "I will give my spark, but I do not know the way." *They are babies and helpless against the evils of this world. I will not let them be beasts for the Dark Order. They are coming with me.*

Al'amire continued, "I will show you. Place a hand on each egg, Torrent. Now establish your connection to the higher reality."

Tara assumed the image in her mind and the war between the Darkness and the Light crashed down around her. She stood in the mists of the torrent of Power, struggling to withstand it and gain a footing. Then she gained her foothold and reality shook as she concentrated on establishing the image of the dragon's eggs in her mind and felt for the unhatched dragons within, with flows of raw Power. As she felt there was an awareness of two highly intelligent and inquisitive minds that reached for hers. When contact was made, the thoughts cascaded in like an avalanche. Tara severed her connection with the higher reality out of self-preservation as she could no longer safely control the flows with all the confusion going on in her mind.

She would have been destroyed, and the two babies would have died with her. Tara fell to her knees and commanded. "Be Silent and Come Forth!" The hall hushed at the sound of the command in her voice, and the troops moved forward as if she was commanding them. But it was the eggs almost six feet in height that shifted and cracked at the top as the hatchlings obeyed their bondholder's first command and pushed hard with their egg tooth to break free.

First, their egg tooth at the top of their snouts emerged, followed by their snouts and then their heads, which pushed through and settled, taking in the breaths of air. They were translucent at first as they rested. Their gleaming gold eyes never left Tara. To them, there was no one else in the world except her. All others diminished in comparison, even their mother only a distant voice. As they rested, their lungs heaved with an effort to gulp the air for the first time. They did not break eye contact with Tara. They were sizing her up, and as they did, their skin changed. One's scales took on the white color with gold trim and the other black scales with a gold trim, remembering their mother as they added her color to their own.

Al'amire uttered the prophetic words imprinted in her genetic memory by the first dragon. "*Two shall Be Silent and Come Forth! One of Darkness and One of*

Light and they shall serve her, even until death and the world will quake with fear as it is torn asunder once more. Oh, that hope could prevail and fate has its way. Oh, that balance be restored with the coming of the Night and the Day."

As she finished her utterance, the younglings made a massive effort and broke free, falling to the floor covered in the remnants of the yoke. Tara crawled to them and cradled their heads in her lap as best she could as the young dragons' lungs labored, and then they rested, comforted by Tara's touch, and closed their eyes.

Al'amire looked hard toward the door that led to the first chamber as if she could see through the walls. "Those Zoruks are coming now. I smell the hate they have for you, Torrent, but hidden beneath that hate is the fear you placed there in their minds. You have given your gift, Torrent, and I will give mine." Her lips peeled away from her teeth and droplets of acidy drool smoked as it fell on the dusty stone floor. "Now these Zoruks will know why they fear dragons when I am done. They will fear even to whisper your name, Torrent, that I might hear it and come. They must know that I am awake and that your hatchlings are my brood." Her eyes flashed a golden light that duly illuminated the room before her, and the great dragon stood and walked toward the Dwemerin statues on each side of the door, her back spines brushing the ceiling.

Chapter 13 Be Silent and Come Forth!

"Where have you gone, you Warrior Mages, famed dragon riders of old? Have your losses confounded your heart? Are they greater than the world? We played our strings with our whole hearts, and you did not listen. We wept for your loss; but your hearts were not moved by ours. If you cannot be moved by love for the ones you have adored or by the pain of their loss, how then will you be moved by the suffering of the world? You are lost and thus, we are lost with you."

Ahead Ivan and the dire wolf watched silently from the shadow of the Lost Road as the first of the scout Zoruks entered the Dwemerin estate, following the scent of their prey. The shadow seemed to reach out to Ivan, call to him, but he did not know how to answer. The shadow's beckoning stirred within him, tugging at his doubts and insecurities. But could he truly entrust his faith in it? No, he could not force himself to trust the shadow. The dire wolf, sitting on his haunches, watched as the light from the Zoruk's burning sticks created moving pools on the Lost Road. He stayed perfectly still next to his war brother, waiting for the sign to attack.

The main body of Zoruks advanced toward the entrance of the abandoned stronghold. The first scout paused, sniffed the air, then slipped inside. Then in a single file line the lead Zoruk, a Sargent led the way followed by troops, then a captain riding a lizard, and then rear guard. Finally, the last Zoruk soul slunk into the passage.

Ivan moved like a bolt, shadowy wisps trailing behind him like smoky spiderwebs. The dire followed, struggling to keep visual contact with his brother. Ivan did not make a sound. The speed and violence of his attack on the first Zoruk were so predatory it left the dire wolf awed. Ivan struck the first Zoruk just as he passed an open door off the entry hall. The weight and momentum carried both into the room, out of sight of the Zoruk troop. Ivan slammed the Zoruk warrior into the wall, driving the air from its lungs with a thud.

It was dark inside of the open room except for the shadow of a huge dire wolf crossing the doorway, moving to take the next prey. Ivan's struggle with the breathless Zoruk was short. While a Zoruk warrior is large and powerful, this one had been stunned and stunned hard. Ivan held its hands at bay, head-butted the thing, and then sunk fangs deep into the creature's jugular. Zoruk blood, while not preferred, would serve.

The dire had seen his war brother slam into the first Zoruk, removing it from sight in a burst of supernatural speed and power. The dire could see him feeding as he passed the opening. He did not interrupt him as it would be impolite. There were rules about eating that must be kept. If he wanted to enjoy that one together, he would have allowed him to share in the kill, but there would be no time to wait.

Just then, the next Zoruk in the rear turned to look and found that he was now the last man in a shrinking rear guard. To the Zoruks' surprise, he was not alone as a giant black wolf some six feet at the shoulders was watching him a span away, yellow gold eyes aglow and lips drawn back, exposing dagger-like teeth. A Zoruk's roar turned into a cry as he swung his cleaver defensively at the wolf.

The dire leaped forward at him, snapping and avoiding the shiny stick, allowing it to pass over his head and then sinking his teeth into its arm in a vicious vice-like clamp as it was on the downward stroke. The Zoruks in the rear turned at the cry and were greeted by the sight of a dire wolf dragging their fellow Zoruk back down the hall and out toward the entry, his victim crying out for help while kicking and flailing about.

Captain Um'elik rode upon his color-shifting lizard, surrounded by Zoruk warriors, front and rear. He was frustrated. These Zoruks gave a strong show of doing his will and yet slowed at every opportunity. It was a battle of wills. He had ordered them not to bunch up in the hall, but here they were pressing in upon him, front and rear. What's more, this riding lizard was dragging his feet and kept trying to turn around in a hall too small by half with Um'elik's knees dragging on each side of the damn wall. Just then, a cry reverberated down the hall from behind. The rear guard turned and then backed up, pushing against his Camolisk Lizard whose color-shifting skin had taken on the craven color of red. The color of a defeated foe.

Um'elik bellowed, "What's happening here?"

The Zoruk responded, "Attack, attack!"

Um'elik bellowed back. "Then attack back, you fool!"

The Zoruk warriors ebbed back towards the fight. Um'elik continued giving orders. "Sargent, lead the front contingent into the open room and space out to defend." The Zoruks in the front, based on how they had been acting, were more than happy to move away from the battle to the rear and give space to fight, or in Um'elik's opinion, to run if they got half a chance. As soon as the front troops broke into a run following his orders, his mount fast on their heels to avoid the drama playing out at the rear. Clearly, the beast was conflicted, seeking a means of escape. One thing was for sure, there was dying going on back there, and being crammed in a hallway like a cork in a bottle was not high on his list of places to be.

An authority filled bellow rang down the hall and from the sound of it, the Zoruks that had been staggering backward like drunken sailors now moved back toward the entry. Ivan saw the dire wolf moving down the hall dragging a hapless flailing Zoruk. The dire wolf ignored the Zoruk pounding on his flanks. Ivan's mind was ablaze with vitality from the Zoruks' fear-filled life's blood. He moved like a ghostly blur as he slipped out into the hall and stopped between the retreating wolf and the onrush of the Zoruk rear guard. The Zoruk, seeing the form of a legendary Half-Dead appearance in the hall, went nearly out of their minds with fear and rage. All movement in the hall stopped for a breath as they sized up the foe.

Ivan was deadly calm in the stillness before the rush. His mind was fog-like. He was only watching what was going on, but not in control. The first Zoruk burst forward, wielding a half-spear and a shield. It stabbed at him and, to Ivan's horror, he just stood there as the point of a jagged half-spear slid slowly through time toward his throat. Then, just before the spear point could strike, Ivan moved without warning. A marshal form he was unfamiliar with. His hand swept out in a fanning motion, thumb to fingertips intercepted the heft of the spear only milliseconds before the blade went home. At the same time, he found his other hand resting on the handle of the ornate two-handed long sword at his side. The blade slid smoothly from its sheath in a rasp. The pummel first struck the Zoruk spearman under the chin, causing his eyes to roll up in his eye sockets. Then, as the limp Zoruk was falling to the ground, Ivan's left hand found purchase on the handle of the blade. Suddenly it spun in an arc, slicing the falling Zoruks head from its neck. Now as Ivan held the sword before him, tip down with knee bent, the blade's blood gem pulsed red with light and new life.

Ivan's eyes did not move from the onrush of Zoruk. The only thing that had confirmed the kill was the satisfying thud of the corpse as it hit the stone just behind his feet and he was now poised in a swordsman stance. The rush came and the swordsman's blade met each weapon with a smooth, efficient economy. No movement wasted; Ivan gave ground ever so slowly, forcing the enemy to work each inch like a farmer worked his field. Just as he took a step outside of the stronghold, the last of the Zoruk rear guard fell.

The dire stuck his head in the opening only to survey the hall. Seven dead Zoruks lay in sequence as if on the stone floor every fifth step one had fallen. The war brothers moved back down the road into the shadow.

Va'Yone watched as Al'amire moved cat-like, amazed to see an Old One of this size possess such grace and power. One moment's failure to note their position on the floor below her as she passed could have ended them all. Al'amire looked down at them as she passed over and lifted her great spiked and bladed tail to ensure she did not injure anyone.

When she arrived at the statues, she called for Antoff. "Priest Knight, come and see." He was astonished when he saw the image burst into his mind, *his form moving toward the dragon's position near the door.* Her call was compelling. "Come, Priest Knight, there is little time!"

In his vision, a sunset and Zoruks streamed through the statues, roaring with hatred. When Antoff reached the dragon's head, she gazed through the doorway at the statues and said, "The statue on the right is DuRRam'Dal the Hero of the Light, and the other is EL'ALue, as you know her, Priest Knight."

Antoff stammered, "This cannot be! EL'ALue is a god of Light."

Al'amire calmed the thunder in her voice and spoke, like speaking to a confused child. Antoff could see himself as a child sitting in a chair while his mother schooled him in the proper behaviors after misbehaving out of ignorance. She went on, "EL'ALue is a goddess of Light, Priest Knight. She was always for the children of our planet."

Antoff cut in, "This cannot be. They teach us EL'ALue does not have a gender and..."

The voice of the gold stormed through his mind. "Now, Priest Knight, I will do for you what your Torrent Arcane Mage has done for my children, if not to a lesser effect. EL'ALue is very much a female of your species, and unlike my bondholder, she will awaken if a true Priest Knight of her order calls on her. You, Knight, now only have access to whatever her vessel, the dragon De'Adin the White, cannot hold. Like a rain barrel overflowing."

He could see all the imagery in his mind. Al'amire went on, "When the Order of the Light, out of male pride, no longer acknowledged her gender, when they refused to see her for who and what she was, she stopped supporting the Order of the Light directly and slept, only giving them the leavings of her Power. But you, Priest Knight, now know. These creatures who dwelt here are just like you. They refuse to acknowledge her for who she is and have only ever received her leftovers." The image of the water from a light rain flowing over the edge of a barrel, being divided between the numbers of her wayward followers.

"If you love her, Knight, you must acknowledge her. What I tell you is true. I swear it on the lives of my children, Priest Knight, and the life of my bondholder."

Antoff shuddered when he heard this. He could not speak. The oath on the lives of her children and bondholder was too powerful, and he could tell in his core she was not lying.

Then her voice trickled like a stream in his mind, and the images of Tara's command to her babies rang out inside. "Be silent and come forth, Priest Knight. EL'ALue, the goddess of Light, awaits!"

The glyph on the black table no longer pulsed, and the black volcanic sand no longer gave form to the Torrent's location. Lord Modred was in a panic when the ribbon of purple light split the air of his room and then formed a globe large enough for the two mortal-sized figures to step forth. Their shadows flickered on the walls as The Great Lord Amorath and EL'Keet stepped into his chamber. His master brought with him the cold fear of the undead and the smell of the open grave; only the sound of the staff tapping on the floor gave testament that he was carrying that legendary instrument of Power.

The Great Lord EL'Keet, on the other hand, was the image of a high-born lord with all his finery and noble bearing. Dark chestnut brown hair tied at the neck with a golden cord. A burgundy jacket, cuffs stitched in golden scrollwork to his elbow, covered a white puffy shirt laced at the front. Pants that matched the jacket that covered to the knee in tooled black riding boots, the tips done in silver.

At once Modred took a knee and bowed his head, awaiting what undoubtedly would be his death. His master's voice was an icy shiver that ran across his body and into his depths.

"I see Forge'Wrath has done its work, Lord Modred. Well, no surprise the keep is awash with wards against such things. Nonetheless, Modred, we have a bigger problem."

Modred responded, "Yes, Great Lord."

Amorath continued, "We have some mice in our grain bin, it seems. The Dragon Hounds are not responding to our calls. That means a Great One is awake and already passively swaying their loyalties. It appears we have also been slacking in our counterintelligence, as it is quite clear the Light has somehow penetrated not only our security but that of the Dark Order itself. The help the Torrent received likely came from a member of the Dark Order, and while we have not yet ascertained the identity of that member, you can be very sure we will, Lord Modred. Thus, as it is clear to me that you are as much a victim of this act of betrayal as the rest of us, I will not be replacing you today, as this failure is as much ours as yours."

Modred gave an involuntary breath detected by his lord.

"Did you think you could have this level of epic failure alone, Modred? Did you think the little things you try to hide from me are not visible? Let me assure you that you have many underlings waiting to take your place and would want nothing more than to see you fail. If for no other reason, then to take your place at my table. It is no different for each member of the Dark Order. Let me assure you we will find our mice in the bin, and you will do the same or suffer the consequences of your failure. Do you understand me, Modred?"

Lord Modred, the Great Black Demon of Legend, inclined his head, "It shall be as you command, Great Lord. All betrayers shall be flushed out and brought before you for punishment."

His master nodded his satisfaction. The gateway still shimmered within his chamber. The two Great Lords of the Dark Order turned and entered, and it winked out. While the stench of the open grave remained, the chill of the undead lord had vanished. Modred stood and threw a fresh log on the fire. He would find these little mice, and they would pay for disturbing his plans. Now the only matter that remained was what manner of trap he would use. He sat down in his high-backed chair, placing his elbow on the armrest. He rubbed his elongated chin with his hand in deep thought. And as for his underlings, those little rats would have their backs broken in a rat trap as well if he had half a chance to find out who they were.

The Stingers were brought into the furnace hall with considerable effort. Tara and the hatchlings slept together, curled on the floor in a heap. Anytime someone would try to check on her, the baby dragons would wake and hiss at the approach wearily, but not viciously. They were just saying, let her sleep. One at a time, each baby got up and finished the remnants of the yolk that had remained in the upright egg and then consumed the shell.

At a distance, there was bellowing and the clanging of swords. Then, after what seemed forever, it stilled to silence. Al'amire spoke. "Remain at the back of the hall, children, and keep those beasts of yours under control or they will probably suffer the same fate as your pursuers."

Captain Um'elik had dismounted his craven lizard and handed the reins to a Zoruk that looked like it needed something to do. The combat at the end of the dark hall had gone silent and not a Zoruk had returned. *Not one.* They waited for what seemed like forever and nothing came. Indeed, when he sent a scout to look for the missing Zoruk, on their return, they reported them all dead or missing in action.

Um'elik harrumphed, "Likely ran off is more like it. All right, let's get on the heels of my prize, Zoruk. I will not lose them now because of laziness or worse yet, craven fear. Sergeants whip these Zoruks like the beasts they are, if you must. I can smell our prize not far off and I have never had the nose of a scout."

A scout quipped to his sergeant, "But sir, it smells like a Dragon Hound mating pit in there!"

The sergeant slapped him with the loops of his whip, snarling, "Move, you craven dog, or I'll split you in two."

Golden Al'amire crouched like a cat, her tail whipping with anticipation as she peered into a door for her the size of a mouse-hole that led to the furnace hall. Her snout covered most of the opening, and her golden eyes could only catch the area directly ahead, but it was enough. First came the sound of whips, stinging flesh, and angry bellows, followed by the clanking of armor and weapons. The Zoruk stopped just inside the opening, like young snakes testing the air with their tongues.

The sergeant's bellow was interrupted by the retort of an old one. "Who dares disturb my slumber?" The sound of Al'amire's voice was all they could hear, but there was one among them so twisted with desire even that voice was not sufficient to stop him.

Captain Um'elik said, "Please pardon our interruption, Old One, but our prisoner has snuck into your sleeping place and... and..."

Al'amire cut off the noise. "Nothing sneaks into my den unless it is invited, Zoruk. Therefore, it is clear to me you are speaking of my guests, *fool*. The bearer of my brood's spark, the Torrent Arcane Mage. Is that who you are referring to, upstart?"

His reply was hesitant, but still came off as arrogant and demanding. "Yes, Old One, that is my prize, and I shall have her now, so long as you are finished with her?"

Al'amire cut him off again. "And what if your plans for her would cause her harm or death? Do you not understand you would cause pain to my brood or kill them?"

The Zoruk replied, "That is for my master and the Dark Order to decide, not me and not you, with all due respect, Old One."

Al'amire spoke with an air of final judgment as she chuckled. "With all due respect, really? You do not have the slightest idea what respect is or, for that matter, who you are speaking to. I am Al'amire, the Golden Shadow, a vessel to De'rious, the god of Dismay and Sorrow! Do you think your will or your master's Dark Order can rival that? It does not. Now, I shall teach you why you will leave my brood's bondholder alone. And now, for the first time, you shall know the meaning of fear and respect!"

With each word, the Zoruks retreated further down the hall, leaving Um'elik standing there alone. Al'amire breathed in deeply and exhaled, letting her gas bladders expel at the same time. Then, the striker in her throat gave a spark, and a rancid, acidic gas turned to liquid fire. And Um'elik, the self-proclaimed respecter of dragons, turned to ash and was no more.

Emerging from the Dwemerin stronghold came a lumbering riding lizard, as red as a blood moon, followed by the few Zoruks that had fled the chamber. They furiously slapped at the burning remnants of the cloth now hung about their blackened forms, smoking. Plunging out onto the Lost Road, they ran as hard as they could back in the direction they had come.

Al'amire chuckled to herself, but she let the others share in her mirth. "By the gods, that felt so good. Do you have any idea how long I have been in hiding? Well, too long!" Tara and the babies were sitting up like youngsters watching a puppet show. Tara clapped, and the brood hissed. Al'amire's voice saddened. "Children, it is time for me to go. And you must go likewise, or this brief respite will have been for nothing. Remember the price, Torrent. These are your dragons now." Her mind said this, walking toward the destroyed wall that opened up into the vent. At her last words, she spread her wings and leaped upward, flying out of the vent into the open sky.

Tara's voice rang out, a heartfelt cry that echoed through the hall. "Goodbye, Al'amire. I will keep them safe. I promise!"

Al'amire's voice returned to her. "I know you shall try, child." And then she was gone.

Chapter 14 Waking of the Light

"What shall I say to you? How shall I say it? Can I tell you how cold it was in my age of solace? You could break the heart of gold and I see not one cheek wet with tears. But I will have none of you. You shall hear even less of me until you turn and declare yourself for the Maid of Light! Until that day breaks do not seek me, for I shall not answer you! Your cry shall resound down the vacant halls of the Darkness that consumed you! But if you turn towards me and acknowledge me, I will acknowledge you. Yes, even I, the Maid of Light, will turn towards you and answer you. Let those in all the heavens and the lands of El'idar tremble, and let the Darkness flee your sight, for the glory of the Light shall burst forth brightly in a Priest Knight once more!"

Antoff, touched by Al'amire's words, slept after his watch and dreamed. A maid stood upon a hill facing the rising suns; her silvery-white armor trimmed in gold emblazoned in the light. Her blonde hair waved in the wind, the color of hay. She turned, and as her ice-blue eyes fell on him, her rose-colored lips spoke. "Can you see me, Antoff? Will you accept me as I am?"

"Yes, EL'ALue. If you will have me, I will take you just as you are." He reached towards her as she walked forward. Her hand stretched out towards his. Just before they touched, he was startled awake and covered in sweat. In his dreams, he had seen EL'ALue as the Maid of Light. A longing stirred within him, a yearning for the dream to be reality. *I want her to be real. I need her to be*, Antoff prayed, his heart aching.

Those awake talked quietly in soft murmurs amidst the occasional clank of gear. Ivan slipped in during the watch and sat with the dire wolf. Ivan's spirits looked uplifted, but that would have to wait until later. Even in the heat, Tara and her hatchlings played together. They chased her and snapped at her as she ran. It was good to see her laugh after all the fear. The defeat of the Zoruks was a fleeting thing; much worse was coming. Antoff rested for a few more minutes, letting her enjoy a carefree time before the seriousness of their plight surfaced once more.

All made ready, the troop moved out of the stronghold. The bodies of dead Zoruks lay piled outside the door. Tara looked at them as she passed by. She was angry, and the air stirred. With a whisper in the Old Tongue, the dead burst into a white-hot flame. She turned her back on them, mounted her Stinger just ahead of Va'Yone, and rode away. She fell in with her troop, young dragons in tow. Cur'Ra was on her right and Edward on her left; Ivan and the dire wolf brought up the rear as the young dragons played in and out of the party. And, of course, Antoff led the march.

Her troop smiled at the scene as they trotted down the Lost Road toward the Spring Tide Valley. In less than a day, they reached the exit from Forge'Wrath mountain, still sealed and barred from the inside. It took Edward, Ivan, and Antoff to lift the bar that had lain in its cradle for many generations. With the bar thrown aside, they pulled the massive bronze doors inward and were greeted by the early spring air and the bright light of the binary suns. They journeyed down the Lost Road toward RavenHof, only two or more days away—a short time compared to the darkness of the mountain. Dragons romped in the fields of grass until they saw their first rabbit. That was just the start. They stalked it like cats until they killed it. They ate one and then another like it. Then they spotted a wild goat and killed and ate that. Their hunger was insatiable. Even the dire wolf had no respite from the young dragons. When he went out to hunt, they went with him, and when the kill was made—a small deer—they ate half of it. Just as astonishing was their growth. They played within sight while the troop rode in a line two abreast.

Edward spent most of the day riding behind Tara and Cur'Ra, grappling with a growing need to be near her and puzzling over what to say to engage her. He just could not think of what to say. This kind of problem normally did not happen to him with other girls. Was it because of her incredible Power, or maybe because he owed her a debt of gratitude? It was both of those things and more. The difference between Tara and the other girls was that with them, he had not really cared about anything, but now, with her, he did. With that, he touched his Stinger with his knees, and the Stinger sprang into a canter, bringing him up beside her.

Cur'Ra shifted her gaze from Edward to Tara; her expression revealing more than her words. Her knowing, almost motherly smile suggested she had an inkling of what he was up to, but wanted to play along. "Yes, Edward?" Cur'Ra asked with an indulgent grin. "Do you require something of us?"

Edward's mind raced, struggling to find the words. Why had he approached them without thinking? *I am an idiot*, he thought. *That's what he should say*. But, he blurted out, "I was getting a little bored riding by myself." His words spilled out faster than he'd wanted, and he felt his face flush.

Cur'Ra raised a questioning eyebrow. "Well, if you want to chat, you'll have to speak with Tara. I must check on the animals. If you'll excuse me." With that, she spurred her horse into a trot, heading toward the front.

Tara sized him up, her gaze expectant. "What did you want to talk about, Edward?" Her lips twitched into a slight smile.

"I just… I wanted to get to know you better, Tara." Edward cringed inwardly at his clumsy phrasing. *She's going to dismiss me now*, he thought, feeling defeated.

Tara's steel-grey eyes searched his, as if trying to decipher his sincerity. "Edward, you don't need an excuse to talk to me. Just talk to me."

Edward hesitated before confessing, "It's been gnawing at me all day. We are almost back to RavenHof and the job I was hired for will be finished. I want to stay with you,—with everyone. Gods, Tara, I can hardly find my words around you." He laughed, aware of his fumbling but no longer caring.

She smirked. "Lost for words, Edward? How unlike you. Did you hit your head when you fell?"

Struggling to put his shame into words, he wanted to let her into his life. He just couldn't do it. "Perhaps I did," Edward conceded, "but I felt foolish years before that happened. I have failed people before. I don't want to fail you too, Tara."

Tara placed a hand on her hip and chided him gently, "Stop putting yourself down, Edward. You're not a fool. You belong with us. Now, tell me you believe that."

His defenses crumbling, he took a deep breath. "I do want to stay."

She raised an eyebrow, pressing further. "Are you sure, Edward? Many things have caught your eye before."

Edward looked her squarely in the eyes. "I'm certain. I acted carelessly in the past because I was indifferent to life. I was just existing. But now, I care, Tara. Truly. I had something happen, and it destroyed a piece of me. And while I don't feel like I will ever get it back. I've found something else, something I didn't know I needed." He flicked his eyes away from hers. "I was not always like that, you know. There was a time when I had a near-normal life. Before everything went away." Edward fumbled, struggling to communicate something he could not put into words.

Tara squinted at him through a bang of white that had slid in front of her face. She brushed it back. "Before everything went away?" Tara gently pressed him.

"My family cast me out. They blamed me for a horrific crime, something so terrible I don't even want to remember it. I swear, I didn't do it."

Tara looked mystified. "Everyone has dark secrets, Edward."

That was the question he was dreading. He was not going to lie to her. She had saved him, and she deserved more than that. "I was blamed for murdering a woman from my father's court. I did not do it, Tara." Edward pulled his eyes away. *Now she will get rid of me for sure.*

Tara watched him for a long moment before answering. Her voice was low and tinged with compassion. "Everyone I know, Edward, has done terrible things. Things without thinking, most people never learn the secrets held inside another person. You have shared it with me in honesty, and that is better than keeping secrets." Tara waited for his eyes to return to hers. "I know better who you are now, Edward. You have a chance with us so, I am glad you are staying. I will see you as the man you are from here on out, not the one you are pretending to be."

"I don't know what to say, Tara," Edward confessed, his face betraying a turmoil of emotions.

"Say you want to be that man of honor. I know you can be, and then be it." Tara stared off, like she was looking into the distance. "Edward, all my life, everyone close to me has died. My parents, well, who knows where they are and then Master Duncan... I'm afraid to lose you too, but I can't..." She looked away.

"You can't what, Tara?" Edward gently seized her chin between his forefinger and thumb, turning her head so she'd looked into his eyes.

"I can't lose any more people in my life, Edward. I'm tired of being afraid, so you promise me, promise me you won't leave."

Edward released her chin. "I don't make empty promises, Tara, and at the best of times, all I can do is try to keep them. I want to stay."

Tara nodded slowly, still somewhat guarded, but she allowed the scales to tilt a little more his way. They continued to chat with Antoff and Cur'Ra, observing from a distance.

Eventually, Cur'Ra approached again, her expression unchanged. "You seem to have found your voice, Edward. Did you two have a pleasant talk?"

Edward grinned confidently. "Yes, I believe we did. Thank You."

Cur'Ra smiled in return. "Good. Head up front. Antoff mentioned he has some tasks for you."

He acknowledged with a nod and spurred his Stinger into a run.

As he galloped away, Cur'Ra turned to Tara. "That young man is spirited. He'll be quite the handful," she remarked, pausing for a moment before adding with a playful tone, "He's rather handsome, isn't he? I can see a twinkle in your eye."

Tara's cheeks reddened immediately. "Mother, please! It's not like that. I respect him, that's all."

Cur'Ra chuckled, her eyes sparkling with amusement as she teased a daughter.

Tara rolled her eyes, trying to hide a smile.

"Don't be silly, Child. Of course, you have," Cur'Ra added.

***

In just a day, the dragons, once the size of large, scrawny dogs, had grown to half the size of a horse. They ran alongside the troop with wings spread wide, beating at the air, sometimes lifting off the ground ten feet or more before touching back down. But always before doing something, they looked to Tara, craning their necks with their eyes locked to hers. Tara was more like a proud young mother than a bondholder at that stage, and there was little question, but she spoiled them. However, when she drew them up short, they listened and listened well. She was their bondholder, and they knew it.

They stopped just before nightfall to eat and make camp. Usually whatever game the Elp'harean warriors could scare up, which was a testament to their hunting prowess given that the two dragons ate everything they could find, and they did not miss much.

After eating and caring for the animals, the children were sent to bed, and the remaining troop divided up the watch. When Tara watched, the dragons watched too. When Tara slept, the dragons slept as well. Usually, you'd find Tara and the dragons sleeping in a tangle.

Tara also complained to Cur'Ra about being tired all the time. Cur'Ra said she was always in contact with the dragons, and it was a mental drain she would have to get used to. There was no getting around the fact it would be lifelong. Tara revealed the higher reality did not disconnect anymore. The image was always in her mind, with the Power flowing constantly between her and the two dragons. They were bottomless pits, absorbing the raw flows, one the Darkness and the other the Light. It did not disturb the dragons in the least. They were vessels, and vast vessels at that. She wondered how long it would take to fill them.

However, on the second day, the pull on the flows ebbed to small trickles, and Tara felt somewhat rested as the higher reality slipped into the background of her mind. This day was different. On this day, they saw lush forests, and the occasional farmstead dotted the countryside. The dragons spotted a farm animal and thought of eating it. Tara put a stop to it and explained animals could be owned, and it was not allowed to just take them.

The dragons stopped dead and stared at each other in shock, asking, "They are not their own?"

"No," she said. What's more, they would have to buy the meat they ate in the towns and cities where the game was not present. She sent images of a transaction between herself and a local butcher from her past. The dragons seemed confused but followed her instructions, always asking before taking an animal.

The questioning seemed to go on all day. "This one?" A picture of a deer would form in her mind.

"Yes," Tara replied.

"This one." A picture of a farmer's animal pulling his plow in the fields.

"By all the gods, please no!" she sent back. When Tara sensed a snicker, she was sure they had the idea and were just testing her. However, the game did not cease, and the questions kept coming, just to be sure.

Finally, when the forests of fir trees gave way to oaks and Redleaf, and then the forest turned into stands of trees dividing the farmlands, RavenHof came into view in the distance beside the LeafWater to the west and near the Garden Wood to the south.

Antoff held up a fist, and the troop came to a halt. He had been dreading it, but he knew he and Tara would have to talk now. He rode his Stinger next to Tara, and they put their heads together in a spirited conversation.

"Tara, you cannot hope to bring those dragons within the walls of RavenHof; the townsfolk would go mad," he said.

She huffed and placed her hands on her hips. "Well, they can go mad for all I care, Antoff Grant, Priest Knight. They are coming if I am coming with you."

Cur'Ra suggested they make camp in the Garden Wood and keep the dragons there, but Tara would not hear of it. "We are one troop and one family, and I will not divide us up to comfort the townsfolk. There are plenty of old buildings we can make camp in that are not in use."

Antoff let out a long breath and said more to himself than anyone else, "You have been spending too much time learning from Cur'Ra. All right, Tara, at the very least let me go into RavenHof and get it set up before we go stomping in there, scaring the gods out of everyone?"

She smiled at him while inclining her head. "Of course, you do what you think is best, Priest Knight."

Chapter 15 Home For Dragons

"A building becomes a home not by its structure but by the souls that inhabit it. The priceless moments and treasured memories are stored in the people that lived there. When they are gone, the memories of their loss remind us of what a home truly should be."

The air was rich with the familiar fragrance of towering trees, verdant farmers' fields, and blossoming flowers of the meadows. With a puzzled grunt, Antoff rode towards the city. Ivan fell in next to him and signaled to the dire wolf that it couldn't follow, then pointed it back towards the camp.

Antoff leaned back in his saddle, "I don't recall having these difficulties before I left RavenHof. Now I have to beg just to enter and find a place for us to stay in an abandoned building."

Ivan shrugged, "Well, things change, Antoff. When you left, there were just three of you and four warhorses." He glanced back, smirking. "Now you've got twenty-one souls, a herd of horses, two dragons, and even a dire wolf. Quite the company you keep."

Antoff chuckled, his eyes twinkling with amusement as he waved a dismissive hand. "Okay, okay, Ivan. Enough about my pains and grumbling. What about you? What's been on your mind?"

He furrowed his brow and gave Antoff a puzzled sidelong look, lips parting as if he needed to say something and was debating whether he should do it. "What do you mean?"

Antoff noticed a subtle change in Ivan's demeanor since Forge'Wrath. The usual coldness in his eyes had given way to something not softer... but he was warmer now. He studied Ivan, leaning closer. "You've changed since Forge'Wrath. What's going on?"

Ivan's attitude darkened only a little. Antoff waited for him to speak. He knew not to push him.

He finally replied, "I can't explain it, but when I hit the Zoruks from behind, my plan was just to take one or two for survival's sake, if you get me? But... something happened."

"What?" Antoff asked.

"I wasn't in control. It felt like me, and yet... different. I fought with the sword, not the axe, Antoff, and I was good—I mean very good. I killed seven Zoruks in less than thirty strides," he said, his voice a mix of awe and disbelief. "Not a scratch on me. I didn't have one injury. What's more, my unarmed combat skills seemed far more advanced than anything I know. I'm sorry, I'm sounding like a braggart. I'm just trying to tell you what happened," he added defensively.

Antoff thought for a moment before replying, "I believe you, Ivan. Remember what De'Nidra said about the sword?" Ivan's eyes narrowed at the name of that witch. "She knew something about your past. She was afraid of what you could become. What do you think of that?"

He rasped his agreement. They rode in silence the rest of the way to the gate, deep in thought. Ivan finally replied, "Well, I, for one, am good with it. Anything that scares De'Nidra, Daughter of Shadows, is good in my book." He let out a low chuckle. His mind churned on his missing past. On the images of a life that was as blurry as looking through a dirty mirror.

"Now, that is a pleasant change. I don't think I've ever heard you laugh before," Antoff said.

Ivan felt his chest loosen; he hadn't realized that the tension was there. Antoff was trying hard to be his friend in a world that feared and hated him. "I don't think I ever have," Ivan said, his voice softening. They shared a genuine laugh, a rare moment of connection between them.

The city gates stood open, propped by beams used to bar them at night. The traffic, both on foot and beasts pulling carts, was busy. Trade between the Harbor City, Black Stone, and Luc's Ranch was brisk, and RavenHof set in the middle of the crossroad between these points, making it the central hub for trade in the Grey Area. While the farms are months away from harvest, this usually brings with it a flurry of activity before the freeze sets in, causing the roadways and harbor to ice over in an almost impossible state. Spring always brought with it the urgency of an almost empty larder and the need to bring in goods such as fresh meat, dairy, and cloth.

In the Harbor Cities, much of the wealth of the Grey Area had long ago divided neighborhoods into districts dominated by lords, masters, and gangs. There was a balance maintained, and no one wanted that balance disturbed, as it had worked for centuries after the breaking and bloodshed had occurred before what can be described as a shaky peace. Commerce was part of that agreement. City stocks could not grow too low, and the commerce guilds had the sole responsibility for trade.

Contracts awarded to the guild by the districts were based on the previous year's performance, and the district clerks and secretaries made it a top priority to keep these facts ready for inquiry. RavenHof was the benefactor of that system. As they passed through the gates, the mood of the city was darker than normal. Antoff sensed something else tugging at him, that he just could not put a finger on. They trotted straight to the City Master's house, winding their way through the cobblestone streets, thronging with the townsfolk to the sound of steel-shod hooves ringing their approach. The residents were always bustling about the day's tasks, surrounded by the tightly packed two- and three-story homes and storefronts. Yet, amidst the bustle, hawkers and shopkeepers bartered with locals, heedless of the broken gothic towers looming overhead—a dark reminder of a distant and ancient past.

The City Master's house was a grand old mansion constructed of the same dark gray stone color as the remaining gothic architecture that dotted the city. Massive columns supported a large, railed balcony that stretched out over the lower floors' porch.

Dismounting Stingers and handing their reins to a stable boy waiting just inside the imposing black iron gate, Antoff seemed weary to Ivan as they walked up the steps of the grand house. Met by a doorman who offered to take their cloaks, but when the Priest Knight told him no, thank you, the thought of requesting the weapons hidden under the cloaks seemed even more unlikely. Ivan lent his air of cold death, which cut the conversation short. "Just get the Master, thank you," Antoff said.

The doorman asked them to wait in a sitting room as he hurried out. Of course, it was obvious from his sniff they smelled somewhat gamey and offensive to the nose. Antoff had no intention of taking the time to bathe, not while Tara was waiting outside the city. It wasn't long before the City Master saw them.

He was a balding, portly man of medium height wearing the velvet red robes of office and greeted them while eyeing Ivan with mild skepticism. "What a pleasure to see a Priest Knight of your stature in my home. It must be very important indeed, having come straight here from the ride. What news do you have, Priest Knight, and who is your companion?" His expression held a look of superiority.

Antoff responded. "This is Ivan, my friend. The issue at hand is the need to use an abandoned building within the city walls for my troop."

The City Master's face paled as he gasped, "I will not hear of it, Priest Knight! You and your knights must stay at the Inn at the very least."

Antoff took a slow breath. "These are not Priest Knights, and the animals we have with us will undoubtedly scare the city folk. That is why I am requesting a less formal setting. Believe me when I say it is for the best, Master." Antoff nodded after each word to stress the importance of the matter. *This man is acting differently than normal. Something is going on here; I feel it.*

The City Master lowered his voice to a whisper, and his eyes twitched nervously towards the upper floor while he talked. "Naturally, if there is any damage, the church will be responsible for the cost?"

Antoff sighed and looked at the City Master with narrowed eyes. "Naturally," he said, his voice dripping with sarcasm. *At least, that was normal.*

The City Master agreed, and after his clerk fetched a map, they chose a large, abandoned church building on the southwest side of the city. "So, you are unconcerned about the beasts to which I refer?"

The City Master replied. "Not at all, Priest Knight. That is church business." He waved it away with a careless gesture.

Antoff grunted, "Very well, City Master. Then, I believe we have concluded our business here. May the gods of Light be with you," Antoff said, making the sign with his hand.

"And with you," the City Master replied. His face outwardly appeared placid, but his eyes had a hint of fear. He let them go with a bow.

Antoff blew out a breath when they remounted their Stingers. "That was easier than my dealings with him in the past."

"He is definitely hiding something," Ivan said, narrowing his eyes and casting a glance over his shoulder.

Antoff looked at him, feeling a nagging uncertainty. He couldn't shake the feeling that something was indeed amiss.

Above, in the big stone house, the City Master watched them exit the circular driveway from the security of a parted curtain hung in front of a balcony door.

From behind him, the silky allure of De'Nidra's voice spoke. "And so, he believes he can hide inside this decrepit ruin? That the Dark Order will not look here? That it is not already here. Antoff, do not be a fool. Flee!"

The City Master's voice shook, the words catching in his throat as he responded, "Great Mistress, why help them if the Dark Order seeks them?"

Her voice turned to ice. "Do you question me, Ja'Rid? Have you forgotten your place? Let me even suspect you would, in some tiny way, hinder my plans. Let me believe your use has ended and you will be no more."

Ja'Rid, the City Master, threw himself on the floor at her feet. "Please Great Mistress, I can serve. I will never betray you; I swear!" He blubbered.

Her beautiful dark eyes fell on him. "See that you don't. The punishment for betraying me is without equal. That includes anything the Dark Order could do to you. Very well, Ja'Rid. You are still under my protection. *For now.* I have a personal stake in this Torrent and anything that opposes my plans will get dealt with. You would be wise to remember that."

Ja'Rid trembled with anticipation, waiting for her to give a command. He took a long time to lift his eyes from the floor. His brow dripped with sweat by the time he did. He looked around, but De'Nidra, Daughter of Shadows, was no longer there.

Chapter 16 Maid in Need.

"Prayers whisper our deepest hopes to the universe; they are bridges between desire and reality, echoes in the chambers of destiny. In the silence of a prayer, both blessings and warnings dwell. Ask with wisdom, cross with care, for what you ask may bear a price, awakening paths unforeseen. Prayers are always answered. But, not always in the way we mean."

Guiding their Stingers, Antoff and Ivan traversed the city's bustling streets, eventually reaching the dilapidated districts—remnants of a once-great metropolis. Abandoned, except for the few squatters and thugs lurking in shadowed alleys, these crumbling structures whispered stories of an era long forgotten. Feral creatures darted across streets, their fleeting shadows barely noticeable amid the rhythmic clatter of hooves.

Ivan became cautious, his eyes darting to every flicker and sound, while Antoff maintained an unyielding posture, embodying the stoic image of a Priest Knight lost in thought. Beneath that calm exterior, Ivan detected an undercurrent of readiness. A promise that Antoff could swiftly shift from benevolent priest to a disciplined warrior.

Breaking the silence, Ivan remarked, "You seem familiar with these ruins."

Antoff met Ivan's gaze. "A friend, Duncan, and I explored this area extensively. Fascinated with past eras, he hoped to uncover answers not found in our order's teachings. While I respected the writings of previous Priest Knights, Duncan believed that simply accepting the past without inquiry could lead to ignorance. Some in our order viewed his quest as almost blasphemous, but I knew his heart. He was driven by love for the Light and a wish to heal the breaking. He even theorized about an entrance to a 'Lower World' here. We never found it."

Ivan gave a raspy snort. "That is an interesting thought. Legend says there were two cities here. The Upper City and a Lower City. So, your friend Duncan may have been onto something. The legends say the city above was for mortals, and those who had lost their mortality through unnatural experimentation created the city below out of an underground. It is the legend of where the Vam'Phire dark lineage got its start. Indeed, it is the birthplace of my progenitors, or at the very least half of what the mages of the Light called my construct."

Antoff responded, "Well, that would have been just the kind of legend that would have had my old friend the cleric up all night doing research. Then, at the cresting of the first sun, I would be drug out of the bookshop on some adventure. Mostly adventure for him and a lot of 'go fetch a pick and a shovel for me, boy.'" He concluded with a laugh.

They rounded the corner at an intersection, turning northward, avoiding centuries of fallen debris that had lain undisturbed, broken on the cobbled street. There, just beyond an open square except for a single large fountain, were the remains of a cathedral. They trotted past the fountain into the square. Ivan could see a figure of a Priest Knight astride a proud mount as the centerpiece of the fountain.

The statue carried a banner with the blazing binary suns, chiseled out of grey stone, in one hand and an upraised sword in the other. The clanging of shod hooves echoed back at them.

Ivan looked on in wonderment. "What must this have been like back in its day?" The cathedral, a relic of its former glory, stood mostly intact. A sweeping stairway, thirty steps high, led to grand columns supporting a steep stone roof. The landing of the stairway was also thirty feet deep and ended at an enormous doorway whose door and frame had long since rotted away. And that was only the entry. Massive stone block walls rose skyward two hundred feet, supported by carved colonnades and buttresses reaching down to the square. Ivan could only make a sound akin to a whistle. "Yes, this will do fine."

Antoff chuckled. "You approve then?"

Ivan was still in a state of raspy awe. "You could hide a thousand men and a hundred dragons in there, and no one would be the wiser."

Antoff answered. "Let's just hope Tara likes it as much as you do. I don't want to linger any longer, as I want a bath and a hot meal, and that's not going to happen, my friend, until Tara and Cur'Ra get one." He gave Ivan a sidelong look. "Of that, you can be sure."

Antoff led the way around the aged ruin, whose grounds butted up to the walls of the city. There was a large stone stable, constructed architecturally similar to the church, stood next to the old city walls with a bronze gate that led outside to an overgrown meadow just off the main road, obscured by a thicket. Antoff dismounted his Stinger and led the way to the gate. He laid hold of a handle and slid back the bolt with a loud squeak.

"In the day, the old city is not too bad, Ivan, but at night you can feel its memories, and it still has eyes. That is to say, you never feel alone. Something still lives here. What it is, I cannot say." They passed through the bronze gates, leaving them ajar. Letting the old gate close all the way would have allowed the bolt to drop back into place, and this would save the time of riding back through RavenHof while everyone waited outside the gate in the dark.

They rode across the meadow called Dan'Nor's Field, and through the thicket, turning west onto the Great Road. The second of the two suns, called the Little Sister, had already crested mid-sky. Heading towards the Springtide Valley, where they had left Tara and the troop, or as Ivan called it, "*The Zoo.*" It was growing warmer, and there was a breeze that only lightly stirred the air. The Leatherwings, with their malty-colored scales, buzzed about with wings humming, taking up spring mating calls.

A league away from RavenHof, they saw a wagon lying on one axle, with a yoke of two Hurdbeast tied off to one side. A young woman used a scavenged roadside branch and rock as a lever, working intently to lift the axle and replace the broken wheel. Antoff rode forward and looked down at the young woman who spied them over her shoulder as they rode nearby.

Antoff spoke first, "May we be of help, miss?"

She stiffened, pausing in her work.

A small reply came back, "You won't harm me?"

Antoff only sighed, wondering if this was what the world had come to. "I give you my oath, my lady."

She looked over the cart, and her cheeks colored deep red, clearly embarrassed by her failure to recognize a Priest Knight.

"I'm sorry I didn't realize when you rode up. The suns had blinded my eyes. Forgive me, Priest Knight." She said.

Antoff got a better look at her as he dismounted his Stinger. It was clear from her dress and cloak she was a local woman, most likely from a nearby farm. But beyond the dirt that streaked her face and the axle grease on her hands, she was a vision. Her long hair gleamed in the sunlight like golden strands tied up in a bun in the back to keep it out of her eyes. Those eyes, deep pools of blue water, had captured him and wouldn't let go. He found himself still holding onto the stirrup and lost in her gaze when he came back to reality, to the sound of her smooth voice. "Are you okay, Priest Knight?"

He released the stirrup. "I'm fine. Sorry if I offended you. You look familiar. Have we met?"

She laughed a warm musical laugh. "We haven't met before unless you traded Hurdbeasts on the side of your priesthood."

Antoff let out a low laugh, shaking his head. "No, I haven't tried the Hurdbeast sideline yet. Does it pay well?"

She responded with a chuckle. "Sadly, not well for me. This is all that's left after creditors took my ranch and sold everything. I came to RavenHof for a job, but being a woman, it's hard to convince a man you can handle beasts."

Ivan, already dismounted, watched them with a subtle smile.

She was tall for a young woman and somewhat broad at the shoulders, showing she was indeed strong and willing to work. Yet Antoff noted quietly to himself she was all woman; of that, he would indeed give his word. She also had a warrior's way, and from the looks of her, if things got out of sorts, she could handle herself.

Antoff introduced himself, putting a hand on his chest. "I'm Antoff, Priest Knight, at your service. This is Ivan, my friend."

Antoff walked up to the cart and looked. "This axles broken, Al'len, and replacing the wheel won't do any good. Maybe you could hire a carpenter in RavenHof to cut you a new one."

She sighed. "I was just trying to limp the old thing along for a little while longer until I could get a job and earn the money to have it fixed."

Ivan gave Antoff an evil smile. "You know..." he drawled, "Antoff was just saying the other day how we could use another hand to help with all the animals we have."

Antoff's face snapped towards Ivan, giving him the—*I never said that look* before recovering. "Yes, it's lucky *indeed* to find someone with your qualifications, my lady, given we have quite the menagerie now."

She eyed them a little suspiciously before responding. "My name is Al'len, not 'my lady,' and if you're serious about the offer, that's one thing, but I don't want any charity. I work for my keep, or I go my way. Understood?"

Antoff responded like a soldier following an action command. "Yes, my lady... I mean, of course, Al'len, I would expect no less. For now, let's get your belongings on your beasts and we will lead them back to camp. We will have to leave the cart here for now, but we can hire a carpenter in the morning to pick it up with a team and get started cutting you a new axle." She opened her mouth, but he held up his hand, cutting her objections off. "And for this, you will take care of our animals until the cost of repair is paid for."

Antoff raised one finger. He then went on. "And when it is paid, you can decide whether you want to remain with our troop any longer. Is that fair?"

Al'len nodded.

His eyes met hers. He raised the second finger to denote the second stipulation of the arrangement. "You will eat what we eat, ride what we ride, and sleep where we sleep." He raised a third finger. "If you can agree to those terms, we have a deal."

She squinted her eyes at him, sizing the deal up in a way that made Antoff's heart pound in his chest with anticipation. "Very well. It sounds like work and not a charity, and the terms are fine. Until the wagon is fixed, then we will renegotiate terms or go separate ways. In either event, I am thankful for the job."

He approached the rear of the wagon. "Let's load these onto the beasts. We have a ride ahead to the troop and then a few leagues back to RavenHof." The three of them got to work loading her belongings in two heavy-banded trunks onto her animals, which she was going to lead on foot while they rode their warhorses ahead of her on the road. Antoff mounted his Stinger. He reached out a hand to her. She acted as if she might refuse, but Antoff cut her off gently. "Al'len, 'ride what we ride' is one of the terms, remember?"

She squinted piercing blue eyes at him. They chilled his soul, and then she took his hand. He pulled his foot from the stirrup so she could use it, and when she was ready, he supported her while she smoothly mounted with an air of expertise and fluid grace. In Antoff's heart, he was glad she accepted his offer and his hand. It was strange, but that touch, even with a gauntlet-covered hand, was electric, and it signified some greater bargain kept.

While the thoughts were still forming in his head, she held the yoke of the Hurdbeast with her left hand, placed her right hand on his side, and gave him a tap with three fingers to let him know she was ready. They journeyed slowly down the road at the pace of the beast. Al'len answered a few questions on their trip back to the Spring Tide Valley. While she was not unkind with her responses, she was just a little elusive and maintained a mystery about personal information. This was nothing new to Antoff; Tara did the same thing if she felt he was digging into a business that was not his own.

Tara sat amid tall grass, blades swaying gently as the twin suns bathed the world in warm light. The whisper of grass accompanied by the distant laughter of the Elp'har children. On either side of her, she could feel her dragon's presence. They were her eyes and ears, and seldom left her unattended.

The image of a higher reality raged around her, a constant battle between Darkness and Light. These battles threatened to overwhelm her, but the dragons acted as her anchors. They allowed her to tap into the Power birthed from the ceaseless clash of energies. The Dark Order's search for her was a constant weight on her psyche, though their recent journey beneath Forge'Wrath had obscured her from their gaze.

As Tara reveled in her surroundings. The sounds of nearby playing children broke her solitude. She opened her eyes and watched as they ran through the meadow, their giggles echoing across the hill. Their sheer joy was infectious, and Tara couldn't help but smile. Soon after, the mothers joined her, taking a moment's respite while keeping an eye on their playful brood.

One of the young mothers, Darnie, shot Tara a curious look. "Tara, have you ever thought about having children?"

Tara chuckled, her eyes twinkling mischievously. "I'd need to find a man I actually like first."

The women exchanged glances. Tara realized it wasn't mere curiosity; they genuinely wanted to understand her better.

Cur'Ra, approaching the group, remarked, "Ah, here you are. It wasn't hard to find you. Just had to follow the children's laughter."

"We were discussing Tara's thoughts on family. She says she'd need to find the right man first," Darnie playfully relayed.

Cur'Ra, giving Tara a motherly wink, added, "Well, Edward seems quite taken with you. He would be a perfect match for the vows, and it doesn't hurt that he is handsome."

Tara looked aghast. "Mother. I hardly know him. He acts so immature. I am trying to keep him from killing himself needlessly."

Darnie chimed in, "They all do, Tara. At least until they grow too old and then they try to act dignified." This elicited nods and chuckles from the other women. The conversation soon shifted to playful jabs at men, but Tara sensed an underlying encouragement regarding Edward.

The evening advanced, and the children, exhausted from their play, sought solace in their mother's laps. Little Joya, Darnie's daughter, approached Tara with hopeful eyes. "Can you tell us a story?"

Tara hesitated momentarily, then began, "Near RavenHof lies the Garden Wood. As a girl, I dreamed of building a home by a pond there, where the water flowers grow." With her finger, she traced the imagined pond and house on the ground, captivating her audience.

The girls inquired if Tara dreamed of living there alone, while the boys were more interested in the wild animals of the woods.

"The world can be an interesting place," Tara assured them. "In my dream, I wasn't alone. I hoped to share it with someone special and perhaps even have children like you. And as for wild animals," she tickled a boy, "The children would have to do."

The boy pointed out, "Well, you have dragons now, horses, and a wolf!"

Tara giggled, "You are right, I do. I have a whole family now, a big one, and I love it too. Sometimes, living life can be better than dreams if you accept change." Inside Tara's heart, she felt the fear. *If I can protect it.*

Static hissed, and a streak of light split the air, forming a ribbon, and finally congealing into a purplish globe, a manifestation called forth from the minds of those who still have the talent to use the Power. It was a Mage Gate, and out of that gate stepped Lord Modred, the Great Black Demon of Legend. An undead voice called from behind him, "See that you do not fail me further, Lord Modred!"

He responded, "It shall all be as you say, Great Lord Amorath."

The cold, dead reply came, "That would be better for you, as disappointing me, Lord Modred, will end in your demise. I will not deal with it so mildly next time."

The dust curled around him mystically as the Mage Gate winked out behind him. He stood on a sandy cliff overlooking a canyon pass that snaked a jagged path around Forge'Wrath mountain, belching its volcanic ashy smoke into the atmosphere in a black inky plume. His army, cobbled together from the Dark Order, moved in a long stream below.

From behind him, he could hear the approach of Narean's red, leathery wings as they spread wide, and he landed upon the rocky cliff, adding a bluster to the already dusty air. "Report!" Lord Modred's voice cracked like a whip. He did not need to look to know Narean knelt just behind him. Nor was it necessary to turn to know he had not yet moved his eyes from the grey stone beneath his feet.

"My Lord, there are now five fists of mortal and Zoruk cavalry at your command, and a like number of Zoruk ground troops. The Lords have been gating them in groups of ten and twenty, not wanting to alert the Torrent with huge spikes of Power. Lord Modred, a Great One, has awoken and left Forge'Wrath. My Lord, she burned Captain Um'elik alive after he demanded she give 'her guest,' the Torrent, to the Dark Order."

Lord Modred chuckled darkly to himself. "Then he received a far kinder death than he deserved. We will put an end to the rest of this game soon. Hand down orders to move the army under the cover of terrain and darkness toward RavenHof. All reports say the Torrent's Priest Knight protector has secured a location inside the abandoned section of Coth'Venter and will be hold up with his ragged troop of vagabonds there. We will slip into the abandoned area and take them by force long before any Army of the Light can muster to answer. Or, even know what it is they have lost."

The red demon's voice behind him shook with anticipation or fear. Modred was not sure which. "Lord, it's also babbled by the few Zoruks that survived the encounter with the Old One. The Torrent now travels with two hatchlings of her own."

Modred brought him up short and cut off further conversation. "No mage has ever successfully bonded with more than one dragon, fool. Now carry out my orders. I grow weary of this foolishness."

Narean the Red spoke, "It shall be as you command, my Lord." And with a gust of wind and the beating of wings, he was gone.

The Dominion was angry. *I'm still trapped in this old bastion of Light within these Twisted Lands.* His eyes smoldered with a deep red glow as he watched the old dead remains of the High Mage Co Ádean who had first been his kidnapper and then later Lord De'von, harvesting them for their material without permission.

Now charred and wounded by that Torrent and Va'Yone that upstart Darkling, he sat on his haunches before the compression portal door. It was far too small for him to enter; he was just their brooding. He stared into the opening at the back of the old, dead wizard who had called him forth out of the abyssal realm. It was pure hate. He was the king of his realm! Now, he was nothing more than a lab experiment.

He had commanded millions before his capture, and now the best he could do is have the few darkling he had captured working on clearing the lower halls. They had been at it for some time now, and the work was almost done. He could access the larger portal room, but much to his frustration, it was inert. And it would take a sizable talent to use it. And use it, he would. Oh, he had no intention of going back to his realm permanently until this world paid in full for disturbing his rule. He did, however, intend to use this portal to bring his followers in and then open a Gate to the surface of this planet where they, and this whole broken world would feel his wrath and rue the day that this High Mage took him from h is home.

The problem was the knowledge and talent he needed all existed outside. There was a lot of knowledge here, but he did not know how to get at it. It was all locked away in that thing they had called the Well. He would have to keep his temper a little while longer. Before the Torrent, there had been no way in and no way out, but now she had changed all that. He had already sent scouts, and while only a few of them had returned, he was gaining an understanding of the authorities and powers that ruled the lands surrounding the desolate location of his prison. They had brought back maps and names. He also knew how to motivate them: *greed*. Lord De'von had educated him on the trinkets they called gems and precious metals, of which were supplied in vast amounts. Also, the amulet and the book needed recovering. The bothersome Torrents had taken that as well. While He was not sure what it did. The Dominion knew he was going to need it to get home. That point Lord De'von was explicit about.

While the old, dead thing that was his mentor could communicate with his mind, he was immune to the mental persuasions it used on everyone else. Since Lord De'von's untimely death by the intruders, he had continued to interrogate these weakly talented darklings on the Power to gain a better understanding of what it was. He had destroyed two of them, trying to make the portal work with no success. This resource was far too precious to waste further, and he had too few to risk. While he had encouraged breeding by the populace, it did not produce talented ones quickly. Thus, in the past, he resorted to forced breeding of the talented together, accelerating the results. So far, it had been favorable, with the strength and utilization of the Power doubling approximately every generation. However, that had come with some risks. The more talented they were, the more of them broke free of his grasp. He now had an open rebellion by a small but growing group. The problem was he could not tell the difference between the ones who had the talent and the others who did not until they use it.

Nevertheless, he had no intention of waiting for whatever additional generations necessary to gain the Power to use the portal. Some outside talent was needed, and if Lord De'von's tutelage was as effective as he believed, he had all the resources he needed to obtain it. If greed was what motivated them, then he would use all these resources and take all the rest he needed from this world when liberated from this cage. He needed the energies that came with the sun to heal, and if the reports were to be believed, it was a binary system. The power he could pull from them would be awesome indeed. He watched the dead figure as if expecting it to answer. It kept its back to him and remained still and out of reach.

It was approaching the second sun's noon when Antoff returned from RavenHof. Tara had spent her day in meditation, and Cur'Ra had prepared everyone for the march to RavenHof. Antoff introduced Al'len to Cur'Ra, who welcomed her with a hug and immediately put her to work as if she had always been part of the troop. As Al'len left, she looked back at Antoff with a smile, seeing he had been true to his word, and he needed her to manage *"the zoo,"* as they affectionately referred to it.

Tara was absent, but a gesture from Cur'Ra directed him to a nearby hillside. He rode his Stinger up the hill at a run. Things felt urgent now. He needed to see her with his own eyes. He knew she was safe, but he had to be sure. It was his responsibility, and he was determined to fulfill it. The warning from a god of

Light was like a sound that would not go away, and it was growing more intense with each passing day.

Antoff galloped over the crest of the hill and through the tall grass of the field, dirt spraying from the clawed hooves of his Stinger. The warhorse was eager to after not being let loose for some time. He abruptly reined him in, causing another spray of soil. Tara sat in the tall grass, still with her eyes closed, enjoying the breeze. Her dragons didn't stir at the approach of Antoff's steed, but they alerted her to his arrival well before he reached the top of the rise and dismounted in a gallant display.

His voice carried a fatherly tone, gently informing a child that it was time to come inside after playtime, yet it also held firmness in his loving way. "It is time to go, Tara."

She opened her eyes and smiled at him. "That means you found us a place to take shelter."

Antoff only grunted, understanding she was teasing him again. "Well, I did what I could, Tara. The day is growing late, and we should try to reach Dan'Nor's Field just after dark if we can."

Tara stood up, and her dragons matched her every motion. She brushed off her soft thieves' armor and walked towards him slowly, then embraced him. "I missed you, priest," she whispered, her voice carrying the weight of the time they'd been apart. Her heart soared at the feel of his embrace, as if the world had suddenly become right again. She held him tighter, reluctant to let go, cherishing the rare moments of closeness they shared in the midst of their challenges.

His voice was soft. "I will be by your side as long as I can, Tara. They will have to take my life for me to leave you. But if that ever happens, I give it willingly and out of love. You have my heart and my sword. Now, let's get moving. Time is running out." Antoff tried to sound stern, but his voice had a catch at the end, as if he was trying to control his emotions. His eyes shone with the love he had for Tara. He gave her head a loving pat. "Come on, child, we have much to do." She hugged him tighter, and her eyes were wet when she let go. Turning, they walked towards the camp.

Chapter 17 The Field called Dan'Nor

"Drawn by the drums of war, I remember their beat leading me to a place now lost, a field that is no more. King Dan'Nor gave grim tidings of the numbers opposing us. There was no winning. Nor would there be the glory of a type we had in the engagements of the past. This was the end, but the choice of the end was what I pondered. What kind of end would I bring myself to? If I were to live long enough to merit remembrance, old soldiers that had stood beside me would not do that commemoration in some later year with a cup of ale. No, we will all fall in this field. Thus, if the tale was to be told, the enemy must tell it. The fury of my death and its cost would be so high that they would tell the grim tale. Having come to such a bleak conclusion, with my death assured, I sally forth without fear, only purpose."

Al'len assisted the troop in finishing the packing of the equipment into leather-lined travel bags. It was always the same, regardless of the troop size and the surrounding noise. The last item to be packed was usually the first to be unpacked, typically related to the soldiers' stomachs, which meant the cooking gear. Just like in any other camp she had been in, Al'len hurried to pack it up. Being around warriors again felt good. It had been a long time since she had company to spend time with, and it felt refreshing. Antoff kept an eye on her, and she kept one on him. So far, he was living up to her hopes. That's how a Priest

Knight should be, and it was plain he had no intention of causing discomfort. He was simply interested. On the other hand, Al'len wanted to know what kind of man he truly was. Every time he caught her watching him, and she knew he had noticed, her cheeks would involuntarily flush, and her face would grow hot. *For god's sake! Am I just a girl fresh off her mother's apron strings?* She observed Antoff letting his charger head up the hill at a run while glancing back at her. Their eyes met.

Cur'Ra interrupted. "Is everything alright, Al'len?"

Al'len looked up quickly from her thoughts. "Huh, what?"

Cur'Ra's eyes went to where Antoff had been and looked back at Al'len, understanding. "Ah, I see, a certain Priest Knight holds your interest."

Al'len blushed once again. "I just want to know what kind of man I am working for."

Cur'Ra interjected, placing a warm hand on her shoulder, "Al'len, there is no need to worry. He is a good man. Like the rest of them, he can be stubborn and won't admit to any injury, but I have been observing him for days now, and Tara has him well under control. He doesn't do everything she says, but to his credit, he listens."

Cur'Ra ended the moment with a smile, resembling a mother who knows her daughter's intentions. "Now let's finish packing. We'll be departing soon."

Al'len nodded, saying, "Yes, ma'am."

Cur'Ra started walking away, but turned back momentarily. "He is quite handsome for a man his age, don't you think?"

Surprised, Al'len answered. "I'm not sure," she stammered.

Cur'Ra smiled in a motherly manner. "Oh, I think you are, girl."

Al'len had yet to decide whether she liked that woman. Once again, her cheeks grew warm, and she scolded herself for revealing such vulnerability. *I must have appeared as though I were pining after him instead of focusing on my duties. I am just evaluating him. Goodness, woman, act your age*, she chastised herself.

Edward sat on his charger next to Ivan, while the dire wolf lay not far off in the tall grass with its tongue lolling out of one side of its mouth. Edward leaned over to Ivan and remarked, "Looks like you guys found another stray on the way back, huh?"

Ivan rasped a quiet reply. "Antoff seems to want to help everyone. Besides, I think he's *interested* in this one, if you get me?" He gave Edward a sly smile.

Edward gave him a sidelong glance, a disbelieving look on his face. "Really? *our* Antoff?" He gave a low whistle. "Well, she *is* pretty, for sure, but if he's interested, thanks for the warning. I'll stay well clear of her."

Ivan gruffly retorted, "Yes, sure friend, you'd be interested in her if you could take your eyes off a certain Torrent mage."

Edward flushed.

Tara and Antoff walked together, with his Stinger obediently following behind. Two dragons, one with black scales edged in gold trim and the other white with gold, played around them. They had already grown larger than the Stinger and appeared much more muscular. At first, Al'len thought she was seeing more Stingers following them, but then one Stinger, opened large semi-translucent wings, and her mouth fell open. "This cannot be. One, yes, but two? It has never been done! Never, not in thousands of years of trying!"

Cur'Ra's motherly voice came from behind as Al'len was packing a horse. "It's all right, girl. Just take a breath. They are real, and they are dragons."

Al'len stammered, "But there are two of them. How in the name of all the gods is that possible?"

Cur'Ra sighed. "With this group, young woman, you will witness things you never thought possible. You will probably meet them soon enough, but Tara takes care of them, and they take care of her. So, it is very unlikely you will have to look after them at all. I am sure Antoff did not hire you to look after dragons."

Spring was already well underway. Ruby throated Leatherwings with multicolored scales flashed, chasing in and out of the treetops, displaying their mating rituals. The air filled with chirping calls, their determination and purpose apparent. The Hornbee, its round body, and four wings, resembled a red and yellow striped ball with a horn and six spindly legs dragging lazily beneath it. It busily moved among large blossoms, that begun closing as the day grew late. The blooms reached out for the waning energy of the binary suns, struggling to sustain their efforts. The wind picked up, and the dragons ran alongside the troop, occasionally spreading their large wings and soaring above the treetops before gracefully descending back to the ground on powerful legs.

While Al'len observed the unfolding scene, Tara and Va'Yone rode alongside her as she sat behind Antoff.

Tara leaned in close, nodding subtly towards the dragons, and whispered, ensuring no one else could hear, "They like you, Al'len."

Al'len shook her head modestly. "Everyone here is kind."

Tara persisted, "No, I mean, yes, they are kind, but the dragons say you smell good and your mind is open to them."

Al'len thought to herself, *Be careful, woman. Your ease around these dragons might give you away.* She made her face placid. "Cur'Ra said they are yours, and I needn't worry about them," Al'len answered.

Tara giggled, "As for who belongs to whom, we are still figuring it out, but I believe Antoff holds you in high regard, and you handle the animals well. I think this will work out for all of us. However, I must warn you, we seem to attract many creatures that wish us harm. I told Antoff he can't protect everyone in the world, and you need to know there are dangers if you choose to stay with us."

Al'len had decided. She liked this Tara. "Antoff is a true Priest Knight. That's the truth," Al'len mused aloud.

Antoff growled, "You two realize I'm right here, don't you?"

Al'len turned her head towards him and smiled. "Yes, but I would expect someone of your age to distinguish between two women talking *about* you and two women talking *to* you."

Tara coughed and covered her mouth, poorly disguising her laughter.

Al'len then turned to Tara as if Antoff hadn't spoken, "I can handle myself, Tara. I have a sword, an heirloom, in my trunk. I rarely need it, but sometimes I wear it to let curious eyes know I possess it."

Antoff grumbled, "Do you know how to use it?"

Al'len responded, "I haven't needed to for some time, and I'm sure my skills don't match those of a legendary warrior like a Priest Knight, but I know how to put on a good show if necessary."

Antoff replied, "You'll need to do more than just put on a show if you're going to stay with us, Al'len. You can join Tara for sword training. She's working on a two-weapon form called At'Aelcontoe, but I've always preferred the sword and shield style."

Al'len teased, "I never thought I'd receive lessons from a venerable Priest Knight like yourself, but I'm honored."

Antoff growled, "I'm not that old."

Both women laughed.

The day wore on until nightfall, as the last of the suns fitfully slipped beneath the horizon, leaving its memory painted on the cloudy sky in a reddish-purple hue that fought against the encroaching night, slowly fading away. In the countryside below, lights from small farms, then houses, and finally RavenHof came into view. The lamps of the small city illuminated every street corner, inviting locals and visitors alike to partake in the entertainment offered by the inns. Innkeepers went to great lengths to maintain a good stock of drinks, food, and talented singers and storytellers to entice their patrons to spend their hard-earned coins.

The chimneys below emitted wisps of smoke as innkeepers and household members laid fires in their hearths. The last pedestrians and merchant wagons rumbled towards the gate, where guards shouted calls to urge stragglers. "Gates closing! Hurry along! Come on now, don't drag your feet! Let's go!" Just as the last fortunate soul entered the city, the gate slammed shut, and the bar went home, sealing off RavenHof for the night. Behind the lit city loomed the dark ruin that remained untamed. It sat like a black mausoleum, attempting to engulf the small friendly lights with its darkness.

The troop moved off-road, hidden by the thicket that ran along the highway. Then they crossed well before the intersection to the other side, continuing with the undergrowth concealing them from the open road. That is until they reached the field still remembered by the locals as Dan'Nor. The meadow spread out like a lake of waving grass, with only a few bushes and sprigs breaking the clear expanse from the walls to the trees. The wind blew fitfully here, and the grass rippled in response, reaching out towards the ancient walls of the dead metropolis, jutting out into the meadow defiantly. Wounded battlements and broken towers reached toward the heavens.

Antoff led them through the thicket to the wall. Above the center most point of the wall rose a tall, sharply pointed roof, spires, and the dome of the abandoned Cathedral of the Light. It sat there alone and unwelcoming. True to Antoff's word, the old gate remained ajar. Antoff dismounted and pulled it open, revealing a view of a cobbled, stable yard. Across the yard, some fifty paces away, three flights of stairs climbed the face of the church's raised foundation. Three landings needed before reaching a sizable metal door that led into the building. He whispered orders to the troop, directing them to the stables. With the finality of a squeak and the bolt sliding home, they had arrived.

It took no time at all for Al'len and Elp'harean troops to commandeer the old stable. The packs and equipment offloaded outside, and the animals led into stalls to be rubbed down, fed, and watered for the night. The Elp'hars were already setting up camp in their usual fashion on the cobblestone paving of the yard. Va'Yone was sore from the ride and tired. When Tara pulled him down from their mount, he went with the Elp'harean women and young ones to bed down in the stables near the animals, where they would benefit from their heat and the small fire set in the forge.

Like clockwork, the troops ate and set the watch on the grounds and above on the wall, keeping well out of sight using the broken tower and remnants of battlements to obscure their presence. Above the church, a cloud of blood bats fluttered. They had burst forth from the cathedral the moment the invaders had discovered their tranquil lair.

The dire wolf's black form disappeared into the shadows as he secured the grounds for his pack. But he wasn't alone; the dragons loped along behind him, afraid of missing out on a potential meal. Tara watched them go, knowing they would alert her if any problem arose. She had already explained to them they had to stay out of sight and remain within the confines of the grounds.

Antoff instructed his troop to re-saddle six animals. He pulled a tarnished key from a chain hanging around his neck, lit a lamp, and climbed three flights of stairs that led to the rear of the rectory. Tara, Ivan, Edward, and Cur'Ra followed him.

With a click of an old, unoiled lock, it groaned from years of neglect. The door opened, revealing a hallway that passed by the kitchen and dining hall. Dark wood paneling lined the halls, sourced from a tree whose seed had long since vanished from the land of El'idar. The hallway led to an area divided into single cells, each containing a small fireplace, a slab serving as a bed, and a stool accompanied by a writing table chiseled from the same gray stone. There were approximately fifty cells in each hall, and there were twenty halls with cells like this on each floor.

Tara exclaimed, "This is how the Priest Knights lived? This is all they received for their service?"

Antoff replied quietly, "It is how we still find lodging, regardless of rank. The only possessions we have are our armor, weapons, and a few portable belongings. The clergy are the ones who enjoy opulence." His words tinged with a bitterness. Soon after, a familiar voice echoed through the hallway.

Al'len had followed, and she leaned against the doorway. "I can see how you've maintained your humility, Priest Knight."

Antoff grumbled as he threw his bag onto the stone slab in the first cell. "Everyone take a cell; there is no shortage. We're going into the city tonight to have a bath and a hot meal,"

Cur'Ra started, "I should stay here…"

Anticipating her objection, he continued, "You're all coming, every single one of you." He sensed her raised eyebrow without looking, but she remained silent.

Each member of the group tried to cleanse themselves of the grime accumulated during the past weeks, before donning fresh clothing. Antoff dressed in black britches, a dashing white shirt, and his four-winged hawk buckle securing his ornate two-handed longsword at his waist. He added a leather purse that made a hefty clank and draped his black cloak over his shoulder with a flourish. He waited outside his cell. Ivan was the next to step out, standing a head taller than anyone else with skin as pale as white flour. He wore a nondescript outfit of brown britches, an earth-tone shirt, a wide-brimmed hat, and a dark brown cloak that concealed the curved blade with the blood gem, which Antoff was certain now had become his weapon of choice.

Edward dressed in noble finery. He still aimed to impress the local women, hoping to reel in a kiss. But beneath his cloak lay a wicked-looking broadsword, causing Antoff to reserve judgment about the lad. Perhaps Edward was simply fulfilling the locals' expectations.

Tara wore black britches, and a blue blouse adorned with sewn-in flowers. Cur'Ra emerged from her cell wearing a spring dress she must have borrowed from Tara, paired with low-cut shoes. Al'len, however, stepped out of her cell in an all-tan leather ensemble that did nothing to hide her ample curves. Her face held a hint of sultriness. She wore an ornate two-handed longsword belted at her waist, with a white dragon buckle, and a light tan cloak with gold fringes. Her hand rested comfortably on the hilt of her sword, and her cloak swept back in an almost cavalier fashion. Antoff's heart pounded. His face was growing hot, and maybe other things long since forgotten as she spoke. "Do I look the part, Priest Kni ght?"

Filled with wonder as he responded, "I think that will do the trick." And then he cleared his throat.

Tara and Cur'Ra gave each other knowing smiles from behind. It was like they could read each other's minds. *Al'len had him. That man is done for. He just doesn't know it.*

Antoff mounted the Stinger. It sensed his mood, and it danced beneath him, on one side of the yard. Al'len professionally mounted her horse and held the reins with her right hand while resting her left hand on the hilt of her fine blade. After they all settled into their saddles, they rode two abreast in a short column. Antoff and Al'len led the way, followed by Tara next to Cur'Ra, and then Ivan and Edward as rear guard. Edward's eyes searched the night. He knew the locals would still look at him as they always had: *the disgraced noble son.* For him, it was the best disguise he had. Now he served Tara, and if it meant being met with the usual disdain and disregard from the locals, he was fine with that. For him, there was only one thing that mattered: keeping Tara safe. He had pledged himself to her service, and nothing else held significance for him.

Ivan rasped quietly, "You have changed, boy. I can see it seeping out of you like rainwater sheeting off a roof. You are truly her oaths man now, aren't you?"

Edward kept his eyes searching and answered with a curt nod and a brief statement, "I serve the Torrent alone and have abandoned any thought of myself. She saved my life. I have pledged this new life she has given me to her. I would rather die than fail her."

Ivan rasped, "I can see that she will make a man of you yet." Ivan gave a strong, friendly pat on his back. However, as much as he may jest, Edward knew Ivan was watchful for anything. They both understood this respite would not last long.

Ivan was well aware he would not allow the darkness to claim her any more than Edward would. He was distant because he had to be. How could he know her when he did not even know himself?

They crossed the square, moving toward the centerpiece: a figure of a Priest Knight on the back of a proud mount, the central figure of a fountain. He held a banner with the blazing binary suns chiseled out of grey stone in one hand and an upraised sword in the other. Seeing it for the first time, Tara exclaimed it looked like Antoff. In many respects, it did. It represented the image of what Priest Knights should be: *strong and resolute in faith, quelling any challenger of the Light.*

Al'len spoke so quietly to herself, Antoff barely caught it. "That is exactly how Ram'Del was. The Defender of the Light, and it was to the exclusion of everything else. One may choose to honor him or even grant him a kind of godhood, but for him, the loneliness drove him to death."

Antoff's head whipped towards Al'len in surprise. She had a faraway look on her face, her blonde hair reflecting in the light like a golden waterfall, and for one second, to Antoff, she looked like a goddess and he could almost kneel at her feet. He cleared his throat...

Al'len thought quietly to herself, *I have slept for far too long. My mind wanders between the dream and waking. Even with full awareness, I must choose my words carefully with this knight. I must focus, but I dare not fully awaken, or I will awaken the others with my presence.* They cautiously made their way down the thoroughfare, sidestepping fallen debris and skirting around ancient, crumbling structures that bore the weight of centuries.

The people of RavenHof renewed the nearby buildings and streets of old Coth'Venter as their population required it, and although the progress had been steady, the recovery had been slow. Echoing rings sounded as hooves struck the worn cobblestones. Their movements became swift and cautious as they approached the inhabited section, where dark figures of men in small groups could be seen, to be sizing them up from hidden lanes. Yet, there were no takers. No one dared to challenge their passage. But, as with all things, someone eventually would. The gear they carried would be worth a king's ransom in a place like this and could provide a temporary break until the next opportunist took it from them. Antoff's heart ached as he watched. What kind of life could these people have had if someone in their lives had given them a helping hand? How many of them wouldn't be out in the darkness, struggling to survive?

Al'len watched him from the corner of her eye, noticing his stoic expression and the underlying sadness. "What is that I see? Pity for the downtrodden? You would gather them all up and save them if you could. Antoff, you are like Ram'Del in so many ways."

Antoff could also sense the hatred emanating from those who were watching them. Whether it was the hate stemming from envy, he did not know. "Life is about the opportunities that are presented. These poor souls didn't receive the same opportunities we did because society didn't care. Well, I care about them. These people have potential, just like everyone else, and to deny them the opportunity to develop in life is a crime."

Still led by Antoff and Al'len, the cavalcade turned the corner onto the bustling main street that cut through RavenHof. Wagons pulled by large teams of animals were a common sight, and disputes rarely escalated beyond spirited exchanges of words. They rode past two other inns, The Fat Hound and The Grey Mount, before reaching the renowned Rusty Bucket, the oldest inn in town. Unassuming from the outside, its true charm lay in the vibrant lives of the people inside—a second home to many, filled with laughter and song whenever the doors swung open.

Antoff led the party through an alleyway between the buildings to a wagon yard behind the inn. A yard stuffed with wagons and stable hands sprang into action upon their arrival. They were well-organized, both in their actions and manners, as they bowed upon their entrance. One of the younger hands sneered at Edward but received a cuffing from the older man for his behavior.

Edward's reputation had preceded him. The older man stepped forward as they dismounted.

"My ladies, Lord Priest Knight, and good men, welcome to the Rusty Bucket. You'll be wanting warm meals and music, and we offer the very best in RavenHof. Our esteemed innkeeper, Mrs. Devens, will take good care of you right away, as you shall see. Just go straight through the back to bypass the stairs to the rooms on the right and the private dining areas on the left. Keep going straight, and you'll reach the common room."

Antoff slipped some small coins into the older man's hand, allowing him to decide how to distribute the tips among the other hands working under him. The older man expressed gratitude for Antoff's generosity, claiming it wasn't necessary, but the coins disappeared into his pocket as he motioned them toward the door. As they entered the inn, they could hear the older man saying, "Are you a fool, boy? That young Lord spends good coin here at the inn, and Mrs. Devens would be put off if she knew you were sneering at her customers like that."

The boy protested, calling Edward a lout. Edward chuckled to himself, deliberately slowing down to be the last one through the door. As soon as the door opened, the sound of music and laughter washed over them. A young woman's voice sang, recounting a tale of a man chasing after the fairer sex. On the high notes, the tambourines shook loudly, prompting the crowd to erupt in laughter.

Chapter 18 The Dance of a Thousand Years

"There is but one love that can change a person forever. It can reveal itself in the gentlest of touches, soaking in and awakening a hunger. The awareness of what had been missing and the yearning to be whole again. It is the rain that nourishes the wilting plant in the garden. Once missing, only half of your being is truly living."

The last heat of midday dissipated as the second sun slowly slipped over the horizon. Fading light cast purple-red across jagged peaks, sending shadows like long fingers stretching to touch the barren landscape. Already, stars were visible in the night sky, beyond clouds resembling dirty cotton. A plume of ash from Forge'Wrath mingled with them, rising high into a vast canvas of the lonely heavens. Lord Modred watched as a long line of horses and foot soldiers approached, marching two abreast. They snaked their way toward RavenHof, a cloud of dust billowing out behind them in the chilly night air. Normally, his underlings would conduct an action like this one; however, given the stakes, he was leaving nothing to chance. The Great Lord had commanded him to see to it personally. And see to it he would. Any failure to acquire the Torrent would end with his demise. Oh yes, in the past, when a high chance of failure had presented itself, it was common for him to pick some fool bucking for a promotion to take the fall. Not this time. This time, he had little choice. It had become necessary to emphasize to the military leadership that any lack of discipline or failure in carrying out orders would be dealt with swiftly.

Wind rustling, expensive fabric alerted him to the presence of the forgotten War Mage Mel'Temdel, who still awaited his permission for dismissal. Modred turned slowly to address him. First taking in the view of the burned husk of the irksome lieutenant, who had failed to properly motivate his troops to pick up the pace. With a kick from Modred, his ashy form collapsed into dust and dispersed into the breeze, one fiery cinder at a time. Modred had employed the mage to no small effect from the top of the cliff, and the lieutenant's shrill cries still left a weak smile on his face as he stared down at him.

Modred eyed the War Mage. "Work well done, Mel'Temdel. You may return to your enclave."

Mel'Temdel bowed low, exposing the balding crown of an ancient skull and the finely worked dark metal staff carried in his right hand. His reddish finery rustled with an overly marked swish of his arms as he took notice of his lord's dismissal. "We live to serve, my lord."

Behind the mage, a ribbon of purple light split the air and then formed into a great globe of pulsating Power. Modred turned back toward the troops below the valley just as the War Mage stepped through, and the Gate winked out.

Modred spread his black leathery wings, stretching them widely to relieve the fatigue of a long and demanding day. *This day is far from done*, he told himself. *I must march this army through till morning and only then give them a rest. They will require strength in the coming days.*

Normally, Modred would care little for the plight of the lowly warrior, but in this case, he would give them every chance to succeed. Their failure, this time, would also be his end. That changed things for Modred. For the first time, his fate was tied to theirs, and for the first time, he cared whether all his troops made it fresh to the fight. He had to manage this situation. They dare not tarry too long. Who could have said how long the Torrent would remain in RavenHof? That Priest Knight, who was traveling with his prize, was well known to them. He had proven himself to be formidable in battle over these long years. Likewise, this Priest Knight, Grant, had shown a vestige of his order's old Power. This was troubling, to be sure. He was connected to the old gods of Light somehow. While it was well known the old gods slept, one of them still granted him favor. Yet, an old god in slumber had taken note of him. That was a subject of concern and made for interesting discussions among the leaders of the Dark Order. Nevertheless, it changes nothing. The die is already cast. Succeed or be destroyed by his master.

He spread his wings wide; his banded muscles ached as the last vestiges of his fatigue lingered. With his large bat-like wings held wide, he leaped from the ridge, purposefully haunting the night sky above his troops, adding more menace to the threat than they had already seen from the ridge. He was watching them, and with any failure there would come an even swifter punishment.

De'Nidra, the Daughter of Shadows, wore a fine-cut dress of light blue, splashed with cream, silver stitching down the sleeves, and a single dark braid thrown over her shoulder. She sat with her back to the corner nearest the fireplace of Val'Etor, now known as the inn of the Old Rusty Bucket. Her dark brown eyes studied the room. The Dining Hall of Warriors had been reduced to a shadow of its former self. The whole world was like that, a shadow and dream of forgotten glory since the Shattering of the Balance.

No one could know her for who she was. She could wear any of a thousand faces, a thousand masks of people long dead whom she had once known. It was not just a matter of Power; it was more than that. It was an issue of craft. She prided herself on being believable and tangible, and required a legend of some kind to pull it off. Modeling her appearance, outward behavior, and bearing on the actual people she had studied before taking over their lives. She kept these personas throughout the kingdoms everywhere. Granted, it took work—the occasional appearance here or there. The duties of the individual legends had to be maintained. Everything had to be perfected, right down to aging and the final act of dying. Body doubles did that part down through the generations, whose identities of powerful families she kept for herself.

In some cases, members of the Dark Order came to her legends to conspire, completely unaware they were revealing all their secrets to De'Nidra, the Daughter of Shadows. A smile curled her lips. She imagined the shock on the faces of the Dark Order members if she ever exposed all the treachery and betrayal that had gone unreported over the centuries of conniving. She held onto these small tidbits like trump cards to be played in a great game. Little did the players know she was not only playing as they surmised, but also played the house and the dealer at the same time. She hid a small smile by sipping what was barely passable as wine.

Today, however, she was a merchant from the Harbor Cities on her first of two annual trips to RavenHof to buy goods required by her guild contracts. The House of Deepwater never failed a contract. De'Nidra clandestinely eyed the rear entry to the common room as the next group of travel-weary patrons entered the inn seeking refreshment and perhaps entertainment, if that's what you wanted to call this. The girl standing on the chair singing the stories belonged to her as well. She was useful. The Dark Order seldom paid much attention to the common people. However, De'Nidra knew that even tiny nudges to the average folk could plant ideas that would grow, eventually changing the direction of an entire town and spreading far beyond with great effect. These ideas and rumors legitimized things she did elsewhere, and the townsfolk depended heavily on the word of merchants and entertainers to keep up with events happening throughout the kingdoms.

De'Nidra had servants like this everywhere. It was necessary. The webs she spun were too grand without delegation. However, with delegation also came failure, and with failure came punishment, and with punishment came the desire to please. De'Nidra mused on how even the most powerful individuals could quickly be bent to her will using that simple formula. Failure, in many cases, had become as important to the success of the overall scheme. Without failure, the system De'Nidra employed could not work. The crucial aspect was the planned tasks had to be completed in small pieces, so each individual task had only a small importance to the overall scheme. When failures occurred, the plan had to be flexible and be able to ebb and flow with mortal frailties.

De'Nidra was not concerned with how many lifetimes it took to complete each phase of her plan, or how the mortal theatrics played out. It was all about steering events to the outcome she wanted. Further, this kind of plotting meant no one except her knew the plan, or how what they were doing affected it. All they knew was what they needed to know and nothing else. If you tortured any of them, or even all of them, you would learn nothing.

Over the rim of her wineglass, she watched Antoff, the Priest Knight, enter with his party of travel-weary companions. She knew all of them, except one. That one she could not read, regardless of how hard she pressed with her mind or Power. She heard Antoff say her name, *Al'len*.

Al'len wore an all-tan leather outfit, highlighting her allure, with a two-handed longsword belted at her waist with a white dragon buckle and a light tan, almost white, cloak fringed in gold. Matching her long, beautiful hair. Those standards tickled the thoughts in the back of her mind.

Al'len's deep blue eyes delicately scanned the common room, feigning a casual survey but keenly aware of unseen dangers. But De'Nidra wasn't fooled. The woman had detected her probe and was now conducting her own investigation. De'Nidra's head started pounding, and a drop of blood fell to the tabletop. She touched a finger just below her nose and drew it back, wet with blood. Quickly, she grabbed a white cloth napkin from the table and wiped away the blood before using a thread of Power forcing it to clot.

Who is this woman, and why can't I penetrate her mind or sense her presence using my Power? De'Nidra wondered.

Behind the bar, Mrs. Devens poured drinks and directed staff with the assurance of a general overseeing troops. Their entry did not escape her attention. She wiped her hands on her apron, lifted a small section of the bar, folded upward, and then closed it behind her before effortlessly moving through the press to where they stood. Mrs. Devens was smiling and cheerful, but beneath was a hint she would have no nonsense. Her black hair framed a pretty face, and she wore a bright green dress that came to her ankles with a splash of white at the shoulders and hem. Over that, she wore a white apron with a pocket sewn to the front to hold paper and writing stuff for taking orders or making notes.

"Look at you!" Mrs. Devens clucked while warmly hugging Tara. She looked over Tara's shoulder as if she were simply surveying her inn for needy customers and lowered her voice after releasing the embrace. "Back from your ride, I see. Well, you will be wanting hot tubs and a good meal, no doubt. You certainly have come to the right inn for that." She took them all in with a satisfied smile as they gave voiced agreement or nods. Mrs. Devens seemed to gather them into a line like a mother duck does her ducklings and guided them through the common room and out to the bathhouse that lay just behind the stable.

A narrow, serpentine pathway of gray cobblestone wound through the vast stable yard, leading to an aged wooden fence behind the stable. As she opened the gate, a bathhouse revealed itself, its roof stretching over the cobbled patio, upheld by sturdy wooden posts. Round wooden tables, chairs, and benches provided a place to relax. Divided for males and females, the bathhouse had separate entrances, one in white and the other in green.

Mrs. Devens guided the ladies through the white door on the left. Inside, a well-lit room revealed elegant floor tiles, with benches and hooks lining the walls. A picturesque mountain scene adorned the bright white walls, creating a soothing ambiance. Beyond the entrance lay a hall for private access to the rooms, attended by the inn's staff for patrons' comfort. Baths and laundry services were available upon request. Copper tubs steamed, awaiting them.

Shutting the door behind her, Mrs. Devens opened the green door for Antoff and his friends to enter. Already the staff had been hard at work setting tubs and filling them with steaming water. The fresh towels, cakes of soap, and brushes waited in a warm well-lit room with green walls and the same tile with a central floor drain. Other than the color of the room and a picture of city life with men jubilantly eating and drinking at a party, it was the same.

Mrs. Devens addressed Antoff. "How will you be taking your meals tonight, Priest Knight?"

Antoff responded. "Private room well away from everyone, if you have it."

She nodded. "If you need anything, there is a bell and these good men will take care of those needs while I get your table set. All will be in readiness when you have finished here." With that, she bustled out to see to it. Before the door closed, Edward was already stripping for the tub he picked out. Unbuckling his sword belt, he leaned it against the tub so it was within reach. He tossed his cloak on a hook and pulled off his shirt. When clothed, Edward's physique was commendable; but shirtless, his rippling muscles, shaped from years of hard training, revealed a form that could easily be underestimated. Ivan was not far behind him and Antoff got to it as well. Ivan's skin, almost white, belied the lethal grace of his form that even unclothed bespoke an almost animalistic quality and power. Antoff, while being the oldest of the men, did wear his age well, his body strong and well-muscled from years of battle. His grizzled back and arms showed the crosshatchings of injury that had healed to scars.

Where the men had been less neat about the process, the women had folded their small clothing and hung everything orderly. They laid back and soaked the worries of travel away.

Tara commented casually, "Antoff is very taken with you, Al'len."

Al'len was taken aback, and her cheeks flushed. "I think he is just keeping an eye on me."

Cur'Ra chortled. "Is that what you think, girl? Half the time the man can't see anyone else and the other half he hardly can string three words together when he looks at you. And you are not very good at keeping it secret either. You are pining after that man as well, and you are both acting like the other does not know it."

Tara giggled, "It is a good thing, Al'len. We are happy for you, that's all. I, for one, am enjoying it. I have never seen that ice exterior so melted before. All we are trying to say is everyone already sees it and we are just hoping it works out. He needs you, even if he can't see it for himself yet."

Al'len, still blushing, said, "I didn't realize it was obvious. I do think he is handsome in a rugged way. I don't think he is interested."

The other women laughed.

The sounds of women's laughter carried into the men's side of the bathhouse. Edward smiled while scrubbing the remnants of the ride away. "They certainly seem ok over there."

Antoff rested his arms on the side of the tub, easing aching muscles and listened to the laughter for a moment. "It is good to hear them laugh after the last two weeks."

Ivan rasped, "Al'len is fitting in fine, don't you think Antoff?"

Antoff cleared his throat, "She sure knows what she is doing with the animals. That much is plain. Tara and Cur'Ra like her."

His complexion darkened a bit. "Cur'Ra is like a mother hen, always clucking about how nice a girl she is and I could use her influence in my life. Tara is not much better. Trying to push the two of us together all the time."

Ivan replied, "Listen, my friend, they just see what the rest of us do."

Antoff growled, "I am a Priest Knight, not a farm boy. My life has been dedicated to the service of the people for almost as long as I can remember. Right now, I have one mission. We all have *one* mission. *Keep Tara safe.* I have no intention of letting my devotions be diverted in what is the most critical and deadliest time in her life."

Edward put in, "I agree with all of that too Antoff, we are all thinking about that and ready to do whatever is needed. All we are saying is, life is short, and you should get whatever happiness out of it you can for yourself. Al'len is beautiful and smart and women like her don't come around very often, if ever, and you shouldn't eliminate that opportunity if it is there. Besides, we all see it. Maybe you should too."

Antoff jumped in, "Tara is a Torrent. Don't you understand? A living myth. Legend from prophecy come alive. The one hope we have seen from prophecy for a thousand years. Master Duncan believed she was the one who restores the balance to this shattered world. I believe that too. Do you have any idea what that means? If she dies, we lose all hope. But, know this gentlemen. That is not the worst of it. If the Dark Order gets her and turns her, the devastation that happened in the Shattering is a pittance next to the destruction that would be loosed on our world. I will not let that happen." Antoff's stone wall was up now, and he would hear no more of his happiness while the world teetered on destruction.

Edward and Ivan gave each other an exasperated look, but let it go.

The men exited the bathhouse first and waited on the patio for the rest to finish. After a few minutes, Tara and the others came out looking refreshed. Al'len's and Antoff's eyes met for a brief second and then he broke eye contact. He cleared his throat. "Let's see if our table is ready, shall we?" Motioning the others toward the inn. Ivan took the lead, followed by Tara, Cur'Ra, and Al'len. Antoff fell in and Edward brought up the rear. To the trained eye, it would look like what it was. A protection detail. But for most, it would be some patrons heading into the inn for supper. They passed the kitchen stairway to the bedrooms and into the common room where Mrs. Devens was waiting to usher them to a private dining room.

Their room was the furthest from the busy common room, and while you could still hear the roars of laughter and storytelling, it was bearable. The room was large, with a well-set table, high-backed padded chairs and a fire set in a hearth at the rear of the room. Polished brass wall lamps provided a bright warm light and the smells of the beast roast sat as the centerpiece of the table flanked by steaming bread just out of the oven, a bowl of vegetables, and one of a meat gravy made their mouth water. Antoff took the head of the table closest to the fire and stood waiting for the women to sit, as did the other men. Tara and the other women sat, and the men took their places. Mrs. Devens was pleased, and the serving staff came in just behind them with wine to fill the glasses. "I hope all is to your liking. If you need anything, just ring the bell, and we will get it for you. Please don't fail to ask."

Antoff replied warmly, "It is a feast, Mrs. Devens. Thank you." Mrs. Devens hustled the staff out and left them to their meal.

Edward stood and served Tara and then passed out the meal to others. Antoff took notice but said nothing. Here was a lad until recently, had servants to care for his every need, and now he happily served Tara.

Tara smiled at him, "Thank you Edward of Haven."

He leaned in close to her ear, "you know, you could just call me Edward." His eyes twinkled as he gave her a little wink. She flushed.

He put a hand on his chest and gave a little bow of his head. "It is an honor to serve you, Tara."

Antoff could also see he meant it. His loyalty was to her, and he served Tara before himself. That took some weight off Antoff to know his sword may not be the first to the fight to defend her. This lad would be at her side while he was taking care of other things. Ivan politely sipped wine and had some of the roast beast, but his body only required a small amount of mortal food to sustain it.

Cur'Ra spoke first. "This was needed, Priest Knight. I am glad you offered it." She smiled at him slyly to remind him he had given her little in the way of choice in whether she was coming.

Antoff inclined his head in acknowledgment.

Al'len added, "I was longing for a hot bath and a good meal; this feast is perfect."

Tara sighed hopefully. "They were clearing the floor for dancing in the common room. There may be a little time for it later before we go back." She said the last part, but it was with a daughter's pleading in her voice.

"Let's enjoy our meal first, Tara, and then we'll see what the night has in store for us," Antoff said.

Tara smiled at him. Antoff responded with a thoughtful grunt.

De'Nidra sat alone to wait for some sight of Tara. In many respects, she was as interested in the girl as in the Power she could bring her. The girl had no idea what was bearing down on them. If they did, they would not be at an inn having a meal. What they had dealt with before was children's play when compared to the threat that was only a day or so away. Antoff should have known better. This Priest Knight had fought in the campaigns and yet he was dragging his feet and waiting on the women, acting more like a father giving into a daughter than a warrior ready for battle.

No, there was something else he had up his sleeve, and she was curious to find out what it was. De'Nidra was not alone. Of course, she had a merchant guard sitting throughout the hall that could be employed if needed and while the Dark

Order would not attack here; they were watching. An agent of the order sat not ten strides from her, a corrupted host of the creature that inhabited him. A local man, a tradesman of one type or the other, he watched and waited. She had not found out the name of his inhabitant yet, but it was there. She could see that demonic intellect peering out through the windows of that soulless man.

And what of this other problem now that had presented itself? *Al'len.* Who in the name of all the gods was she, and why was she so unreadable? No, this woman was a problem, a powerful problem. Caution was required now. There were too many eyes watching to risk exposure, but she would discover her secret as well.

Ja'eam sat at the corner table of the inn nearest the door, sipping an ale, or at least it was his body. It was Sam'Ieal that stared out. Be'elota had done good work preparing this vessel, and while some rules had to be abided by to continue the authority he had. Rules that could not be violated or the vessel would slip out from under his control, and he would be expelled. Allowing his vessel to spend time with his family. That was part of it. Not only that, but Sam'Ieal could not interfere with, or hurt, Ja'eam's family in any way. So maddening to give up time to such trivial things as are required by mortals, but a deal is a deal, and he could not violate it.

This Torrent was important to the Dark Order, which Be'elota served. Sam'Ieal had to make a deal with him to gain access to this sweet mortal life. How frustrating! The cost of being pulled out of the depths of darkness was high, but well worth the sacrifice. For now, he was just to watch and report on the Torrent's movements, but he could be used by the Dark Order anyway they wished. That also was upsetting. Sam'Ieal could see how many of his kind had grown annoyed with the Dark Order. He would never be on his own. He would always be beholden to them. They believed he would never be free. But one day he would be. He promised himself.

He watched the mortals dancing about like fools, laughing and carrying on. When he realized he was tapping his foot in time with the music, it perturbed him. Why? There was an element of power this host kept beyond the deal.

Now that was troubling. Even more troubling was the fact he was not even aware he was doing it. What if he found out? Should he start focusing his efforts towards regaining full control? Did Sam'Ieal even dare let the Order know? No. If they thought him too weak to manage his host, he would be expelled and then replaced. Back to the void and eternal disembodiment.

Antoff could hear the sounds of music playing and the dancing of feet. Their meal finished. Tara looked at him pleadingly. He growled. "All right Tara, but not too long, ok?"

Tara stood and nodded, then flung herself at him in a laughing hug. "I will. I promise."

She turned to run for the common room, but Edward caught her hand. "Not without me, Tara. I am coming with you. Someone must keep an eye on you." She smiled at Edward and led him by the hand toward the common room in what was almost a run.

Al'len leaned in, her eyes amused. "They seemed to be quite taken with each other." Antoff still glared at the door Tara and Edward left through and only grunted. Al'len and Cur'Ra shared a look of amusement and held in their laughs.

It was a rough country song. The kind made for careless dancing and singing along. The kind that made Edward feel like he was a beacon, holding Tara's hand, his heart beating louder than the band, the singing voices, the clinking of ale mugs. They were a world within a world, standing amidst the crowd but feeling alone. He lifted her hand, inviting her to the dance floor. Though his lessons in dance had been of little use, he knew his aim wasn't the perfection of steps, but the perfection of her joy. He yearned for her laughter, her smile, and if he only got one, it would be worth it.

Tara's steel-grey eyes met his, dipping into the depths of his soul. They echoed an acknowledgement that she knew he was there for her. As they moved to the rhythm, Tara was a ball of energy and delight, her spirit echoed by the tempo. Edward was not the best dancer, not by her standards. But in this dance, he wasn't merely a man; he was the instrument, the conduit for her elegance and grace.

She moved like a dream, never missing a beat, while Edward, in contrast, was more akin to a swordsman in battle than a partner in dance. Yet, Tara relished Edward's clumsiness as much as she did the dance itself. His awkward steps were testament to his devotion to her joy, his determination to be by her side, regardless of any potential embarrassment. His eyes were for Tara alone and the love he showed stole her heart.

As the music ebbed, she stood flawlessly in the silence, radiant in the warm lamplight. Rising on the tips of her toes, Tara tenderly brushed a kiss against his cheek. In response, he turned to meet her lips with his own. Tara's eyes widened. She had never been kissed by a man, much less one as handsome as Edward. She leaned in further, hoping to capture his lips with her own. The unspoken yearning in her gaze was visible to Edward, fueling his desire. Just then, his attention wavered at the sight of Antoff emerging from the dining room. *By all the gods, why now?* Edward hoped he hadn't said that out loud.

Tara's eyes sparkled at him with a note of irritation that said she was thinking the same thing. They both let out a sigh. Edward's hand found Tara's, his warm, calloused hand engulfing her smaller one, pushing his fingers through hers and he gave a little squeeze. Tara gave a squeeze back, and they both huffed a laugh, shaking their heads at Antoff's lousy timing.

The others were not far behind Antoff. He did trust Edward to watch over Tara. He could hardly believe he heard himself say that. The boy had been such a terrible lout and his reputation with the local mothers had hit the point of scandal and infamy. Antoff kept one eye on the youngsters at the same time as he approached the bar where Mrs. Devens poured ale from casks and placed them on trays for her serving girls to pass out to waiting customers.

She smiled at him and directed his attention toward Tara and Edward, spinning with the other townsfolk and patrons. "It is so good to see them having fun." She said.

"It is," he agreed. "I wanted to ask for your help with a service I need done."

She finished placing the ale from the pulls on the trays and sent the next girl out to her customers. "How may I serve you, Priest Knight?" Mrs. Devens still observed the formalities of title and place even after five years of retirement and despite Tara and him inheriting Master Duncan's bookstore.

Antoff went on, "Al'len's cart broke an axle a league away and I was wondering if you would be so kind as to arrange for it to be picked up and repaired?"

Mrs. Devens smiled past him to Al'len where she, Cur'Ra, and Ivan stood not far away watching Tara and Edward. "Of course. First thing in the morning." Antoff pulled out his map and showed her where it would be.

Mrs. Devens lowered her voice almost to a whisper and leaned in closer to Antoff, holding Al'len in her view. "You do realize she is lovely, don't you?"

He cleared his throat. "That seems to be the consensus, yes."

Her smile deepened and her voice stayed low, and she continued to nod as if she was settling the cost of service for the night. "Maybe that lovely girl would do with a dance as well?"

Antoff dug coins from his purse as if on cue and added more besides for the cart. He gave her a small bow. "Thank you for the wonderful service, Mrs. Devens." He said as he stepped away from the counter.

Antoff turned. His eyes swept over the common room like a warrior about to charge into battle. He steeled himself and walked over to where Al'len stood with Cur'Ra and Ivan and bowed formally, extending his hand.

Al'len was taken aback again for the second time this evening and blushed. She froze. *I cannot act like a foolish girl*, she told herself. Cur'Ra placed a firm hand on the small of her back and the vile woman gave her a shove forward.

Antoff caught her hand. It was electric. Her mind spun. She was in a dream with him again. She was the maid standing upon a hill facing the rising suns, white armor trimmed in gold emblazoned in the light. Her long blonde hair waved in the wind the color of hay. She turned, and as her ice-blue eyes fell on him, her rose-colored lips spoke. "Can you see me, Antoff? Will you have me for who I am?"

Antoff spoke. "Yes, EL'ALue. If you will still have me, I will take you just as you are." He reached towards her as she walked forward. Her hand stretched out towards his. Already committed now. She fought to remain in slumber. She did it only by raw strength of will.

She came back to herself. It was all becoming so confusing. *Was she the Maid of Light or Al'len?* She cursed to herself as she allowed Antoff to lead her into the din. Mercifully, the other dance had ended and something slower she almost recognized as they began to play. Antoff put his other hand on Al'len's waist and began the lead. She followed and found a smile. She was dancing again for the first time in a thousand years. Her Priest Knight was all she hoped he could be. A brave warrior. A priest of the people. Kind and generous. Charitable. Hard as a stone and his heart as deep as an ocean.

Tara's mouth fell open. Edward was not far behind her. He was just standing there staring when he felt Tara give him a nudge. "Don't act like a boy, just dance, Edward. And stop staring!" She breathed.

De'Nidra could see Tara burst into the common room, dragging Edward by the hand. They laughed and danced as younglings do. Edward, now the disavowed future lord of Haven, was not a good dancer, and he knew it. While Edward may have been embarrassed and red-faced, De'Nidra could see much more. Yes, *much, much more.* Tara's face was beautiful but marred by the myriad of markings that would only darken and become more pronounced as her Torrent Powers grew. Edward was completely unaware of the thing that would scare the seven hells out of any man who understood what she was. Any other man who knew would run and keep on running. Not Edward. It was already too late for him; he was far too lost in her. Edward was more than loyal. He was taken in by Tara, and neither one of them had seen it yet.

De'Nidra could see it. Now, it was only a matter of how she could use it. The boy was so intent on the girl a dark demon's vessel just sat and watched unhindered by the Light's notice. Just when De'Nidra didn't think it could get any more interesting than the youngsters, Antoff and his troop filed in. Antoff paid his bill while the others watched. Then he turned and walked to Al'len and begged for a dance. Oh, this was indeed a priceless gift. A gift that would not be wasted on De'Nidra.

Ivan watched, grateful that mortals couldn't see through his eyes. Their blood pulsed and writhed in their bodies, calling to him seductively. The blonde girl sang her song, and the musicians played their harps and lutes, keeping time by tapping a tambourine. But it was the pulsation of their blood Ivan was listening to, until his eyes fell upon a well-muscled tradesman sitting near the door, quietly tapping his foot. It was this man's eyes that interested Ivan the most - they never left Tara. Something odd about him struck Ivan: his blood flowed in a slow, emotionless rhythm, akin to what Ivan had seen when mortals slept. Furthermore, the flush of the man's cheeks and the gritting of his teeth bespoke some kind of internal struggle. No, he was not there for the drink or entertainment - he was there for Tara.

Ivan moved with the grace of flowing water through the crowd. The vile man, whatever he was, did not see him coming, so fixated on Tara. Ivan's voice was low and threatening, like the growl of a wolf. "I don't know what you think you are doing, but I suggest you leave." The man's eyes met Ivan's with an unnatural rage, a detail not lost on Ivan.

"Mind your own business, friend," the man sneered, his voice smelling of ale and his mind slumbering like someone, something else, was driving the coach.

"I am not your friend." Ivan's eyes swirled from silver and gold to gold and blood red, his very presence exuding danger, "However, I am a friend to that girl over there whom you can't seem to take your eyes off of." Ivan leaned over him, making a show of his elongated fangs glinting in the light. The man's eyes widened as if he truly just coming to realize that the creature that standing before him was not mortal. "And if you mean her any harm, I will drain you dry here and now.

Just so that you understand the situation you are in. She is not alone. She will never be alone. I will be there with her, always."

The man tried to speak, but Ivan wasn't hearing him. He strolled back to the bar, took a stool, and sat down, watching him with ashy, white-muscled arms crossed on his thick chest.

The man or thing. Whatever it was. It got up under his gaze and left.

Chapter 19 Where are the riders?

"Where were the dragon riders when they swept down the valley? Did the call not go out? Did the horn not sound? Every time heretofore they came and threw back our foes. The riders are no more! The riders are no more!"

It was late, and the night was clear and crisp, with only the slightest breeze stirring the air. The moons passed overhead, casting a cascade of colors across the night sky. First light blue, then pink, and finally red as they began to slip below the horizon. Insects hummed their nighttime greetings, and Torchflies flew about, blinking their silent mating songs. Most townsfolk had gone home, leaving only the most stubborn inn hoppers about. Antoff smiled inwardly as they wearily rode two abreast toward the Cathedral of Light. The sound of Stingers echoed down the street, rebounding off the buildings. Except for the occasional passerby, they were alone.

Al'len rode her horse beside Antoff. Occasionally, his gaze would drift toward her, and he would be met with either a reassuring smile or her eyes locked onto his when he turned. Their eyes continued to meet. An undeniable attraction existed between them, one that neither could resist. Antoff squirmed uncomfortably in his saddle.

Tara, Cur'Ra, Ivan, and Edward all wore satisfied expressions or were in deep reflection. Their quiet reveries broken by a spontaneous discussion about the night or someone poking fun at Edward for his dancing, but it was all in good-hearted humor, and Edward took it well. The soft musings continued until they turned and headed into the old city. Riding through the ancient metropolis during the day awakened memories of old tales. At night, the city took on a unique aura. It had eyes at night, and occasional voices, and sometimes even feral animals roamed the darkness of obscured alleys.

No lamps were lit here, just darkness and the echoing of horseshoes on the wide streets. Gothic towers rose, crumbling and broken, lit on one side by moonlight. A stone tumbled from the heights of an abandoned building near an intersection just ahead of the group. The rasp of swords leaving sheaths came from Antoff's companions, and he found Al'len's sword had leaped into her hand as well. Shadowy figures with bows stepped forward and lined balconies, and a single man treaded out onto the street, holding up his hand.

"You can pass, but you will have to pay the tax," he commanded. He was tall, his skinny frame clearly underfed, clad in a ragged grey cloak over a disheveled white shirt, and brown pants, ill-fitting and filled with holes. There was a kind of desperation, a need on the man's stubbled face.

Antoff dismounted, the only one who hadn't drawn his sword yet. He advanced toward the man, who stood some twenty strides down the street. Tara had positioned her horse slightly to the side, likely to maintain a clear view to use her talents. "Stay here," Antoff ordered in a hushed tone. He heard Al'len's sword slam home in her sheath with more force than needed as she dismounted.

"Not tonight, Priest," she said as she stepped next to him. He grunted, "Okay, then the rest of you stay with Tara."

They walked about halfway to the man before he yelled to them. "That is far enough."

They stopped. Antoff inquired, "Are you the tax collector?"

"I am tonight," he answered.

"And how much are these taxes of yours?" Antoff asked cheerfully.

"Well now, that depends on how much you got," he said.

"You can't perform an audit from that far away, friend. How will you know we are giving you your fair share?" Antoff asked.

The man retorted, "You become adept at estimation in this line of work."

Antoff reached down, producing a purse heavy with the sound of fat coins. He dug into it and pulled out a gold piece, tossing it to the man. "I think that will cover it, then. Have a good night," Antoff stated firmly, his tone leaving no room for argument, as he turned to leave. But Al'len stood her ground, and the man took a step forward. She gracefully swept her cloak aside, revealing the hilt of her fine blade, which had an immediate effect on the man, stopping him in his tracks. The tension on bowstrings pulling to cheeks was audible.

"It is not enough!" The thug growled.

Antoff turned back to face the man. "You are aware I am a Priest Knight, aren't you?"

"Yeah, we know, and what of it? The Order of the Light has done nothing for us. Is that supposed to give you some kind of holy man's discount or something?" Laughter erupted from the darkness above.

Antoff let out a sigh. "No, I was just making sure you knew what you are getting into, that's all."

Tara sat astride her horse to one side, deep in the greater reality as it shook in a wash and time froze. While her body remained stationary, her mind moved disembodied along the balconies. Dirty-faced people in tattered clothing lined the floors with bows drawn to their cheeks. Some were old, some young, and some were little more than children. She remembered what it was like to run the streets as a child, scratching for life. Her heart went out to them, but she would not let them harm her friends. Concentrating on the string of each bow until they glowed hot as forge fire at the point where the arrow touched fingers and strings, she knew this would be the limit of what she could do without killing anyone. The Power roared within her, and her dragons answered with a roar of their own as they took sustained flight.

Ivan slowly slid from his mount, his hand creeping to the hilt of his sword. Beneath his cloak, the blood gem pulsed hungrily. His eyes glowed gray, spotted with gold, giving off an angry light. He had to make a choice, not one he would choose for himself if time allowed, but there was no time for such luxuries now. His eyes changed to blood-red, swirled in gold. He could see each person along the balconies lit up with life as the blood pounded in their forms. Tara sat on her horse, shining with Power like the sun. He knew he would never reach Antoff and Al'len in time, not even with his speed. He called to the shadows, and they answered him. Surrendered to them, and they slid forward and took him.

Edward held his sword to the side, and his Stinger pranced beneath him. He steered his mount with his knees, so it danced just ahead of Tara. If an arrow came for her, he would be the one to receive it.

Antoff fixed his gaze on the man. A part of him sighed in pain at the sight. Haggard and beaten, he couldn't let this man harm his...*family*. It wasn't just Tara he was protecting anymore; it was Al'len, Cur'Ra, even Ivan and Edward. Antoff's jaw clenched; a vein pulsed in his forehead. "Lad, I suggest you take the coin and move along. You do not understand what's happening." Antoff hoped he would listen. He had no desire to cut this man down, but he would. He would do it. As he expected, he only got mocking laughter in return. Resolve took place within Antoff. Desperation turned people into fools. This man was one of its victims.

The man reached beneath his cloak. All along the balconies, flashes of fire flared. Voices cried out with fear and pain as fingers were burned and bowstrings turned to ash with a snap, arrows clattered to the stone floors above. Al'len's and Antoff's swords flew into their hands. Ivan was spat out of the shadow below the building, just across from the man. He moved in a blur of supernatural speed, shadow trailing after him in wisps like spiders' webs as he appeared behind the tall man, drawing his sword to the man's throat. Overhead was the beating of wings. Two young dragons, one white the other black, folded wings tight to their bodies, rolled and dove toward the heat signatures lighting up the night below them. Their wings opened with a pop just before hitting the street. Powerful wings beat the air as they landed hard on the street before Tara. They roared in fury and the sound of it shook the air. Moments later, a dire wolf six feet at the shoulders rounded the corner just behind where Ivan stood. The great wolf's golden eyes took them all in. His hair stood up on the back of his neck. Lips peeled away from dagger-like teeth. He lowered his massive head and gave a deep, predatory growl.

Antoff barked at the man, "Are you done now, or do you wish to continue this silliness?"

The tall, skinny man spoke, his voice strained and weak. "We are done, Priest Knight." Antoff sensed a trace of respect in his tone as the man withdrew an empty hand from beneath his cloak.

"Release him," Antoff commanded. Ivan did reluctantly. "Have your people come down so I can have a look at them." Antoff ordered.

The man was reluctant, "I told you we are done Priest Knight."

Antoff understood his need to protect his people. In fact, that's exactly what he had been doing. "No harm will come to them. I give you my word." They both stared at each other, Antoff willing the man to see the truth in his eyes. The thug finally agreed.

He yelled for the others to come down and Tara, Cur'Ra, and Edward collected the horses and moved to join Antoff, Al'len, and Ivan. Dragons moved with their heads swaying back and forth, watching the road from twice the height of the Stingers. By the time they got to the others, a small mob of twenty or more crowded the streets around Antoff and Al'len. Ivan stood back with his dire watching.

Antoff's voice was harsh, "What were you thinking? You could have been killed. Or you could have killed someone. Is it worth all that?"

The crowd answered him, voices tumbling over each other, "We were hungry, no one cares about us, we have to take to live. Please forgive us, Priest Knight. You don't know what it is like to be hated for having nothing, to be cast out for being poor."

Antoff sighed quietly and spoke in a whisper, forcing them to strain to listen. "I can give you all I have, and perhaps it might feed you for a month, but then what?" He shook his head, his regret palpable. "Still, you would be just as lost as you are today. And in time, some number of you would be dead as other takers took from you." Antoff's voice grew stronger as he went on. "And so, what shall I do with you? Shall I give you an offer of service, or shall I turn you away?"

The mob's voices cried out desperately, "No, don't turn us away. We can work, we can serve."

Antoff's voice lowered again to a whisper they strained to hear, "You cannot serve me. I serve EL'ALue the Maid of Light."

Al'len stared at him. *Such a statement would have him stripped and flogged by the Order of the Light.* Her mind whispered.

His voice strengthened again, and he turned and pointed his sword at Tara. She froze. "But you can serve her! She is the only thing standing between you and these streets. I am not telling you that it will be without danger. Or some of you will not die. I am telling you. That if she will have you. If she will take your service, you will be cared for and loved. If you lose your life for her sake, she will not leave you in the street or a field. You will be mourned, missed, and remembered. You will eat what we eat, ride what we ride, and sleep where we sleep."

The mob ran toward Tara and fell in front of her. They cried out and their voices tumbled over each other desperately. "Please take us. Let us serve!"

Tara could barely breathe. Her voice shook. "I will. Go get your things. You are coming with me." *Now what am I going to do with all of them?* She thought. Outwardly she looked calm, but inwardly she was on the edge of panic. *I have no experience managing so many people. Feeding them, and clothing them. Does Antoff realize the needs of these people and the danger he is putting them in? But, I am committed now.*

The tall, skinny man started moving. Antoff's blade swung back to his neck. "Not you though. I have other plans for you. Do you care for these people? Would you give your life for them?"

The man firmed his voice. It shook a little, but he had steel behind his words. "I will." The thug said.

Antoff went on, "Do you see who they serve? Without her, what do they have? Do you swear to defend her with your life? Do you swear to come when she calls and go where she sends you without thought for yourself? Do you swear it before a Priest Knight of EL'ALue, the Maid of Light?" Antoff's sword burst into a bright radiance. "Swear it now, by your life or your death. If you can save her, you will!"

The tall man yelled, "I swear by my life or death if I can save her, I will. I will come when she calls and go where she commands me without thought for myself."

Antoff firmed his jaw and stared into the man's eyes so that ice shivered down his spine. "Very well then," Antoff lifted his left hand, placing his thumb on the man's forehead. "What is your name?"

Power surged through the man's body where Antoff's thumb touched his forehead. "I am Mikael."

Antoff's voice grew harder, "Mikael, I charge you in the name of the Light and bear witness before EL'ALue that you have sworn these things and I have marked you in your spirit that it will recall." Antoff recognized the man had his faults. Indeed, there is little question he would have killed one of them to get whatever coin he could to feed and care for his troop. Would he do something similar if he had been in the man's place?

Antoff brutally backhanded him across the face with his sword hand. The man crumpled to the ground. "And that is so your mind and body will remember it and keep your honor clean from this point on. What you do now is in the service of Tara and reflects on her." Antoff swung his sword to Edward. "That is Edward, her champion. Obey him." His sword swung back to the man lying on the ground, blood trickling from his mouth. "Kneel and look at me."

Mikael scrambled to one knee, his gaze locked on Antoff. The sword lowered to his left shoulder, tapping it. The brightness of the blade was blinding, and the tap vibrated throughout his form. "I name you Mikael, first of her guard." The blade swung over his head and tapped him on the right shoulder. "Defender of her life, honor, and keeper of her faith. Now rise and be recognized."

The man stood shakily, so that Antoff gave him a hand up. When he stood, he raced for Tara and knelt on one knee before her. She placed her right hand on his head and said, "I receive you."

Mikael's voice rang with strength. "Command, my lady."

Tara instructed, "Rise and attend me."

Chapter 20 The Legacy of a Pale Man

"Where are all our lost ones? They are more than gone. Have they fallen from our thoughts and our hearts? They become as lost in our minds as they ever were in the world. How have we put them aside? How did those lives mean so little?"

Va'Yone slept deeply. Though fully grown, Va'Yone's dark grey and small, much like a child. His dark black-brown hair was a messy mop to his shoulders. Pronounced ridges traced his face from his nose to the length of his long eyebrows. In deep brown, rumpled leathers, he had fallen asleep in the stable. The kind of sleep that comes from a long and uncomfortable ride in the open air. It was the sleep that comes after finding safety following a period of intense fear. A fire set in the forge had burned down to charcoal ash long ago, with only occasional embers giving a quiet pop. Aside from the stomp of a stabled beast or the smooth breathing of others sleeping, there was no disturbance in the stillness of the night. The only interruption was the outside breeze that rattled the walls of the aged structure.

A tickle deep in Va'Yone's mind did not wake him. It was like a light brush, and had he not felt it years ago, it may have gone unnoticed. Someone, or something, was ever so lightly searching. It was like a feather touch, swishing away some dust. There was a mind behind that touch - a very old and powerful mind. Unlike his childhood master, Lord De'von, this mind was not malevolent. It was dark, distant, and even lonely. Knowing he was being read, Va'Yone felt the presence doing the reading leave something of himself behind, like a signature that politely told him who was there.

Courtesy was something young Vam'Phires learned from the old, and it was done out of a traditional form of communication. Va'Yone, being a darkling, whose material had been drawn in part from Vam'Phires, knew the history of their communication traditions and was reinforcing lessons from the past. These gave inference to guide actions if he ever found himself alone and needing to endure. Va'Yone brushed back lightly. *I know you are here.*

"*Do you?*" the voice replied, only a little taken aback and with mirth. *Then perhaps you can tell me why you have an acquaintance with someone I know, and have missed for some time, left on your mind?*

"*Lord De'von?*" Va'Yone inquired politely.

"*Yes,*" the voice replied just as politely.

"*He is lost to you,*" Va'Yone replied sympathetically. Indeed, loss did travel across his mind - the loss of a stolen child and the loss of a pupil pulled away before needed knowledge could be passed.

"*Where? How long?*" the mind brushed back, questioning.

Va'Yone replied guardedly, but honestly. *No more than a ten-day. His death was a result of his behavior.*

The old mind came back with some confusion. *How can this be? I have lost all sense of him now for more than an age.*

Va'Yone stumbled with his reply. *I don't fully understand how it works. I will try to explain. There was a portal and wards made by mages. He could not communicate outside of the complex we were in. The portals were such that he could not cross the compressed time and his mind could not reach you because of the wards.*

The touch was still as light as a feather. *We should meet soon so we can converse in a more normal manner for you. I would like to see you with my own eyes, hear your voice, and meet your other friends.* The last part was said with mirth as well.

I did not mention friends, Va'Yone responded.

No, you did not, but I can see their images in your mind shrouded to protect them. With a little training, I would not have seen them. Your mind is very open. I know everything you told me was true, but I have an advantage in communicating this way. It would not be proper for me to continue like this. It is too much of an advantage and robs you of your opportunity for expression. Do not fear. I promise none of you will receive harm from any of mine.

Va'Yone took him at his word. *Very well, I will tell them you want to meet. If I reach for you, will you hear me?*

The mind replied, *I am not far. I will watch and listen.* The touch was gone.

Tara sat on her horse quietly. What was she going to do with all these people that kept coming one way or the other? More importantly, what was she going to do with Antoff? The man was like a father to her, but he seemed to draw lost souls out of the world at will. That, by itself, was not the problem. The problem was after he drew them, he promptly deposited them at her door with no more than a nod and some honor-bound words. *In the name of all the gods, what am I going to do with them?* She asked herself.

"What is the matter, Tara?" Edward asked. He saw she was upset.

She was trying not to show anyone her concern. These people needed her to be sturdy and assured of what the future would hold in her service, not more fear and certainly not added to the turmoil that was already present in lives being uprooted. She watched all the people calling friends and family to collect everyone and everything. A woman passed, hauling her husband behind her by his coat.

"Never you mind what we are doing. You just do what our lady commands and be quick about it, El'erl. That's no business of ours. Lady Tara knows what she is about. You just hop to it and tell your friends they better get it together quick, or I will come and help you men get it together. Ya, got me, El'erl!" He fended her off with a forced smile while pulling his stained jacket free, trying to wipe away an appearance of a man who had eaten a bad turnip. Schooling his face, he trotted over one street to fetch the others.

"Edward, what do I do with all these people? I expected twenty or so, but they've brought their families, relatives, and friends. The gods only know how many that is going to be! Edward, what am I going to do with all of them?" Tara's eyebrows furrowed, her forehead creasing with concern. She let out a tired sigh.

Edward cleared his throat and leaned in closer, acting as if taking instructions from her. "Tara, you are not alone, you know? After all, I am your champion." He gave his best smile and a flourish of his cloak. "Besides, I am going to start training these men and some of the younglings to hold a spear and use a bow, so they are not defenseless if something happens. You need to get everyone started on a normal routine of some kind. Once you separate who among them has trades and skills we can use, set all these people to work, and it will start to fall into place."

She looked at him pleadingly. "Edward, can you show me? You've known these things from youth, but it's all new to me."

Edward gave a beaming smile. "Whatever you command, my lady." He said this with more voice than was strictly necessary so the others passing by would hear him, and then he inclined his head and bowed in his saddle the way a warrior would who just received instruction from his queen.

Mikael moved his people along as Lady Tara had instructed. He had a purpose and duty pressing down to his bones, and it was heavy. He did not understand it. Everything had happened too fast. The power of his oath throbbed deep within him, and it consumed him. A glyph had risen on his forehead where the Priest Knight had touched him, and it was as if a god of Light looked down upon him, judging his heart and service. If this was a tenth of what it was like to be a Priest Knight, he was glad he was only in the service of a fine lady like Tara.

"Get your hides moving there!" He had already left Lady Tara out of his sight for too long and needed to get back. His people, no, *her people*, had finished filling an old wagon with belongings and were slowly pushing it out of an abandoned stable yard. They did not have a horse between them, but that did not stop more than a dozen men and women from pushing the thing out onto the wide street and around the corner, back towards Lady Tara. He sighed to himself and strolled over to the wagon. Placing his hands on the wagon's gate, he put a shoulder into it and pushed.

Antoff led the way back toward the Cathedral of the Light. A line of people followed behind them. Al'len had ridden up next to him. She said nothing, but it was obvious she was deep in thought and working something out. She rode in a warrior's way, with her hand on the hilt of her sword, back straight. Moving as if she had become part of the horse. She must have been born in a saddle, and she didn't seem to even notice it.

Antoff cleared his throat. "You know if something is troubling you, Al'len, I am always happy to listen?"

She turned her face toward him, and her ice-blue eyes swallowed him up. "Would you now? Antoff, you are all Priest Knight, aren't you?"

He smiled back, "Sorry, it's a habit, but I am quite happy to help if I can. Nothing you tell me will be passed to another. You have my oath on it, Al'len."

She raised an eyebrow at him. "Antoff, you can't keep swearing yourself to the Maid of Light in front of people like that. If it got back to your order, they would charge you with heresy."

He nodded his head. "You are right about the liturgy and how the Order of the Light would see it, but that does not change the facts, Al'len. EL'ALue is the Maid of Light. I saw her. I gave my word I would take her as she is and not how men want to see her. To do less is a betrayal of that oath."

She became stern with him then. Her voice was hard. "And if they charge you with treason, Antoff, what then? I will tell you what, they would kill you just to protect what they want everyone else to believe!"

His eyes regarded hers, and his face became like stone. "So be it if that is how they want it. I know the truth, Al'len, and I will not deny it. EL'ALue is the Maid of Light, and I follow her. She can dispose of me in whatever way it pleases her."

Her eyes still froze him in place. "However, she sees fit." She mused, "and you don't think she will abandon you in your time of need?"

His face was still stone, "I said. However, she sees fit, Al'len."

She gave herself a shake. "Well, whatever happens, Priest, you can be sure I will be there to see it."

A knot in Antoff's stomach loosened. He had not even realized it was there. "You are staying, then? You have seen the danger, and you know at least, *in part*, what is at risk, and yet you are choosing to expose yourself to that risk, knowing it could cost your life?"

Her eyes did not leave his face. They swallowed him and held a promise. "I do."

In the darkness of the night, they rounded the corner into the square of the cathedral. The dominant figure of the central fountain was a lonely Priest Knight on the back of a proud mount. Ram'Del, the Defender of the Light, stood alone, holding himself separate from the world, just as he had in life. He still tried to bring hope, and no shadows of the night could diminish him. A banner with the binary suns in one hand and an upraised sword in the other completed the picture.

Tears leaked from Al'len's eyes as she passed by. *Never again*! She told herself. *I will fill this one with more than selflessness. He will know he's loved, needed, and valued beyond a vain idea of sacrifice. This one shall not die. This one shall live.*

The sounds of hooves and unfamiliar voices entering the square stirred the watch long before they came into view. It was not as if no one knew something was going on. Va'Yone drew his cloak around himself to ward off a chill, what with dragons taking to the skies and dire wolves leaping about. It was getting so a respectable Darkling could hardly sleep at all, with voices in the night tickling your senses. Every time Tara or Antoff went out of earshot, things categorically went wrong.

Va'Yone stood alone in the stable yard, at least to the casual eye. He scrubbed his hand through his black hair; the wind whipping it into a messy mop. Not alone exactly, the desert Elp'hars were slinking about as they always did, but to the casual eye, he was alone. And he had learned others lived here beyond bloodbats and scaly eight-legged rodents. The Elp'hars had claimed they were "good eating," but he had found the meat stringy and the flavor off, even with all the spices. Elp'hars had a peculiar sense of taste. What was more disturbing, based on his nighttime conversation, there was a nest of Vam'Phires close by. Deucedly polite Vam'Phires, but it was unsettling to be sure.

The troop, followed by a bedraggled band of ruffians, sauntered around the corner. It became plain to Va'Yone Antoff and Tara had been at it again. As the troop dismounted, Va'Yone went to report the "meet and greet" with the Vam'Phires.

"Va'Yone," Antoff gave a nod. "You look like you didn't get any sleep?"

Va'Yone wanted to give this Priest Knight what he had coming. Especially after leaving him behind with the Elp'hars and their rodent stew. "No, I did not sleep well with all the uproar. Dragons roaring, wolves growling, and Vam'Phires talking to me while I was trying to sleep."

Antoff investigated his face. "What's this about Vam'Phires now?"

Well, he heard that part at least. "Yeah, that's right. An old Vam'Phire was rummaging around in my head while I was sleeping and wanted to set up a meeting between us. We killed one of his flock, and he is wants to get to know the ones who did it. Before you get your armor in a bunch, he was sad. Not angry. Very polite."

The conversation did not escape Ivan's ears. He handed his reins to one of the new band and walked over. "Well, the old stories are true, then. There is a population living nearby. Funny, I could not sense him, but you did."

"He can hide from people he doesn't want to see him. He has a very skillful awareness," Va'Yone said. "And who are all these people? Looks to be more than fifty, and they are still trickling in?"

Ivan's eyes swept the stable yard and rested his gaze on Antoff. "Take it easy, Va'Yone. It was that same compassion that snared you. Antoff can't help himself."

Va'Yone watched the din pass by.

The dragons watched the whole procession stream into the stable yard while lying beside the wall near the gate to the rear exit. Tara directed the women to the rectory kitchen and lower barracks where the Priest Knights once took their lodging. Edward likewise set the men and older children to quietly gathering wood outside the wall in the thicket, obscured from view. Beast-less wagons were pushed into the yard and unloaded; belongings being carried into the cathedral. The wind still moaned and gusted. Voices called with a hurried insistence. Life had returned to a dead place, and it seemed to Va'Yone the ancient structure had brightened somehow to receive them.

Antoff placed a hand on Va'Yone's shoulder, walking him up the stairs toward the rectory. "Va'Yone, let's meet your new friend."

Antoff, Al'len, Ivan, and Va'Yone ventured deeper into the cathedral's halls. Their footfalls echoed off the walls, trailing through the dust that had remained undisturbed by mortals. Small animal tracks were everywhere, evidently exploring the interior for any food that had long since vanished. Ivan walked along behind them gravely. Al'len did not appear to be the least bit ruffled by the prospect of an undead any more than Va'Yone was. When the light from the lived-in area had diminished, they stopped.

"Can you call for him now?" Antoff asked.

Va'Yone nodded. A solitary man stepped into the dark hall from an adjacent room. Tendrils of smoky spiderwebs still clung to his seven-foot-tall form. Dressed in an all-black leather long coat, tooled in silver along a burgundy lapel and upturned cuffs. *Pale* did not describe his complexion, as his flesh was almost white. The eyes, however, glowed with an angry light, and his presence emanated awe and fear. All but Antoff and Al'len began drawing blades instinctively.

Antoff raised his hand and whispered, "peace," and his companion's blades slid home again.

Al'len smiled as she thought of how Antoff's voice commanded with a whisper.

The tall man swept an elegant bow. "Allow me to introduce myself. I am the chronicler of our clan. You may call me Da'Vain if you are so inclined."

Antoff and Al'len returned the old form with equal respect, bowing with the same depth and a sweep of the arm, ending with a fist pressed to the heart. "Honor and Truth," they spoke as one. Antoff and Al'len caught each other's eye. Al'len smoothed her face. Ivan's hand still rested comfortably on the hilt of his sword. He had not taken his eyes from the ancient Vam'Phire, nor even moved a muscle.

Da'Vain smiled a bloodless smile. "Honor and Truth, yes, we should try to keep those words with one another."

"I am Antoff Grant, and this is Al'len and Ivan. We likewise will give only honor and truth." Antoff's voice still spoke low. "Though I did not know

Darkness can know either honor or truth." Antoff ended his sentence with a raised eyebrow.

Da'Vain replied hushed as he slowly closed the distance between them. "Just because we hide in the darkness does not mean we are neither civilized nor lack enlightenment. Nevertheless, it shall be honor and truth between us, Priest Knight, so long as it holds. How shall I say it to you, then? Honor binds me to be civil and truth compels me."

Ivan was watching Da'Vain with inquisitive eyes, but his stance was still predatory, looking for signs in case of an attack. "Why did you want to meet us?" Ivan asked. Da'Vain's eyes found his and paused briefly, then went on, addressing all of them.

"Lord De'von was our child, Knight! He was our prince! What can you call a thing that steals children in the night from their loved ones? Steals the passing of treasured experiences and needed life lessons? Can we call that an act of the Light? Even with the passing of time, it has not dimmed the pain or the sorrow of that loss. And what do I find now but the child we lost, held prisoner and experimented on by the very order that claims the Light and a superior code of morality? Here stand the very mortals that found our stolen child, if only to inform me you have taken his head!" Sorrow and anger were apparent in his tone.

Antoff felt deeply ashamed of the depth of folly his order had fallen to. "I cannot fix this wrong. I cannot undo the pain it has caused you and yours. I can only say I am sorry. It does not fix it. It does not bring him back or change the travesty of the wrong done. However, I stand with you in this judgment. We, meaning my order, were wrong, and you are due repentance, and I will do whatever I can to give it to you when my task is done."

Da'Vain smiled bloodlessly. "I have time, Priest Knight, and I can afford to wait." He backed away as the shadows reached for him, and he was gone.

Chapter 21 To Haven

"Emotions, like materials, are both rough and smooth. Their surfaces, light and dark. Having peeled away the layers of each feeling, word, and look. I've sanded and polished their surface, painting them in colors both vivid and subdued, and I have placed it in the sun. I see my work's imperfection. My failures to catch the light. Still, I sculpt and refine with a more focused sight. This sculpture is my journey. My search to see you clearly in a perfect light."

Antoff sat alone on the dark stone steps at the rear of the Temple of Light. He had sat down before reaching the ground floor of the stable yard, well below the foundations of the abandoned church. The night was chilly, and sitting on the gray stone pulled the heat from his body. The air smelled of new spring, filled with the scents of freshly planted farmers' fields and the decay of a lifeless city. Unable to sleep, Antoff pretended to check on the horses. He never reached the bottom of the three flights of stairs, stopping in frustration at eye level with the stable's roof. Beyond the battlements, the field of tall grass swayed with the wind, and the trees sighed as the waves reached them.

I have run out of time. I avoided the decision, and now fate has made it for me. He must seek the help of his friends in the Order. Like him, they had all gotten old, and most retired to the Haven Rectory. He could not hope to keep Tara alive alone. He needed more help than a collection of wayfarers could offer. *I don't doubt their hearts.* Antoff knew everyone, if needed, would give their life to save Tara. The problem was that they would all die, yet the Dark Order would still take her. He had to protect Tara first, but there was no way she would abandon these people now that she had accepted them as her own.

Dammit! Had I been more selfish, just this once, we might have fled faster and further. That never was going to happen, dragging this circus with us everywhere. Furthermore, he had a responsibility to everyone here, and he could not abandon it now. He dare not take anyone with him, and not because they should stay here and watch after Tara while he is gone. Edward could not go. Banished by his father, who is also the ruler of Haven. No, he would pull the guard down on them before he got a hundred paces from the city gate. Ivan was definitely out. Explaining away consorting with a Half-Dead prodigy of Vam'Phires and demons wouldn't end well for either of them. Al'len? No, he couldn't involve her in this. Besides, Tara leaned on Al'len and Cur'Ra for everything now. Managing the day-to-day operations of caring for the troop and the animals. No, he would have to go alone. There was literally no one he could take with him.

Antoff stood up, brushing himself clean of the gray dust that coated everything around him, and walked towards his horse to saddle it. He quietly opened the stable door, which was left ajar for warmth from the forge, and slipped inside. Flame flickered in the forge as he gently closed the door behind him. As he saddled his loyal Stinger, it nuzzled him and greeted him with a soft nicker. Antoff touched the plated snout and patted it to calm it down.

Sneaking away wasn't easy as the stable was being used as a sleeping area for those who needed the warmth from the forge. Yet, Antoff planned to leave a message with one of the desert Elp'har before riding out of the gate. He planned to reassure them he would return in a few days and there was no need to worry. As he turned to lead his Stinger out of the stable, he almost collided with Al'len.

"You're going for a night ride, Priest?" she demanded, her bright blue eyes shone in the darkness.

He almost jumped out of his skin, but he recovered, hoping she wouldn't notice. She smiled at him. She had noticed. He led the Stinger out with Al'len in tow.

Al'len quietly closed the door behind them. "Well?" she demanded.

Antoff quietly replied, "I've got to go to Haven for a few days. I was going to leave word. Tara needs everyone here with her, and I didn't want a debate."

Al'len's eyes widened in disbelief. "Debate!" she huffed, her voice tinged with a mixture of concern and frustration. "You are worried about everyone and afraid our blood will be on your hands if you don't get help."

Antoff felt an unnerving chill, as if Al'len could peer into his very soul. "Yes, Al'len. Tara will stay here and try to protect these people, and you will all die, and the Dark Order will take her! I cannot let that happen." He breathed a ragged breath and calmed himself. The last thing he needed was everyone coming to investigate raised voices. "I had thought about asking you to come. Really, I did, but Tara needs you."

Al'len's eyes narrowed intently. "Did you now? She needs me? What about what you need?"

"Tara needs to be protected, and she needs you. She comes first, always." Antoff spread his hands.

Al'len recognized the conviction in his voice. "All right, Antoff, I will let you off for now, but don't think we are done with this. I am going to bring this up again when you get back. You need to leave your beliefs about EL'ALue out of your conversations, Antoff. I am not asking you to lie. Just don't bring it up." She was pleading with him now. "They will arrest you. Promise me, Antoff."

"I will not deny EL'ALue, but I will be careful. Al'len, cover for me with Tara. Just tell her it couldn't wait until morning."

Al'len was still staring at him. "Oh, I will tell her, Priest Knight, but you are going to owe me, and I always collect." Her eyes were like deep pools, and he forcefully pulled his eyes away from hers before he could get lost in them again.

Antoff swung into the saddle, and his Stinger danced beneath him. "I am sure you will." he said, yanking his prancing Stinger around and booting him into a trot.

Al'len met Tara at the door. She was already hustling toward the stable to ride after him. Al'len placed herself firmly in the doorway, blocking her way. "He wants you to stay and care for your people while he rides alone to Haven for help. Tara, he wants to go alone."

"Why?" Tara cried.

Al'len grabbed her chin and pulled her eyes up to investigate them. "You know why, Tara." She drew her close and hugged her. "Don't worry, child, his goddess will watch over him. She has watched him for a lifetime. You can be sure of that."

"What about what I want!" Tara said.

"What do you want?" Al'len whispered.

She pulled away from Al'len with her fists balled at her sides. "Fine, I'll tell you what I want. I want to have a little piece of land in the Garden Wood or Leaf Water. I want children, a garden, and a man who loves me. But I didn't choose any of this. It chose me and stole every dream I ever had."

"I understand," Al'len replied calmly. "Is that why you push Edward away?"

"What!" Tara shouted. "I don't love him like that! I told him so."

Al'len laughed quietly. "Yes, I know. I listened to your proclamation."

"No, I mean it!" Tara railed. "He is a reckless boy I am trying to keep from killing himself over foolishness."

"You're yelling." Al'len said, placing a finger to her own lips in a quieting motion.

"I am not!" Tara yelled. She said it again, this time in a lower voice, "I'm not."

"Yes, you are. Your problem is you love him, and you are afraid to let yourself fall any deeper in love because you don't want him to die, not on your account. You want to live with the illusion that if he dies, you will hurt less. That is childish. That is not how it works. Tara, I loved a man once. I poured all I hoped he could be into him. But I withheld what he dreamed of, my true love. And when he died for me, I was so deeply cheated, robbed. I robbed him as well. He wanted more from me. He wanted to hold me and love me and be that great man for me. In the end, all he could offer in demonstration of his love was his death. He gave himself to me in death, and I robbed us of what we both wanted, what we both needed most."

She was weeping now openly, and the tears ran and did not hold back. "We both needed each other." Tara's eyes were running too, and she hugged Al'len.

"It's okay," Al'len whispered, her voice trembling. "Don't make my mistakes, child. Love your man."

"I will if you do," Tara said, her eyes welling up.

Al'len hugged Tara close. "I promise."

EL'ALue slumbered deeply, lost in timeless dreams. She saw the desolate shrine atop the Steps of Glass. From her vantage point, gazed out over the glassy peaks, and down to the charred fields where her beloved had died.

Ram'Del, Defender of the Light, rode astride his white dragon horse gallantly, leading his Army of the Light into battle. Their golden-trimmed white banners, emblazoned with binary suns, whipped in the wind as Ram'Del thundered with divine Power, fueled by his love for a goddess and his desire for the woman who refused to confide in him fully.

Suddenly, the Torn Flowage erupted with a horde of nightmare creatures, pouring onto the battlefield like black oil spilled on the ground. Their howls for blood echoed across the land as they charged forward, driven by their relentless savagery and thirst for violence.

Ram'Del raised his banner, rallying his troops for the fight ahead. "This day we fight! Whether we survive or die will never be forgotten! We are fighting for the truth! We are fighting for the love of all we dare not lose! So, whether we live or die, all we love will be preserved! Henceforth, no one will forget we gave our all, for the Light and for Love!"

The call rose like a wave from the Army of the Light. "For Light and Love!" they shouted, charging forward to meet the black mass in one last flash of Light upon the field. Ram'Del, thoughtless of himself, bravely rode, dirt spraying up around him. He gave himself one last longing look toward EL'ALue, the Maid of Light, before dying. He could not see her, but he knew she was there. EL'ALue the woman, not the goddess, reached out in her pain and regret. She struck with all her fury and love. The field exploded in a flash of Light and flooded the Vale Lands, accompanied by a blast leveling the outskirts of Coth'Venter. A cloud rolled upwards brightly toward the suns, climbing high into the atmosphere, consuming the clouds, and leaving circular rings in the strata of the heavens' rose-colored sky.

Winds rose over gray stone battlements, blowing across the stable yard and down the cobblestone path that led around the Cathedral of Light to the square. The statue of Ram'Del stood atop the fountain, making a good, mustering point for the volunteers. Wooden swords clacked and arrows thumped home into targets made of burlap stuffed with straw in the shape of a man's torso, backed by wood hung on a tripod. Edward was shirtless and held a wooden sword opposing his challenger. Sweat dripped from Edward, but he did not seem affected by the heat. A man who stood across from him was older, larger, and well-muscled.

"Again!" Edward yelled. The larger man moved forward, swinging his practice sword. Clack, clack, clack, and slap, as Edward repelled the blows, sliding below his opponent's sword and finding his flesh with the final blow. "Don't hack at me like a side of beast! Do it as I showed you. Again!" Clack, clack, clack. "That is better. Who is next?"

Tara leaned on the balcony rail well above the square. The roof of the cathedral covered her in shadow. In days gone by, the bishops addressed crowds and armies from here. Tara was watching Edward. Tara's gaze lingered on him, her thoughts swirling as she contemplated how to approach him now that she had decided on him. But what would she do if Edward didn't feel the same about her as she did about him? She saw all the people in the square practicing. "There are like seventy of them. Where are they coming from? Every day I wake up, and more keep sneaking in right under my nose. How many did she have now? If these were new, there would be almost two hundred now, including children. How am I going to feed all these people?"

"Mikael," she said. She knew he was there, standing in the hall. He only left her when she sent him on missions. She smiled at the word she used when she needed to be rid of him for a while. This time she was killing two Hornbees with one arrow. The last thing she needed was him watching her 'review the troops' when what she wanted to do was moon over Edward. The other thing was she needed to talk to him, and a summons would work better than sideswiping him in a dark hallway. "Please go down and request Edward to give me the pleasure of his company at a private dinner to discuss important matters this evening. I will send you with the location once I am aware of where it will be later. He is to make himself ready for our meeting."

"Yes, my lady," Mikael answered, already at a run.

Mikael ran as fast as he could to Edward to inform him of Lady Tara's command. Edward watched him coming at a run. "What is it, Mikael? Are we under attack?"

Mikael's sides heaved. "No, my lord. Lady Tara has commanded the pleasure of your company tonight at dinner, and she will send you word of when and where. She commands you to stand ready for her summons, my lord."

Edward wiped his brow with the back of his hand. "Why? What did I do?"

"I don't know, my lord, but she's serious."

"Well, whatever I did, I will be ready when she calls. Tell her I said that," Edward commanded.

Mikael started to run and yelled over his shoulder, "I will tell her, my lord!"

Tara and Cur'Ra cooked a meal for Edward and had set a simple table in an unused dining room. The local ladies cleaned and freshened the room, all the while asking her all kinds of questions, trying to drag her plans out of her. Tara took her leave to get dressed for dinner. When she reached her cell, she could hear Al'len quietly humming to herself.

"Tara, is that you?" Al'len asked.

"It is," Tara replied.

"Well, since every woman in the temple is already gossiping about what they think you are up to, did you get everything ready?"

"Yes," Tara answered. She could hear the splashing of water and smell rosewood soap mixed with lavender. "Mikael's wife Sylara made me a dress, but I have not had time to try it on until now."

"Let me see then," Al'len called.

Tara's cell was only steps from Al'len's. She was, in fact, surrounded most of the time, day and night.

"Here I am," Tara said, stepping in front of her door while standing in the hall.

Al'len's breath caught. "Tara, you are stunning."

Tara's dress was of a simple cut - above the knee, reddish-purple with a rose-colored blouse that may expose more bosom than Antoff would find proper. And matching slippers. Cur'Ra had done her hair in the fashion of the Elp'harean girls. The way mothers do when giving permission to find a life's mate. Hair long and flowing naturally like a river with moons stones bedded in a thread, fine silver mesh woven in.

"It is perfect," Al'len said.

Tara giggled and hugged Al'len.

Al'len sighed, "Well, almost perfect, it's missing one thing." She went on in a flatter tone.

"What is it?" Tara exclaimed.

Al'len held out her hand, unfolding her fingers to expose a necklace and earrings set with fire opals. "These." Then Al'len helped her put them on.

"Thank you," Tara said. "I promise I will not lose them, and I will return them when I am done."

Al'len laughed. "Oh, lose them if you want to. They are yours." She said as she turned and hugged her. "Now, let's have a look at you." She held her at arm's length. "Yes. You are way too lovely for that lout, but since you are set on him, I guess he will have to do."

"Mikael?" Tara called.

"Yes, Lady Tara," his voice came from the hall.

"I am ready for you to escort me to dinner."

He turned into the open cell hall and answered, "Of course, Lady Tara…" He stammered. "My lady, I have no words."

"That's a pleasant change," Tara said, while holding out a hand and giving him a fond smile.

Edward received his summons from Tara shortly after. Mikael stood at his door. "Lady Tara will receive you now, Lord Edward."

"What is it?" Edward asked. "Am I in trouble for something?"

Edward had a white shirt on with puffy sleeves in the style of Haven gentry, black leather britches, and matching knee-high boots.

Mikael looked him up and down and cleared his throat. "Oh, I think you are definitely in trouble."

Edward hastily buckled on his broadsword while following him down the hall.

"I can't say what her plans are for you, but they appear to have changed. Lord Edward, we best not keep her waiting."

They walked at a deliberate but sullen pace. The doors to the dining room were closed, except for a local woman with a cart and trays coming towards him. Mikael pushed the door open, and Edward went in.

Tara was standing with her back toward him, facing a fire crackling in the gray stone hearth. A silver mesh held moonstones that sparkled in her hair. As she turned and faced him, the fire drops caught the reflection of light and her eyes burned his words to a whisper. "You summoned me, Tara?" he swallowed hard.

"I did. I summoned you to ask you something and to have dinner with you."

Edward stepped forward. "You can ask anything of me, Tara, you know that," he replied.

She gave him a nod. She rung her hands together, a habit Edward noticed she did when she was nervous.

"I wanted to tell you-" She started pacing near the hearth. Edward's heart was in his throat. He went to her and closed the distance between them, putting his hands on her shoulders, stopping her from pacing.

"Look at me Tara." She did, her eyes shining with unkept emotions. "Now breathe." He commanded in a low tone. She did just that. "Whatever you have to tell me, just say it."

She gave a nodded. "I wanted you to know that- that I don't love you as a member of our group and I don't want you to think of me like that either, like I'm a lady you just have to serve." Her voice stayed strong, though there was a little shake and fear that he would reject her. *What would she do if he did that?*

Edward gaped at Tara. "What do you mean by that? You can't send me away. I swore my blade to you," Edward protested. *Did she not know how much he needed her? How much being with her meant?* Edward's heart thundered in his chest, "Just tell me what you need from me. What do you want me to do?" His eyes took her in. She was a vision, an angel. The woman he loved, and she did not even know it. He was a warrior, and this was a battle he would fight. Everything hung on what she wanted, but if she tried to send him away. He would resist.

Tara's eyes focused on him, her voice certain. "I will need more than your blade, but only if you want to."

"What is it, Tara?" he asked, his voice trembling.

Tara stepped forward, an unseen cord controlling her, drawing her towards him. It had always been there between them, this filament, connecting them like a string between their two hearts.

"Tara, you're scaring me," Edward whispered, his voice betraying his vulnerability.

Tara stepped forward, her heart pounding like the rhythm of a battle drum. Her voice trembled with unspoken longing, yet it held a resolute determination. "Edward, you're scared?" She drew near until he could feel the warmth of her breath mingling with his. Her scent, a delicate blend of lavender and rosewood, enveloped him, grounding him in the moment. Her hands found their place on his chest, and the sensation was electric, sending shivers down his spine.

His eyes locked with hers, revealing not only desire but also a deep yearning for something far more profound.

"I want you, Edward," she whispered, her voice a fragile echo of her heart's desire, "and I want it to be as a man. I want to love you as a man. Do you understand?"

A fleeting smile tugged at the corners of his lips, though his eyes were earnest. "You already have me, Tara, you know that."

"No, I want *you*, Edward, as everything. Warrior, friend, protector and most of all, as a lover," she repeated, her words like a mantra, a plea to the fates themselves.

He gently took her hands, holding them as if they were precious treasures. "I want you too," he confessed, his voice filled with a mix of longing and certainty.

Without hesitation, she pulled him close, her heart beating in rhythm with his. "Then kiss me," she entreated, a mixture of anticipation and vulnerability in her voice.

He chuckled softly, a sound of both amusement and tension. "Antoff is going to kill me, you know that," he playfully warned, though his eyes held a fire that matched her own.

"I know," she replied, her voice a whispered promise, a secret pact sealed in the space between them. And then, as if the world had shrunk to just the two of them, he kissed her, and everything else faded away in the rush of emotions that surged between their lips.

Chapter 22 Lies of the Ages

"Truth? What is the truth? It is pure and cannot be tainted by personal selfishness, nor can it be altered to make it more pleasing to the ear. The truth about us does not bend to the lie. Thus, changing the truth's meaning to make it more palatable is to change its essence. The truth is not here to please us. It is here to lay us bare with a surgical blade and expose our deepest insides to the Light so Darkness has no place to hide. The truth shines, and those who have the humility to embrace it shine with it."

Antoff rode urgently toward Haven. He did not push his Stinger beyond its limits, but he also did not slow down. He had ridden without stopping since leaving RavenHof over a day ago. The road flanked a deep, lush forest, ending one league before the shining white walls of the Lands of Light.

As the suns rose, the walls shone with a luminous glow. Antoff straightened his back and firmed his jaw, and his Stinger pranced in response to his mood.

When he approached the gate, he was not alone. He knew she was there. EL'ALue was watching him, and he felt a sense of mutual trust and faith between them. He had stood before her in a dream, but it was real to him. *Yes, EL'ALue. If you will still have me, I will take you just as you are.* Suddenly, the sound of his warhorse's hooves resounded and echoed off the walls. He shone like a blazing paragon, and the guards stood aside, not daring to challenge him. They placed their right hands on their hearts in salute of the true Priest Knight of the Order of the Light.

Antoff sensed EL'ALue's gaze and the trust she placed in his devotion. He tapped his mailed gauntlet over his heart and gave the guard a distinct glance in review, then a crisp nod to show they were to his satisfaction as he passed. He knew they would stand taller and prouder and speak with kinder resolve for the rest of the day.

The passing of a true Priest Knight left the folk astonished. Such things were told in a story, but never seen in this day. Not like this. News of his arrival would spread like wildfire through Haven. It became easy to say a person was a Priest Knight because they could say the words, or clad in armor, and looked the part. Some see the garb, and it is sufficient for them. But when you see purpose driven by truth, it is like an arrow seeking the target. Released, it will always hit its mark .

Al'len was humming the song from their dance and smiling to herself while working on a wagon harness in an empty stall in the stable, feeling the trust and love Antoff had for her pulse through their bond. As EL'ALue watched, she stirred. Al'len wondered what would become of their relationship. Would he see EL'ALue only as a goddess, or would he also see the woman that loved him? She made a vow to herself: *I will not let him forget the woman. I will not repeat the mistakes of the past. This one will recognize me first as a woman, above all else.*

The reality of how she saw him was already affecting him. The image in her mind was becoming a construct intertwined with his understanding of the world and himself. As they reached for each other, the wave of reality took shape, and they were both changing. This was why the old gods had agreed to sleep - the shape of reality depended on who their lives became intertwined with.

Cur'Ra's voice interrupted her thoughts. "Al'len!" Al'len startled and blushed. "I see you smiling and daydreaming. I know what you're doing."

"Don't sneak up on me like that!" Al'len said breathlessly, her hand at her heart.

Cur'Ra sighed, "I have been standing here, listening to you humming and daydreaming, wondering if I should interrupt you while you are pining over that man or just leave the wagon master sitting in the stable yard. You ordered grain for the animals, did you not?"

Al'len stormed out. "I will take care of it!"

Cur'Ra smiled. "I'm sure you will, and the gods help him when you finally do."

Antoff rode towards the rectory. Mothers nudged their children forward, men bowed their heads, and even the elderly strained for a clearer view, every face painted with quiet reverence. Some reached out, trying to touch his foot or leg as he continued down the cobblestone streets. His warhorse pranced high, each step echoing past parades and royal processions, with the crowd parting and closing behind him.

In the bustling market district, he caught his reflection in a large window. It mirrored back not just an aging priest, but a formidable Priest Knight. An unspoken aura seemed to whisper, "This one is my chosen!"

He rode past the imposing Haven Cathedral with its powerful stone arches and twin spires, towards the rectory on the opposite side. This smaller temple, with its adjoining stable, hadn't changed in eons. Much like the historic Temple of Light in RavenHof, clerics and knights came and went, their deeds inscribed in the library's sacred books. Antoff had often sought guidance and inspiration from these tales of old.

Rounding to the stable yard, a young awestruck monk approached to take his spirited steed. Dismounting, Antoff gave a nod of thanks, then entered the rectory's rear. He had just missed the morning prayer.

"Well, the air in the Grey Area has done somebody some good!" A familiar deep voice echoed. Turning, Antoff faced a towering figure in a cleric's robe, Mel'Anor. The two shared a hearty embrace, Antoff grunting at Mel'Anor's strength. Pulling back, Mel'Anor appraised him, "I heard you'd entered the city during Brother Dor'rean's oft-repeated sermon on 'Pride the Ruin of Mortality'. I can now recite it verbatim! Yet your arrival seems to have stirred more excitement. Our god has been distant lately, but word of a 'True Priest Knight' passing through spreads fast ."

Antoff replied, brushing off the implied importance, "I simply rode through the gate, as I have countless times."

Mel'Anor, wearing a broad toothy grin, clapped him heartily on the armored shoulder. "Back for good or just visiting?"

"I have a problem, Mel'Anor. I need your counsel."

Understanding filled Mel'Anor's eyes. "Come, let's find a quiet place."

Ivan practiced his sword forms in the depths of the lower temple. His blade moved fluidly between various styles, relying on muscle memory to recall the old techniques.

"Those are old forms," Da'Vain replied from the shadows. "Is this the blade taken from our lost child?"

Ivan tensed at his voice. "It is."

"May I see the blade?" Da'Vain asked.

Ivan spun the sword, so the blade landed in the crook of his arm, and the pommel faced outward in his hand. Da'Vain stepped out of the shadow to examine it. "I wonder, do you know the story behind this weapon?" he asked.

"No," Ivan admitted. "But I would very much like to learn whatever I can."

Da'Vain smiled. "Very well. It will be my pleasure to teach you. Before the Shattering of the Balance, it was not just the mages of the Light who wanted to capture us for their use, but also those of Darkness. One night, the Dark Order sent demons to take us to use against the Light. We were beaten. Beaten until one of us, who had been well-trained with the blade before he had undergone the change, took up his sword. He defeated the strongest of the demons and took this very blade. The minions of Darkness retreated, taking the injured with them. They have never returned. From that day until this one, the overlord of our coven has carried that blade."

Da'Vain handed the blade back to Ivan.

Ivan took the blade and thought better of it. "Here, you take it."

"Should I?" Da'Vain asked. "I think not. You are aware of the intellect and hunger your sword has?"

Ivan nodded.

"It is for this reason the blade can only be passed to the next in line or taken by one who is worthy to assume the position should his mind begin to fail. You did the latter by taking it from the former. I don't want it, and there is no one else to take it that has the strength to deny the hunger of the blade or its lineage." Da'Vain began backing away. "For tonight, that is sufficient." He bowed low formally, and the shadows took him. In Ivan's mind, he heard the whisper. *I bid you good night, Lord Ivan.*

Chapter 23 Falling Night

"The world is a canvas; interactions are our brush, having the power to shape how others perceive reality. Thus, it's crucial to approach our speech and hearing with mindfulness, as they can leave a lasting touch, like ripples on a pond. Each of us is a storyteller, embracing our inner selves and directing our influence through words. Let us treat lives like gardens. Our speech and deeds grow life, and death's power is pulled like weeds from our words, our actions, and our life."

As Antoff and Mel'Anor spoke, and their numbers gradually increased, their brethren silently took their seats, extending invitations to trusted friends and loyal armsmen in a steady flow. Whenever a newcomer arrived, an informed individual would discreetly brief them, ensuring they were up to speed before they contributed, answered questions, or dispelled any misunderstandings. Soon, the library was no longer occupied solely by aging clergy and knights; those present who trusted them had also invited younger members. Of course, not everyone in the order was called to share in the conversation; in fact, within the city, many were not invited at all. Nevertheless, the room grew uncomfortably crowded.

A young woman stood. "If this girl hasn't chosen between Light and Darkness, why should we intervene?" she addressed Antoff. "Shouldn't fate decide the course?" Silence enveloped the room; even EL'ALue seemed to listen.

Antoff scrutinized the young Priest Knight, pausing before responding. He attempted to recall his own youth. *Have I ever been that young?* He asked, "Your name, Knight?"

"I am Tes'sus of the Third Order of the Light," she replied.

"Well met, Tes'sus," Antoff acknowledged her with a nod. "If we are to stand in the Light as EL'ALue does, then we advocate for the sake of truth. We cannot idly watch as Darkness engulfs a people in distant lands. Our actions are not self-centered; but compelled to confront Darkness wherever it seeks to overshadow the Light. The Light embodies truth and love. Therefore, I submit I genuinely care for Tara and her people. If I pass judgment on them and, by my failures, they perish, the Light that shines upon me will, likewise, judge me. I am a Priest Knight of the Order of the Light, sworn to protect those threatened by Darkness. So, if the Dark Order appears and we do not resist the Darkness, what does it say about our Light?"

Antoff gestured toward the sky. "Each morning, the suns rise and shed Light upon our world, and we do not question whether they will rise the next day. Each day they faithfully appear, and we trust in their Light. But if those suns do not rise, how could we look towards morning? How could we trust in their Light?" He paused, allowing the room to hang on his every word. "I must return to RavenHof before Darkness descends. But I have not come here to persuade you. I have come so that you may answer your calling. Rise! For the sake of Light, Truth, and Love!"

The room stood in unison. "For the Light, Truth, and Love!" The resounding call reverberated through the square, and once again, EL'ALue had shaken the Haven Cathedral of Light.

De'Nidra, the Daughter of Shadows, reluctantly whispered into the ears of sleeping, greedy men. She had no choice but to follow the instructions of the

Dark Order, lest she lose her position. Her informants had overheard Antoff Grant professing his loyalty to EL'ALue, the Maid of Light. De'Nidra cared little for such distinctions; what mattered was the bishopric of the Order of the Light had turned against the Maid of Light, seizing her Power after the Torn Flowage incident and the death of Ram'Del, the Light's greatest hero. EL'ALue, devastated, destroyed leagues of the Grey Area. Wary of mortal greed, the elder gods slumbered, leaving mortals to exploit the gods' Power for their own desires. The gods, whether through gift or action, became entangled in civilization's petty struggles. Mortality, as always, stained everything it touched.

A man knelt, shivering before the High Bishop Er'laya of the Order of the Light. The Grand Hall of Light was very large, with scaffolds of seating lining the walls for those in attendance and an expansive gallery above for a more private arrangement for those with the credentials to use it. The ceiling displayed vast murals painted in gold, clad with glorious scenes of battle and dramatic compositions of divine Power. Here and there, scenes of mercy, forgiveness, and love dotted the vision that lined the Grand Hall. There would be none of that mercy on this day. The heresy this man spoke of needed a swift conclusion.

High Bishop Er'laya stood from his elevated gold-worked dais, some five spans higher than the man who knelt. His blood-red gown dripped with golden fringe and jewels, and his overweight, overfed bulk nimbly navigated the marble stairs to the huddled man. "These accusations are gravely serious, and because you were delivered here in bonds only exacerbates the concern. Antoff Grant had always maintained the reputation of purity and favor in the eyes of EL'ALue. But this notion he has feminized our great god disgusts me. EL'ALue is what EL'ALue is, not male save in battle and neutral in all else."

"While we have allowed females to continue to hold rank as Priest Knights out of regard for old traditional historical views, they do not occupy elevations of the clergy or have access to the canonical writings beyond the limits of that station. Antoff Grant, a full Priest Knight of our very order, that has so defamed EL'ALue in public, is grave indeed. Therefore, it is the judgment of the bishopric that Antoff Grant is to be arrested and brought here before us to answer for these crimes. It is further our judgment that he be stripped of the title and position of Priest Knight and banished from the Lands of Light until such time as he is brought before us in chains. That this excommunication shall be posted and abided by in the Lands of Light, and a price be placed upon his head for this grievous insult to our god. Let this serve as a warning and an example to all that would harbor or follow this heretic and let them be judged under this same judgment should they fail to repent and comply with our most righteous commands."

The wind sighed through the Redleaf, rustling the waist-high yellow grass that rippled like waves with each gust. Va'Yone sat under the shelter of the trees that lined the Dan'Nor meadow, feeling the grass with his bare feet, outside the protective walls and battlements of the Coth'Venter Cathedral Of Light. He glanced up from the ancient tome he had borrowed from Da'Vain to see Tara playing with two juvenile dragons, who were chasing a dire wolf through the tall grass. To anyone else, the sight would have been madness, but these creatures adored Tara, and she fearlessly ran towards them, laughing as they feigned attacking her before scampering away.

As the dragons grew larger, their feeding requirements became more demanding. The two now had to venture out beyond the Steps of Glass to get enough meat to sustain them. Tara approached. Va'Yone returned his attention to his book, trying to make sense of the diagrams explaining the inner workings of a Mage Gate. Tara nudged him in the ribs and grinned.

"Hey, I thought you were going to help me figure out this spell?" he said.

"I am," she replied.

Va'Yone smiled. "Okay, see here. I believe I grasp the diagrams, but the symbols don't make sense to me. No one speaks this language anymore."

Tara peered at the page. "Let me see. Do you agree that to use the gate, you must know your starting location and your intended destination?"

"I do," Va'Yone concurred. "But these symbols are perplexing."

Tara pointed, "Take this formula:

$$ds^2 = -e^{(2\Phi(r))} dt^2 + (1/dr^2) dr^2 + r^2 (d\theta^2 + \sin^2 2\theta \, d\varphi^2).$$

And $\Delta x = \sqrt{(\Delta t^2 - [(1 - 2r)/c]^2)}$, then lines link each symbol to an image.

This one," she pointed to ds^2 =, "must signify distance and speed, and t is for time. This line that leads to r likely denotes a location on the map or in space. θ and φ are at an angle to it, and the line leads to a point on the map or in space. Φ is the shape of the gate opening. On the other side of the page, the same symbol, but the shape of the opening is different."

Tara was clever, but Va'Yone struggled to follow her explanation. "I'll have to take your word for it, Tara," he conceded.

Tara closed her eyes while the Power raged all around her and focused her thoughts, envisioning the complex equations and symbols in her mind. She pictured the gateway as a twisting tunnel, a bridge between two far-off points. The equations reflected the curvature of space-time created by the massive gravitational fields of the two endpoints, and the symbols described the geometric properties of the tunnel itself.

In her mind's eye, Tara perceived the Mage Gate as a ribbon of pulsing energy, enveloped in a shimmering halo of strange matter. The ribbon bent and flexed like a living thing, stretching through the fabric of reality to connect distant places. She channeled raw flows of Power into the strange matter halo, stabilizing the gate's fragile structure and preventing it from collapsing in on itself.

Tara opened her eyes, and two small orbs of light floated above her palms, connected by a faint ribbon of energy. "This is the Mage Gate," she explained, holding out her hands for Va'Yone to see. "It's a shortcut through the fabric of reality, a bridge between two points in creation. With enough energy, we can open it up and step through to the other side."

"Now I'll just feed them with Power." Then the two lines split the air where the lights had floated, and small purple globes of light snapped into place and hovered above Tara's hands, pulsating. She stepped back and picked up a small rock. Walking over to one globe, she tossed it in. It appeared from the other globe on the opposite side and fell to the ground. She let the Gate wink out.

Va'Yone handed her the book. "Here, you need to study this and teach me, because I don't understand it." he started walking back to the cathedral.

She called him. "Va'Yone, where are you going?"

"My head is killing me and clearly this book hates me, so I think I better lie down for a while. I have had too much sun because it's way too bright for me," he replied sarcastically.

Tara laughed at his antics and acted like her hands were claws and started to chase him. "Do you want me to carry you?" She swung her claws.

"No, Tara, leave me alone!" He laughed while she raced him to the gate.

Edward was talking to Cur'Ra and Al'len. He risked a sly wink at Tara, which earned him one raised eyebrow as she passed the gate with Va'Yone. Edward went on, "We are going to need a lot more arrows, so I have set some guards to make them. However, we will need more than they can produce if we must defend ourselves. Cur'Ra and Al'len agreed to pitch in and volunteer anyone with idle hands to craft fetching and shafts."

Al'len nodded. "Yes, but we will have to forge the heads or buy them. We could send our people out who know the city to find all the metal scraps. They can melt it down with the forge and pour our own."

Cur'Ra agreed, "Sylara will know who to send out and get them working on it. She will have them pouring arrowheads by afternoon if I risk a guess."

It was not long before wagons full of metal started returning, full of every type of scrap the pickers could lay their hands on. Edward was betting there wasn't a hinge, doorknob, or gate left anywhere in the city, and that may include RavenHof as well. He felt it best not to ask if he didn't want to know the answer. A group of people worked on heating and cutting the metal, while another group poured hot metal into sand molds made of clay. Around the corner, a group worked on purifying local clay to surround sand packed with wax broadheads that melted away when the metal was poured in.

By the end of the day, the speed of production was such that any smithy would have been proud. By the time the next day arrived, there were bundles after bundle of arrows in barrels all along the battlements and in the towers. With baskets of arrowheads, shafts, and fetching still being processed into arrows. Al'len had suggested they start producing boar spears using the same method. She thought they might get thirty to fifty done by the end of the day.

Edward had managed to buy, trade, or steal thirty more horses with saddles and tack, and had begun training some guards as light cavalry the next day. The smithy scraped together wooden shields with metal strapping, which would serve to deflect arrows and light blows. It was the heavy spears with long shafts Al'len had designed that made them deadly if he could manage to teach them to hit anything. He also outfitted them with horse bows, but had completely depleted his savings. He could borrow more if needed on his stipend, but he wanted to leave that credit open in case he needed to hide Tara.

Modred descended purposefully, his powerful form landing on a mesa overlooking the vast sea of troops marching towards the vale. His gaze locked onto the War Mage. "Mel'Temdel, send scouts to the outskirts of Coth'Venter. I want to know everything about the Torrent's position by nightfall."

Mel'Temdel nodded, his voice steady. "As you command, my lord."

Modred surveyed his horde. Five hundred heavy horses, twelve-fist-strong of Zoruks, and fifty Camolisk riders. In addition, eleven of his brothers stood at his side. Against so meager a foe, now an unstoppable force. He knew the city and temple well, and he knew he and his mages would crush anyone who dared to oppose them. Modred smiled confidently, his victory over the Torrent already assured.

Chapter 24 Truth Rides Again

"Some speak of the evil of the world as if it dwells in the land, sea, or air. The foundations of El'idar do not bear its weight. Nor the sky, or the winged creatures within its embrace. Does the sea bear its mark of evil? No, it doesn't lurk in those briny depths. You cannot find the evil there. We must look within ourselves. We alone have the power to choose between good and evil. It is our responsibility to wield that power well, to do what is right, and to keep our world free of all that has dwelt in you and in me."

Lightning forked across the sky, its distant thunder shattering the night's silence. The storm began gently, like a feather's touch, then escalated to an icy gust. Events build slowly that way; we rarely stretch our view beyond ourselves to see the signs of the coming storm.

Rain pelted down, droplets pinging off armor and splashing up in Antoff's eyes. The heavy horses' hooves thundered, splashing mud in a wide arc. Occasionally, the odd pedestrian got the full effect of fifty-five Warriors of the Light passing by. Yet they withdrew their curses, hands clutched to their hearts. Hope still rides.

Antoff rode at the column's front, scanning the road. As he had done so many times, but never in such weather. This rain was coming down in sheets, making it difficult to see more than a span in front of him.

The storm drowned all else out; thoughts drifted back to words spoken earlier, just before the breaking of this day. He knew the real battle was not against external forces, but against the Darkness that dwells within each of us. He had waged this inner battle countless times and would continue until his last day. The untamed thoughts and feelings released into the world. But tonight, he rode through the storm with his comrades at his side. He felt a sense of peace. He knew that despite the Darkness and evil in the world, there were still people willing to fight against it. As long as there are men and women of conscience, the Light will never die.

They approached the city of RavenHof. Antoff could see the flickering fire, hear battle and people shouting. He hoped they had arrived in time. With a renewed purpose, he urged his horse forward. Hope still rides.

Tara slept. In the background, the higher reality raging within her and all around her. Light and Darkness fought, trying to tear each other apart.

"Wake up, child," Cur'Ra shook her.

"What is it?" She helped Tara up and began pulling Black Thieves' armor from a grey stone shelf.

"The enemy is here," Cur'Ra said as calmly as if she was saying the weather had changed.

Tara worked quickly with her help, putting on the armor, belting twin short swords on her hips, and slinging her white-bone short bow and arrow-laden quiver over her shoulder. Images flashed in Tara's mind as her dragons spoke of the coming doom, sending vivid visions of hot life pouring from the vale in a long stream. A second group, though not as large as the first, moved towards the far northern side of the abandoned city, attempting to find a way inside.

Cur'Ra wore earth tones, with a short sword at her hip, a longbow held in her right hand, and a quiver of broad-headed arrows stuffed full crossed her back.

Her defiant green eyes showed no fear. The sleeping cells and halls were empty; not one person remained inside. Tara didn't wonder where they were; they had planned for the defense of the grounds. Everyone knew their place, even the last defenders of the children.

Tara exchanged glances with Cur'Ra but spoke few words. However, not everyone adhered to silence. The rain poured down, accompanied by lightning and thunder. Al'len stood at the top of the battlements, unfazed by the storm. She wore a white cloak trimmed in gold, with a white dragon outline in gold flapping in the breeze. On her left hand was a knight's shield, also white and trimmed in gold, while her heirloom sword hilt and buckle bore the same signet. She still wore the tight-fitting tan leather outfit that had made Antoff stumble over his words, but tonight, she looked every bit the warrior.

"Where did you get that shield and cloak?" Tara asked with surprise.

Al'len smiled back. "What, this old thing? I must look the part. Besides, it's likely I'll need more than just appearances tonight, so there's no sense sparing the good stuff. Listen, Tara, don't use your magic. I believe they will have magic of their own, and you'll shine as bright as the suns to those mages if you throw fireballs and lightning around."

Tara turned her head and looked straight into Al'len's deep blue eyes. "You seem to know a lot about magic, battle, and Priest Knights for a ranch hand, Al'len." She finished with a smile.

"Yes, I do," Al'len answered simply, not bothering to explain further. A look passed between them, one of understanding and trust. Tara knew this wasn't the time to ask questions, so all she did was nod.

Atop the towers and battlements, Elp'har archers stood with bows in hand, arrows knocked, their gazes fixed on the night. Volunteer guards stood scattered along the wall.

"Where might Edward be?" Tara questioned Al'len, her gaze darting about.

"He's led his light cavalry to scout the grounds' perimeter. And he's placed some archers on the front balcony, a spot you seem fond of mooning over him," Al'len noted teasingly.

"That was strictly uncalled for." Tara grinned. "Not all the time. Not more than you daydream over Antoff."

Al'len wiped the rain from her eyes and chuckled.

Strange as it was, amidst the army advancing toward them, Al'len stood there on the wall, unchanged. When she said she was with them, she truly was.

"My Lady," Mikael's voice called from below. "You'll get yourself killed out here. Please come inside, and I'll stand on the wall in your stead."

She smiled down at him grimly and shook her head. "Regrettably, I am afraid you all will need me tonight. I have seen this host from far off. I am not sure I can do all that will be needed. There are so many."

"My Lady, what of Antoff, our Priest Knight? He has not yet returned?"

It was Al'len who answered. "If I know the man, he is riding hard for us as we speak."

Edward rode at the head of two columns of light cavalry. He had drilled them mercilessly for ten hours the previous day. While they weren't as skilled as seasoned riders, a lucky charge could still inflict damage. The thundering hooves of their horses nearly drowned out the tapping rain on Edward's armor. His shield still bore his father's house symbol—a fist holding two lightning bolts—on his left arm. Like his lancers, he held the long-handled boar spear tipped up, securely set in a lance cup attached to the right stirrup.

However, one lancer had decorated their spear with a pennant—a new standard featuring a black and white dragon facing a fist with two lightning bolts. It came as no surprise Tara's ladies had been spreading gossip far and wide. Every woman he encountered seemed to know what was going on, making it clear he would suffer a terrible fate if he broke Tara's heart. Well, he had earned that reputation; he had been a lout. The good wives of RavenHof had a valid point.

Halting the column just past the fountain, Edward barked out an order, "Lance, shift abreast!" The two lines of lancers neatly fell into formation, fifteen on each side, shoulder to shoulder with him.

As the Zoruk scouts skittered into the square on the slick cobblestone, a tight knot of anticipation formed in Edward's stomach. Memories of past battles flashed before him, and the weight of leadership pressed down. Whispering to his lancers, trying to maintain a steadiness in his voice, "It has begun. Post Arms!" Boar spears swiftly pulled from the stirrup cups, and the broadhead tipped down, maintaining a uniform angle along the line. The horses frisked anxiously. "Hold the line!" he ordered.

The disorganized group of thirty or more Zoruks was difficult to count. Despite their chaotic movement, their hodgepodge of armor and weapons—spears, cleavers, axes, and crossbows—were undoubtedly deadly. The Zoruks surveyed the square and the fountain, with Ram'Del, the Defender of the Light, sword raised high. They seemed as if they might turn and run until fifty Camolisk riders emerged into view. The commander's guttural scream sent the Zoruks charging toward Edward's lance.

Edward's Stinger warhorse pranced and strained beneath him, eager for its rider's command. "Death or victory! We fight for Light! We fight for Love and until our last breath! Charge!" Edward cried out. The warriors called out, thumping their fists against their armor, the sound echoing like a drum around them, and then the lance charged.

Wherever the minions of the Dark Order moved through the town of RavenHof it burned; its buildings consumed by voracious flames twisting like whirlwinds. Thick smoke billowed into the sky in acrid plumes, choking the air and obscuring the moons. The Zoruks had descended upon them with brutal force, breaching the main gate and leaving a wake of destruction in their path. They littered streets with the fallen bodies of both Zoruk and the townspeople, their blood staining the cobblestones. Townspeople, their hearts filled with fear and anger, fought back valiantly. Gripping any weapon they could find, they stood united against the overwhelming odds. The Zoruks, driven by a relentless hunger for conquest, had set their sights on the abandoned city, and the people of RavenHof feared it was only a matter of time before they returned. Determined to protect their town and their loved ones, they wielded makeshift weapons, ready to confront the enemy once again. Their lives and freedom hung in the balance, and they refused to surrender. If the battle were to be lost, the cost would be immeasurable—their homes razed to the ground, their lives shattered, and their spirits crushed.

Va'Yone perched on a wooden stool, balanced below a narrow crenel spaced between two merlons on the high battlements. Behind him, an Elp'har stood with a smirk.

"Oh, go ahead. Laugh it up, pointy ear. You'll be grateful to have me when the Zoruk's start climbing the wall," Va'Yone jested, his eyes scanning the horizon for any sign of danger.

Hoth'Le, the Elp'har, chuckled softly. "I'm sorry, Va'Yone. If you find your viewing angle lacking, please let me know. I can adjust your stool."

Laughter erupted down the wall as the soldiers awaiting the upcoming battle joined in, releasing their nerves before the imminent fight.

Tara watched from the tower above, her heart swelling with pride as she glanced down at Va'Yone. He had become like a little brother to almost everyone, and it was hard to believe he was a grown man, young though he may be. Often, in the past, the children who had played in the stable yard stood head and shoulders taller than him.

As Tara steadied herself against the rough surface of the tower, letting her fingers feel the chisel marks to keep her mind grounded, her dragons flew high above the enemy forces, obscured by the clouds and out of arrow range. Despite the wind and rain battering their wings, they kept a steady flight, their movements graceful and majestic.

Tara focused on the mental pictures streaming into her mind—a dizzying mix of heat and cool vaporous images. She could feel the wind and rain on her skin, even though she was safely ensconced in the tower. The images flooded her mind while the dragons were in flight, were still new to her, and a particularly dynamic move could make her stomach churn.

More than a thousand enemy soldiers flooded onto the field opposite the road beyond the tree line that sheltered the meadow of rolling grass known as Dan'Nor. What made it so challenging was not just one stream of images, but two. At first, it overwhelmed her, but gradually she learned to separate and even blend the streams. The dragons communicated with each other in images that created a mental resonance, which could be almost unbearable, but they used it to find each other in flight.

Despite the minuscule time lag it took for the images to travel and seeing the others' perspective of the lay of the land, they could still get a good sense of their location. Understanding the dynamic was complex, but Tara had figured it out. One dragon had gone hunting in the Steps of Glass, and the other was about halfway between them. It took a little more than one and a half seconds to reach the first one, and then about three seconds for the image to reach her. That means the first dragon was about ninety Leagues away, and the second dragon was about forty-five Leagues away. Before long, the time lag did not mean much as her mind, like theirs, automatically calculated the time lag as it related to distance and the speed of flight.

To her white dragon's eyes, a bloom of light appeared like a ribbon on the field behind the main army, blossoming into a sphere, then riders poured from it like a flood. Now that Tara did recognize. She remembered it from her and Va'Yone's study only a day or so ago. *Good Gods, It was a Mage Gate*! They were using a Mage Gate to summon more troops.

In the stable, people diligently followed Cur'Ra's instructions. She utterly dreaded the battle and injuries that were going to come. *Can you prepare for so much death? Battles, though necessary, are such a waste of life. There were always wounded, and being connected to the strings of life when they failed was a loss that stripped away something deep. A part of me died with every spark of life that was blown out. The memories of their injuries never truly left. The process of healing and the intimate bond between us, how life flowed through their bodies like a symphony that had gone awry when they are hurt.*

The victims, when injured, lacked the energy to repair the damage. I had failed Tara in her guidance. I had taken from my energy reserves to heal them, despite having taught Tara that one should never drain energy from oneself, as it could be fatal. I had broken the rules so many times; this battle could very well be my last. Telling Tara about my condition, knowing she would not have let me take part in the battle, was out of the question. Someone might need me, and these people could not rely on this power to heal. No, I would rather spend my last moments in love and lose this life than live knowing I had failed them and abandoned myself.

Cur'Ra and her team collaborated to establish a triage system, with Cur'Ra's understanding that she would prioritize her loved one's over herself if they got injured. Backboards and clean bandages, compresses, and hot water were like the herald that comes before the storm.

Chapter 25 The Coming Storm

"Amidst the trumpet's call and the fury of war, bravery and cowardice stand exposed."

The storm raged on, rain poured down in buckets, and Edward's heart pounded in his chest as his light cavalry charged forward. Arrows whistled through the air as they approached. Out of his peripheral vision, he could see the line still holding strong. Hooves of the horses splashed and rang in unison on the cobblestones of the square. His charger tensed just before lowering its head, unleashing the full force of its mass into the Zoruks' front line, trampling them down like fallen hay. Mortals and horses alike screamed as spears struck home, and they wheeled away six riders short of their original number.

Amidst the chaos, Edward's voice rose above the din. "To the Cathedral of Light!" With determination, they rode hard across the square, dodging arrows whipping by. Suddenly, a fleshy thump and a scream echoed as one more victim fell to the hard stone and lay motionless. Twenty-three plus himself. They were now twenty-four.

Edward spun his mount just before the grand stair leading to the cathedral's entrance, the wet stone causing his Stinger to slide and nearly lose its balance. "Ship spears and pull bows!" The line reformed next to him, shields sliding to their backs as the warriors on horseback smoothly knocked arrows with the butt of their spears cupped in the stirrup, and heft leaning on their shoulders. Edward surveyed the fallen on the square. While the charge had been costly, it had a good effect, reducing the thirty-plus Zoruks to only seventeen. Even though bodies lay motionless on the stone, the seventeen Zoruks still charging were ready to strike. The fifty Camolisk riders counter-charged on their giant color-shifting lizards, blending with the gray stone square as the Zoruks split around the fountain, screaming their vengeance.

"Ready!" Bows drawn to their cheek. "Steady!" Edward commanded. "Fire!" Arrows flew in arcs, not just from his twenty-three riders, but from ten more on the balcony above. Four more Zoruks fell, squirming. "Fire at will!" and the arrows flew once more.

The Warriors of Light galloped through the destroyed gates of RavenHof, their well-drilled warhorses jumping obstacles and the dead without slowing. Antoff took in the burning buildings and charcoal-smudged faces, but he did not slow. A cheer from the townsfolk went up as they rounded the corner, heading for the Cathedral of Light. The warhorses galloped, the anticipation for the coming action plain in their step and arch of neck. They passed by the familiar balconies where he had collected the wayfarers and turned the corner on the last stretch before the cathedral square. Ahead, the street was plugged by a throng of Zoruks spilling into the main square where only the statue of the Champion of Light, Ram'Del, opposed them. Yet there was a voice rang clear through the din. It was Edward's, "Arrows Loose!"

Edward watched as the last of the enraged band fell, only strides from the front of his shrinking line. Yet all was not done; the fifty Camolisk riders were at a full run, their bodies snaking towards his line in a dizzying array of colors, shifting as they surged ahead. The Zoruks that sat on these oversized lizards were larger and better armored and armed than the ones had been on foot. While the armor was still a mixture of what could be scavenged, it was clear they were much higher in the picking of the prizes that came from battle. And undoubtedly, they had been in many. The weapons they carried were of a higher quality as well. They did not own crude cleavers or rusty spears, but true swords, broad-headed spears, and metal round shields - not exactly exceptional quality, but good.

"Fall back up the stairs and hold them at the top!" Wheeling his Stinger, it jumped, taking the steps seven at a time with each jarring bound until he reached the top. "Dismount! Shield wall!" The last of the cavalry reached the top and slapped the rumps of their horses, sending them running into the cathedral. The line fell in and locked shields, their boar spears nestled atop. Edward threw the spear behind him and pulled his sword. He thought only of Tara. Wanting to keep her safe. He desired to give her everything she wanted out of life and out of him. That was over now; the best he could hope to do was slow them before he fell. The arrows from above still flew, and a few had fallen, but death was almost on him. From behind him, he heard steel dragging on the marble floor. He turned his head fast to see.

Ivan and the great dire wolf were on a hunting expedition once again. This time, not in the depths beneath the land of El'idar, but above and here, the hunt was hot and savage. Horses galloped all around them, except for one, a Stinger still hanging just inside the door in case its rider called. Ivan held his sword tightly, feeling the blood gem pulsing with hunger. The sword felt heavier than ever before, its tip dragging on the ground as he walked towards Edward and the tiny shield wall that was soon to be overrun by the Camolisk riders. "What's wrong with me?" Ivan thought, struggling to maintain his focus. He felt himself drifting away, and his heart began to race as his feet moved uncontrollably. He was losing himself again, becoming someone else entirely.

Suddenly, he moved with blinding speed. The sword swung above his head as he vaulted over the shield wall. Just behind him, he heard the great wolf taking off from the ground. Everything seemed to slow down as he flew through the formation of Camolisk riders. They were positioned in a line, at least five riders deep and ten across. Ivan's sword cut deep into the neck of a lizard as he passed over its body. The lizard's rider was thrown forward, flailing its arms in a futile attempt to stop his fall. Ivan didn't look back, knowing a wall of spears awaited him. As he landed on the stairs, Ivan spun in a low circular arc, his blade pulsing with hunger as it sliced through the next Camolisk rear leg, sending both the rider and the lizard crashing down. With each strike, he felt his strength grow, and the blade exacted its toll. The next Camolisk rider charged towards him, but Ivan didn't even slow down. The blade spun, and first the rider and then lizard were beheaded. Ivan heard his dire wolf behind him doing its dreadful work. Some of the Camolisk riders swung around to deal with the attackers from behind, but Ivan didn't care. He wondered if this had not been his plan all along. The dire wolf had pulled a large Zoruk from its saddle, dragging it down the stairs by its throat. The Zoruk kicked its legs in its final throws as the wolf shook it violently, savagely spraying blood, before dropping the motionless corpse.

Antoff did not need to issue orders to his Priest Knights and Clerics. They formed the line without slowing. His sword appeared in his hand with a rasp. The black hawk shield pulled close, and to each side of him, silver armor gleamed with swords, maces, and lances tipped down. Horses strained and leaned as they hit. "Crash!" They struck the rear of the Zoruks, penetrating their line six deep. Five Knights with lances wordlessly wheeled away as the remaining fifty went to work on their hapless prey. "For the Light, Truth, and Love!" Antoff roared, and his companions took up the call.

Every warrior of EL'ALue ignited with Light. Antoff's blade fell in smooth, flowing strokes, parrying, and hammering blows in a godlike, blinding Light. These Zoruks were numerous, and more than a fist remained as a rear guard, and the rest ran forward into the square. One Knight, then two, fell, yet their companions did not decrease their efforts. If the loss of a friend did anything, it only increased the violence from the Warriors of Light. Again and again, Antoff struck and parried the blows that reached for him. He swung at a low arc that connected with a cleaver wheeling Zoruks' blade, batting the attack away. "Crash!" The five Priest Knights struck with heavy lances, shattering the Zoruks' rear guard before it could completely reform again. The Priest Knights, young and old, finished the remaining rear guard as clerics dismounted to pray for their glorious dead. They lifted them onto their horse and tied them in place. At the same time, the lance reformed and prepared to charge once more.

Al'len stood on the battlements, cloak waving with the wind. "Tara, they are here," she announced, her lips pressed together in anger. The first line of enemy troops breached the trees and flooded into the field called Dan'Nor. They ran with ladders and grappling hooks toward the wall, spreading out like a flood coming down a wash. Behind the first ranks came crossbow troops, one fist deep. Al'len started the call. "Ready bows!" The bows lifted down the battlements. "Steady, fire!" Her strong voice rebounded down the wall. Arrows arced and struck. "Fire at will!" Because of their elevation on the battlements and the reach of their longbows, the arrows found their mark five volleys before the Zoruk crossbowmen came into range.

Zoruk bodies littered the field, disappearing in the waving grass that had not yet been trampled by the rush. Still, one-third of the Zoruks lifted ladders and began the climb. Crossbowmen fired a vicious volley in revenge, striking four soldiers who fell backward off the wall or slumped to the stone floor.

"No!" Tara cried and tried to move past Al'len, who barred her path.

"Healers!" Al'len called, and Cur'Ra's team went to work. She moved with efficiency, placing her hand on each, helping the ones who could walk and carrying the ones who could not with backboards. Al'len held Tara with an iron grip by the shoulder. "You have your job, and Cur'Ra has hers. Now stand the wall!"

Cur'Ra pulled off armor and cut clothing to find the wounds. She was deep in search of her patient's injury and cut the shaft, only leaving space for a hand to grab the heft. "Sylara, you have to pull the arrow straight out." Mikael's wife pulled it out, doing as little damage as she could. The Elp'har screamed in pain. Cur'Ra's hand covered the wound, and the Elp'har arched his back as the cold heat shocked his body. The wound closed with accelerated healing. She pulled her hand away, and all that remained was the blood and a small scar. "Place him in a stall," she called. Two men came and carried the Elp'har away to rest.

"Mikael!" Al'len called.

He appeared with a bow in his hand and an arrow knocked on the step that led to the level below where they stood. "Yes, my lady," Mikael replied as Al'len began to move past him to the battlements below.

"Watch after Tara," Al'len said as she moved by.

"With my life, my lady." Mikael confirmed.

Tara's eyes were wet with tears as she watched in horror while people died, and she couldn't stop it. *I can't use my Power and I am helpless to save them!* The dragons rolled in the air, moving away from the enemy's position and back towards the Cathedral of Light, feeling distress from Tara. Beyond the trees in the field of Dan'Nor, volleys of arrows traded deadly blows as the Zoruks climbed the battlement. Tara yanked her short bow from her back and went to work, her arrows flying. She may not be able to use the Power, but she still had her bow and swords.

The Black kept flying straight toward Tara, and the White-winged fast, then made a wide curving turn, bringing him parallel to the field. The Black tucked his wings tight and fell towards the wall. Just above, his black translucent wings snapped open in a resounding pop spanning twelve meters. They beat like a hurricane above the climbing Zoruks as the young dragon struggled for hovering flight. His neck arched, and head stared down at the Zoruks as gas bladders filled with rank acid. The gas expelled with a massive push from his lungs. He roared, the striker in his throat struck a spark, and the rancid acid burned in a lengthy liquid flame that billowed out white hot, his fire turning the falling dead to charcoal. Its fire clung to the attacking Zoruk below the wall, and they screamed. The Black struggled to gain altitude and barely cleared the wall.

The crossbow Zoruk thought to shoot at the hovering black dragon breathing death on the Zoruks below the wall. They sighted him in and fired. They could hardly miss the mass of the creature's bulk. All bolts but one bounced off the Black's armored scales. One penetrated low on the trunk of his body, burying itself deep, leaving only half of the shaft protruding from the dragon's flesh. The Blacked bellowed and climbed. The White glided down, wings spread wide, its rear clawed feet extended like raptors, raking the length of the crossbow line before climbing high into the air beyond a bolt's reach, bodies falling screaming from its grip. The damage to the Zoruk crossbow line was not definitive, but at least twenty of those Zoruks would never see the suns rise again, and double that number had been sent flying, crushing, or mangling their bodies to the point of no longer being able to fight.

Al'len reached the battlements below the tower just as she heard the screams of Zoruks below. The black dragon's bulk cleared the top in a wave of heat and smoke. She watched it wheel to the right around the cathedral toward the square. A large Zoruk climbed onto the wall between two merlons. Its greenish skin slicked with rain glistened, and in its right hand, it held a cleaver. There was little question in Al'len's mind, but its job was to clear the wall of archers. The Zoruk turned toward Va'Yone.

Al'len bellowed at it, "Hey, how about some of this?" Her sword leaped into her hand. It turned to face her. She was not a small woman, but this thing was huge, easily towering over her head and shoulders. The Zoruk grabbed the volunteer from the next slot and threw him from the wall with its free hand while advancing on Al'len. It swung a massive blade at her in a sidestroke that should have split her in two.

Tara looked on in panic. "No. Al'len watch out!"

Al'len ducked low, and the blade crashed into the stone where she had been standing. She stepped back, gaining more room. There was a grim smile on her lovely face. The towering Zoruk roared and swung his blade at her the other way. She used her shield to glance the massive blow, sending the cleaver harmlessly away from her body. She stepped back again, leading it away from Va'Yone. *Now it was mad!* She laughed audibly at it, her face now in a dazzling smile.

Tara was in fear for her, but Al'len appeared like she was enjoying it. It bellowed, lashing out with its cleaver, enraged. Al'len parried each blow but now attacked, having gained the room. The Zoruk was starting to be pushed back. Her blade came faster and faster as she closed the gap between them. She deflected a blow with her shield. She could have stopped with her sword, but that was already spinning following the cleaver blow, removing both Zoruk's hands. The cleaver cleared the battlement and clattered to the cobble below. She finished in a flourish and sliced the Zoruk's throat. As it staggered, she walked past it and pushed it from the wall. Tara's mouth fell open with awe.

Va'Yone smiled up at her. "If you are a ranch hand, I'm a bloodbat!" Al'len reached down and ruffled his dripping hair.

Modred observed Mel'Temdel as he stared into a glowing glass ball, searching for the Torrent. The rumors of her bonding with two dragons were true, and she was hiding from them. "She hasn't used her talents yet, my lord. There are no signs of power being used anywhere in the battle, except for a small band of Priest Knights. We dare not cast spells until we're certain we won't accidentally harm her. Furthermore, her dragons are surveying the battlefield, putting us at risk of being detected. Our dragon hounds have refused to respond to our summons. In short, we are blind while they possess sight. I am relying on a method that has been dismissed as irrelevant for centuries."

"Damn it, Mel'Temdel! We are losing troops as quickly as I send them to the wall. Pray our encirclement plan succeeds and they locate her, because if they don't, we will have to go and find her ourselves. Deploy the remaining troops to the wall!"

"Yes, my lord," Mel'Temdel bowed.

Less than a league away, five hundred heavy horses stood ready. The remaining Zoruk foot soldiers had breached the killing grounds before Coth'Venter Cathedral of Light. Following them were two strings of battering rams. If these failed, the only option to enter the temple grounds would be to ride through RavenHof, a convoluted path at best.

Mel'Temdel relayed Lord Modred's plan to the commander of the heavy lance. Tem'Aldar, the former Priest Knight, who had surrendered himself to Master Tormenter Be'elota after the fall of Ram'Del. Now he battled for control within this vessel. The agreement was he would not directly harm those he loved in exchange for information about the authorities controlling the Order of the Light.

Tem'Aldar had long been taken and had revealed every crack of greed within his order. He exposed every instance of faith and power that had corrupted his brethren. The Dark Order, naturally, had exploited this knowledge, infiltrating and fueling the flames of greed. With the loss of his commander Ram'Del, he was devastated. It was he who was supposed to bring the reserve legion to reinforce them. Yet, he had lingered needlessly, ensnared by the love of a woman who had toyed with him until that fateful day.

Later, during his captivity, he had glimpsed her dark beauty haunting the halls of his cell beneath the fortress of Are'Amadon. De'Nidra, the Daughter of Shadows, swore to Tem'Aldar in the depths of his chains that she loved him. If he surrendered, she would find a way to set him free and reunite with him. She cast a powerful spell, freezing his aging in time and binding herself to him eternally. She vowed to keep her promise, locking him away within her love. And so he now slumbered, awaiting her call.

However, the dark presence reclaimed control. Gilli'med, the deepest of spirits that had dwelled within the Dark Well, possessed this vessel and would never relinquish it. No muse of any witch could steal his freedom or his life. He kept the conflict hidden for obvious reasons. The Dark Order was not known for its mercy, and tales from those who had ventured into its Darkness were conclusive. This struggle belonged solely to him.

"Prepare to charge! Lines five abreast!"

The Warriors of Light gleamed brightly as they followed the remaining horde of Zoruks into the square. The Zoruks were yet more than three fists and moving toward the road that swung around the cathedral to the stable yard. Edward was at the top of the stairs, holding the shield line while Camolisk riders were trying to swarm him and fend off an attack from a Half-Dead and dire wolf that had gone mad with a killing frenzy. It was obvious what the course of action must be. He charged toward the Camolisk riders, his companions at his side. As hard as Edward struggled, there was no way he would survive; he was being overrun. The arrows rained from the balcony above.

The Camolisk riders were on him, even with Ivan and the dire wolf pulling five away; it was not enough. A Camolisk jammed its wedge-shaped jaw against the wall, bashing two of the shields back and stepping into the opening, lashing its body back and forth, buckling the line. Its rider plunged a spear through the chest of the guard directly ahead and removed it in a spraying twist. The guard collapsed in a heap. Edward was next on the huge Zoruks list, and his spear struck. Edward used the shield to deflect the blow and cleaved the broadhead from the shaft with his counterstroke. The Zoruk dropped the shaft and reached for a sword, but before he could clear the sheath, the guard's women's spears sunk deep into his neck, and another stabbed his arm from the opposite side. He fell, and Edward jammed his sword point through the lizard's eye. It fell writing and clawing at the air before going still.

"Reform the line and push!" Below, Edward watched a flood of Zoruks, with at least three fists, heading for the stable yard. If they hit Tara from the rear, she would not survive. Edward redoubled his effort. Then, from the street, a group of warriors entered the square on warhorses at a gallop. They gleamed with a bright divine Light as they charged toward the Camolisk.

Antoff was in the center of the lance line. Ivan sensed the distance of the incoming rush as his blade bit deep into the head of an oncoming Camolisk lizard, and the dire wolf leaped, sweeping its rider from the saddle with a vicious bite. The Warriors of Light thundered up the steps. Their warhorses lowered their heads in time with the collision, "Crash!" the hammer stroke fell, and the Camolisk rider's rear lacked the line to endure the impact of their warhorses' momentum. Edward's line was also pushed back with the collision of the mass pounding the Zoruks between them. The Light was so bright Edward could not see, and when Antoff wheeled his lance away, only twelve Camolisk riders remained. Antoff's lance was at full gallop again, their chargers strained to catch the loping Zoruk. They were already out of sight around the other side of the Cathedral of Light.

Chapter 26 Sparks of Glory

"What is glory? The pursuit of honor or reward for achievement? If too cheap, it fails to balance the scale; if too high, what's its value? Glory mustn't compromise character or moral depth. It's not an end, but a consequence of principles. Without them, glory is hollow, meaningless, and glory cannot exist."

The black dragon banked, its wings straining with powerful strokes, gaining speed for an effortless ascent. Soaring over the stable yard, the glowing heartbeat of life spilled out before its gaze, shimmering. From the tower, Tara watched the image the dragon sent her, her heart filled with fear for her family.

Antoff rounded the corner just in time to see the Zoruk horde, three ranks deep, descending upon the stable yard. Lightning flashed, casting the black dragon's shadow—a manifestation of Tara's pain. The dragon descended upon the Zoruks and breathed out upon them, the expression of her grief for all her losses in one long fiery rain. The heat was so intense, its roar shook the earth. A liquid hell of dragon fire consumed them from a wrathful shadow in the sky.

"Two abreast!" Antoff yelled, and his companions charged the enemy's rear flank in formation. The remnants of the dragon's fire guttered on the stone, leaving behind ash melting into watery streams. These flowed down the cobbled path toward the stable yard.

Tara felt every inch of a bolt tearing through the body of her dragon. The pain was so agonizing that it dropped her to her knees. She felt the dragon reach his neck around and pull the bolt from his flesh with his teeth. The pain burned like molten metal, forcing a scream from her lips. The black wings strained and pulled its bulk into the air toward the fists approaching the rear.

Tara's senses, overwhelmed by the resounding roar of the black dragon as it scorched a path through the heart of the Zoruk horde with its living fire. Amid the cacophony of Zoruk screams, she strained to make her voice heard, "Antoff is here!" She pulled herself to her feet, the dragon's pain still throbbing in her side.

"I know!" Al'len yelled. Her words were barely audible above the chaos. "The time for hiding is over, Tara. You must unleash the Power now. Keep a vigilant eye on any signs of their mages using their energy."

Something inside Tara shattered, as if a thousand panes of glass had broken simultaneously. For too long, Tara had held back, forced to watch as her family perished before her eyes, feeling utterly powerless. "No more," she whispered with resolve.

Surrounded by a heightened reality, she felt the surge of living Power raging between Darkness and Light, connecting with the very essence of the elements within El'idar and the vastness of the sky. The force of the storm surged within her like molten lava pulsing through her veins. At this moment, creation itself seemed to shudder, and time threatened to slow to a standstill.

The rain fell with otherworldly slowness, each droplet reflecting the vivid images of countless worlds ablaze. Downward they descended, landing upon the stable yard's stone, each microcosmic world disappearing in a splash.

Tara had known fleeting moments between heartbeats, but this was unlike anything she had experienced before. It was an image of desperation, a raw manifestation of her unwavering will to bring forth that which did not exist, yet lay complete in every intricate detail within her mind. In her Power, she conjured a world of her choosing, as though it already existed, as though it was reality itself.

Fueled by love for the living and burdened by her loss, her heart throbbed. At that moment, she became the very embodiment of the storm.

Within the depths of her mind, the image spun and danced with an otherworldly vitality, until Tara could contain it no longer. With a surge of Power, she released it into the fabric of time and creation, setting in motion a chain reaction that reverberated like a resonating bell before gradually settling into a semblance of normality. The sky seemed to respond, thundering and flashing with electric intensity, while the clouds swirled and morphed, shifting from shades of gray to a foreboding blood-red hue. The rain descended in fast, heavy droplets, as the wind howled and roared with unrestrained might, lashing the fields of grass and treetops back and forth.

Tara's envisioned spectacle played out before her eyes. She channeled the storm's furious energy, drawing on the interplay between Darkness and Light. The lightning, thick and formidable, writhed with dense cords of electric Power, striking down upon the hapless Zoruks. Wherever it touched, it consumed them, reducing their forms to nothing but ash.

Chaos erupted among the Zoruks, who scattered in panicked disarray, their desperate screams piercing the air. Clawing at the ground, they sought refuge from the unrelenting wrath of the storm. In their frenzied retreat, they attempted to retrace their steps, trying to flee the scene of this calamity, of this chaos, of the living hell that had manifested on the surface.

Tara was the sky; she was the Land of El'idar.

Taking charge of the moment, Tara summoned her dragons, steadfast allies bonded to her through an unbreakable connection. She commanded, "Find those mages!" And so they took to the clouds, soaring high above, unbothered by the lightning that answered to the will of their bondholder. Together, they pursued the elusive enemy mages, determined to bring an end to the Zoruk threat once and for all.

Modred and Mel'Temdel felt time rebound as the sky turned to blood. "No one who has the talent to see can mistake what is going on. She is raw Power, brighter than the suns," Mel'Temdel said, admiration in his tone. He watched the huge cords of Power feeding the storm and the lightning twisting and thrashing. "She has already used more Power than all of us have used, gating your army here, my lord, and it has only begun. If we use one drop and she sees us, she'd fry us to ash where we stand."

Modred yelled, "Is there no shield to be employed? Do you have knowledge of no Power that can counter her spell?" The High Mage looked at the members of his conclave standing a short distance away. They were not eager to turn themselves into beacons for dragon fire or the Torrent's vengeance.

"There is, my lord, if we were ready, but she froze time itself and prepared all this between heartbeats. Any of us can slow time locally, directly around the space within reach, or even in a small room. But we do not have the Power, not even with this," he shook his staff in front of Modred, "we cannot effectively stop time for leagues. My lord Modred, this is madness, folly to try any shield or spell when she is so aware. Lord Modred, we should withdraw," Mel'Temdel said with solemn finality.

"No!" Modred raged, his face contorted with anger. He stabbed Mel'Temdel in the chest with a finger, voice dripping with contempt. "We will finish this. You had better do something!" He called to his brothers as he took flight, "Follow me! We will complete this task ourselves." Modred spread his wings and leaped into the air and the eleven other demons spread their leathery wings and followed him to the fight.

Mel'Temdel watched Modred and the other demons fly toward the Coth'Venter Cathedral of Light. The High Mage Mel'Temdel walked only a span to his mages conclave. The six of them ranged from Middle Mage to High. "Lord Modred said do something, and there is something we can do to help him and cover our escape. The timing will have to be just right or we will be smoked meat."

De'Nidra, the Daughter of Shadows clad in black form-fitting silks, her long black hair trailing down her back, sat on the ledge of an empty window facing the stable yard below. She watched as Tara turned the world upside down. Her Power was growing exponentially. *How long would it be before this Torrent ascends? One year? Two at most? Tara is the one. She must be.* Tem'Aldar was heading this way and this girl would burn him, and all the pain and suffering they had endured would be for nothing. *No, that is not going to happen! I will either save him or I will strike you down. To the Darkness with prophecy and hell with the balance. I tried to save you. I tried to force Antoff to take you elsewhere, but you would not go. But if you try to take Tem'Aldar from me. I will destroy you*!

Tem'Aldar, Gilli'med's vessel, rode effortlessly as his charger jumped through the treelined thicket and into the killing field before Coth'Venter Cathedral of Light. Arrows rained down and Zoruks clawed over the charred bodies to reach the ladders and ropes filled with the long lines of creatures climbing toward the top of the battlements. Two strings of rams slammed the gate mercilessly, trying to open it before their charge reached it. Only one third of the crossbow still fired bolts at the defenders above. Nevertheless, their deadly thorns were doing decent work. Gilli'med looked right and then left and saw his lines were with him four abreast, flowing out behind him in a thunder of five hundred heavy horse carrying men in black full plate.

Blinding light lit the bleeding heavens as lightning fork down thick and drove writhing like a living thing. It stabbed the ground behind him. Gilli'med felt the atmosphere charge with Power and heard the screams from the line behind him. Static crawled across the ground, seizing his vessel's body with a force that caused him and his mount to tumble. As he fell, he could see the line directly behind him had been thrown into the air where the bolt had struck, blackening the earth in a two-span smoking hole. Horses and riders screamed as they tumbled to the ground. He hit and slid in the wet grass and mud; the blackness took him.

Edward batted away the last feeble stroke of a Camolisk rider who had fallen as Ivan ran him through. The last of the Zoruks were fleeing from a world that had turned to blood. "To the gate!" He whistled for his Stinger. It trotted out, and Edward vaulted back into the saddle while his cavalry, now on foot, charged into the cathedral. Booting his charger into a gallop that struggled to descend the steps without a fall, he headed heedlessly through the square toward Tara. His warhorse strained, neck stretching, as its steel-clad hooves pounded the ground towards the stable yard, ringing like a hammer on stone. Edward's heart pounded in his chest for Tara, though he could still feel her warmth.

Ivan followed the shield line through the cathedral with the dire on his heels. He was about to call to the shadows when he saw the form of a woman in a window. He might have missed her entirely if he were mortal, but to the eyes of a Half-Dead, her life energy gave her away as blood pounded in her body like a sweet song. Ivan called to the shadows, and they took him.

Below, the gate buckled and heaved as Zoruks battered it with rams. Rain-slicked green bodies crawled between merlons on walls, cleavers in hand. Va'Yone's hands slinked a ball of blue fire back and forth, electric energy crawling up his fingers. The cleaver-wielding Zoruk lunged and swung a blade that would cleave him in two, but he did not give him the chance. He flung the blue bolt of fire, and it struck the Zoruk mid-chest, flames and electrical energy spreading outward from the burst. The Zoruks' body smoked where it was hit and struggled to move.

Hoth'Le looked back and forth between the smoking Zoruk and the darkling. Va'Yone yelled, "Don't just stand there, pointy ear! Shoot 'em!" Hoth'Le responded with action, smoothly pulling his knocked arrow back and shooting the jerking Zoruk in the face. "You've been shooting stuff all night, and I have been standing on this stool. When the time comes, you freeze up! Pull it together, Elp'har, would you? We've got work to do." A blue ball of fire formed in his hand and crackled as he began to roll it back and forth with a smile.

Tara's heart swelled as she watched Edward gallop into the stable yard and throw himself from the saddle. He charged on foot and ran for the stairway of the tower. Edward took the stair three steps at a time, his smoked plate and shield trying to pull him down. When he reached the height of the battlements, he glanced at the wall, seeing Al'len easily dislodging a Zoruk from the wall with a sword strike that sliced him from chin to chest. Seeing that the wall was still clear, he climbed two more flights and planted himself at the top of the stairs. Mikael stood behind Tara, wounded, holding his side with one hand, blood leaking between fingers, and a long bloody blade in the other. Two Zoruks lay at his feet, unmoving, green blood trailing in the rainwater that drained from the tower scuppers. The relief that was on his face when he saw Edward was clear.

"Mikael, are you okay?" Edward asked with concern.

Staggering, Mikael dropped to one knee. "I don't think so, my lord." The stress in his voice and on his face was plain.

Edward urgently yelled for healers, but the battle was far from over. Cur'Ra's bearers removed Mikael to the stables. The remaining members of his shield wall, now reduced to twenty, ran down the stairs from the top of the rectory. Antoff organized them well back from the gate, prepared to charge if the Zoruks managed to breach it. Meanwhile, ten bowmen kept watch over the square, and Antoff couldn't help but be impressed by Al'len's skill in dispatching the Zoruks attempting to climb the wall.

Mel'Anor, amused by Al'len's prowess, jokingly asked, "Something wrong with your horse, Antoff? Every time a Zoruk scales the battlement, you look like you need to dismount!" He chuckled along with the companions. Al'len's display of skill was truly awe-inspiring; she effortlessly dealt with Zoruks, creating a literal pile of bodies beneath the wall.

Ivan sauntered into the yard with a black silk bundle over his shoulder. "Look what I found spying from a window right up there." He pointed to the window overlooking Tara's tower. Al'len hissed, "De'Nidra, the Daughter of Shadows, you snake." Ivan laid her on the stone next to the others. "She was so engrossed in spying and unwilling to use her Power lest she be discovered, I would guess. I knocked her out with the butt of my sword. She is still breathing, but she will be out for a bit, I think." He rasped.

"You know this Half-Dead creature, Antoff?" Mel'Anor asked, an eyebrow raised.

"I do," Antoff affirmed. "He is one of ours and my friend. He has proven himself dependable." Ivan felt his chest tighten at his words, at Antoff Grant's, Priest Knight of the Order of Light, not shying away from his friendship in front of his brethren and claiming him as....family. He turned away, lest he do something weird...like hug the old man.

Ivan carried De'Nidra into the stable so Cur'Ra could make sure she was not permanently injured and would live.

As the conflict raged on, the dragons sent Tara a horrifying vision. The terrain transformed into a Mage Gate, a semi-circle of mages unleashing a giant black ball of molten shadow that streaked toward the cathedral. Mages entered the gate, and it vanished as quickly as it had appeared. The ground was left cold and lifeless, except for the remnants of the defeated Dark Order army retreating.

Tara kept the fire burning in her veins, unwilling to release it until she was certain they were gone. She was in the higher reality beyond the mortal coil, standing amid the battle between Darkness and Light. And though more than anything she wanted to let go of the image that was overwriting creation's normal flow, she would *not* until she was sure it was safe. Edward watched his love, her hands reaching for the sky. A thing that would scare the seven hells out of any other man, but he did not care. He would love her every day until the day he would die.

Amidst the chaos, Al'len urgently called for Antoff's attention. Her face showed strain, and her beautiful long hair flowed in the wind, reflecting the brilliance of the lightning illuminating the dark sky.

Antoff noticed something unfamiliar in her expression - *fear*.

The black ball smoldered, casting a shadow as it increased in size, approaching the cathedral. When it hit the top of its tower, it didn't explode like a fireball. Instead burst and unleashed a glowing black, dusty smoke that spread like a fog of darkness over the square and battlements, out into the field, engulfing everything in its path.

Voices cried out, muffled amidst the eerie silence, broken only by the agonizing screams of something else in the darkness. Antoff urgently asked, "What is it?"

Al'len's muffled voice reached through the darkness, "It is a construct! Something from the War of Breaking, designed to fulfill a purpose for a set time or until its mission is complete."

As the smoky fog cleared, figures of dead friends and foes stood up, breathing the dark mist in and out. Blood spilled from their wounds as their eyes remained closed. Al'len sprang into action, swiftly dispatching the reanimated dead before they fully awoke.

Tara, watching from above, witnessed the haunting scene. The mist dissipated, revealing a field of the dead, animated by the inky darkness. Their eyes opened, and a purposeful energy filled the air as they ran toward the gate and climbed the ladders beneath the battlements. Al'len kicked away the closest ladder and moved toward the tower with determination.

Suddenly, Edward's voice rang out behind Tara. "We have a problem!" The sounds of steel clashing against armor and flesh followed. Turning around, she saw Edward fiercely battling the Zoruks, the ones Mikael had killed.

Drawing her short swords, Tara moved to help Edward. She knew they would have to hold their position alone, with the dead surging up from below. "Edward, they are coming through from below. The passage is filling with the dead. We must hold them here." They ran down the stairs, pushing below.

With resolve, Edward fought back the undead, determined to block their ascent either at the tower or the doorway below. Meanwhile, Antoff and the Warriors of the Light formed a shield wall alongside Edward's remaining light cavalry, fighting valiantly against the throng of undead before the stable where Ivan had taken De'Nidra, the Daughter of Shadows. The battle was far from over, and the fate of all they love and protected hung in the balance.

The black and white dragons flew above the clouds, covered in a hue of blood. Ropes of Power danced, weaving a fractured lattice against the tapestry of the night. From high above, mortals scurried below like ants, their movements aglow with the heat of life and the chill of death. They felt the fear surge in Tara and answered it with a roar, turning and diving toward the Cathedral of Light. Throngs of lifeless, cooling corpses lumbered towards the searing warmth of the living. They sent a message to Tara, "We are coming."

As they broke through the dense clouds, low over the city of Coth'Venter, twelve creatures flew toward the cathedral in a formation, low and fast, heading for the stable. The black dragon sent the image to Tara.

Tara moved to Edward's side, her twin short swords spinning. She deflected the blows he could not. The undead were a flood overwhelming them, plugging the stairway that led down to the wall and out to the cobblestone yard. Tara had seen arrows still raining from the battlements and the blue flashes of Va'Yone's Mage Strike. Al'len had battled her way out and fell in with the warriors below, but they could not hold the entry to the tower. The dead had become a flood. Edward and she were backing their way toward the stair that led back up to the top of the tower. What they would do once they got there, Tara did not know. They would be out of space.

Edward was exhausted, a weariness that penetrated to his very bones. This was the second battle of the night, and his arms felt like stone, barely able to intercept the blows. His shield arm was bleeding, and he clung to his chest plate with that hand, keeping it from falling, but he could not use it anymore. He felt the hot warmth of blood flowing down his side. Without Tara, he would have been gone. Tara was like a blur of steel. She slid in front of him, taking the brunt of the battle.

"Up the stairs, Edward," Tara commanded, her voice strained as she deflected blows, slicing through the flesh and bone of both friends and foes turned undead. Teeth gritted with concentration, she backed into Edward, forcing him back up the stair over his objection. He had taken the main burden of the fighting before and now was injured, and Tara did not know how bad. He was moving so slowly that he would not be able to parry the blows without rest. "Move, soldier!" Tara's voice filled with urgency, her eyes locked on Edward's as he reluctantly backed up the bloody stone stairs toward the tower's top.

Modred, alongside his brothers, flew low over the side road that led to the stable and touched down with a purpose. With a sense of grim determination, he drew his curved, bejeweled sword. It pulsed angrily in his hand, reflecting the dark fury in his eyes. The yard ahead swarmed with undead constructs, their only goal to kill. *Mel'Temdel, you fool! You will kill the Torrent!* The thought echoed in his mind.

"Spread out! Find the Torrent and kill anything else that moves!" Modred bellowed in the guttural speech of the demons. Towering at over seven feet, he led the way, his brothers a head shorter, their dragon-scale-like armor matching the color of their skin. Amidst the blood-red sky streaked with lightning, his black armor reflected the ominous flash.

They surged forward, ripping through the rear flank of the undead horde. He had to eliminate everyone except one, and he would get that Torrent even if he had to slay every creature on the grounds. Besides, how long could this dreadful construct last? The High Mage and that ragged conclave had likely created it hastily and then departed. "*Cowardice.*"

Modred's mighty voice boomed above the din of battle. "Give me the Torrent if you want to live!"

Antoff fought fiercely against the oncoming undead, holding his shield wall like a bulwark against a flood. The deafening bellow of the black demon reached his ears as he cleaved through the relentless foes. In defiance, Antoff yelled back, "You want her? Come and get her. But know this, demon: you'll have to come through me first!"

"DONE, Priest Knight! I am coming for you. I will take pleasure from cutting you down!" Modred answered. The legendary black demon exploded into motion, and Al'len, on the other end of the shield wall, rushed to aid Antoff.

Meanwhile, the black dragon swooped toward the tower, its wings creating a loud flapping sound. Edward and his bondholder were in dire straits, surrounded by the dead. The dragon landed on the tower's edge, blocking the way, and used its formidable jaws to fend off the attackers, sending some tumbling down the stone stairs. With a deafening roar, the dragon released its gas bladders and ignited a deadly stream of fire, incinerating the falling corpses.

"Take Him!" Tara commanded, determined to save Edward.

Edward protested, "No! Tara, No!" But it was too late; the dragon's clawed talons grabbed him, lifting him off the ground. "Tara, no!" he screamed, reaching toward her.

Tara's eyes met Edward's, a loving smile on her lips despite the surrounding chaos. "Go!" she urged, her voice firm, but her eyes betraying a flicker of fear. The black dragon obeyed, delivering one last blast of fire down the hole before beating its wings hard, ascending into the sky. As the white dragon saw its brother and the unfolding scene, it swiftly approached the tower's top. With a powerful swoop, lowering his neck for Tara, she climbed on, and together they took flight, pursuing the black dragon.

Tara clung tightly to the white dragon's neck, feeling the immense power of its flight. They soared above the treetops of the field, disturbing the branches with their massive wake. Tara held on with all her strength, determined not to let go. The wind buffeted her, but she clung on, gripping tighter than before.

The black dragon appeared above the tower top, and dragon fire billowed into the tower's interior. Flames shot out of every murder hole, blasting the molten doors off as if bellows were pumping a forge fire. Modred was horrified. The dragon breathed again, and the smoldering remains of the dead were flung from the door like coals from a campfire caught in a gust of wind. The acrid stench was overwhelming, almost causing Modred's stomach to turn. A sickening smell of raw, fouled meat and death hung heavily in the air.

The black dragon ascended in a whirlwind of smoke and dirt, carrying away an injured man. But Modred didn't care. His focus was on the Torrent.

Then, a second dragon, a white one, landed sideways on the tower top. Lowering its neck, it rose again with the Torrent on its back. The white dragon took off from the wall, its wings carrying its bulk effortlessly. "The Torrent is getting away!" Modred gestured with his weapon and commanded, "Follow them!" Some of his brothers, who were not engaged in battle, took flight, pursuing the Torrent. As others finished their combat, they leapt into the air to give chase.

Modred planned to kill the troublesome Priest Knight Grant and then join his brothers. This service would restore some of his credibility with the Dark Order.

Antoff watched as Tara was lifted to safety from the top of the tower by her white dragon. He wiped the dirt from his face just as the image of a colossal black demon filled his view, charging towards him. He whispered, "EL'ALue," and she answered. Bright Light erupted from him, illuminating the courtyard. The dead fell before the wave of Light, the construct dismissed, the Power of an elder god coursing through his veins.

Modred deflected a warrior's strike, dispatching her with a swing of his blade that cleaved her in two. Her blood sprayed, and his gem pulsed, absorbing the last of her life and filling him with energy. The Light from Grant was blinding as he ignited. Modred struck out instinctively, his blade connecting.

Al'len watched in horror as the blade descended towards Antoff, her Priest Knight, *her love*. Time seemed to slow as she realized she was too late to prevent the strike. Modred's massive sword broke through Antoff's longsword and struck him on the shoulder. The blood gem pulsed, absorbing Antoff's life force, and he crumpled to the floor. His Light went out. "No," Al'len roared, rushing to save him. *No, no, no, she kept chanting in her head.*

Ivan saw Antoff fall as he pushed through the doors of the open stable. He watched Al'len racing towards Antoff, but knew she wouldn't make it in time to stop the demon from finishing him. From the corner of the stable, the shadows pooled. He called to them and they reached and took him, spitting him in wisps of smoking spider webs out before the demonic monster. Ivan then intercepted the blow meant for Antoff, swords up, blood stones pulsing. His eyes, a swirl of gold mixed with blood, met Modred's. "Save Antoff, Al'len. Save my brother!" Ivan ordered.

Taken aback, Modred studied the creature before him. He had found himself in a similar situation before. "You're seeking death, slug, if you think you can stand between me and my prey," he said, stepping back and swinging his sword.

Ivan felt a sense of disorientation. His mind spun, dreaming. He was somewhere else, in another time, another fight. *He moved fluidly through the ranks of the night's minions, tearing through flesh and bone to reach his objective. Suddenly, the Great Lord Amorath appeared, raining darkness and fire upon the Warriors of the Light. Ivan raised his sword, and fire engulfed him. He screamed.* Then the world refocused, and the demon Modred came back into view.

Modred stood ready. Barely a second had passed. Ivan closed his eyes and held his sword tipped down. He bent his knee and took a deep breath.

Modred sneered, "Fool!" He struck like a viper.

Ivan opened his eyes, a fierce Light within them. Modred's blade swung with a power that could decapitate him. Time seemed to stretch out as Ivan moved with supernatural speed, his own blade flashing. The gem pulsed and sparks flew from its twin on Modred's sword.

"Where did you get that sword, slug?" Modred sneered, his eyes narrowing dangerously.

"I took it from one of my kind. As for how he got it, I don't know. Are you here to make conversation or fight?" Ivan asked, hoping he was buying Al'len time.

Al'len reached Antoff. His body lay unnaturally on the ground; he wasn't breathing. The wound on his shoulder was deep. "Get him to the stable," she ordered the Warriors of the Light. Four of them lifted him and carried him inside. As tears streaked her face, Al'len murmured, "Don't you dare die on me, Antoff." Hearing EL'ALue's questioning rumble, Al'len responded aloud, "Because I love him." She followed him inside, and the door closed behind them.

The remaining Warriors of the Light fanned out in front of the door.

Chapter 27 Knight Terrors

"Beneath consciousness, echoes of loss and voices of the abandoned create an aura of careless disregard. True, we may misplace an item, even one of importance, but love cannot be lost. It is a choice. Choose wisely, lest your fate becomes a lonely one."

The white dragon flexed its mighty muscles, hoisting its imposing body into the skies. Tara's connection with the dragons was second nature. Yet, as she gazed through the dragon's eyes, the shrinking world below made her throat tighten. Her fingers clung to the dragon's scales, the only anchor amidst the perilous ascent.

The black dragon veered towards the white companion, projecting fleeting images of their distant pursuers. Within moments, a second layer of magnification dropped in as her dragon blinked, offering a close-up view of the approaching red and black demons. With determination, the black dragon surged forward, its talons clutching Edward's still form, a mere silhouette in its grasp.

"Is he okay? Is he alive?" Tara's urgent plea echoed in their telepathic bond.

Gliding above the white dragon, the Black transmitted a reassuring image: the thermal outline of Edward's body. "He yet lives, but his injuries are grave. Unconsciousness has claimed him, a sanctuary from the unrelenting pain," the black dragon conveyed through fragmented mental images.

"We must use the clouds for cover. Ascending further is too risky; the air grows too thin for your lungs above them," the white dragon relayed, illustrating its warning with a rapid flood of images.

Blood-red clouds drew nearer. The ground below faded into a cold, foggy haze. Tara, perceiving the world through the minds of her dragons, extended her will towards the storm. Her mind crafted an image, and lightning flashed in response, transforming the clouds into a brilliant pink curtain. If demon vision worked like that of mortals, they would be blinded.

Deepening her connection with the dragons' minds, Tara sensed the chilled, viscous air around them. Shifting their focus rearward, the demons radiated like beacons, their forms dancing amidst the frigid sea of vapor.

They leveled out, gaining distance before they came about, turning back towards the Cathedral.

Ivan's body moved with muscle memory as their blades flashed, their blood gems pulsing, hungry for any misstep. Modred employed every trick he knew, but Ivan pressed on with his blade—a blur of precision and skill that Modred hadn't witnessed in a long time. He marveled at the economy of motion, with nothing wasted. Sweat glistened on Modred's forehead, and a whisper of familiarity crept into his mind.

Ivan thought, *If you wait too long, one of us will make a mistake, and it may not be him. Every moment this continues, Antoff is dying.* Ivan attacked full force, closing the distance between himself and the demon, forcing Modred to retreat defensively.

Ivan drove closer, his blade striking from every direction, but then he deliberately broke the attack, moving to the side, sword held low. Modred, familiar with the rhythmic pattern, swung his blade down to finish Ivan. Yet, with supernatural speed, Ivan stepped in and under the swing. Time seemed to slow as Ivan's blade sliced smoothly across Modred's chest, ripping through armor and flesh. The blood gem pulsed, drinking deep of Modred's life force.

The Great Demon of Legend staggered back in shock. Ivan hadn't killed him, but he had dealt a significant blow. "I know you. I know that move. Only one person could have pulled it off, and he is dead," Modred whispered, creating a distance between them.

Filled with his life energy, Ivan gasped for air, his sides heaving. "We have more in common than you care to remember," Ivan began, his voice filled with a certainty. "You'd better leave. I'm growing tired of playing, and if you press me, I'll take the rest of your life. I will drain you and let you wither in the heat of the morning suns." The angry Light in Ivan's blood-gold eyes pierced through Modred. *I have Antoff's life back. It is within me. If I die, he dies. Every moment I spend here, he is slipping away.*

Modred sheathed his sword. "Next time," he declared before taking flight.

"I will be here, waiting," Ivan said, his voice dripping with defiance. He turned to the astonished looks of the Priest Knights and Clerics of the Light, walking past them and into the stable.

The deafening wind roared, drowning out any attempts at communication. It underscored the necessity for the type of communication that had developed in the dragons. Their bond granted her this heightened sensory experience. Feeling the cool prickling sensations of the wind not only on her flesh but also on theirs, the lift of the air under their wings, and the rush of air drawn into their massive lungs awakened something in Tara she didn't even know lay dormant.

Unified with the dragons, Tara sensed the weight of Edward in the talons of the black dragon ahead. Images flashed vividly—the silhouettes of attacking demons against the backdrop of lightning-streaked, blood-red clouds that lit up like a lattice.

Tara had considered controlling the wind or wielding lightning, but one would affect both dragons and demons alike, and the other would lack precision. She would have to be creative on this flyby, and it would need to remind them why engaging dragons in their native environment was not just a terrible idea. It was insanity.

She planned to use her abilities in conjunction with her dragons', and it would have to be so devastating that it drove the demons away. Edward was dying, and she needed to get him to Cur'Ra. Time was running out.

The Black banked upward as they closed the distance. Tara didn't think that the demons could see in this thick, viscous cloud cover. They certainly gave no signs that they could; the Black dove hard for the attack, angling Edward to the side in an effortless aerobatic display that, if he were conscious, would have seen his stomach emptied.

The white dragon sent an image of the maneuver it was about to execute, and Tara swallowed hard. It claimed the move would keep her secured to its back and yet allow a clear view for her to act when they got close. All she had time to do was scream, "Oh No!" As her stomach dropped, she felt as if she was falling. The White ignored her. Tara closed her eyes, struggling to regain control—it was far from easy.

Flying through the atmosphere, everything felt alien. Her perceptions of reality still held, and the construct she had created was playing out the overwritten scene. The scrollwork tracing from the corner of her eyebrows to her cheeks came alive, ashy fire outlining them. Time shuddered in a ripple expanding outward like a pond. The breathing of the dragons, the beating of their wings, and even their movement became slow.

The Black approached the first demon in the line, its body hot as fire. As the dragon's bulk rolled over, soaring above the black-clad demon, its massive maw, brimming with spear-sized teeth, lashed out like a striking snake, crunching down with force. The demon's wings flapped on each side, and the sword fell from its hand as it was ejected from the dragon's mouth with as much casual disregard as a creature tossing a bit of shell from its nest. The body windmilled down and crumpled. The black dragon climbed once more.

Narean's translucent red wings beat hard behind his brothers. Three of them had already entered the crimson vapor, and he was the next one in line. Only a few more moments, and he would reach it. The logic of following dragons into the clouds struck him as highly flawed. The image of his brother pinwheeling from the sky told him that his thoughts had been correct. *This is madness!* Having the ability to fly did not mean you mastered the environment. *We're merely food for these hunting beasts!*

The White dove toward the next one in the line, just inside the cloud's vaporous outline. It was like a slow fall; she was upside down, but the momentum of the dragon arching inwardly toward the forge hot demon held her firmly to his back. Time slowed. Tara concentrated. A liquid sphere of molten energy formed, crackling the size of a melon, blue lightning crawled across its rippling mirrored surface.

They fell, everything was slow. Tara watched the winds slow, their patterns rippling across her skin as they closed in on the demon. The demon's wings beat rhythmically as they passed it in an inverted arc. Tara released a bolt of power, directing it at her target. On impact, the demon's red body arched, and its wings tangled as her white dragon burst through the cloud cover in a swift motion. Tara let the sphere vanish and then nestled her face against the White's neck and gripped his scales.

The white dragon spun and pulled up in a climb that, even in this slowed environment, nearly tore her from his back. The dragon could feel her weight lifting and compensated, keeping her butt on the hard ridges of its scales. Her dragon's wings beat hard for cloud cover.

Narean was growing tired from the climb, but the fatigue melted away as he watched a flash of light strike and radiate out in the blood-red clouds, and a white dragon emerged with a dragon rider followed by another of his falling brothers. *Ok, that's it; this has moved to a level of insanity even Modred would not ask of anyone. I don't see him anywhere near this madness. We are not apprehending*

a Torrent. We are a sacrifice up here. I am out! Narean dove for the mountains below.

With Modred wounded, it was an effort to fly. He watched black dots in the distance falling from the sky as dragons emerged from the clouds like Crag Lions playing with beasts in a trap. It was madness, and his brothers were right to give it up. He flew toward the Twisted Lands. There would be no capture tonight. Too injured to fight, let alone playing with dragons in their native habitat.

Antoff lay motionless on the stable floor, his chest bare and vulnerable, as Cur'Ra worked in silence. Al'len was at his side, gripping his hand tightly, the sense of his fading life force like the last ember of a once roaring fire being snuffed out. "Cur'Ra, can you save him?" she pleaded.

"I cannot, Al'len. The demon's sword has drawn deeply from his life force. I have none left to spare, or I would gladly give it," Cur'Ra's voice was choked with sorrow. "You must believe me, Al'len, I would." Her eyes, brimming with tears, met Al'len's and reflected nothing but sadness.

Al'len was desperate. "Can you take mine?" She knew EL'ALue would not allow it. *No Antoff Grant, you listen to me, you will not die, I will not allow you to. We still have unfinished business. You and me. So live. I command you to live.* She said it so low, merely a whisper, her voice braking at the end in a sob. "Please don't leave me."

Cur'Ra hesitated, her expression fraught with uncertainty. "I cannot. It is not allowed, Al'len. It is forbidden, considered evil." Her face became twisted and her eyes conflicted.

Antoff was in darkness, falling into the abyss. He could hear voices around him, but they were distant and sliding further away by the moment. If he had had a choice in how to die. It would have been in the manner he did. Giving himself for the Light. For the world and for Tara. Yet, deep within, he felt the loss of what could have been with Al'len and the love he bore her. He still reached for that love out of the depth of the blackness. A hand as blinding and as bright as the sun's grasped his and held him on the brink of winking out. Al'len's voice whispered. *I command you to live.*

The stable doors were thrown open abruptly as Ivan strode in, shutting them with a loud thud. He moved with the ferocity of a wolf, his eyes ablaze with anger. "You don't need to do that, Al'len. I've retrieved his stolen life energy."

Cur'Ra looked at Ivan, her eyes filled with relief and a new sense of worry. "I can try to return what was taken from him, Ivan, but nothing more. If that is insufficient, it means it's his time. Agree to this, and I will attempt the transfer. I have never done this before and I do not know if it will work. I could kill you both."

Ivan nodded, moving closer to kneel by Cur'Ra. She extended her hand, which he grasped firmly.

"Your life energy pulses strongly, Ivan. Are you ready to begin?" Cur'Ra asked, her tone cautious.

"Yes, save him. Save Antoff." Ivan's gaze unwavering on Antoff's pale face.

Meanwhile, Tara called upon the dragons to land in the stable yard, pleading for aid as the Black carefully released Edward from its talons.

"Help me!" she called out, sliding down from the White's neck. Two warriors responded swiftly, picking up Edward with great care. Tara followed them into the stable, where Cur'Ra was gripped by trying to save Antoff. The warriors gently lay Edward down.

Tara approached Cur'Ra, her eyes shifting from Antoff to her. "Will he live?" Her voice trembled.

"I need your help, Tara. I can't save him." Cur'Ra replied softly. "Kneel by Antoff's head. Take Ivan's right hand in your left, and place the other on his chest, as I have taught you. You must guide the flow of energy from Ivan into Antoff, and I will replenish his life force. Be extremely careful, Tara, or we can kill them both ."

She complied. Tara's heart skipped a beat as Ivan extended his hand without hesitation, a testament to his willingness to risk his life for Antoff. Closing her eyes, she attuned herself to Cur'Ra's work, allowing herself to feel the moving energy as she had been taught. It was like a delicate dance, with Cur'Ra maintaining Antoff's dwindling life force with a trickle of Ivan's energy.

Adjusting her focus, Tara turned to Ivan. His energy was overwhelming, a violent storm compared to the mere spark that was Antoff's. She connected with his energy and then delicately tied it to Antoff's life force.

"Slowly, Tara, gradually increase the flow until I tell you to stop. Once I say close, you must immediately sever the connection." Cur'Ra instructed.

Tara nodded, "I understand." She adjusted the flow of energy, her mind filled with a singular thought–*I cannot lose my father or Edward.*

As Cur'Ra took control of the energy flow, Tara monitored its rhythm. The rush of power was reduced to a more manageable flow that looped in a cycle through Antoff, invigorating his life force. As the flow continued, Antoff's life force started glowing brighter, pulsating with renewed vigor.

Cur'Ra, weary but determined, spoke. "Tara, that's enough. Shut it off."

Tara complied, severing the connection with Ivan. The abrupt disconnection made Ivan sway, nearly collapsing.

"Will he live?" Ivan asked, panting.

"All I can say is that we have a fighting chance now, Ivan," Cur'Ra replied. Her hand moved to Antoff's damaged shoulder, emitting a soft, healing green glow. Antoff's body arched in response, his muscles convulsing briefly. The wound began to close, and his breathing steadied. "He will live," Cur'Ra gave a sigh of relie f.

Cur'Ra, Tara, and Al'len, all overcome with emotion, shared a tight embrace over Antoff's still form.

Tara's voice trembled. "We have to help Edward now. He's badly wounded too. He can't die."

"We'll do what can be done," Cur'Ra said, moving to kneel beside Edward. Tara worked swiftly to remove his armor under Cur'Ra's direction. With a stern reminder from her mother to focus on the task at hand, Tara applied herself diligently to clean Edward's wound and prepare him for Cur'Ra's healing. His body arched when she touched him and then relaxed.

Edward, his eyes barely open, recognized Tara's presence. "Tara?"

"I'm here, Edward," Tara reassured him, gripping his hand while blinking back tears.

"Next time, tell me before your dragon snatches me up. Scared me half to death," he mumbled before slipping into unconsciousness.

She wanted to slap him. "Shut up, Edward, you scared me." Tara retorted, her eyes running wet. A fond smile appeared on her lips. She kissed him as he drifted off to sleep.

Cur'Ra, Al'len, and a group of clerics exited the stable, their faces solemn. They set about finishing the wounded Zoruks and transporting any survivors to the stable yard. "These individuals are all possessed," observed Mel'Anor.

"Yes," Al'len agreed, "likely victims of the recent campaigns. We have to save as many as we can. Move them to the stables."

Chapter 28 Honored Rest

"Brokenness and humility shield me from words that hurt, harm, or wrong. I know the song in my heart, and the power of each uttered phrase. When selfishness rises—once revered—honor's call is an imposing path where my desires disappear. Thus, my warden is honor, keeper of keys, and selfishness imprisoned, and selflessness set free. Let brokenness be the sentinel. A heart's pure song. Humility is my memory of all those whom I have wronged."

The rain stopped falling, and the world had become quiet. Life sang, dashed, and flew about. Tara watched this harmony while also watching over the living as they worked to separate the dead. The field called Dan'Nor burned with funerary fires fueled by the Dark Order's minions. As dawn approached, a cool breeze swept over the walls and across the meadow. The wind could not remove the scent of fire that smoked black, belching ash towards the light of false dawn. The first of the sun's rays crested the treetops, and the sky slowly changed from light pink to the blue of a new spring day.

Edward had not left Tara above in the tower, except to get a towel and a warm blanket to cover her. He held her now and did not let go. Neither did he care who would see or whether Antoff would have his hide. That was a certainty. Antoff was going to have words with him. Of that, you could be sure.

Al'len, Antoff, and the Warriors of Light had set up the location for the services for the honored dead. They would take place in the Cathedral of Light's main temple later in the afternoon. Those who found missing family members mourned their loss, and all awaited Lady Tara. But first they had collected in the stables where the prisoners were held. The Clerics of the Order of the Light readied themselves to pull the entities from the bodies of the warriors in dark plate. De'Nidra, the Daughter of Shadows, was in black form-fitting silks, yet lay sleeping in fresh straw under guard.

"Mel'Anor, how long do you think it will take before these warriors will be clean?" Antoff asked.

"It depends on the entities that are inhabiting them. Normally, they don't like to come out easily, and sometimes it takes several sessions. You must cleanse yourself, you know. What we did last night may take some time to deal with before we are ready," Mel'Anor replied.

Antoff nodded solemnly. "Very well, Mel'Anor. Let me know when you are ready. I want to be here."

Antoff limped out on a walking stick to help carry his weight, and Al'len walked with him up the flights of stairs to the rectory and up to the sleeping area where their cells were. They both wanted to wash and put on fresh clothes before the service. Antoff and Al'len went to their cells.

"Hey! Where's my gear?" Antoff exclaimed. He could hear Al'len splashing in the water and smell the rosewood soap and lavender.

"Oh, I think Mel'Anor and the Priest Knights moved you out."

"Why would they do that?" Antoff asked.

"It had something to do with your stuff being in the wrong room because the captain sleeps in larger quarters."

"Oh, for EL'ALue's sake!" Antoff cursed.

Al'len huffed. "Watch your mouth, Antoff! EL'ALue might make you pay for that. Besides, you don't get to pick; they do."

Antoff cleared his throat. "We are almost all retired, and the handful of young ones are going to have to go back to Haven."

"Oh, I thought you came out of retirement when you swore to EL'ALue, the Maid of Light's service? I don't think she will let you out of it that easily," Al'len said, stepping out dressed in a fresh outfit. This time, she was wearing all leather, white, fringed in gold, with a matching cloak and her sword with the white dragon buckle and matching leather boots. She flipped the cloak over her sword hilt and rested her hand on it comfortably.

"What do you think, Antoff? Do I look the part? Maybe later, if the Lord Captain gets time, he can give me that sword training he promised." She looked into his eyes, smiling warmly and a bit seductively.

Antoff eyed her with a stoic expression, "After watching you on the wall, I am fairly sure you've been holding out on me, and I might very well be the one learning the lesson by the end of the class," he jested. There was a little smile there playing on his lips like he may still be willing to try.

She leered at him, and her ice-blue eyes smoldered as they held him. "You may yet win indeed, Priest Knight," she taunted, her voice ringing with a playful challenge. "If you are brave enough to embrace the fight with your whole heart."

Antoff had never felt that kind of challenge before. His body shook with every heartbeat, resisting the urge to kiss her soundly on the spot. *She needed a sound kiss*! He cleared his throat again and bowed his way out. "I am going to find my things, Al'len," he said. His brow was perspiring when he left, and he found it hard to string words together in his mind. His thoughts kept resting on Al'len. *How does she do that*? He had questions for Al'len about her skills and how she seemed to know so much about the Order of the Light. She knew things about the liturgy of their order. Most knights never got to learn because of their station. She was a woman who could only reach the rank of Priest Knight, and she knew so much more.

Antoff searched for his gear. He found it in a larger room with a bigger slab for a bed, an elaborately carved gray stone desk, and dark wood paneling lining the walls. All his stuff was neatly placed on his bed. He couldn't help but think about Al'len and her knowledge of the Order of the Light. He had long been curious about her origins and her profound knowledge of their traditions. He decided to ask her when they had a quiet moment alone.

Tara, with tears glinting, watched the warrior's cleansing ceremony, feeling the burden of mourning for the honored dead. The Priest Knight's songs of mercy filled the vast hall of a temple designed for self-reflection and memory, not worship.

As the ritual ended, Tara faced the gathering of family, warriors, and clerics. Her voice trembled with emotion as she acknowledged the brave warriors' sacrifice.

"Shall I say what's expected of me—that we are grateful for their loyalty?" Tara began, her voice breaking. "Our grief is not only for the brave actions they took but also for the unique individuals they were. We'll always honor their memory, keeping them alive in our hearts." Her tears flowed freely as she continued, "No. That's not enough! I loved them, beyond these simple words. This waste of life. This loss of unfulfilled promise. I will never see their creativity or the love they gave again."

Tara's heart was breaking, yet she found strength for those people still left alive. "Let us not dwell in Darkness. In Darkness, they found Light; in struggle, strength; in death, immortality. Their memories will guide us; their sacrifice will not be forgotten." Her voice rose as she spoke to the room filled with soft crying, "Look around. This is their legacy. We are their legacy."

She pointed to the children. "Their laughter, their joy, and all of their dances. This is what our heroes fought to protect. Every smile, every child's triumph, is their victory. They gave up their tomorrows for our today's. Let's honor them in celebration of the life they gave us. Remember them as heroes who stood tall in the face of danger. Keep them alive in our hearts, tending it so love blooms their memories eternal." Tara wept for them. She wept with t hem.

The remainder of the day was spent in quiet reflection and mourning. The Cathedral of Light was filled with the sounds of prayers and hymns as the warriors and their families paid their respects to the fallen. Antoff and Al'len stood guard, watching over the proceedings with solemn reverence.

As the day ended and the last of the mourners filed out of the cathedral, Antoff turned to Al'len. "I've been meaning to ask you." His ice-blue eyes met her deep pools. "How did you come to know so much about the Order of the Light?" Antoff asked, his voice tinged with curiosity.

Al'len smiled mysteriously. "I told you; my family and I have a long and complicated history with the Order," she said. "But that's a story for another time. For now, Antoff, just take me for who I am."

Her words stirred a hidden memory, some deep promise that held him to her. Antoff saw the hidden secrets in Al'len's eyes, but she wasn't ready to tell him... not yet, at least. So he nodded in understanding and gave her hand a gentle squeeze.

As the last of the two suns set on the Cathedral of Light and the city of RavenHof slept, Tara stood alone in the meadow, looking out over the burned and scarred field of Dan'Nor. The air had not totally given up on the scent of wet charcoal. The wind sighed, and the grass rippled. She knew the war was far from over, but she also knew the memory of the honored dead and their sacrifice would give her strength to face whatever challenges lay ahead.

When they reconvened in the stables, they found the Clerics of the Order of the Light had already begun separating the entities from the living bodies of the fallen warriors. It was a solemn and sacred task, and everyone present was quiet and respectful. They extracted every demon and dark entity, save for one.

"There is nothing for it, Antoff, this one is lost. We do him a mercy and a kind release if we just put him down." Mel'Anor answered.

Al'len asked, "Is there nothing more to be done for him?"

"No," Mel'Anor said. "There was a time before the Breaking when such things could not stand to be in our presence and would flee on their own accord when they became aware they had been discovered. But we have grown weaker, and they are stronger. All we can offer now in these cases is the mercy of quick steel."

De'Nidra was awake, listening, pretending to slumber until that moment. At that moment, spurred by the grim reality, she knew she had to move.

Chapter 29 Broken Gods

"You are magic and fire. My universe. Your eyes, my bright stars, pools of light and wonder. I am drawn to what lies inside. The fires of your suns warm me, and your moons at night illuminate and ground me to you. I have mapped your very surface, every line, and every curve. What is life without you? No magic, no fire, no universe, no wonder in life, no stars, suns, moons, no El'idar, a world bereft of life."

"*No*! Don't slay him!" De'Nidra, the Daughter of Shadows, begged. She crawled to him across the dusty straw strewn floor of the stable to cradle his head in her lap. "It was me. I am the reason Ram'Del died."

Al'len raised her hand. "Wait!" she commanded, and the Warriors of the Light obeyed. "Why should you receive mercy when you have given none?"

De'Nidra wept. "I didn't want to do it. I loved Tem'Aldar. He had already won my heart months before his capture. I tried to resist his advances for his own safety. But the Dark Order saw he was smitten and used me to destroy him. I hoped to save him. I promised to protect him forever. But I ended up killing Ram'Del to save my love, Tem'Aldar."

Al'len's hand shook on the pommel of her sword. "So, you killed Ram'Del, the Hero of the Light, for love?"

De'Nidra wept openly, releasing deep sobs of long-suppressed pain. "Yes, I did it for Tem'Aldar. And I hid my crime to prevent his captors from discovering his possession by their demon was part of my ploy."

Al'len struggled to resist the urge to kill De'Nidra, but it faded away. "You are guilty," she declared.

The Warriors of the Light advanced, ready to perform their duty.

Al'len commanded once more, "Hold." The warriors paused. "You are guilty, just as EL'ALue is guilty. Both chose love over reason and caused great harm. EL'ALue denied the love she and Ram'Del needed. Ram'Del died for the love he could not have. Love can make a mess of everything, but without it, no achievement or desire can fill the void left by love. And what shall I do with you now? We have all fallen and done things that reason cannot forgive. Things that have caused pain. But there can be no justice without mercy. Mercy is the proof that we have known love, the symbol of a truth born out of loss, and our deepest hope to redeem something of that loss for the sake of love and a better future. Living life is complex and filled with nuance and purpose, and this discovery makes life worth living. Love is the beginning and the ending of that tale. Without love, you have nothing. Life is an empty room filled only by the ghost of ambition, an unfinished song."

"This is a truth of a broken balance, one we have failed to see until now. And I will have no part in perpetuating the cycle of this lie any further." Tears streaked Al'len's face. "Antoff, free that man from this Darkness. They have suffered enough. We have all suffered *enough*."

Antoff placed his left thumb on the man's head and whispered to the entity, "You are not of this man's body; you have no authority here. Your lease and agreements are dissolved. Get thee hence, for this is a Priest Knight of the Maid of Light who made his oath first to EL'ALue." The spot beneath Antoff's thumb glowed white-hot, and Gilli'med cried out. Tem'Aldar opened his eyes. "The deal was you would not hurt the ones I love. De'Nidra is injured by your actions; our deal is over, and your lease is done."

Dark smoke, like black oil, gushed from the man's mouth and slithered, slinking through the cracks in the cobblestones beneath the stable yard.

Tem'Aldar sat up and held De'Nidra, weeping, against his chest. "You kept your promise to me."

"Of course I did, you fool. I love you," De'Nidra replied, finally holding the face of the man she loved.

Tem'Aldar peered up at Al'len. "I remember you."

Al'len smiled down at him. "Shut your mouth, lieutenant."

That night, there was a meal held in the grand dining hall, and apart from the guards still on duty, everyone was there. The dining hall was large, with five rows of stone tables made to feed hundreds in shifts. Fires crackled in fireplaces set on each end, and Mel'Anor sang in deep tones of joy, adding to the hospitality. There were new, fresh faces, as the words of Lady Tara and the Warriors of Light had spread like wildfire. Now, every person without hope had found Tara.

To everyone's surprise, De'Nidra stayed and lodged with Tem'Aldar, and he had retaken his oath, asking Antoff to administer it, and Al'len to bear witness he had given it. Tem'Aldar bore a deep purple bruise on his left cheek. He wore it with honor; his spirit was marked, and his body would never again fail to remember it. The request of Al'len at the ceremony was unusual, but accepted.

Antoff looked at the tables full of people and said, "We should take our meals in the evening like this so long as we can. It is good for us to see each other and talk in a setting with good food and family."

Al'len stood and repeated it aloud. "Our Lord Captain has said it is good we are together in this way. And from now on, so long as we can, we should take our evening meal together, and it shall be as a family."

The Warriors of Light all stood with Al'len and, with one voice, said, "The Lord Captain commands, and it is so!" And so, the first tradition of the Knights Meal was established.

Tara appeared to eat with everyone. She moved from place to place, with Cur'Ra and the desert Elp'hars sprinkled throughout the hall. Hoth'Le and Va'Yone sat together, laughing like old friends. Edward watched Tara while standing at the fireplace, sharing a cup of ale with Ivan, Mikael, and his wife.

It was getting late, and many bid their goodnights. Antoff wished everyone peace, then retreated to his room. Feeling guilty about being given a larger cell when the other cell had been more than big enough for him. He stripped off his shirt, washed, and shaved his face. Just as he was finishing washing the shaving soap from his face, there was a rap at the door. "Come in," he said.

Al'len stepped in. "I see you are almost ready for bed. I should let you rest." She began to back out.

"No, please come in," Antoff replied. He finished wiping his face with a towel, his back to her, revealing the crisscross of old scars covering his back from the campaigns of his youth.

She walked over to him and said, "You have taken many injuries in the service of the Light, or at least what you perceived it was while you were young."

Antoff could feel her eyeing him, smelling the scent of rosewood and lavender. "We all bear wounds of service that have left marks."

Antoff cleared his throat. "What can I do for you, Al'len?"

She smiled at him, stepping close, and then began tracing his jawline with her finger. "Do you recall what I told you before you left for Haven? You know when you asked me to cover for you with Tara?"

Al'len was doing it again. Making him a confused bundle of emotion. "Yes, I recall that you threatened me. Told me it was not over and you would bring it up again, and that you always collect your debts. Is that what you are here for? To scold me?"

She was still smiling at him as she turned and walked back toward the door. Antoff watched her, about to leave. He wanted to stop her, but lacked the courage to say it. *She is all woman; of that, I will give my oath.*

But she stopped as if she had heard, closed the door, and turned to face him. "No, I am not here to scold you. I am here to collect your debt," she said mysteriously as she walked to his desk and blew out a candle.

Antoff woke early the next morning, and Al'len had already gone. He could still feel her with him, her smell, her warmth, and her touch. He lay upon his cushion. The sun's light streamed in, revealing the layers of dust that drifted and floated on the warming currents of air. He breathed in deep the memory, the scent of her hair, and closed his eyes, hoping the dream was still there.

Al'len stood alone on the battlements. She stared out across the field. The wind brushed against her long blonde hair; it glittered in the sun's light, the color of hay. She smelled the scent of De'Nidra's perfume. "Good morning, De'Nidra."

De'Nidra stepped closer and lowered her voice. It trembled. "I know who you are. I tried to read you once and could not. You are EL'ALue. You are the Maid of Light."

"I am her construct. The essence of what she dreams and who she will be when she is here."

"I swear I will not betray you. Please let me stay." De'Nidra pleaded softly.

Al'len turned and faced her. The light of the binary suns lit De'Nidra's dark beauty to a glow. "You cannot know how I hate you for what you have done. I would kill you with my own hands. Nevertheless, just as I had a choice to hate you, I chose now to forgive you. Your service to the Dark Order has ended. I receive you." she placed her left thumb on her forehead, and it glowed. Her glyph rose beneath it. "Attend me."

Antoff woke up for the second time. The morning was quickly ending. The second sun, called the Little Sister, had already peeked toward midday, and her light pooled at the window ledge as a tender breeze gusted in with a refreshing spring sigh. Throwing off his covers and placing bare feet on the cold stone. He felt energetic. He walked to the nightstand to wash before dressing. The water in the pitcher was ice cold. Filling the washbasin, he splashed water on his face before taking the towel and wiping the sleep from his eyes. He dug his travel mirror from his bag and investigated it. First, there was a moment of shock as the bags that were normally under his eyes were completely gone. He plucked at his skin. It snapped back with a level of elasticity it had not had in years. In fact, if he were to put a number on it, he would say he had gained back ten years in one night.

There was a knock at the door. "Just a minute!" He hurried to put his clothes on; he was still completely naked. *That Al'len has absolutely left me unsettled.* Tucking in his shirt, he called, "Sorry for the wait. Please come in." Tara came in, leading a reluctant Edward by the hand. "Well, good morning to both of you. And what are you both up to?" That last part was said with the note of a father who could decide to be less cordial should the conversation take an unexpected turn. *Yes, these younglings are definitely up to something,*

Tara started, "Now don't be angry, Antoff."

Antoff's eyes went flat. "You know, Tara, when you were young, you always started your conversation that way with me when you knew I was not going to be happy with something you did. Right?"

She steadied herself and stared him down. "I am no longer a child. I wanted you to know that I love Edward, and he loves me. We are giving our life's vows soon. I would like you to give your blessing. This is not a debate or a childish thing. It is happening Antoff and I want you to be a part of it. Now tell me you will, and that you will love him like you love me." Edward stood there rigid, like a man about to go to the gallows.

Antoff grunted while waving any objection away. "I knew what you two were up to when I watched Edward make a fool out of himself just to make you smile at the Rusty Bucket while you danced. Furthermore, you two have been staring at each other like Leatherwings in the spring for days. Not to mention you have been mooning over him every spare moment of the day. Well, Edward, what about you? Speak up, son."

Edward felt like his tongue was wrapped with linen. "I love her, Antoff, and I want to give her my vow. I want your blessing. We both want your blessing."

He grunted again. "Very well, I will."

Tara flung herself at him and hugged him. "Thank you, Priest Knight. You must administer the vows, and Al'len should witness. Please?"

"Ok, Tara, it would be an honor to administer the exchange of your vows, providing you both are absolutely sure. This is not a game. Once the Vow settles on you, it is for life. You both are going to want to think about that."

Just then, Al'len walked in, followed by Mel'Anor and three other Priest Knights carrying her trunks. "You can just drop them over there. Thank you for your help," Al'len said.

Mel'Anor knuckled his back. "You are very welcome, Al'len. As it appears to be quite busy here. I will take my leave. Antoff, you appear very well-rested. This air is doing you wonders," Mel'Anor said, giving Antoff a smirk and a nod before promptly leaving him at the mercy of the attackers.

"Ask Al'len whether she wants to witness the vows while you are here," Antoff suggested.

Al'len gave him a knowing look. "Of course, I will. The exchange of vows when two people love each other is a blessed thing, don't you think, Antoff?" She smiled at him with a beautiful grin.

"Yes, it is," he replied, looking like a cat that had eaten the grain mouse. "Okay, *Out children*," demanded Antoff, "I want to talk to Al'len."

Tara led Edward out by the hand. Antoff couldn't help but think the boy looked like a man who was heading for the gibbets. Al'len, on the other hand, was still grinning at him.

"I assume you're concerned about how the other Priest Knights and Clerics might react to my moving in with you," Al'len stated with an air of nonchalance.

"They probably won't understand it, and it might cause me some issues with them. But I want you to stay with me here. This room isn't just mine; it's ours. The bishopric may require me to withdraw completely from the order, but I have no regrets, Al'len."

Al'len walked over to him and traced his jaw slowly with her finger. A chill ran through Antoff's body. "Antoff, the Order of the Light has corrupted the liturgy in so many ways, controlling every part of the faithful," she said, leading him to the bed. They sat down together, and she looked into his eyes. "But it wasn't always like this. Mortals should acknowledge their basic needs. *Love*, and everything that comes with it, was never disallowed, Antoff. These vows lie next to the oath of a Priest Knight when they decide to share their life with someone. EL'ALue wants you to be a man in every way, Antoff. So long as you remain honorable, true, and transparent about your actions, you are staying true to the principles of the Light.

Isn't the Light about truth and love? You could say EL'ALue is encouraging you to love me, Antoff."

"I'm not going to ask how you know that." Antoff shook his head with a smile, leaning in to steal a kiss.

The cathedral was always dark, just the way Ivan liked it. Shadows were necessary now that he relied more on his dark gifts. In his cell, he spread out the contents of his travel bags on his bed. Some items came from the dead Vam'Phire behind the portal where his old friend Co Ádean had died: a heavy gold signet ring, a bejeweled dagger that glowed red near those with sway over the Light, an amulet with a teardrop-shaped quartz, and a small book.

He would leave the quartz amulet and the small golden book on his bed as they had not yet discovered their uses, but the other items had to go back to Da'Vain. "I don't feel right keeping them. Selling them would be wrong. They clearly belong in the city below with the Vam'Phires," he mumbled to himself.

He packed the other items into his leather travel bag and threw it over his shoulder. As he walked into the lower halls, he knew Da'Vain would come. He always did.

The shadows moved into the sleeping hall at the cell that Ivan had occupied. It writhed for a second before solidifying and expelling a young female. She was thin, dark-skinned, and with fine, lithe wings, she folded up behind her like a cloak. She wore little in the way of clothing, small swatches of leather and silk covered all the right places, but beyond that, she was bare as the day she was pulled from the Well. Gracefully, she glided to the bed and scooped up the quartz in the shape of a teardrop necklace and the small book. She had haunted these halls at significant risk for almost a week now, and the Half-Dead's carelessness had finally paid off. Down the hall, footsteps came closer. She folded herself in shadow and was gone.

The sound of boots echoed down the dark marble floor as Da'Vain appeared out of darkness, shadowy spiderwebs trailing from him like smoke as always. His mind only revealed his presence when he wanted it to. "Lord Ivan, I heard your thoughts. You were looking for me? How may I serve you?"

Ivan wondered whether he would get Da'Vain to teach him the listening-to-thoughts thing. "I have some things that belong below with you, and I should have given them to you earlier, but it takes me a while to trust people sometimes."

Da'Vain smiled and gave a formal bow. "I am pleased we have gained trust with each other, Lord Ivan. Let me see what you have." Ivan produced the heavy gold signet ring with a bloodstone, a necklace of gold linked with a medallion in the shape of a bird's claw clutching a large diamond, and a bejeweled dagger out and handed them to Da'Vain one at a time. "I see," Da'Vain said. "Well, these are yours, not ours. They come with a sword and the chair, I'm afraid." He said the last part with delight and a smile.

Ivan was surprised, and he didn't want the items. "What do you mean, a chair?"

"I must give it back to you. All of this stuff. It belongs below." Ivan said.

"I see you do not understand what I am telling you now, just as you did not before. There is a chair below in the depths of the lower city, and that chair is, in fact, a throne. You took that sword from the prince, and now it and all he had belong to you, along with his subjects. Lord Ivan, it is time for you to visit the lower city. I will have to guide you the first time." Da'Vain stepped toward him and grasped his hand as a friend. "Let the shadows take you but let me direct your path." Da'Vain's mind became open to him, and the image of an open bridge above a large gorge came into view. The shadows slid over them, and they were th ere.

Lord Lars Haven, mounted on his white charger, reviewed his armsmen. They stood alongside the Priest Knights, clad in burnished silver armor atop their warhorses. His host's son had become an even bigger issue since he allowed him to live in the Grey Area. He had hoped to banish him until he needed a younger body with the right lineage to take control of the throne. However, now that was not going to happen. He had made sure the lad had enough coin to drink and defile himself properly each month. Yet he still fell in with this ex-Priest Knight, Grant. Grant had been excommunicated and is wanted to boot.

He still hoped to convince the bishopric to give him charge of his son until the change could be made. Yes, there would be a matter of clearing the boy's name, but he had the means to find a "volunteer" to take the blame and clean it up for the young Lord to assume the throne. However, if everything went badly, he could father another one. The time it would take to raise him to the proper age would be a problem, as this body was feeling the stress of supporting him with its life energy. Even that could be overcome with the proper incentive, and there was always someone trying to lick his boots. He would just have to allow it, at least until its energy depleted.

"Are you ready, your Lordship? We are assembled and ready to move at your command."

Lars flinched, but the priest did not seem to notice. *The Order of the Light is truly weak and ripe for the plucking*. He thought. "Of course, Priest Knight, lead us out."

"As you say, my Lord. Move out!" The line of three hundred Priest Knights and Clerics of the Order of the Light snaked through the city of Haven towards the gate.

In the great fortress of Are'Amadon, deep in the heart of the Blackened Lands, Modred, the Great Black Demon of Legend, brooded. His room was dark, lit with a single lamp that produced a fitful glow; it smoked and sputtered, emitting a sweet, nauseating, corrupt smell. No comfort was found while sitting in the black, high-backed chair. His chin was propped on his hands, and his elbows were planted on the lavishly carved, demon-headed armrests. Its wings spread wide, finishing the chair-back that broadened out above his head.

A fire blazed on a black volcanic stone hearth, casting shadows that leaped and played on the gray stone walls. Heat radiated from the fireplace, leaving the air of the room hot and dry. A haze hung eerily from back drafts, the wind constantly gusting and changing directions, blowing smoke back inside.

Modred stood and walked to the balcony. Against the backdrop of the murky soil spread out beneath it for leagues, a carpet of dark red and black. Like ants, Zoruks moved across the plains that stretched out into vast fields where innumerable slaves worked to produce a meager crop. Banners flapped in the wind, with symbols of the Zoruk tribes proudly defining the boundary of their territories.

The room filled with the chill of the undead mage and the scent of an open grave. Shadows boiled from Great Lord Amorath walking out of a hole in the darkness, "You must be wondering why you still draw breath. Why have I not drained you of your pathetic life and had your husk thrown from this tower?"

Modred spun with fear and knelt, staring at the stone floor. "Yes, Great Lord."

"It is because while you have failed to take the Torrent at Coth'Venter, you completed a task I could not. You found our little mouse. De'Nidra, the Daughter of Shadows, was that mouse. She is the traitor on the council. Her schemes have been revealed to us. So, as troubling as your failure is, I see your greater worth. Her spiderwebs are long and deep. And you, Modred, are going to continue your investigation until you have found every rat in our grain bin. Do you understand me, Modred?"

"Yes, Great Lord. It shall be as you command. But what of the Torrent?"

"The Council of Shadows has many secrets, my naïve Modred. Now, you had best continue your investigation. Remember, your life depends on your success."

Modred nodded, muttering his understanding once again, and he exited the room as fast as his legs would carry him, feeling a peculiar mix of fear and relief.

Amorath walked to the demonic chair, sat down, and laced his fingers. A smile crept across his pale face, highlighting his yellowing teeth and the dark pits of his dead eyes. It was not a pleasant smile, but one that promised suffering and torment.

"In the end, there is only death. Everything falls into the hands of Darkness," he whispered to himself, and then filled the room with cold, echoing laughter.

As the echoes of Amorath's laughter mingled with the sound of the dust blowing, an unnatural chill settled over the Blackened Lands. Far beyond the fortress, within the heart of the Grey Area, a strange glow emanated from the fractured focal point where the battles once began. It was a faint but persistent glimmer, unnoticed by all but perhaps a select few who were attuned to the delicate fabric of creation.

The glow pulsed, an ancient rhythm long forgotten, a whisper from the past hinting at untold secrets of a fractured balance, so long shattered, seemed to beckon, calling out to something—or someone.

A storm was brewing, not just in the skies, but in the very essence of the world. The dark and stormy night concealed more than the wicked games of gods and mortals; it hid a promise, a perilous path that would either restore balance or plunge everything into oblivion.

A new chapter was beginning, full of danger, intrigue, and darkness, and the fate of the world hung in the balance. But for now, only the ominous glow remained, a chilling reminder of the dark times that were upon them, and a harbinger of something even more profound.

As blackness descended, the only sound was the chilling echo of Amorath's laughter ringing out into the night, leaving a haunting question.

Tara closes the stained cover of the ancient book, feeling a shiver down her spine, as if the words she had just read had seeped into her very soul. The books that had captivated her pulled her into a world of dark secrets and hidden truths. It was a tale that spanned generations, a tale now etched in her spirit.

Lost in thought, she looked around the small, dusty storeroom housed within Master Duncan's beloved bookstore, Lost Lyrical. This place had drawn her back. It had been her sanctuary since childhood, where stories whispered from yellowing pages, and characters sprang to life with each turn of the cover. But now, something had changed. Something had awakened a longing within her—a desire to seek her own adventures once more, beyond the confines of the familiar shelves.

Her gaze fell upon the table where the ancient dark metal chronicle rested alongside other weathered tomes. Each book held a tale; each tale promised a discovery. The bookstore, once a haven of comfort, now felt like a threshold to a world of endless possibilities.

Leaving the bookstore behind, Tara stepped out into the night with a newfound clarity that tingled in her very depths. She had no map, no predetermined guide, but the world stretched before her, a mysterious canvas filled with secrets and possibilities. As she embraced the shadows of the evening, embarking once again on her own epic adventure, a thrilling realization washed over her: her story was not over. Master Duncan's killer is still out there, and her mission was far from done. The end of one chapter was merely the beginning of another, and she stood on the precipice, ready to shape her destiny, driven by whispers of ancient wisdom and the echoes of a broken balance.

THE END.

Afterword

Thank you for reading the book Between the Darkness and the Light, Chronicles of the Night Book One. The second book will be released soon and if you would like to preorder, please check it out at https://books2read.com/u/b6WEVM.